What Others Are Saying about
Sharlene MacLaren and *Abbie Ann*...

Multitalented author Sharlene MacLaren has once again given readers a story that artfully blends excitement, humor, and romance. It isn't every writer who can pluck every human emotion and deliver the promised happy ending, but this one can! If you can afford only one book this month, make it *Abbie Ann*. You won't be sorry you did!

—*Loree Lough*
Author of more than seventy award-winning inspirational romances, including *Love Finds You in Paradise, Pennsylvania*

With the skill and flair her readers have come to know and love, Shar weaves yet another wonderfully captivating historical tale in *Abbie Ann*. This third book in her Daughters of Jacob Kane series will thrill and delight, as each character learns obedience to God and discovers triumph over tragedy.

—*Jean E. Syswerda*
Best-selling coauthor, *Women of the Bible*
Author, *NIrV Read with Me Bible*
General Editor, *NIV Women of Faith Study Bible*

A delightful voice in the CBA market, Sharlene MacLaren captures the true essence of God's restoring power. *Abbie Ann* is a must-read.

—*Debra Ullrick*
Author, *The Bride Wore Coveralls, Déjà vu Bride, and Dixie Hearts*

A fast-paced, gripping historical romance with true-to-life characters and lively dialogue, filled with surprising twists and turns, *Abbie Ann*, MacLaren's third and final installment in The Daughters of Jacob Kane series, will have you rapidly turning the pages. Absolutely captivating!

—Cindy Bauer
Author, *Chasing Memories* and *Shades of Blue*

With entertaining and emotive prose, Sharlene MacLaren's historical romance novels hold their own amid this ever-popular genre. Her characters have spirit and passion in abundance, and Michigan in the early 1900s is brought to life with her vivid and authentic descriptions. *Abbie Ann* is another feather in Sharlene's auspicious author's cap!

—Rel Mollet
Professional book reviewer, relzreviews.blogspot.com

Abbie Ann offers it all—adventure, romance, and the rewards of seeking God's will. As always, Sharlene MacLaren pens a story that will pull you in and not let go.

—Roseanna White
Senior Reviewer, The Christian Review of Books

Sharlene MacLaren has written a story rich in emotion that will tug at your heart with characters that will live on long after you reach the final page. If you love historical fiction with a sweet romance beautifully woven into a captivating story, then you will love *Abbie Ann*.

—Miralee Ferrell
Author, *Love Finds You in Last Chance, California* and *The Other Daughter*

Abbie Ann

Abbie Ann

A NOVEL BY SHARLENE

MACLAREN

WHITAKER
HOUSE

ABBIE ANN
Third in The Daughters of Jacob Kane Series

Sharlene MacLaren
www.sharlenemaclaren.com

ISBN: 978-1-60374-076-0
Printed in the United States of America
© 2010 by Sharlene MacLaren

Whitaker House
1030 Hunt Valley Circle
New Kensington, PA 15068
www.whitakerhouse.com

Library of Congress Cataloging-in-Publication Data

MacLaren, Sharlene, 1948–
  Abbie Ann / by Sharlene MacLaren.
    p. cm. — (The daughters of Jacob Kane ; 3)
  Summary: "Abbie Ann, Jacob Kane's youngest daughter, is a busy woman
with little time for frivolous matters, including romance—until a handsome,
divorced shipbuilder comes to town, his young son in tow, and God changes
their hearts"—Provided by publisher.
  ISBN 978-1-60374-076-0 (trade pbk.)
  1. Fathers and daughters—Fiction. 2. Shipwrights—Fiction. I. Title.
  PS3613.A27356A63 2010
  813'.6—dc22
                                                2009053168

1 2 3 4 5 6 7 8 9 10 11 12 **W** 18 17 16 15 14 13 12 11 10

To my beautiful mother, Dorothy,
and my precious mother-in-law, Chrystal.

In so many ways, you two fabulous ladies, by SHINING example, have shown Christ to countless others. I love you both and thank you from the deepest regions of my heart.

Chapter One

Sandy Shores, Michigan • February 1907

Abbie Ann Kane marched through the blinding snow on her way to her family's general store as howling winds curled their icy fingers around the buildings of downtown Sandy Shores, hissing and spitting and stinging her nose and cheeks. She pulled her woolen scarf tighter about her neck, but the bitter air still managed to find a hole through which to pass, making her shiver with each hurried step.

The Interurban railcar rumbled past, its whistle alerting pedestrians and horses to make way for its journey up Water Street, Sandy Shores' main thoroughfare. Through its frosty windows, Abbie made out a scant number of passengers and even caught a glimpse of someone drawing letters on a foggy pane. *Probably some bored youngster*, she mused.

Turning her gaze downward, she headed into the strong, easterly gusts, passing the Star Bakery, Van Poort's Grocery Store, Thom Gerritt's Meat Market, Jellema Newsstand, Moretti's Candy Company, Hansen's Shoe Repair, DeBoer's Hardware, and Grant and Son Tailor Shop. Two more doors and she would reach her destination—Kane's Whatnot. Normally, her oldest sister, Hannah, would be working there, but Abbie had assumed primary responsibility for Kane's Whatnot since the birth of Hannah's daughter on January 15. RoseAnn Devlin was Hannah and Gabe's third child, and Hannah had her hands full also caring for eighteen-month-old Alex and their eleven-year-old adopted son, Jesse. Taking responsibility for Kane's Whatnot was the least Abbie could have done, never mind that she barely had time to turn around, what with her teaching Sunday school, serving as president of the local Woman's Christian Temperance Union, assisting Grandmother Kane with the household chores, and visiting the elderly Plooster sisters as often as possible. Poor things depended on her to keep them abreast of all the news in town.

The bell above the wooden door tinkled as Abbie pulled it open, a cold blast of air scooting past her ankles. Her father looked up from his place behind the brass National cash register. "Ah, you're back from lunch, and not a second too soon. I have an appointment with a client at one o'clock. Can you take over from here?"

"Of course, Papa. Just let me hang up my wrap." Besides owning Kane's Whatnot, her father also partnered with Leo Perkins in the insurance business, and the Kane and Perkins office was conveniently situated directly across the street from the Whatnot. Both businesses thrived in this lively, little resort town on the beautiful shores of Lake Michigan, where the winters could be bitter, but the summers were delightfully warm and cheery.

The line for the cash register wound around the center aisle. There were Maxine Card and her young daughter, Lily, their arms full of candles, two loaves of bread, a wooden bowl, and an eggbeater; Landon and Florence Meir, each toting grocery items; and Fred and Dorothy Link, Fred hefting a sack of flour over his shoulder, Dorothy holding some canned goods and a few other items. Abbie moved past her father to hang her winter gear on a hook in the small closet behind the counter, which also served as a washroom. After a quick glance in the tiny mirror on the wall to rearrange the side combs in her flowing, black hair, she rubbed her icy fingers together and joined her father on the other side of the curtain. She felt slightly perturbed that the stove at the back of the store was not giving off nearly enough heat to quell today's subzero temperatures.

"My stars in glory, it's cold," she said. "In fact, I do believe I saw some icicles shivering on my way here."

Precocious Lily Card caught the joke and giggled. "You're silly, Miss Kane. How could icicles shiver?"

"Oh, but they can! And not only that," Abbie added, leaning over the counter to tap the little girl's nose, "but I heard that when the farmers have been milking their cows, they've been getting ice cream!"

This remark earned another rousing giggle from the child, as well as a few good-humored chuckles from the adults within earshot.

"Abbie Ann, where do you come up with these things?" Jacob Kane asked his daughter, shaking his head with a smile.

"If you ask me, it's the worst winter we ever had," Landon Meir groused, obviously finding no humor in Abbie's remarks. "Got more snow out there than Mr. Bayer has aspirin. Probably won't melt till June, neither."

"Or later," his wife countered, ever the pessimist. For as long as Abbie could recall, the woman's face had been pinched in a tight scowl.

Jacob finished ringing up Maxine Card's order, put the items in her burlap sack, and then immediately set to ringing up the Meirs' purchases. Maxine and Lily waved good-bye and exited as two more customers entered, ushering in with them a blast of cold air. Saturdays in winter were usually like this, with folks considering the weather and feeling the need to stock up on supplies. Why, one turn of the wind could make for an all-out blizzard!

"You go on now, Papa. I'll take over," Abbie said, edging her father out of his place behind the cash register.

"All right, then," he said, tallying up the last of the Meirs' purchases. Abbie began stack each item in a small crate. "You'll find today's receipts in the bottom drawer," Jacob told her.

"Fine, Papa. Go, or you'll be late." The clock on the opposite wall registered two minutes till one.

Florence Meir stretched out a palm for her change of two dollars and some odd cents, which Abbie found interesting, since her husband had been the one doling it out. Jacob handed it over, and Florence dropped it into her little drawstring purse. "Come along, Landon; you've got wood to chop and stalls to muck and cows to milk and feed," she murmured through pursed lips as she turned to go. "Best get your chores done 'fore this weather kicks up."

Landon shuffled along behind her. "Crack that whip, Mother."

"Hush up, you ol' fool." The two were still going at it when they stepped into the arctic air, the wind catching the door and closing it with a loud whack. Jacob raised his eyebrows and shook his head, then donned his winter gear and left in the Meirs' wake.

"Ain't them Meirs the happiest pair?" commented the middle-aged Fred Link as he laid a twenty-five-pound sack of flour on the counter.

Dorothy Link set her grocery items beside it and nodded. "I think they love each other in their own way, but Fred here thinks they drink vinegar for breakfast."

"Oh, my goodness!" Abbie covered her mouth to hide her spurt of laughter. "You two behave yourselves."

Behind them, Reba Ortlund chortled. "I'd guess the last time Florence Meir smiled was that Sunday Tillie Overmyer tripped on the top step on her way to the organ. There she was, all sprawled out like a gigantic tortoise on its back, her petticoats fanning her chubby—"

"Mrs. Ortlund!" Abbie cut in, her eyes traversing from Reba Ortlund to her young son at her side. The woman looked only a little sheepish. Fortunately, it seemed that Robert was paying no heed to the conversation, his attentions focused instead on his peppermint stick, which was creating a pink smear across his face that grew with every lick.

Abbie proceeded to tally up the Links' items as quickly as she could with hands that were still thawing, biting her lip to hide her smile. Then, all of a sudden, a thundering crash outside the store shook the building's foundation, shattering the front window and sending store merchandise in every direction. Abbie jolted violently and shrieked, Dorothy Link screamed, and little Robert Ortlund leaped into his mother's arms, his eyes as round as pie shells. It took several seconds to figure out what had happened, but the tongue of a wagon and a bent wheel protruding through the broken window signified a buggy mishap, whether from the icy road conditions, poor visibility, or, perhaps, a spooked horse.

"What in tarnation?" Fred Link bellowed.

Hardly knowing what to do first, Abbie instinctively left her station and ran around the counter, but Fred snagged her by the arm. "Just a minute, there, Miss Abbie. There's shattered glass everywhere. Best hold back till we find out the damages."

"Oh, my London stars!" Abbie gasped, borrowing one of her grandmother's favorite phrases of exclamation and then covering her open mouth. Icy blasts and bursts of snow blew in through the cavernous hole in the wall where a large display window had once been. Outside, a horse gave a mournful whinny, and a soothing, male voice said, "Easy, Ruby Sue." Another male voice asked, "What happened here? Anybody hurt?"

At that, Abbie twisted out of Fred's hold and rushed toward the front of the store, stepping over debris and nearly twisting her ankle as she picked her way through a pile of potatoes that had tumbled out of an overturned barrel. The frigid winds continued to howl, exposing everyone and everything to the outside elements.

Suddenly, folks seemed to come to life as frenzied voices started speaking all at once, and several customers emerged from the far corners of the store to investigate what had happened. Through the yawning hole in the wall, a tall, strapping man materialized, with a young boy clinging tightly to his thigh. "Everyone all right in here?" he asked, bending over at the waist to see inside. His striking, blue eyes came to rest on Abbie, and, despite her tangled thoughts, she couldn't help noticing the way they pulled at her. She'd seen him before, but now was not the time for trying to remember when or where. From beneath the rim of his worn hat, a thick tuft of chestnut-colored hair fell across his forehead.

"I—I think so," she managed, pinching the bridge of her nose in consternation. "What—what just happened?"

"Another rig slid out of control and nearly hit me head-on. I had to swerve to avoid a full-out collision. My horse panicked and went up on the sidewalk, veered off, and sent my rig through your window." He gave a heavy sigh. "Looks like we've done some serious damage." As if on cue, the horse whinnied in loud protest, its hooves pounding on the walkway. Someone on the other side of the wall spoke in steadying tones to the animal, probably to try to keep it from going completely berserk.

"Oh, my goodness! Are you all right? Was—was anyone hurt?" Abbie wasn't sure where to put her eyes—on him or on the little fellow still clinging to the man's leg.

"We're fine. Can't say for sure about that man who almost hit me, though. What about you folks?" At last, he looked away from Abbie to peruse the group of wide-eyed bystanders.

Fred Link stepped forward. "Thank the Lord no one was standing at the front of the store when that window came crashing in—or walking through the door, for that matter. An instant sooner, and the Meirs or Jacob Kane might well have met their ends." Abbie shivered at the very notion of such a tragedy, the bitter air accentuating her chills. Some kind soul retrieved her coat and threw it around her shoulders. She muttered her thanks while trying to collect herself.

Just then, Jacob Kane rushed through the door, his eyes wild with worry. "Abigail Ann! Oh, thank God you're standing."

"Of course, I am, Papa." Like a mere child, she wilted into his open arms, thankful he'd arrived to see to things.

She didn't mind the day-to-day responsibilities at the store, but the business end of things—along with major crises— belonged to Hannah Grace and her father. In fact, if all went as planned, Kane's Whatnot would one day fall to Hannah, who truly had a heart for entrepreneurship. Abbie would stick around for as long as necessary to help run the store, but she had no interest in owning or maintaining it.

"Is everyone all right?" Jacob asked, setting Abbie back from him to assess the matter.

"That seems to be the standard question, Jacob," Fred Link answered. He frowned and scratched behind his ear. "I do believe we're none the worse, but I wouldn't say the same for that window or the front display table, Jacob."

"Ah, well. People are far more important than property," Jacob said, his eyes making a quick scan of the place before focusing on the tall man who had yet to introduce himself. The fellow wiped a gloved hand across his clean-shaven, square-set face, then ducked all the way through the opening. The young boy followed him but stayed in the shadows, probably still frightened nearly to death. Praise God his little body hadn't been thrown from the wagon. The man removed his glove and extended a hand to Jacob. "Noah Carson, sir. You must be Jacob Kane, the owner of this store. I believe you know my uncle, Delbert Huizenga."

"Del Huizenga, of course. We're old friends." Jacob pumped the man's hand. "So, you're Noah Carson. I hear you used to come here about every summer as a lad. Your uncle told me you'd moved to town a few months back, said you'd joined him in his window and door business." Jacob made a half-turn and gestured toward Abbie. "This is my daughter, Abbie Ann. She's been running the store pretty much on her own for the past few weeks."

Noah tipped his hat at Abbie, giving her a better glimpse of his sea-blue eyes with their ocean depth. If he planned to smile, one never materialized. "How-do, ma'am," he said in a stiff manner, his gaze flitting over her face. Despite his formality, she offered a pleasant smile and mentally berated herself for noting his wholly masculine deportment. Her best friend, Katrina Sterling, would say he was like candy to the eyes— never mind that Katrina had a husband and twin girl toddlers, to boot. Whenever she saw a nice-looking man, she'd say, "I may have spent my money all in one place, but that don't mean I can't still look at the merchandise." Of course, everyone knew that Katrina Sterling loved to say brash things. Good thing her husband, Micah, never took her too seriously.

"You really couldn't have avoided that mishap out there," Jacob was saying. "I witnessed the entire thing from my office door across the street. Was just about to step inside when I saw Shamus Rogan barreling up the road, his horses at a full canter." He shook his head. "If you ask me, he was driving that wagon of his far too fast for these weather conditions. Matter of fact, it almost looked like he was heading straight at you with the intention of ramming into you. Thank God things didn't turn out any worse."

"Wouldn't doubt ol' Shamus just pulled out of some saloon," Reba Ortlund offered, sticking out her pointy chin with the declaration. "A body can spot his bloodshot eyes a mile away." Little Robert had resumed work on his peppermint stick, fully engrossed in the gooey substance and seeming to have fully recovered from the shock that Abbie had only now started wrapping her mind around. "Seems like he's always comin' or goin' from one o' them dens of iniquity."

Despite the woman's lack of tact, she did speak the truth. Shamus Rogan was a menace to Sandy Shores and a terror to his family. According to Hannah, over the past year, Arlena Rogan had come into the Whatnot bearing suspicious bruises on her arms and face but always attributing them to her own clumsiness. Hannah had believed her, but Abbie hadn't bought it. Just a few weeks ago, when Arlena had come in bearing bad scratch marks on her neck, Abbie had pressed her for specifics, and she'd relented, her eyes moist in the corners. "My Shamus gets a bit carried away with his temper. 'Fraid he drinks too much, and I complain that he's lazy and doesn't give me any grocery money, even though he makes a decent paycheck at the leather factory…and, well, one thing leads to another, and he puts me in my place." She'd fidgeted with her grocery list, looking down at her shoes. "I must learn to keep my mouth shut, I guess."

The door had opened just then, ushering in several new customers, so Abbie had leaned forward and whispered, "You must take care of yourself and your children and get out of there as quickly as possible. He could kill you in one of his drunken fits."

"Oh, I couldn't divorce him."

"No, I'm not suggesting that. I'm saying you should go to a safe place."

"But I have no place to go. Besides, he'd chase me and the girls down. He wants to be the one pulling all the strings." At that, the woman had gathered up her purchases and headed for the door.

"Mrs. Rogan," Abbie had called after her. "Anytime you need to talk, I'm here."

And that had been invitation enough. Since her initial disclosure, Arlena had come back a number of times to talk to Abbie about her desperate situation. Unfortunately, Abbie had no real solution, other than to tell her she would pray for her.

Indeed, Sandy Shores had far too many drinking establishments, which was the very reason she'd joined ranks with the Woman's Christian Temperance Union a year ago to fight against the town's unbridled use of alcohol. Of course, educating folks about the destructive powers of alcohol wasn't all the W.C.T.U. stood for. They also fought for women's rights and suffrage, fair labor laws, federal aid for education, bans on prostitution, improved public health and sanitation, and international peace, all things for which Abbie had a growing passion. Some called her radical—Peter Sinclair, her beau of eight months, for one. Peter thought a woman's proper place was in the home, and many were the debates they'd had over the matter. Although Abbie's father didn't go that far, he did worry about her, especially since she and several other members of the W.C.T.U. had started singing hymns and holding prayer vigils outside many local saloons. Last month, a dozen or so of them actually had walked straight inside Ervin Baxter's establishment, known simply as Erv's Place, to hold a peaceful gathering. Of course, Erv Baxter's rude behavior in response to their hymn singing, Bible reading, and praying couldn't have been defined as peaceful. No, he'd screamed to the heavens at them after all but a few of his regulars had walked out.

"You're ruining my business!" he'd shouted. "And you're not welcome here. Matter of fact, women in general are not allowed through these doors."

"But there was a woman singing on stage," Abbie had countered, "not to mention those sitting on your patrons' laps."

"They don't count. We got women comin' in here for entertainment purposes." Abbie's spine had gone straight at the implication. Entertainment purposes? "Simply put, we don't need your kind coming in here creating a disturbance."

"We are not a disorderly organization, sir. We are merely interested in reform, of which this country is in deep need. Why, do you know that American men spend more money on beer than they do on meat for their families? That is a disgrace, Mr. Baxter, and you are part of the problem for peddling that poison."

The man's chest had swelled to twice its size as he'd tried to breathe through his obvious anger. "How dare you," he'd growled, putting a pause between each word. "It's not my problem if folks got a thirst for booze. It ain't like I'm forcin' it down their throats. I'm just tryin' to make a living, like everybody else in this town, and I'd appreciate a little respect."

The W.C.T.U. purposed not to argue or defy, a policy Abbie sometimes had difficulty following, yet it had been clear she'd get nowhere by continuing a dialogue with Erv Baxter. *Best leave before his hostile attitude burgeons out of control,* she'd thought. "We'll be going now, sir, but you can be assured we will continue our campaign. Make no mistake, the prohibition of alcoholic beverages will one day prevail in this country."

He'd cleared his throat and spat on the already sticky wood floor, having no apparent compunction amid the small group of dignified women. "You ladies stay away from my saloon, or I'll—I'll make you plenty sorry."

Ignoring his halfhearted threat, Abbie had turned on her heel, her silent band of nervous crusaders following after her like ducklings after their mama.

"Well, Gabe will get to the bottom of this," her father was saying, quickly calling Abbie back to the present. "Someone's fetched him, so he should be arriving on the scene most any minute, if he's not already out there." Jacob put a hand on one of Noah's broad shoulders. "Looks like we'll be needing your window-building skills around here, young man."

"You've got it, sir. In fact, I'll take full responsibility for cleaning up this place and making all the necessary repairs."

"We'll see about that. Seems to me Shamus Rogan ought to own up to some of the blame. In the meantime, we'll board up the hole and replace the window when the weather calms down." Jacob took a moment to look at the young boy beside Noah. "What's your name, young fellow?"

Noah nudged the little guy forward. "This here is my boy. Say hello, Toby."

The child raised his gaze long enough to peek at Jacob, and that's when it dawned on Abbie that she'd seen him before—in her Sunday school class of six-year-olds. An older woman, Julia Huizenga, had started dropping him off at the door about three weeks ago. As far as Noah's familiarity, she now recalled having spotted him perched on a pew at the back of the church following Sunday school.

Abbie bent at the waist, her clasped hands on her knees. "Well, hello there, Toby. Do you remember me?"

Toby considered her thoughtfully and scrunched his cherub nose, which was covered with a spray of freckles. Then, his blue eyes brightened. "You're my Sunday school teacher. You're the one what taught us about that old fellow who built the big boat before it rained. His name was Noah, just like my dad."

"That's exactly right," Abbie said, her eyes roaming from the boy to his father and quickly back again. "Aren't you clever for remembering that?"

"He's a smart boy," his father said, his voice bolstered by pride, and he pulled Toby to his side.

A gust of wind bellowed through the building. "My sweet sister, it's cold in here!" Reba Ortlund exclaimed. "Can someone ring up my items so Robert and I can be on our way?"

Abbie gave a quick turn. "Oh, mercy, yes. I almost forgot I was in the middle of totaling up the Links' items. Let's finish so you folks can go home and get warm."

"I think we'd best close up the store for the remainder of the afternoon," Jacob said. The customers who had been in the store prior to the accident had wandered out to the street, where a curious crowd had gathered, despite the unrelenting wind.

"What say I run over to the shop and pick up some wood to fix that gaping hole, sir?" Noah Carson said to her father. "Afterward, Toby and I'll help clean up this mess."

Jacob nodded and pulled at his gray beard, allowing his eyes to appraise his surroundings. It took a lot to dampen Jacob Kane's spirits, and this minor setback to his business would not come close to succeeding.

Chapter Two

With precise aim, Noah Carson drove in the last nail to secure a board over the window he'd managed to knock out when his horse had veered off the road, sending his ancient rig careening through the Whatnot's window. At one time, he might have thanked the Lord for keeping everybody safe, especially Toby, but his cynical self said God probably hadn't had too much to do with it. If He'd truly wanted to intervene, He might have considered disallowing the accident altogether. At any rate, Noah shuddered to think what might have happened if someone had been standing in front of the window when his wagon had slid off course, then shook his head in disbelief that neither he nor Toby had been thrown to the ground. Whether one chose to thank God or not, it was a miracle they'd both walked away from the accident unharmed.

A number of citizens had shown up at the Whatnot to lend a hand in the cleanup, which was quite impressive, considering the blustery storm. As evening approached, the wind and snowfall increased, but so did the number of volunteers, a new concept for Noah, who'd moved to Sandy Shores from Guilford, Connecticut, last September. Not that Guilford wasn't known for its friendly, hometown atmosphere. But folks there had considered him less than respectable. All that most people had cared to know was that he'd divorced the daughter of the well-to-do, highly esteemed Carl Dunbar, and that his father, Gerald Carson, was a drunk who'd never amounted to much. Chances were slim that people would have come out in droves to offer a hand if he'd been involved in an accident there. At least, here, in Sandy Shores, his reputation didn't precede him.

Noah tilted his head to look at Toby, who'd taken to following Miss Kane around the store. He bent down to help her pick up a wooden crate, and it was clear her jovial manner put him at ease. Noah would be lying to say the woman hadn't struck him as downright beautiful with that flowing, rich, charcoal-colored hair and creamy complexion, not to mention her lovely, delicate, oval face and slender but observably curvaceous body. She was one of the finest-looking women he'd ever laid eyes on, no matter that he wasn't the least bit interested in learning more about her. He'd had enough of women to take him into the next century.

Shamus Rogan sat in the county jail awaiting arraignment. As suspected, the numbskull had had one too many drinks at a hangout called Erv's Place, and the odds were, he hadn't yet figured out how he'd landed himself in the clink. According to Sheriff Devlin, Jacob Kane's son-in-law, the fellow was still so plastered that he couldn't even recite the days of the week.

The store hummed with the sounds of volunteers picking up broken glass and debris, sorting through strewn merchandise to either pack it in crates or arrange it on the shelves, and sweeping brooms across the hardwood floor. Every so often, someone prattled about the senseless accident and proclaimed his wish to see Shamus Rogan spend a few nights in jail, lamented the swelling winter storm, praised last Sunday's brilliant sermon, or expressed outrage at the price of hogs these days. But Noah kept his comments to a minimum, anxious to fulfill his responsibilities and still get Toby to bed at a decent hour. He also wanted to avoid questions he didn't feel comfortable answering. Since his arrival in Sandy Shores, he'd established few friendships, and, thankfully, his aunt and uncle respected his need for anonymity. The divorce still had his head spinning, and it felt good to be in a place where folks didn't look down their noses at him or speak in whispers behind his back.

"Soon as you get that wind'r replaced and fix some of them boards out front, you should be up and runnin' again, Jacob," said some shabbily clad fellow who'd stopped by the Whatnot to lend a hand after already spending a long day at work.

"And you got yourself a good insurance agent," one woman chimed in from the back, giggling at her own remark.

"He won't be needing to file any claim," Noah heard himself say. All eyes alighted on him, and he cleared his throat. "What I mean to say is, I take full responsibility for the damage done to Mr. Kane's store, and I've already told him I intend to make the necessary repairs."

"And I've told you we'll see about that, young man," Jacob Kane said from behind the counter, his eyebrows arched above his kind, gray eyes, which peered over the hefty crate he was carrying. "If I know Judge Bowers, he'll be putting the bulk of the responsibility on Shamus Rogan's shoulders, just where it should be. Man's got to pay for his own mistakes."

"Maybe, but in the meantime, I'll do my part. No reason why you or your business should be inconvenienced." Noah's eyes traversed the room to an attentive Miss Kane, then to his son, who'd found some wooden blocks with which to build himself a tower on the floor. He made a visual path back to Mr. Kane. "I've already taken the window measurements, and I can check Uncle Delbert's inventory first thing Monday. Might be he'll have the right size in stock, so we won't have to order it. I should have the frame built within a couple of days."

"Well, I appreciate that, son," Jacob said, bending to set his heavy load on the floor behind the counter before bouncing back up. "I presume you've all met Noah Carson and his fine son, folks," he announced. "They come from somewhere out East, isn't that right?"

"Connecticut, sir." Noah swept a glance over the room. "Nice meeting all of you. Toby, say hello to the folks."

His son looked up from his play and croaked a quiet hello. Noah should have taught him the proper display of manners, but he didn't consider himself the most consistent parent.

Several people offered cheery greetings before returning to their tasks. "Nathanial Brayton," a rather bulbous-nosed, middle-aged man said, stepping forward with an outstretched hand. "So, you're the one who joined Del in his window business. Delbert runs a fine operation over there. It's good you came. He gets mighty busy every spring, when all them Chicago folks come up here to work on their lake cottages. Matter of fact, he's replaced a few windows out at my place."

"Mine, too," someone said.

"And mine," another echoed.

"You do that sort of work out in Massachusetts?" Nathanial asked.

"Connecticut," he quietly corrected him. "No, sir, the window business is new to me."

"That so? What sort of business did you do back East?"

It was a fair question but one on which he didn't care to elaborate. One answer would lead to another question—and another. "Manufacturing," he replied, hoping it'd suffice.

He needn't have worried, for, just then, the front door blew open, and in its frame stood Peter Sinclair, vice president of Sandy Shores Bank and Trust. Noah believed the young man to be the nephew of the bank president, Roland Withers. In fact, he'd sat in Sinclair's office just two days ago, filing paperwork on Uncle Delbert's behalf for acquiring a loan to expand his company's building. While his uncle's business was booming almost out of control, he wasn't the best at keeping track of it, and since his former accountant had moved to another state, Noah had been volunteering his limited expertise until his uncle hired someone else. He'd been the brawn behind his successful shipbuilding company back East, and his partner, Tom Grayson, the brains. In a fleeting moment, he wondered how Tom was faring without him, not having the greatest skill when it came to solo shipbuilding.

Sinclair closed the door behind him, shutting out the howling winds that chased around the building. He brushed a layer of snow off his coat, removed his bowler hat, and scanned the place until his piercing eyes landed on Abbie Ann Kane.

"Abigail, you're all right." He reached her in five or six giant steps, even with having to dart around objects and people. "I only just heard about the accident when closing up the bank. Of course, I rushed right over." He tossed his hat on a shelf and wrapped her in a bear hug, albeit a short-lived one, since Miss Kane hastily stepped out of it, her face gone somewhat pink.

"Of course, I'm all right, Peter," she said, speaking just above a whisper. So as not to appear interested in the exchange, Noah started picking up some tools and tidying the space around him. Still, he couldn't help but keep one sly eye on the pair. "And you needn't have rushed over. My goodness, you're soaking wet, not to mention cold as marble."

"You're sure you're fine?" he asked by way of a response, his hands clutching her upper arms. "From what I hear, it was a narrow escape, the way that wagon crashed through the front window. Someone said it missed you by inches, knocked you flat over, in fact."

"Oh, for crying in a basket!" she exclaimed. "How rumors do fly. I was standing behind the cash register, and, as you can see, I'm just fine. In fact, praise the Lord, everyone came out unscathed."

"Well, that's good news." Sinclair pushed out a long sigh and paused to give her an up-and-down assessment. She was something to feast the eyes on, Noah quietly observed, but then reminded himself of his recent troubles and decided it'd be a long time before he looked at another woman. "What blasted, crazy fool did this awful thing, anyway?" Sinclair asked in a scoffing tone.

Noah stood up and made an about-turn. "'Fraid that blasted fool would be me," he said.

"He wasn't to blame," Abbie said hastily. "Shamus Rogan was drunk and nearly hit him head-on. You see, that is exactly why I detest those awful drinking establishments."

"Amen to that," someone in the room called out.

Sinclair rubbed the back of his head, where his neatly trimmed brown hair was parted down the middle. Two days ago, Noah had thought the fellow's dapper looks were nearly impeccable, and he thought it now, as well—from the top of his plastered-down hair to his neat-as-a-pin pencil mustache; from his stylish, buttoned wool coat with the flip collar and his Scottish plaid scarf to his fine, lambskin leather shoes, protected by rubber overshoes. Indeed, the fellow knew a thing or two about style.

Recognition dawned in his smooth, unruffled expression as he pointed a finger at Noah. "Carson, right? Noah Carson. We met in my office a few days ago."

"That's right." Noah stepped over some debris to meet the fellow halfway and reached out a hand. They shook. "Good seeing you again," he fibbed. The guy was probably the nicest kind you'd ever meet, but thanks to the Dunbar family's out-right snootiness, he'd learned to put up a wall when he was around wealthy folks.

Outside, the wind kept up its constant howl. Jacob Kane strode from behind the counter and cleared his throat. "Sorry to break the news to you generous folks, but the time has come for sending you home. I don't like the sound of that storm, and I won't take any chances on your getting caught in it. Besides, there's not much left to do but rearrange vari-ous items, and only Abbie will know where she wants them to go."

"We can come back on Monday, if you like," one kind soul said.

"That's not necessary," Abbie spoke up, sweeping a lock of glistening hair behind one diminutive ear. "Papa and I will handle matters."

A few more murmurs of protest rose up, but most people started moving toward the door after donning their winter gear.

"Think we'll have church tomorrow?" someone asked.

"Don't know why a little storm would cancel services," another answered. "We Baptists don't believe in canceling."

"We Lutherans cancelled twice last year," yet another said from behind a tall shelf.

"Us Catholics got the advantage. We can go to confession any day of the week."

Noah smiled at the banter. There was no help for it.

"The Third Street Church closed in that blizzard of '03, if you'll recall," a man said while plopping a wool cap over his long, mousy hair. At the door, he pulled at his scruffy beard and took a gander outside. "The way that snow's comin' down, we might see another foot of it come mornin'."

At those words, the room cleared fast. Noah gathered up his belongings and took one load out to his uncle's rig, then returned for the rest. The repairs to his own busted-up wagon would take a few days, not to mention a few dollars— dollars he didn't have to spare but would somehow scrape up. There had been a time when he'd had a wad of money in the bank—more than he could count—but, thanks to Suzanna, her high-powered attorney father, and Tom Grayson, those days were gone. Noah had Toby, though, so he figured he'd come out the clear winner.

"Better put those blocks back where you found them, Toby. It's well past your bedtime," Noah said, arranging his hammer and box of nails in his toolbox, then snapping the lid shut. He stood to survey the area one last time before swiveling to look back at Toby, who didn't appear to be in any hurry, his longish hair falling over his blue eyes a reminder that they both needed to pay the barber a visit.

"Can we stay a little longer? Look at my building."

"I see your building, and it's downright fine, but we have to be on our way. The Kanes are anxious to lock up their store."

Jacob Kane had disappeared to the back room, where Noah presumed they stored extra merchandise, leaving Toby and him alone with Miss Kane. Her beau had left with the others after she'd turned down his offer to drive her home, saying her father would take her.

She crouched down next to Toby and rumpled his blond hair. "If you'd like, you can come back sometime. You saw the toy box we keep at the back of the store. This is a fine-looking structure, by the way. It's a shame we have to dismantle it, but...you know what?" Her tone had dipped in a mischievous way, catching Toby's attention.

He tipped his chin up at her. "What?"

With a clever grin, she crouched down further so that she was at eye level with him. "Knocking it down is half the fun."

She glanced up at Noah, her dark-as-midnight hair falling over one shoulder, her brown eyes flickering like summer lightning. He couldn't keep a smile from forming.

Toby's mouth curved up in surprise, and he bobbed his head.

"On the count of three, then?" Miss Kane asked.

"Yeah."

She sucked in a deep breath, as if preparing for a major event. "One...two...three!"

On three, Toby let his arm fly, sending his miniature edifice in various directions and emitting a burst of giggles such as Noah hadn't heard for some time. The fact was, since the divorce and the subsequent move to Michigan, there'd been very little cause for mirth in their little household of two. His smile broadened as he watched the laughing pair set to retrieving the blocks and placing them back into their container.

Noah would have bent to help, but he much preferred watching the clever, pretty woman convince her son that carrying out a simple chore could be downright fun.

Chapter Three

S ometime during the course of the night, the winds died down to a gentle breeze, and what snow had accumulated in Sandy Shores fell far short of Arend Fordham's one-foot prediction. Abbie felt restless, so she spent several hours gazing at the fresh-fallen snow from her second-story bedroom window, noting how a lingering full moon and a smattering of stars cast their shimmery glow across the front yard, where nothing but a rabbit moved about, hopping from tree to tree, no doubt in search of break-fast. She decided to throw some lettuce leaves out there when Grandmother Kane wasn't looking. "Those critters take over my garden in the summer, Abbie Ann," she always com-plained. "They certainly don't need any encouragement from you to loiter in my yard over the winter months."

"But what will they eat, otherwise?" Abbie had once asked.

"Good gravy, I don't know. But they survive somehow, because they never miss a summer banquet at my vegetable garden."

Abbie fell asleep just before five, and when she woke up a couple of hours later, she could smell the tantalizing aromas of cinnamon and bacon wafting through the house's heat registers. Even though just three people—Grandmother Kane, Papa, and she—inhabited the rambling house, Grandmother never failed to provide a daily feast, and for nearly every meal. The woman loved her kitchen and everything that went with it: baking, cooking, cleaning, organizing, and meal planning. Sadly, Abbie didn't share her zeal.

Hannah Grace surely did, maintaining her busy household of five and, until recently, working at Kane's Whatnot several hours a day. When RoseAnn had grown a bit and Hannah could take her and Alex to stay with Mrs. Garvey, the widow living next door to the Devlins, Hannah would resume her responsibilities at the Whatnot. Their father had decided to hire an extra hand or two, which would lighten everyone's load, but Hannah loved the Whatnot, claiming it gave her added purpose. The town library finally had its own building and was no longer headquartered above the Whatnot, which gave the family one less thing to think about.

And then, there was Maggie Rose Madison, the middle sister, who lived in New York City with her husband, Luke, and their brood of orphans, some legally adopted and others fostered, along with baby Lucas, the couple's biological child, who'd come into the world last August. No question, the Madisons' lives were full to brimming over.

Abbie could barely imagine trying to keep up with either of her sisters' busy, family-filled lifestyles. Oh, no one would accuse her of lacking fervor, and she rarely complained about carrying her share of the household chores, but her passions didn't lie in domestic matters—or even in business or industry. Rather, her heart blossomed to its fullest when nurtured by faith-centered causes. She wouldn't say she had a missionary heart like Maggie did; no, Abbie's heart pulsed with a passion to revolutionize the world, beginning right in the little town of Sandy Shores and expanding out as the Lord saw fit. One could do only so much to leave one's mark on humanity, though, and she was just one little woman, emphasis on *little*. In fact, sometimes, she felt so insignificant in the grand scheme of things that she wondered what possible purpose God could have had in placing her on this earth.

She stretched her slender arms skyward and gave a loud yawn, then moved to the bureau. Pulling open a drawer, she took out her silk underthings and walked to the massive closet, which also served as the family's attic. Besides an abundant supply of dresses, hats, coats, capes, and footwear, the room held boxes of memorabilia, blankets, old toys, treasured paintings, rolled-up rugs, countless volumes of books, and an array of items Abbie couldn't even name. Her grandmother and father were, by definition, pack rats, but at least they were neat ones.

From the rack holding all her dresses, Abbie selected a rose-hued, velvet, long-sleeved affair that would serve her well on this cold, late-February morning. It had a belted waist, a button-up bodice, and a high collar trimmed with lace. From a high shelf, she chose a pair of black, patent-leather, lace-up boots to complement the dress, declaring she would be happy when spring arrived in all its glory and she could return to wearing her white, kid-leather dress shoes with rosettes or a lightweight pair of silk, button-up boots with one of her frothy, washable day dresses of linen or cotton trimmed with tiny pin tucks and embroidery.

Sighing wistfully, she left the closet, tossed her clothing onto her yet unmade bed, and began unbuttoning her cambric nightgown. She shivered at the chill in the air, then grimaced at her image in the cheval glass mirror. Her jet-black hair looked disheveled beyond help, so she decided to wear it up for a change, perhaps in a Gibson Girl bouffant, letting half of it fall in soft waves about her face, since that was what it wanted to do, anyway. Miss Ida Sprig, who always stood at the top of the stairs in the church foyer on Sunday mornings—not to greet incoming worshippers but to see who'd failed to show—would no doubt frown at her Gibson Girl hairdo. Depending on her mood, she might even comment with something like, "I don't understand ladies' styles these days. They're almost flagrant. Why, some women are even starting to show their ankles. Can you imagine?" Of course, the forty-something Ida Sprig still wore a bustle under her skirts and a stuffed bird in her feathered hat, so what on earth did she know about fashion? Not that fashion ruled Abbie Ann's thoughts, but she did believe in staying current with the times.

While she worked on pulling her dressing gown over her head, she reflected on what could have caused her poor night's sleep. Deep down, she knew that the dratted accident was to blame. The sight of Peter rushing into the Whatnot and hauling her into his arms in plain view of everyone, and the excitement of meeting Noah Carson for the first time, muddled her thoughts. My, but Noah Carson's arresting, blue eyes did give a body pause. This put her on a path of wondering why she'd never spotted a Mrs. Carson sitting next to him in the back pew.

"Abigail Ann, are you up and about?" Her grandmother's voice carried up from the foot of the stairs, where Abbie pictured her standing in one of her tailor-made, all-wool suits with the perfectly fitted skirt and double-breasted jacket, handsomely appliquéd with stylish, cloth-covered buttons and loop buttonholes. Grandmother Kane was nothing if she wasn't elegant from head to toe. Even pushing seventy, she had a trim figure and a creamy, nearly flawless complexion, and her long, silver hair was always woven into a neat bun at the nape of her neck.

Abbie snapped to attention, inhaled deeply, and gave her head a shake. "Yes, Grandmother. I'll be down shortly," she called out, snatching up her petticoats and hastening into them.

"Breakfast is on the table. You best hurry before it gets cold."

She had little appetite, but for the sake of appeasing Grandmother, she would force down a thick piece of toasted bread with strawberry preserves and, perhaps, a crisp slice or two of bacon.

K

The vestibule of the Third Street Church was abuzz with the sounds of stomping boots and warm how-do-you-dos mixed with moans of complaint about the frigid temperatures and last night's snowstorm. Jacob helped Abbie Ann and Grandmother Kane out of their long wraps, which he hung on wooden hangers in the cloakroom. Abbie removed her wool hat and set it on a shelf, while her grandmother kept hers firmly planted atop her head, since it matched her navy suit.

"Abbie!" The shrill voice resounding through the crowded room came from Abbie's best friend, Katrina Sterling. Abbie whirled at its sound and found the slim-figured girl standing at the top of the stairs, smack-dab next to Ida Sprig, whose owl-eyed expression rained down disapproval on Katrina, no doubt for the way she'd raised her voice in the Lord's house.

Katrina scampered—flew, rather—down the steps like a schoolgirl, another no-no in Miss Sprig's eyes. Predictably, the woman's thin lips tightened with outright displeasure.

"Katrina!" Abbie exclaimed, embracing her friend. The two had been close since grade school and never had gotten over their giddiness at seeing each other, even though Katrina had up and married shortly after high school graduation and, a couple of years later, given birth to twin girls, Cora and Clara. By all accounts, she and Abbie ought to have drifted apart for lack of common ground, but, instead, their friendship had flourished through the years. "Where are Micah and the girls?" Abbie asked, looking around.

"The girls have the sniffles, so Micah stayed home with them."

"Tell me you did not maneuver the wagon through this snow on your own."

Katrina didn't have a dependent bone in her body and often had trouble submitting to her husband's authority, even though she did give it her best effort most of the time. Thankfully, Micah's calm, perhaps even lenient, personality was accommodating of Katrina's overbearing one. Katrina shook her burnished curls from side to side, her green eyes shimmering in the morning light. "I rode into town with the Frandsens. I rang them early this morning about it, and they were more than happy to pick me up. I would've driven the rig on my own, but Micah put his foot down."

"No," Abbie said with mock astonishment. "How could this be, when you seem to have the upper hand more times than not, Katrina Sterling?"

Her friend smiled and leaned in close. "Not so, my dear Abbie. Micah truly does control the reins, but I have some secrets up my sleeve that help steer him in the direction I'd like him to go. I'll share some titillating tidbits with you after you marry Peter."

Katrina may have been her best friend, but Abbie still felt her cheeks warming. "What makes you think I'm going to marry Peter?"

"Well, why wouldn't you? He's a brilliant, God-fearing, Christian man with the means to support you; he's respected in the community, as is his family; and, best of all, he's mad about you! I don't know why you won't just say yes to the poor man, Abbie Ann Kane. You know he'd make a fine husband."

Why, indeed? Wasn't he all those things and more? Still, Abbie couldn't lay aside her disappointment that Peter Sinclair simply didn't set off a wave of sparks when he kissed her. Hannah Grace always talked about how anxious she was to see Gabe every night at suppertime, how he still made her heart quiver whenever she laid eyes on him—and all that after having three children, for heaven's sake! Moreover, in Maggie Rose's letters to Abbie, she talked about how grand it was to be married to Luke, the fun they had sharing life together, and how romantic he could be. It wasn't that Peter made no noble attempts at being romantic. He'd sent her flowers on Christmas Eve, taken her sailing last summer (which was her favorite experience ever, even though he'd rented the boat and hired a skipper), and, once, he'd had his mother pack them a lunch so they could climb to the top of Five Mile Hill for a picnic. Granted, she would have preferred Peter to have packed the lunch himself, but one couldn't be too choosy.

"He's not too fond of my involvement with the Woman's Christian Temperance Union. I know he'd expect me to give it up if I ever married him, and you know I won't do that. Besides," she leaned close to Katrina's right ear, picking up her floral scent, "he doesn't actually, you know, make my heart flutter."

"Oh, well, that is a problem," Katrina said solemnly. "Why, just last night, my Micah came in from the barn all mussed and dirty from mucking stalls, and, would you believe, the sight of his big frame coming through the door set my head to thinking all sorts of foolish things?"

"Please don't reveal anything private between you and Micah, Katrina Sterling. You'll have me blushing. Besides, I have to get to my classroom."

She turned, but as she did, Katrina grabbed her arm and whirled her back around.

"What—?"

"Oh, my stockings and garters, would you look at that? No, don't. Keep talking to me, so he won't suspect," she ordered, gawking over Abbie's shoulder. "Glory sakes, who is that?" she mumbled dreamily and between breathless gasps.

Abbie slowly angled her head in the direction of the double doors, through which icy air was wafting into the room. Her eyes scanned the lobby until they landed on the subject of Katrina's curiosity, not that she really wondered: Noah Carson and his sweet little boy.

"Oh, him," she said nonchalantly. "That's Noah Carson and his son, Toby. He's the one who smashed through the window of Kane's Whatnot last night. Of course, it wasn't his fault. He was—"

"What?" Katrina interrupted on another airy breath. "There was an accident at the Whatnot? Was anybody—? I never heard—You never told—Why am I always the last to know these things?" She actually stomped her booted heel, making Abbie laugh.

"My darling Kat, you hardly gave me a chance to tell you."

"Untrue." She sneaked another peek over Abbie's shoulder and whispered, "You'll have to give me all the details later."

"There's not much to tell."

"Is he married?"

"I have no idea."

Katrina clutched her throat. "Saints above, he's coming this way."

"Would you settle down? You are a married woman, remember?"

"Well, of course, I am—happily, I might add. But just because I spent all my money in one place doesn't mean I can't—"

"—still look at the merchandise, I know," Abbie finished.

"Miss Kane!" The ebullient voice had her turning and staring down into the wondering blue eyes of Toby Carson—eyes much like his father's, now that Abbie saw them in the morning light. But she dared not study Noah's eyes, lest she appear interested, so she merely cast him a speedy look before returning her full attention to Toby. "My Pa brought me to Sunday school this time 'cause Aunt Julia's got a headache," he volunteered.

"I'm so happy to see you," Abbie said, bending down to touch the tip of his freckled nose. Then, she straightened to give his father a perfunctory glance. "Good morning, Mr. Carson."

His greeting sounded brisk but polite. "Morning."

"You plan to attend the men's Bible class, I presume?"

"Well, I...."

"You might as well, now that you're here. It's in that room right there." She pointed down the long corridor. "In fact, my father is going in just now."

Noah's square chin jutted upward with his hurried glance down the hall. "Yes, I see him."

Katrina gave her throat an impatient clearing, and Abbie tried not to wince. "Oh, Mr. Carson, this is my friend, *Mrs.* Katrina Sterling," she said by way of introduction.

"I'm delighted to meet you," Katrina gushed, giving him her hand. "I hope to see you again. Perhaps my husband and I can have you and your wife and son join us for supper some evening."

Noah seemed to force a smile, which failed to reach his eyes. His lips parted, but Toby beat him to the punch in answering. "He don't have a wife anymore. My ma and him got a divor—"

"Toby." Noah placed his hand on the lad's shoulder and— pinched him? Toby clamped his mouth shut and squirmed slightly.

So, he is divorced. How sad for Toby, Abbie thought. To ease the situation, she took the child's hand and pulled him gently toward her. "I'll be glad to take your son to my classroom."

"If you're sure, then," Noah said, stepping back. He looked down at Toby. "You be good in class, now, you hear?" The boy gave a sullen nod and inched closer to Abbie. "I'll pick you up afterward."

"Oh, no need," Abbie said. "I'll bring him upstairs myself. That's how we do it here. Folks usually either bring their children to my classroom door or send them down of their own accord. They know where to go. At the close of class, I deliver them to their parents in plenty of time for the morning service."

"Fine." He made a half turn, then paused. "Very nice meeting you, Mrs...."

"Sterling. Katrina Sterling. My husband's name is Micah. Perhaps you'll meet him next week."

"Perhaps." With that, Noah turned and headed down the long corridor, disappearing into the room to which Abbie had pointed. She pictured her father, the gracious soul, jumping up to introduce Noah to the roomful of men. Or, maybe, Peter would do the honors, since he taught the class. He'd be standing at the front of the room now, gathering his thoughts and reviewing his notes. Peter, capable and intelligent when it came to the Bible, yet lacking the ability to make her heart thrum with romantic notions. Oh, he'd make a fine husband someday, but for whom? *Lord, if it's to be me, would You please plant a fast-growing seed of love for him in my heart?* Abbie prayed silently.

"Oh, as I live and breathe." Katrina fumbled with her white kid glove, fanning her face with it.

Abbie rolled her eyes, then turned to Toby. "Toby, why don't you walk downstairs to the classroom and tell the others I'm on my way? And, if you don't mind, take the pencil can down from the shelf and—oh, never mind that." Picturing a dozen six-year-olds with pencils in their hands and nothing to do with them but poke each other gave her pause. "Just tell them I'll be right there."

He turned and skipped down the stairs.

As soon as he'd vanished, Abbie turned on Katrina, putting her slightly turned-up nose close to her friend's petite one. "Katrina Sterling, I swear I am going to strangle you one of these days, and take my sweet time doing it," she hissed.

As expected, Katrina put on her most innocent expression. "I did nothing wrong. Merely invited him to supper some night."

"Along with his wife."

"Who doesn't exist, we just learned. He's divorced. Did you catch that? His son was about to provide us with that little tidbit."

"Little tidbit? Katrina, divorce is no small matter."

"True, but at least now we know what we're dealing with. Aren't I clever, darling Abbie?"

"Clever? Try conniving, my friend. Anyway, it's useless information."

"But he's an available bachelor!"

A long, breathy burst of air escaped Abbie's lungs. "I have no idea of this man's spiritual state, and even if I did, I'm not interested in a divorced man."

"You don't even know the circumstances behind the divorce. It could be a very sad tale."

"Most are. Divorce is appalling and hurtful, especially when children are involved."

Katrina's eyes softened. "Indeed, but you are a forward-thinking young woman and usually very forgiving."

"Forgiveness has nothing to do with it. I'm simply not interested in used merchandise."

"Abigail Ann, this is the twentieth century, and, unfortunately, divorce is slowly becoming more commonplace."

"You're not accepting of that fact, I hope."

"Of course not. I abhor the problem." Her eyes drifted down the long corridor. "Poor man. You do have to admit he's a fine-looking specimen, though—not nearly as striking as my Micah, of course, but unbelievably handsome nonetheless."

Abbie allowed her eyes to traverse down the hallway. "All right, all right, I'll give you that."

She noted that the place had nearly cleared of parishioners. Even Ida Sprig had vacated her station at the top of the stairs. "Goodness, I've got to go." She put a hand to Katrina's arm. "You are the berries, Kat Sterling, but I love you, anyway." She headed toward the stairs.

"Come see me sometime," Katrina called after her.

"If I can find the time, I surely will."

Chapter Four

Noah spent the better share of Monday afternoon installing the new window at Kane's Whatnot. Thankfully, his uncle had had the correct glass in stock, but he'd had to build the unusually large frame at the shop and transport it to the store for insertion. The job wound up taking a bit more work than he'd bargained for since he'd had to replace the lower supports with new two-by-fours, the others having been cracked at impact. At least the header had not been compromised, a blessing in itself. He still marveled that neither he nor Toby had suffered as much as a muscle ache from the accident; and, to his knowledge, the only thing Shamus Rogan suffered was disgrace, now that he'd sobered up enough to realize what he'd done. According to Sheriff Devlin, the judge planned to make him sit in jail for a good month, given that he'd had previous offenses. He'd also ordered him to pay all damages, including the cost of repairing Noah's rig, which now sat at Jeb's Wagon and Wheel Repair two blocks over. He hadn't expected the judge's ruling to be the first thing on his Monday agenda, so the news had come as a pleasant surprise when the sheriff had paid him a visit at his uncle's shop that morning.

Little conversation had transpired between Abbie Ann Kane and him while he'd worked, which had suited him just fine. She was a chipper little thing when it came to interacting with her customers, even a bit of a jokester, but she'd made a point—at least, that was how it had seemed to him—of ignoring his company. Jacob Kane had decided that, despite the condition of the storefront, it couldn't hurt to remain open for business. "Folks need supplies," he'd said that morning. "Hopefully, they won't get in your way as you work."

Noah liked the man's genial manner. "It's the other way around, sir. I'm sorry to inconvenience your business."

"Not at all. These things happen. Gracious, we're just so thankful no one was injured in the mishap. Isn't that right, Abigail?"

Abbie had affirmed her father's remark with a jaunty nod, her raven hair falling in soft curves about her narrow shoulders. She'd worn it up in some kind of frivolous do for Sunday services, but, today, she'd simply let it hang down her back, pinned up at the sides with shimmery combs. Noah couldn't decide which style he preferred but then quickly checked himself for even giving the matter a second's thought. What did he care how a woman chose to wear her hair? He used to enjoy running his fingers through Suzanna's soft, tawny wavelets—that is, before things had gone sour between them. That was history now. Since then, he'd not given a woman so much as a glance, and he didn't intend to start now.

"Yes, Papa, it is a blessing, indeed. Sweet sisters of mercy, to think what might have been! Oh, I hate to allow my mind to even go there." She gave a visible shudder and favored Noah with the tiniest glance before going back to arranging items on a table. He carefully hid his grin at her euphemism. The girl did have quite a supply of inimitable expressions, none of which made much sense to him.

By four o'clock, with his job mostly complete, save for adding a second coat of paint to the trim work and wall, he stood back to inspect his work.

"It looks very nice, Mr. Carson." He turned slightly, surprised by the acknowledgement from Miss Kane, and suddenly became aware that the store had emptied of customers, for the time being.

"Thanks. I'll put the second coat of paint on tomorrow. That should just about finish things up."

Miss Kane lifted her skirts a notch and approached from behind the counter, where she'd been doing some figuring, her booted heels clicking on the wood floor. "My, you do work fast. To think that was a boarded-up space just this morning, and now there's a sparkling, new window there." She came and stood not two feet away from him, her hands clasped at her slim waist. Some sort of wispy, floral scent wafted off of her as she admired the pane, and he found himself inhaling deeply.

"I never have been one to dally. My mother used to say...." But what was he doing? He didn't cotton to conversing with the woman at the risk of sparking personal questions.

She swiveled her body slightly to look at him, and there came another whiff of that lovely scent. He stepped forward to the new window to run a hand over the fresh-sanded casing, drawing pleasure from its sleek feel with its single coat of white paint. Even with his back to her, though, he sensed her watchful, dubious gaze. Outside, the snow had started coming down again—in the form of large, crystal flakes—as if Sandy Shores didn't already have plenty of the soggy white stuff slowing down traffic. As it was, the storekeepers were running out of places to shovel it clear of their entryways. "You were saying? About your mother?"

"What? Oh, just that…nothing important."

"No, really, what did she used to say?" She joined him at the window now, making him conscious of how he towered over her. Across the street, two men stood under the canopy of the Kane and Perkins Insurance Agency, their gloved hands gesturing in conversation.

Noah shook his head. "She had her little pet sayings, that's all."

"And what did she tell you about dallying?"

He grinned in spite of himself and shrugged. "Dillydally, miss the rally. That's it." He angled his face to gauge her reaction. Her cute little forehead rumpled as one dark eyebrow arched higher than the other.

"'Miss the rally'?"

He rocked back on his heels and let out a small burst of laughter. "Exactly what I used to ask. My mother had a cartload of sayings, most of which she probably coined to suit her particular need."

"Then she's a clever one, isn't she?"

"I suppose she was."

"Oh, then she's…?"

"Yes. She passed on many years ago. Fact is, she was pretty ill for most of my childhood."

"I'm sorry."

He gave a simple nod of acknowledgement, watching her on the sly as her brow creased even more. "I sometimes work so hard at recalling my mother's face that my brain aches with the trying," she said in almost a whisper. "I was just two when she died. I often think about how hard it must have been on Papa, his being shouldered with three little girls. Of course, his mother, my grandmother, stepped up to the plate quick as you please, and she's been with us ever since. I don't know what Papa would have done without her."

Noah nodded, suddenly feeling out of his element. He hadn't expected to have anything in common with Miss Kane. He leaned close to the window, looking east on Water Street.

"Jesse should be bringing Toby along most any minute now," she offered, as if reading his mind. She checked the gold watch face dangling from a chain around her pretty neck. "School let out twenty minutes ago, so if they don't, um, dally," she smiled mischievously and winked, "we'll see them coming up the street in a matter of seconds."

"It was nice of your nephew to offer to walk him," Noah said.

"Jesse comes by after school most every day, anyway, so it was no problem for him to bring Toby. I'm sure he'd be glad to do it anytime if you wanted him to. Do you usually stop your work to go pick him up at school?"

"Generally, yes, but sometimes Aunt Julia offers to fetch him if I'm off working at a site and she's not too busy."

"Do you live with your aunt and uncle?"

"No, we live in that little blue house on Harbor Drive, just north of Highland Park and east of the railroad tracks. It's actually my uncle's house, but it had been sitting empty for quite some time, so he suggested we make use of it. We're renting it, of course." For some reason, he wanted to be certain she didn't see him as some kind of sponger.

"I know the place—sort of an island unto itself, the way it sits there, all by its lonesome. It has a lovely view of the water. You must enjoy that."

He'd had a lovely view of the ocean in Connecticut, but he kept that detail to himself. "It is quite nice."

"It's quaint, the little house."

He harrumphed. "*Quaint* is too kind a word, Miss Kane. Rustic's more like it, but it will serve its purpose till I decide on something more permanent. Until we came along, it hadn't been lived in for a couple of years, unless you count the varmints we chased out of there."

"I bet it rumbles when the trains pass by."

"Shakes to kingdom come, actually. Between that and the ships blaring their horns when they come into harbor, it's a pretty ear-popping place to live. When we first moved in, Toby couldn't sleep for all the noise, but now, the ships and trains come and go, and the foghorns blow, and we hardly notice them."

"Yes, that happens."

They stood a while, watching the snow float slowly to the ground and shoppers navigate the sidewalks, their shoulders hunched against the wind. A few men rode past on horses and mules, moving aside for the oncoming Sandy Shores Interurban. The stretch of silence lingered, becoming an expanse of awareness in which Noah knew he ought to make a move to put his tools away. Instead, he stood there and soaked up her scent, giving her another sideways glance to examine her perfectly formed profile and her formfitting, dusty mauve gown, the lace neckband of which touched her earlobes.

As if sensing his gaze, Abbie smiled up at him, prompting him to look down at the floor, then raise his eyes to look outside again. "Well!" Coming to life, he rubbed his hands together and moved to his toolbox. "I best start cleaning up so Toby and I can—"

The bell above the door jingled, and Noah whirled around, expecting to see Toby. Instead, it was a customer, a rosy-cheeked fellow Noah guessed to be nearing fifty, bundled in a cashmere coat and wearing a wool scarf and a fine crusher hat. His face lit up like an incandescent lamp at the first sight of Abbie Ann, and, with a brisk, sweeping motion, he removed his hat and bowed low.

"Well, if it isn't the fairest lady in Sandy Shores."

With a schoolgirl giggle, Abbie beamed and chimed, "Mr. Clayton! What are you doing out on a day like this?"

The man's brow crimped. "Since when do I let a little snow keep me from my usual Monday shopping trip? You ought to know by now that even when I don't need anything, I'll not miss an opportunity to see you."

She flicked her wrist and strode to the door to meet the man, her skirts sweeping the wooden floorboards. "Oh, pooh! You best not let *Mrs.* Clayton hear you say that."

"What Mrs. Clayton doesn't know won't hurt her."

Abbie laughed, and the tinkling sound was like a measure of grace notes that filled the store from floor to ceiling. "Mr. Clayton, you are the berries, not to mention a jester!"

"Of course, I am. That's what makes me so likable," he joshed, his eyes twinkling like midnight stars.

"And a corker," she added. Their laughter blended in a chorus of two, and Noah immediately sensed the solidarity of their friendship. He wondered how and when they'd formed it. Instinct told him it hadn't happened overnight. Perhaps this Clayton fellow had known Abbie as a child.

Noah coughed quietly as he bent to collect his tools, and the sound made Clayton turn his attentions away from Miss Kane. "Ah, and this must be that young fellow who had the near collision with ol' so-and-so—that drunken bum. Name's Donald Clayton. And you are?"

The fellow extended a gloved hand, so Noah took it, finding his firm handshake backed up with bright eyes and a jaunty grin. "Noah Carson, sir. Nice to make your acquaintance."

"Likewise. I've seen you about town. You're the one working with your uncle in the window business. I've known Delbert and Julia Huizenga for years. Good people, they are."

"Yes, sir, the finest."

His eyes lingered on Noah as if to size him up, and yet it wasn't the sort of gaze that made a body feel uncomfortable. Abbie Ann took to busying herself around the store. "Mr. Clayton's in the furniture business," she offered with a sideways glance. "Besides owning a large company in Chicago, he owns and operates Clayton Furniture Manufacturing, right here in Sandy Shores. They make everything from headboards to fancy cabinets to shelving units. As a matter of fact, Papa's getting his new display table from Mr. Clayton."

Noah gave a nod and shifted his weight. "I think I've seen your building…at the foot of Sixth Street, north of Monroe, if I'm not mistaken. I did some work on a house near there."

"Randolph and Ella Curtsall," Clayton responded with a crooked grin.

"Y-yes."

Noah's confusion must have shown, for Clayton tossed back his head and laughed. "That's my sister and brother-in-law, in case you're wondering. They were mighty pleased with your work, by the way; said you were fast and efficient, yet quite the perfectionist. They bragged how skilled you were, considering your age and all. You can't be much past twenty-five."

Noah never had been good at handling compliments, especially with an audience, no matter how small. Even though Miss Kane had moved on to a display shelf, where she appeared to be rearranging women's pocketbooks, he was certain she had an ear to the conversation. "Actually, I'm twenty-eight," he revealed, ill at ease talking about himself.

Clayton gave a thoughtful nod. "I might have some work for you. My wife keeps telling me she wants a better view of the lake. We live on Mill Point Lake. You think you could give me an estimate on what it would cost to replace a few windows, maybe knock out the three small ones facing the lake and put in a nice, big window?"

"Oh, I…. Are you sure you don't want Delbert doing the work? It sounds like a big job."

"It is a big job, but I'm convinced you're up for it. Fact is, I ran into Del last week, and he mentioned how pleased he was about your coming aboard. I told him what I wanted done out at the house, and he made no bones about how capable you are. Sounds like he's up to his neck in a number of other projects right now."

"That's true. He just picked up several contracts on some cottages up in Highland Park and Stickney Ridge that I've been helping him fulfill."

"So he told me. He also mentioned he employs a good crew of workers, not skilled craftsmen such as yourself, but good laborers. I'd truly like this job done before spring sets in so the wife can have a nice view of the dogwoods and magnolias, not to mention the lake. When she stops fussing, my life will be much easier. You know how that goes."

Noah did, but he wouldn't divulge that fact. "The weather's not very conducive to tearing out windows right now."

"Not to worry. We've got another place we can go to, one of our rentals, sitting empty, just up the road from Tall Oaks."

"Tall Oaks?"

"That's the name my wife gave our property. You'll see why when you come up the long drive off West Mill Point Road."

Noah nodded, imagining the lakefront estate with its massive acreage. "If you give me directions, I can probably stop by there late tomorrow afternoon, if that's all right by you."

"Perfect. My wife will be away, but I'll be there."

"Don't you want her opinion?"

He guffawed. "I've had her opinions for nigh on thirty years." His gray-blue eyes twinkled with merriment. "It'll be pure rapture to make a decision without her."

"Speaking of opinions, Mr. Clayton, you're giving Mr. Carson an ill one of you right now," Miss Kane said while turning her pretty, dark head around and throwing Clayton a scolding glance.

"Pfff! Too late for changing that, right, Carson?" He gave Noah a hearty slap on the back, setting him off balance. Noah chuckled, not yet quite sure what to think of Donald Clayton.

Jesse and Toby finally breezed through the door a little after four, jostling each other playfully and lugging knapsacks on their shoulders, Toby's looking too big for his narrow frame. Several customers also came into the store, so Donald Clayton took his leave, his few purchases under his arm.

"Hey, Pa! I got me a new friend!" Toby squealed by way of a greeting. "His name's Jesse."

Giving the lad a nod, Noah stepped forward and stuck out his hand. "How do, Jesse? I appreciate your walking my son home from school today."

"Aw, it was nothing," the dark-haired boy said with a wide grin as he placed his hand in Noah's for a quick handshake. Next, he shrugged out of his wool coat and stuffed his gloves and hat inside the sleeves. Toby followed suit. "Sorry we're a little late, but I wanted to introduce Toby to my pa, so we stopped by his office."

"Ah. Toby, keep your coat on. We're heading back to the shop in a minute or two."

"His pa's the sheriff," Toby said, dropping his coat in a heap on the floor. "Ain't that somethin'? I got to see where the jail's at!" His eyes grew wide with pure wonder. "It's down in a dark, dungeon place."

"Pa didn't let us go down there," Jesse put in, as if to put Noah at ease.

"'Cause there're bad guys down there," Toby added. "Includin' that one what made us go off the street and ram into the Whatnot."

"Is that so?" Noah asked, deciding to ignore his son's poor grammar but not his lack of obedience. "Put your coat back on, Toby." He angled a look at Miss Kane and found her smiling from behind the cash register, where she was ringing up a young woman's order. Yet her eyes were still focused on her work as she made quiet conversation with the customer.

"How was school today?" Noah asked Toby, bending over to pick up his coat.

"Okay," came the standard answer.

He watched Jesse walk to the door to hang his winter gear on a hook, then step out of his heavy boots. He had a pair of street shoes parked next to the door that he quickly slipped into. Toby followed after like a puppy trailing its master, obviously enthralled by the bigger boy's every move, plopping himself on the floor and proceeding to remove his boots, as well.

"Keep your boots on, son. We're leaving soon."

Once again, his words went unnoticed, for the boy proceeded to remove the wet boots and place them next to Jesse's. Had he gone deaf? Anger boiled inside Noah, and had he not been in a public place, he might well have snatched the youngster by the arm and walloped him on the backside. But what was he thinking? Images of his own upbringing came to the fore of his mind with a vengeance—most vividly, his father's rough handling of him when he'd had too much to drink. Never had Noah laid a hand to his boy, and he couldn't allow himself to start. The problem was that neither he nor Suzanna had ever truly disciplined Toby. Suzanna's interests had been far removed from raising a child, and Noah had been consumed by work every waking hour. He deeply regretted that now, of course.

The woman whom Abbie had been waiting on gathered up her purchases, murmured her thanks, and headed for the door, casting Noah the quickest glance and tiniest nod as she slipped past him. Like a perfect gentleman, Jesse reached the door ahead of her and threw it wide open. "G'bye, Mrs. Taylor. You be sure to come back again."

"Oh, I will for certain, Jesse," she called over her shoulder.

My, Toby could learn a thing or two from watching that lad.

"Y' wanna play somethin'?" Toby asked Jesse.

Jesse's brow crinkled as he cast Noah a questioning glance. "I think your dad said you have to leave."

Toby slanted Noah a pair of pouty eyes. "Can we stay a while longer, Pa?"

Noah whistled a deep sigh. "It's been a long day, son. I need to get you over to Aunt Julia's so I can finish my work at the shop."

"Aunt Julia don't have good toys."

"Doesn't have any," he corrected him. "And she does have several. You took them there yourself."

"But those are old."

"Well, then, you'll play outside on the swing Uncle Del put up for you. Look, the snow's coming down real good now. You ought to be able to build a nice snowman."

"It ain't the right kind of snow, Pa," Toby protested.

He had him there. His frustration must have showed in his face, for Miss Kane emerged from behind the cash register, her skirts hiked above her heels, and said, "If you like, Toby can stay till closing time, and Jesse can walk him to your place—that is, if you'll be home by then."

Noah hesitated. "I'm usually home by six or a little after."

"Perfect. The store closes at five thirty, but there's always work to wrap up and cash to count before I can leave, right, Jesse?"

"Right. Toby and I can help Aunt Abbie."

"Yeah!" Toby leaped up and down like a wired jack-in-the-box, and Noah couldn't help the surge of laughter coming out of him. He hated caving into his son's whims, yet Miss Kane and Jesse had helped convince him.

"I'd have to let Aunt Julia know not to expect you," he said to Toby.

"You can ring her here, if you like," Miss Kane offered, thumbing at the phone on the wall behind the counter.

"You do have an answer for everything, don't you, madam?" he said in a more or less joking manner.

"I wouldn't go that far, but things such as these don't require much thought. It's no trouble at all, really, and it will give Toby and Jesse some time to get acquainted."

Noah studied the boy who stood at least two heads taller than his son. "I'm sure Jesse has more important things to do than entertain a six-year-old."

Jesse shrugged and pushed several long strands of black hair out of his nut-brown eyes. "Naw. I volunteer at the store most nights, anyway, don't I, Aunt Abbie? Usually, my ma is here, but we have a new baby, so she can't run things right now. Comin' here after school is the least I can do. And if Toby wants to tag along, well, that's just fine by me." He stretched out his hand and ruffled Toby's hair. "Fact is, I'll probably put him to work."

Now, that appealed to Noah. The boy needed to learn responsibility, something he'd been lax in teaching him.

"Wow, you're gonna give me a job?" Toby's mouth went as round as a fish's just before biting its bait.

Abbie bent forward to look into the boy's eyes. "There is always plenty of work to be done, so, yes, young man, we're going to give you a job."

"Every day?" he asked.

"Well...."

"Well...."

Noah and Abbie's one-word replies blended, and their eyes met. "If you..." she started.

"We'll see. We'll talk about it later," Noah put in. He brushed his hands together, not exactly sure of how all this had come about. "Now, may I use that telephone?"

Chapter Five

Jesse did walk Toby to the store three out of five days that week, and after they closed up shop, he dutifully walked him home. Once Noah Carson completed his job at the store on Tuesday, he didn't come around again, which suited Abbie fine, even though he did fascinate her for reasons she couldn't quite identify. More times than she could count, his image had surfaced in her mind, making her wonder if she wasn't losing her buttons. After all, Peter Sinclair had been courting her for the better part of a year. What made her think she had the slightest right to think about another man, especially one she'd spoken to only a few times, and who was divorced? Heavens to Betsy, it wasn't even rational—or proper!

She spent Tuesday evening conducting the bimonthly meeting of the Woman's Christian Temperance Union, which met in the basement of the Third Street Church. Roughly twenty-five women attended, if she counted Ada Freefeldt and Molly Staninga's late arrival and Sarah Welling's abrupt leave-taking when her thirteen-year-old son came to fetch her from the room, saying something about his younger brother falling off a stool while trying to reach the cookie jar and cutting his chin.

The meeting certainly started off on the right note with the opening hymn led by Tillie Overmyer and the beautiful, heartfelt prayer said by Gertie Pridmore, the town's new librarian. They'd even made it through the first two items on the agenda: continuing a discussion about finding a vacant house—donated, of course—suitable for sheltering abused women, and conducting a search for the proper persons to act as superintendents of the program. But when they moved on to the third item on the agenda, scheduling a time for another "saloon walk and prayer vigil," a strange, if not alarming, thing happened. A sizeable rock came hurling through the small basement window, narrowly missing Gertie Pridmore's topknot and skimming Jenny Fowler's shoulder, bouncing off the cement block wall, and rolling two or three feet before coming to rest by Gertie's feet.

Gasps of surprise, followed by tense, stunned silence, filled the room, and then there was a sudden eruption of voices at varied pitches and levels. Most of the women jumped to their feet in shock; others reacted in dazed, motionless wonder. Abbie snatched up the rock, unwound the string that was wrapped tightly around it, and removed a note. She took her sweet time unfolding it, perhaps because she felt the need to maintain calmness as the women surrounded her with anxious looks. She studied it quickly yet thoroughly before refolding it and sticking it into her skirt pocket.

"Well?" Gertie asked, wringing her hands. "What did it say?"

"Yes, we insist you read it to us," said Evelyn Merchant, one of their oldest, dearest members. Although nearing eighty, she rarely missed a union meeting, and she'd even acted as chapter president for several years before relinquishing the responsibility to Lois DeVos, who'd served for five years before handing it off to a reluctant Abbie Ann. She'd wanted to attend the meetings, not be promptly thrust into a leadership role. But when no one else had stepped forward, she'd acquiesced and accepted the appointment.

Abbie pressed her fingertips to her temple and tried to push back the dizzying wave of panic that was coming on. Her throat clogged suddenly, and she cleared it before speaking. "It…it didn't say much of anything."

"What?" several ladies said in unison. "We saw you reading it."

"No, I…wasn't exactly reading it. I was studying it."

"What do you mean?"

"I mean, it contained very few words. Mostly, it was a silly picture, drawn by hand." She swallowed and looked into two-dozen pairs of worried eyes, all drilling into her own.

"What sort of picture, dear?" Lois DeVos asked.

Abbie felt her forehead wrinkle into a tiny frown. "It was a picture of a—a gravestone."

"A gravestone? What on earth would possess someone to draw that? Do you suppose the reverend has a disgruntled church member?" someone asked.

"No, I…don't think they intended this for Reverend Cooper." She tried to keep her voice light, free of worry.

"Well, then, for whom? For goodness' sake, someone broke the window. That's vandalism," said another.

Abbie nodded, slowly coming to realize the gravity of the act and its evil intent.

Gertie rested her hand on Abbie's shoulder. "You said the message contained few words, Abbie Ann. What exactly were those words?"

With reluctance, she took the note from her pocket and handed it to Gertie.

Gertie sucked in a sharp breath upon seeing it. Quickly, everyone else gathered around, taking turns looking over Gertie's shoulder.

More gasps and shudders. "This meeting is adjourned," Jenny Fowler announced. Jenny loved being the first one of the group to make a motion, but this was no motion. "I'm marching straight over to the sheriff's office. Anyone coming with me?"

"I'll go."

"I'm coming."

"Count me in."

"Ladies," Abbie said, anxious to settle the waters. "Sheriff Devlin is my brother-in-law. Let me handle this. There's no point in all of us descending upon him. What will that accomplish? Besides, I'm certain he's gone home by now. I'll stop by and file a report with whichever deputy is on duty."

They pondered her suggestion for a moment. "She's right," Lois DeVos finally spoke up. "No point in all of us trudging over there. But, for safety's sake, I'll accompany her to the office and then drive her home."

Abbie tried to downplay the incident. "I'm sure this is just a silly prank—probably some troubled soul I barely even know trying to give me a jolt. Perhaps a customer irate at the rising cost of…of ice picks, I don't know, or buttons, or bread and flour, and he sees me as an easy target for placing blame. Papa did have to raise prices on several items a few weeks ago, you know."

"Abbie." Evelyn Merchant leveled her with solemn eyes, her voice strained. "A drawing of a gravestone with a marker bearing your name is no small prank. This is someone who knew your whereabouts. You and Lois best get yourselves over to the sheriff's office, and the sooner, the better."

K

An icy thrill raced through his veins, making him quiver with excitement over what he'd accomplished. That little Kane woman had another thing coming if she thought she could get away with her calculating schemes, she and that assortment of mostly gray-haired ninnies who'd got it in their square heads that they could change the world. Ha! He'd show them who's in control, starting with that little she-skunk, Abbie Ann Kane. He'd had about enough of her and that women's union group, whatever they called themselves. Rubbish, that's what it was—pure rubbish. Women had their place in society, and it was high time someone put them in it.

Next time, that little piece of whistle bait would find more than a rock with a note attached. Beads of sweat, added to the ice in his blood, created a dizzying effect. Half the fun would be just figuring out what to do.

Yeah, next time, he'd really put the fear of the Almighty in her.

K

February gave way to March, bringing with it three sunny days in a row and a warming trend that made good work of the piles of snow along the streets and on the sidewalks. Since the rock incident, nothing further had transpired to cause alarm. The day after Abbie had reported it to the deputy on duty, Gabe had paid a visit to the Whatnot, questioning her about every aspect of the incident. Had she noticed anyone following her to the church or detected anything out of the ordinary that day, particularly before the meeting? Could she name anyone who might want to harm her? Naturally, she'd told him about Erv Baxter's anger the night they'd walked into his saloon, singing hymns and praying, and consequently causing a big enough stir that all but a few of his customers left. And he wasn't the only saloon proprietor angered by the union's campaign. Gabe had pinched the bridge of his nose and scrunched his brow. "I don't suppose I can talk you into dropping out of that organization, can I, Abbie? Or, at the very least, resigning your position as president?"

"No, I'm sorry, Gabe, you can't. Besides, why should we give in to this—this awful beast's taunts?"

"Because there's a threat on your life, young lady, and you shouldn't take it lightly."

"It's a ploy, Gabe, a direct hit to the union, and we simply cannot surrender to it. Women all over the country receive similar threats, but they aren't intimidated. How would it look if I was?"

He'd tucked his notepad into his hip pocket, sighed, and shaken his head, tipping his chin down at her. "I knew the first time I saw you, that day I came to your house to tell your grandmother that Hannah Grace was sitting in a jail cell with Jesse, that you were a feisty one. Shoot! Both your sisters run a close race with you in that department, but I'd have to say you're a full stride ahead of them. What is it with you Kane women, anyway? You're all as set as cement in your ways. How'd you get like that?"

Abbie had grinned and relaxed. "I don't know. Mama, maybe? Grandmother, for sure. Anyway, you may as well admit it, Gabriel Devlin: you love us just the way we are."

Gabe had chuckled, nudged his hat up, and given his sister-in-law a wondering look. "You're also pretty confident."

"That comes from Papa."

After that, he'd instructed her to pay special attention to her surroundings, to stay on the lookout for anything suspicious or out of the ordinary, and to ride, not walk, to the store for the next few days. She'd complied as best she could but saw no point in continuing the rides when no more incidents occurred. Of course, Papa wanted her to ride with him from that day forward, but she refused to give up her daily hikes to work. She loved the invigoration of the brisk air penetrating her lungs, the songs of winter birds, and the sights and smells of Sandy Shores—everything from the foghorn's early-morning whistle to the chug-a-chug of incoming and outgoing trains, from the Interurban car buzzing up Water Street to the wonderful scents of bread and pastries coming from Star Bakery.

With the slight warming trend, folks' spirits were lifting. It showed in the way they walked with a lilt and smiled their how-do-you-dos as they passed. Business at the Whatnot picked up, despite rising prices, and Jacob hired Rita James, a somewhat plump but attractive widow in her fifties, to help at the store. On Saturday, with the insurance agency closed for the day, Jacob told Abbie he would work with Rita, training her on the cash register and acquainting her with her responsibilities, and that Abbie could have the entire day off to do as she pleased. She rose early, read her Bible and prayed, and then went downstairs to the kitchen, where Grandmother Kane was puttering at the sink. While Abbie nibbled a blueberry muffin and sipped a cup of coffee, she scribbled a to-do list for herself, humming quietly. She wrote, in no particular order, *Write to Maggie Rose, Visit Hannah and the kids, Tidy my room*, and *Ride out to the Plooster farm*. Beyond that, she had no plans, other than to do a few household chores. She decided to wait and see if Grandmother proposed anything.

Tapping her pencil on the paper, she glanced out the window in time to see a black squirrel scamper up the sprawling oak tree situated between the Kane house and that of Ambrose and Norma Barton, their lifelong neighbors. Rays of morning sunlight spread their spindly fingers through the barren branches, casting shadows on the driveway.

"Have you had any more frightening incidents happen to you?" her grandmother asked while stacking saucers and cups on a cupboard shelf.

"Nothing. I think it was a onetime occurrence."

Grandmother paused and then picked up her dishcloth, wiping down the already spotless countertop. "Well, I sure hope you're right. That was such a strange thing to have happen in the middle of your meeting."

Abbie couldn't have agreed more. "I've put it out of my mind, and you should, as well."

Helena Kane resumed her kitchen tinkering, so Abbie thought the matter was closed, but then the woman folded her cloth into a neat square and made an about-turn. "I really don't know why you continue with that temperance club of yours."

Abbie sighed. "It's not a club, Grandmother. It's a national organization with multitudes of chapters in every state. Actually, it's international, if you want the truth of it, but it was founded in the United States way back in 1873. We have a U.S. membership of some 250,000 women, and the organization even publishes a small newspaper that circulates nationwide to keep us abreast of the latest events and issues. You could join, if you'd like."

"Pfff. That's not my cup of tea, dear." Her grandmother sniffed and scrunched her nose. "I'm all for charity, mind you, but I'm not...well, what you'd call an extremist."

"And you think I am, Grandmother? Just because I care about matters that concern women?"

The woman's frown deepened yet softened at the same time. "I think...." She advanced across the room and pulled out a chair, its legs scraping along the linoleum, and sat down, releasing a long sigh in the process. She placed a warm hand on Abbie's arm and swallowed. "I think you're very passionate, dear, and, sometimes, that passion gets you into a heap of trouble, that's what I think."

Abbie smiled and rested her hand atop her grandmother's, noting its softness and lack of wrinkles. She only hoped to look half as good as her grandmother at that age, not that beauty played a large role in her life. Health and well-being, now, those were another matter.

"Do you know Arlena Rogan?" she asked, the question surfacing quite unexpectedly.

Grandmother sucked in another breath, withdrew her hand, and leaned back in her chair. "Isn't she Shamus Rogan's wife?"

"Yes, do you know her?"

"Not really, no. Why do you ask?"

"He abuses her—verbally and physically."

Grandmother twisted her mouth into a frown. "Oh my, that's awful. How do you know these things?"

"Arlena has told me on a number of occasions. Of course, I had to initiate the conversation when I saw her bruises. Hannah's seen them, too, if you don't believe me."

"Honey, I believe you," her grandmother assured her. "I'm sure she's enjoying her reprieve from him as he sits in jail."

"But he'll be getting out before you know it, and then what?"

The woman bit her lower lip and shook her head several times. "I know it's a shame, but there's nothing you can do about it, Abbie."

"I've been telling her she should leave him."

The older woman's face contorted with shock as she shifted forward. "Abbie Ann, you mustn't tell her such things. Divorce is wrong on all counts."

The very word *divorce* made Noah Carson's face materialize in her mind's eye. She gave the image a mental shove aside. What in the world would Grandmother Kane think if she knew Abbie had daydreamed about him on more than one occasion?

"I'm not suggesting she divorce him, Grandmother, just leave him for a time. Someone needs to stand up for her and her children. If I don't, then who will?"

Grandmother Kane pressed her lips together until the upper nearly disappeared into the lower. Her nostrils flared with each slow breath until she sniffed and cleared her throat, fidgeting with the rim of a wooden bowl in the middle of the table. "I understand your concerns, dear, but getting involved in someone else's affairs is…well, presumptuous."

Her stance did not surprise Abbie. Coming from the Old World, as she did, Grandmother Kane believed in preserving one's privacy, especially in family matters. At times, she came off as callous, when, in truth, she merely thought it improper to pry. Abbie hated opposing her; to do so equated to arguing with a mother bear. But on this matter, she couldn't keep quiet.

"Our W.C.T.U. chapter is trying to locate a house we can convert into a women's shelter."

"Oh?" Mild interest lined Grandmother's voice.

"It would be the perfect place for someone like Arlena Rogan and her children to go, if even for a short time. It might be the sort of thing that would give a man pause, make him realize his need for reform if he wants to keep his marriage and family intact."

Grandmother Kane looked thoughtful. "A man like Shamus Rogan isn't a fast learner, I'm afraid. He's been drinking for many years. Lands, I remember him drinking as a young'un. His father was a drunkard, and, no doubt, so was his father's father."

Abbie fingered the hem of her blouse with one hand and took a sip of her tea, now cold, with the other. She frowned and set the teacup in its saucer. "You remember his family?"

"Of course." Grandmother Kane sniffed and stood to her feet. "The Rogans moved to Sandy Shores when Shamus was, oh, a youngster. I recall your father coming home and complaining about the boy's unruly behavior when he came into the Whatnot, always picking up items and tossing them back where they didn't belong. He even caught him in the act of stealing candy a few times." Grandmother's gaze trailed off, then came to rest on the clock over the stove. "My, look at the time. I must get to my bread making. Will you be seeing Mr. Sinclair tonight?"

Actually, Abbie welcomed the sudden change in topics. She had much to mull over. "Perhaps."

"You don't have firm plans?"

"Not altogether," she said, watching her grandmother open a cupboard door and take out a canister of flour. Next, she went for the sugar, setting the container on the counter with a slight thud. After that, she opened the icebox and pulled out a bottle of buttermilk.

"Why is that?" The woman bent over and retrieved a mixing bowl from another cupboard.

Tracing an old scratch mark on the round oak table her grandparents had brought with them when they'd left England all those years ago, Abbie answered, "We're going to discuss things on the phone later this morning. He's invited me to see that traveling theater troupe tonight at the community hall, but I may beg off."

Grandmother Kane's quick turn made her all-wool shepherd's plaid skirt flare at the hem. She pushed up the Nilegreen cuffs of her puff-top sleeves and leaned back against the soapstone sink. Abbie couldn't help but notice that not a single silver hair had pulled away from the simple yet stylishly pinned bun at the nape of her neck, despite the fact she'd probably done it up at six in the morning.

"Ah, the ones performing *The Earl of Pawtucket*. I hear it's very amusing, and the acting is superb. I ran into Myron and Sandra Lucas at Thom Gerritt's Meat Market yesterday, and they very much enjoyed the Thursday evening performance. Sandra said she laughed till her sides hurt. I may even talk your father into taking me to see it before the troupe leaves town next weekend. Why ever would you decline an invitation to attend?"

Why, indeed? Abbie shrugged and sighed. It would be nice to laugh at something refreshing and new, even if Peter didn't join in; his personality didn't easily lend itself to spontaneous bouts of laughter. Oh, he occasionally laughed, or chuckled, rather, at her jokes, and he did find certain situations humorous, such as the time a customer came into the bank expecting a $400 loan when he didn't have a job or the wherewithal for repaying the money, or the instance when he'd seen a big oaf of a dog struggling to walk on an icy patch of sidewalk, his legs sprawling every which direction. And, oh, there was that moment when he'd seen a bumblebee get caught in the ostrich feathers atop old Mrs. Riley's hat during church. Even Abbie had giggled at that one. Still, they rarely found humor in the same things, and she seriously doubted watching a comedy together would be any different. He might give her a gentle poke in the side or whisper in her ear to tone down her laughter, which would put a damper on her spirits.

"For one thing, I'm going out to visit the Plooster sisters this afternoon, and you know how they love to talk."

"Ah, yes, the Ploosters. Another of your passions, visiting those oldsters—although of this gesture I totally approve. I think it's wonderful the way you pay them heed. They rarely get out in inclement weather, and I know they love your visits. Still, that oughtn't to keep you from seeing the play tonight." Abbie thought it humorous how her grandmother considered the sisters elderly when, really, they were probably close to her in age.

She considered Grandmother Kane's words. "Chances are, they'll want to keep me for supper, delaying my return to town. Besides, I have so many things I want to accomplish today." She looked at her tablet, on which exactly four items were listed. "My paper is fast filling up. I fear I'll be too weary for going out with Peter."

Grandmother tipped her chin up, keeping her gray-blue eyes narrowed on Abbie. "It appears to me you're fishing for excuses not to see him, dear girl. Have you forgotten that he asked your father some time back for permission to marry you?"

Abbie felt her face sag into a pouty frown. "No, I haven't forgotten, but just because he asked and Papa gave his blessing doesn't mean I've consented to the idea."

One of her grandmother's sculpted, gray eyebrows arched in question, and an all-new spark of interest took hold in her expression. "You've been seeing Peter Sinclair for a number of months, Abbie Ann. Do you or do you not love him?"

"I have absolutely no idea."

K

With one last nail, Noah finished securing the large piece of canvas covering the gaping hole in the wall where he intended to install the new window in the Claytons' home. The house was quiet, save for the ticking clock in the adjacent dining room and Donald Clayton's footsteps on the floor upstairs. A gentle breeze billowed the canvas, making the cold seep through. Noah had worked up a lathery sweat earlier because he never did anything at a snail's pace, but now with sunset looming and quitting time upon him, an arctic chill seemed to race through his damp body.

After sweeping up a few remaining particles of sawdust, he secured his tools and clamped down the lid on his metal toolbox.

"Heading out?" Don Clayton came down the eight-foot-wide, oak staircase, which was lined with a wine-red carpet runner. The house put Noah in mind of a governor's mansion, with its walls of windows overlooking the wraparound decks and the beachfront at the bottom of a gradually sloping hill, the spacious living room with the redbrick fireplace and ornate mantle, and the French doors that separated the rooms, each of which was elaborately paneled with thick oak on the lower three-quarters of the walls and had a beamed ceiling and an intricate chandelier. Rich, wood floors shone like splendid satin, and the finest tapestry rugs were arranged over them. Truth be told, he'd never seen a house quite like it. Even Suzanna's parents' home on Long Island Sound couldn't compare, although it wasn't too far behind. It made him wonder about the company Don Clayton owned in Chicago. Obviously, it had to be a thriving one.

Rising to his full six-foot-one-inch height, Noah said, "I'll be back early Monday morning, if that's all right with you, sir."

"That's more than all right. Actually, when I said I wanted the window done as soon as possible, I didn't expect you to use your Saturday to work on it."

"That's no problem. I've only been here a few hours. Wanted to tend to a few details before Monday."

Don nodded and surveyed Noah's progress. "That's a nice-sized cutout there. You'll make my Esther a happy woman. This the window in the crate, here?"

"Yes, sir. It took four of us to carry it in. 'Course, the frame alone weighs a pretty pound."

"I don't doubt it. I assume you'll have help with the installation."

He nodded. "Uncle Del and a couple of others plan to come out with me on Monday."

"Good, good. You'll no doubt need assistance putting that monstrous thing in place."

"Yes, sir." Noah glanced at the large walnut clock on the wall over Don Clayton's shoulder.

"I guess you want to get home to your son. According to Abbie Ann, he's a fine little boy. I'm sure he's missing you about now."

Noah laughed. "I have my doubts about that. My uncle took him fishing this afternoon. I'd guess they're still out there trying to catch the big one." The mention of that Kane woman had his mind wandering to places it didn't belong. He quickly reeled it back in.

Don's face twisted into a frown as he shuddered. "Fishing, aargh. Never have understood the draw behind that sport, and especially not in the winter months. 'Course, with spring upon us, I suppose there are those just itching to get out there. Del's been a dyed-in-the-wool fisherman for as long as I've known him. Not me, though. Nope, sailing's my love."

As if he'd been caught sleeping, Noah's senses instantly came alive, but he tried to minimize his reaction. "That so?"

He nodded. "Have you sailed much?"

Had he! He decided to step out on a limb, since Donald Clayton seemed the sort he could trust. "I have. In fact, I used to make my living building boats."

Don's eyes went round like boulders. "You serious? You talking from the bottom up?"

Noah straightened his shoulders. "Yes, sir. I learned the craft by watching my father." He swallowed, his pulse quickening. "Almost as soon as I graduated from high school, I started my own boatworks on Long Island Sound...well, I and another fellow, that is."

"Really? There's a big shipbuilding industry out there. Your pa put up the money for you to get started?"

"Hardly. As I said, he taught me the craft, but he never made much of a living working at it. He's darn talented, don't get me wrong, but...well, let's just say he wasted a good share of his talent and money on booze and fast women. I, on the other hand, saved every cent I ever earned to get my own business off the ground."

Don's grayish brow slipped into a perfect arch. "I like that sort of determination in people. No matter their upbringing, they pull themselves up by their bootstraps and determine to make something of themselves."

"Yes, sir."

"What happened, if I may ask? You sell your share to your partner?"

"No, I mean…not exactly." Noah shifted his weight from foot to foot as a knot tightened in his gut.

Something must have shown up in his eyes, for the man quickly backpedaled. "I didn't mean to infringe on your affairs."

"Don't worry about it," Noah said. "To be honest, it's no secret. Not that I'm broadcasting it, mind you, but, well, I'm—I'm a divorced man."

Don didn't flinch; he merely gazed with softer eyes. "Yes?"

"My former wife had no interest in raising children," Noah continued. "So, it was no problem gaining custody of my son—as long as I agreed to give her the majority of my holdings, that is." He cleared his throat and brushed a hand over his whiskered face. "She and my partner were in cahoots."

"You mean, they…?"

Awkward pause. "Exactly. She got my boatworks *and* my partner; I got my boy. In the long run, I know I came out ahead, but that doesn't lessen my bitterness about the whole situation."

Don nodded, finally setting the small, black suitcase he'd been clutching down on the floor beside him. He scratched the back of his head and frowned. "So, you lost your livelihood to your conniving partner and former wife. You couldn't have gotten a good lawyer?"

Noah chuckled wryly. "Her father's the best attorney for miles around, and he has the money to back up his point of view, not to mention that he carries a good deal of influence in court and with every judge in the state. No one dares stand up to him. Not only that, he dragged my name through the mud with made-up stories that would burn the hair off a goat. Of course, he defended his daughter to the nth degree, saying I'd had an extramarital affair long before she had."

"Had you?" Don asked point-blank. Noah should have resented his directness but, strangely, did not, perhaps because he welcomed the opportunity to clear his name of any wrongdoing.

"Absolutely not. Looking back, I shouldn't have been surprised by the whole business. That woman had a roving eye long before I hitched up with her." He ran his hand through his thick head of dusky, brown hair, straggly after a long day of work. "'Course, you know what they say—love is blind; it's marriage that's the eye-opener. Makes me wonder how long she'll stay with Tom Grayson."

"Your former partner, I take it."

Noah nodded and stuffed his hands deep into his pockets, shocked by how much he'd divulged to a near stranger. Donald Clayton now knew nearly as much as his aunt and uncle did.

"I'm surprised your father-in-law would give up his grandson so readily."

"There was never much attachment. He's a selfish, greedy so-and-so. On the other hand, Suzanna's mother is a nice woman, just clearly missing any backbone. I'm sure she misses her grandson. Actually, my father probably misses him, too. In his sober moments, he paid him a good deal of attention. 'Course, I always discouraged it. Don't ever want my son looking up to his Grandpa Carson like he's some kind of hero."

With the matter out in the open, Noah now wondered if Donald Clayton would shun him, as so many had in Guilford. He braced himself for the rebuke.

Don rubbed his chin and gave a solemn nod. "These things happen—abusive upbringings, poor choices, even divorce. It's what you choose to do with your life afterward that makes the difference. You're young and capable. I've no reason to believe you won't bounce back—if you haven't already. Tell me, what sort of boats did you build?"

That was it? No further questions on the subject? He'd expected something far worse. He took in a cavernous breath. "Mostly cargo schooners," he ventured. "And a few racing boats."

"Racers? That right? Why didn't you take a job over at Rikkers Shipbuilding in Mill Point? They do a pretty good business. Schooners are their specialty."

He'd thought about it, but after the burning he'd taken from Suzanna and Tom Grayson, he'd figured he needed a break from boatbuilding. Besides, after owning his own company, he couldn't quite fathom taking orders from someone else. "My uncle was gracious enough to offer me work, so I jumped at the chance to leave Guilford. He and my aunt have always been like a second set of parents to me." He paused, swallowed, and rubbed the back of his neck. How odd to be telling this fellow things he had revealed to no one but Uncle Delbert and Aunt Julia. "The window and door business is lucrative."

Don eyed him with a hint of doubt. "But is it your love?"

A stony lump formed in the pit of his gut. "You're good," he said, cracking a small grin.

Not missing a beat, Don went on to ask, "You done any racing yourself?"

Had he ever—for almost as long as he could recall, actually. As a tyke, he'd hung out at the docks with his mother, watching the sails flap and rotate like giant angel wings as they headed into the wind. But from age twelve on, he'd raced every year with his grandfather, his mother's father, acting first as shipmate—until his eighteenth birthday, that is, when his grandfather passed away. Then, he'd been appointed skipper and assigned his own crew, using his grandfather's trusty, old schooner. "A good amount," he finally answered. "Before my career went belly-up, I had a new design in mind for a lighter, flatter-bottomed lady with less wetted surface when she's heeled up and less drag to her sleek body. She'd be roughly forty feet long but weigh less than a ton, which would make her ideal for racing. I'd hoped to enter her in this summer's race, but, well, things went sour, and I never got the chance to build her."

Don's eyes narrowed into skeptical slits. "You serious? I'd like to hear more about this so-called plan of yours. Do you have a rendering of it? A sketch?"

Noah couldn't believe it. He never went anywhere without it. No matter what pair of trousers or workpants he stepped into, he always dug into the pocket of the previously worn pants for the folded up piece of paper, frayed around the edges and wrinkled, to boot, to stuff into the hip pocket.

He never knew when a new inspiration might strike him for altering his drawing, which already had been amended more times than he could count.

"I…yeah. Right here, in fact." His fingers were suddenly sweaty, despite the biting air, and he withdrew the sketch from his pocket and gingerly unfolded it. To date, the only other person he'd ever shown it to was Uncle Delbert, giving him the distinct feeling he was about to bare a piece of his soul. He hesitated for a moment at the realization.

Don eyed the paper clutched in Noah's hand. "Want to show it to me?"

What could it hurt? Swallowing a nervous breath, he handed over the crumpled piece of paper.

The fellow squinted at the design, turning it first one way, then another, studying it closely. Finally, he cleared his throat and said, "So, if I'm reading this right, you've cut way back on the sail area. Why's that?"

"Yes, sir; makes for less weight on the hull." Noah stepped forward to point at the sketch and draw an imaginary line from one section to another with his index finger. "I think you'll see we're talking a planing hull, here, as opposed to a displacement hull. That's what'll give her more speed and buoyancy."

"Huh." A thoughtful gaze skipped across Don's face. "What's going to keep it from tipping clean over?"

"Using smaller sails, for one thing, and a shorter bow-sprit…and hollow masts."

"Hollow masts, you say?"

"It's not likely to capsize, but if it should, say, in a really bad storm, the masts will float, and it won't take much for a crew of six or seven to right her and be on their way again."

The older man turned the paper once again and tipped his head to the side. "The keel configuration is completely different, isn't it, with its virtual flat bottom?"

"That's the idea. She'll literally skim the water's surface rather than plow through it. You won't find anything faster, sir."

Don's brows arched over his twinkling, gray eyes, which matched the graying hair at his temples. He raised his gaze to level Noah with an assessing look. "You seem awfully sure of yourself, young man."

"Not to brag, sir, but I've built enough boats to know what I'm talking about."

"Hmm." Don carefully refolded the worn paper and handed it back. "Interesting. Very interesting."

"Thanks." Noah slipped the treasured sketch back into his hip pocket. "I should be going. Mind if I leave my tools here?"

"Not at all. I'm heading over to our other house." He bent to retrieve his small satchel. "I'm sure Esther's waiting on me for supper." With his brow crimped, he stood unmoving for a few seconds, as if mulling something over in his head, and his eyes skimmed Noah's face. Slightly unnerved, Noah turned and snatched his coat from the back of the divan, slipping into it in a fluid motion. "Well, nice talking to you, sir."

"Please, call me Donald. Don is fine, too."

To appease him, Noah nodded, not even sure he'd see the fellow again once he'd completed the window work.

"You know, Sandy Shores Yacht Club sponsors the Lake Michigan Regatta in late July," Don remarked as Noah wrapped his wool scarf around his neck and plopped his cap on his head.

"I've heard some talk about that." He and Don started the long trek through the house, making their ways past the staircase and through the dining room and kitchen, which boasted marble floors, a dozen or so white cabinets with clear glass panels, and all the modern conveniences a woman could want—hot and cold running water, a decent-sized icebox, and a large oven. Noah imagined Mrs. Clayton hosting many a dignified party in the grandiose house.

In the large garden room off the kitchen, he settled himself on a bench to remove his shoes and slip into his heavy, tie-up rubber boots, noting a small pile of dirt on the tile floor where he'd parked them upon entering the house.

"If you'll hand me a damp rag, I'll be happy to wipe this up."

Don waved him off. "Naw, that's why we have a house-keeper. She'll have everything sparkling in a few hours. Back to this regatta talk."

He seemed determined to continue the discussion, Noah thought, so he determined to listen.

Don dropped his satchel on the floor again and joined Noah on the flat, backless bench. "It starts in Saugatuck and ends in Sandy Shores, gathering a good number of spectators from all up and down the coast, and even from as far away as Chicago, Detroit, and Flint. They take the train over, stay in one of our spas, and watch the goings-on from beneath their wide-brimmed hats, always keeping an eye out for the first boat to come over the crest of the waves." He gave his graying head a slight nod. "It's really quite something."

Noah finished lacing his left boot and started on the right one. "That so? You a spectator or a participant?" he asked.

"Bosh! What do you think? I enter the thing every year. Matter of fact, I won it back in '02, then sold my boat for a pretty penny afterward. Wish I hadn't done that. All I have now are a couple of sloops, neither of which has the sleekness or speed of your lady."

Noah couldn't hide the smile that split his lips or the tiny spurt of laughter that escaped them. "She's not my lady, sir. 'Fraid, right now, she's nothin' more than a drawing on a piece of paper."

"But you envision her, don't you?" Don asked, tapping his temple with his index finger.

That he did, but now wasn't the time for dwelling on dreams. His shipbuilding days were over. He removed his gloves from his pockets and got to his feet. Don remained seated, leaning against the robin's-egg-blue plaster wall. Above his head, a framed picture of a snowy scene hung slightly off-kilter. Noah fought the urge to right it. "I wouldn't mind another trophy in my case," Don said, a sly glint flashing across his face, putting Noah in mind of a cunning fox. With his legs outstretched and crossed at the ankles and his arms folded across his chest, he kept his eyes trained on Noah.

Noah thought about the trophies he'd earned over the years, now all neatly stowed in a wooden crate in the shed behind his father's Connecticut house. The time for winning trophies had come and gone. Life had taken a sharp turn on him, making it important to carve out a living doing something more practical.

"I also wouldn't mind talking to you in a bit more depth about this boat design," Don continued. "Maybe we could discuss a schedule, too, and what you think it'd cost to build it."

Noah wasn't quite following him. "Schedule? Cost? I'm not sure I—"

"What I'm asking, in plain terms, is, how long would you say it'd take to get her built, and how much would it set me back?" He narrowed his eyes conspiratorially.

Noah had no idea how long he stood there with his mouth gaping, eyes unblinking, but it must have been several seconds, because Donald Clayton stood and waved a hand in front of his face, breaking his stare and bringing him back to reality. "You all right?"

"I...yes, but, well, I'm trying to digest your questions. I'm afraid I...I don't think I'm the one to...that is, I don't really have the time—right now."

When Don was standing, he still had to look up to see into Noah's eyes. He put a hand on Noah's shoulder. "Don't look so worried, son. We'll talk later, all right? But for now, I best get out to the cottage 'fore my Esther burns my meal. She does have a way of getting impatient when I don't show up at the proper time." He retrieved his small, black bag and opened the door, turning his body so that a ray of dying sunlight shot straight past him, casting its shimmery glow on the tile floor of the garden room.

Noah smiled politely and slipped through the door, murmuring his thanks.

"I'll see you Monday," Don called after him. "How about you carve out a few minutes of your lunchtime to give us a chance to talk? I might have a proposition for you."

Chapter Six

Erma and Ethel Plooster were twins, but they barely even looked like sisters—Erma was tall and as skinny as a bedpost, with beady, brown eyes and white hair she tied back in a bun; Ethel was short and stout, with round, blue eyes (albeit fading to a murky shade) and brown hair, peppered with plenty of silver strands, which she wore in two long braids. The only things they truly had in common were their good health and an affinity for food and chatter. At seventy-two, neither one was able to maneuver the rig in the winter, so Abbie and a number of other folks visited them on a weekly basis to bring them news, groceries, supplies, and the Sunday sermon notes. Of course, that meant paying close attention to Reverend Cooper's homilies, which could be somewhat tedious and dry.

Over a supper of beef sandwiches and tomato soup, Erma's canned pickles, and Ethel's applesauce, Abbie filled them in on the excitement at the Whatnot—how Shamus Rogan had forced Noah Carson's rig off the road, resulting in his ramming straight into the storefront, and how Judge Bowers had issued Shamus a thirty-day jail sentence right off the bat.

"He should've doubled it," Erma said, sniffing. "That Shamus Rogan's nothin' but a hazard to the community. Why, he'll kill somebody one o' these days."

"Erma, don't say such things," Ethel scolded, dabbing at her mouth with her napkin.

"Why not, sister? You know it's true. He's always walking in or out of one saloon or another, and not in a straight line, either."

Ethel furrowed her thick, silver eyebrows as she gave in to a nod. "Well, I suppose that's true. We did see him weaving up the sidewalk last summer. Nearly knocked Mrs. Valkema off her feet when he ran smack into her. If I recall, she whacked him on the head with her parasol."

"Hmm," they muttered in unison, their solemn nods marking the moment of silence as they mulled over the matter.

"And who is this Noah Carson?" Erma asked, breaking the stillness. "I don't believe I've ever heard his name mentioned, not that I know every Sandy Shores citizen, mind you."

Abbie's foolish heart skipped a beat. She finished chewing a bite of her sandwich and licked her lips. "Noah Carson?" Thirsty, she snatched up her glass of water and gulped three deep swallows. "He's new to Sandy Shores...well, new as of last September. He's divorced." Why she'd felt it necessary to blurt out such private information was a bafflement to her.

"Divorced? No. Truly?" Erma's narrow eyes widened as she made a tut-tut noise and shook her head. "I don't believe I know any divorced people."

"I know some that should be," Ethel muttered.

"Ethel Plooster, don't say such things!" Erma exclaimed, then leaned toward her sister and, in a lower voice, asked, "Who might you be referring to?"

"Well, take the Gilberts, for example. They've been arguing for nigh onto thirty years. Why, every time you pass them in the street, they're bickering about one thing or another. And the Meirs—have you ever heard a happy word pass between Landon and Florence?" She leaned back and folded her arms with an air of importance. "I didn't think so."

Erma shuddered. "What is this world coming to? You see, that's why I never married. You just don't know what you're gettin' till it's too late."

"You'd have married Orville Basker if he'd asked," Ethel challenged. "But he up and proposed to Matilda Freeman straight out of high school, before you muttered so much as a single word to him. Not that you didn't have plenty of opportunities, being that Mrs. Silverstone plunked you right down next to him in world history."

"Oh, pooh, Ethel, you always bring that up. I don't know why you think I'd have married him."

Ethel tilted her chin up and out, blinking slowly as she sent Erma a knowing glance. "Because, dear sister, you talked about him in your sleep, remember?"

"How would I remember if I was sleeping, Ethel May? And I never have believed that twaddle, anyway. I think it was you who was so taken with him, and you just enjoyed the chance to blather on about him. He was charming, if you recall."

Ethel pointed a finger straight at Erma. "See? There you go admitting it."

"Uh, ladies?" Abbie cut in. Never had she visited the Plooster sisters without having to settle some sort of dispute between them. It made her wonder how they managed when there was no one else around. She stood up and gathered their plates and silverware on a serving platter, which she carried over to the kitchen sink. It was an unwritten rule that, whenever she visited, Erma and Ethel prepared the meal, and she cleaned up.

She could have dined at one of Sandy Shores' finest restaurants with Peter before attending the stage play; in fact, he'd suggested just that on the phone earlier that day. But, in the end, she'd declined, saying the Ploosters were expecting her. A heavy sigh had traveled over the wires when she'd told Peter her decision. "I don't see why you have to visit them on a Saturday," he'd huffed. "I look forward to spending Saturday afternoons and evenings with you, Abbie. Besides, it's not smart for you to go out there by yourself—especially in light of that rock-throwing incident a while back."

"You could always come with me," she'd reminded him.

"I…that doesn't really appeal to me, Abbie."

"Of course, it doesn't. That's not where your interests lie."

"Why don't you at least take the Interurban?" he'd said, passing over her remark.

"Mill Point's train station isn't anywhere near their house, Peter."

"Oh, I see. Well, at least make sure you're home before dark, then. Promise me that, all right?"

He had so much supposed concern for her well-being, yet he couldn't take the time to drive her to see the sisters himself? Yes, Peter Sinclair was a fine, Christian man, but he was certainly lacking when it came to performing charitable acts of kindness. Perhaps he was what one termed an apathetic Christian—if there was such a thing.

The tinkling of teacups at the table brought Abbie back to the present. "I went to see RoseAnn today," Abbie announced to the Ploosters from her place at the sink. "She is such a beautiful baby."

"Oh, I wish we could see her," Ethel exclaimed, setting down her teacup. "You must bring us a photograph one of these days."

"I will. Papa bought one of those new Kodak Brownie cameras. As soon as he develops the first roll of film, I'll bring you a snapshot. I got some very big smiles out of her today. She seems to appreciate my jokes, unlike most other people."

The sisters chortled. "And what sort of joke did you share with her?" Erma asked. She and Ethel began gathering up what few dishes remained on the table.

Abbie wiped her hands on the apron Erma had insisted she wear and turned around. "Are you ready for this one?"

The women set the dishes in the sink. Erma nodded with a skeptical expression, while Ethel shook her head. They'd heard plenty of Abbie's jokes.

"Okay. Two snowmen are standing out in a field. One says to the other, 'That's odd. I smell a carrot, too.'"

Nothing. Not even so much as a giggle. In fact, all Abbie got in return were blank stares. "Don't you get it? Snowmen have carrot noses."

"We get it, don't we, Ethel?" Erma finally said, forcing a smile while poking her sister in the side.

"Yes, yes, we get it, but can't you do better than that?"

Abbie sighed. "All right, here's another. What did one ghost say to the other ghost?"

Erma sighed. "I don't know. Do tell us."

"Do you believe in people?"

This one produced a small spurt of laughter, albeit feigned. "Oh, you ladies just don't have a sense of humor," Abbie joshed. "I have some more, if you'd like to hear them."

"That's okay, dear. Why don't you save them for next time?" Ethel said. "No point in wasting them all in one visit."

Abbie whirled back around to resume rinsing the dishes. "All right for you, but just know, you're missing out on my best ones."

All of five seconds passed. "Oh, for mercy's sake, tell us another, Abbie Ann," Erma said. "Otherwise, the suspense just may do me in."

Abbie giggled. "Why were the teacher's eyes crossed?"

"We don't know," Ethel said, almost cutting her off.

Abbie grinned, angled her face at the women, and crossed her own eyes. "Because she couldn't control her pupils!"

This time, they did laugh. "Abbie Ann Kane, you are a corker!" Ethel exclaimed.

"What lies on its back, one hundred feet in the air?"

"Stop," Erma said, holding her stomach.

"No, tell us," Ethel insisted.

"A dead centipede."

"Gracious me!" Erma exclaimed.

"That was a funny one," Ethel said, cackling. "Now you're warming up."

Later that night, with her back propped against two thick pillows and her down comforter pulled up to her waist, Abbie yawned and reread the note she'd just finished writing to her sister.

March 6, 1907

Dear Mags,

I just returned from visiting the Plooster sisters. We had a lot of fun, even though I spent a good share of my time refereeing their spats. Tonight they argued over some man from their ancient past named Orville Basker, whom I believe they both had a crush on but neither cares to admit. They do make quite a pair, and I enjoy trying to brighten their days with my repertoire of riddles.

I turned down an opportunity to attend a play with Peter tonight. Oh, Maggie, I do sometimes feel like a floundering fish. You know how I've always said I don't need a man to fulfill me, and that God is all-sufficient. Well, it's true. Not that I don't wish to marry someday, but I also don't want to marry for the sake of it. (I'm sure Grandmother is worried I shall end up an old maid.) I know many think I should up and marry Peter Sinclair, and, maybe someday, I will. But, first, I must have a sense from God that it's the right thing to do. How in the world did you know Luke was "the one"? Did God reveal it to you in some significant way?

Many interesting things have transpired here over the past days. Of course, you know from talking to Papa on the telephone about the incident at the Whatnot. It was really quite something, a mess of broken glass and damaged merchandise, but volunteers from the town, as well as the man whose rig crashed through the window, helped to clean up and repair the damage. This man I'm speaking of is divorced and has a very sweet little boy who's in my Sunday school class. I don't know the circumstances surrounding his divorce, but I will admit to being slightly curious. By the way, he is a very handsome man, but, of course, that is neither here nor there. Divorce is so rare, usually occurring only in drastic situations, so, naturally, I'm somewhat eager to know what went wrong. At any rate, I shall pray for the two of them, but especially for little Toby, his son. In fact, I look forward to seeing him in my Sunday school class tomorrow morning.

Katrina Sterling remains busy as ever with Cora and Clara. I don't know how she keeps up with them, but then, I don't know how in the world you and Luke manage with your brood, or Hannah Grace and Gabe with theirs, for that matter.

And speaking of Hannah, I went to visit her today. I got to hold precious little RoseAnn (I'm still so honored that she bears our middle names) while Alex took his nap. While I was there, Jesse decided to go to the Whatnot. He took Dusty with him, since it was Saturday. That crazy dog loves spending time at the store. He lies on the braided rug in front of the stove, lifting his head only to greet the incoming customers.

Papa hired a new employee at the Whatnot, a Mrs. Rita James. Her husband passed on last year, and she recently moved from Mill Point to the east side of Sandy Shores. She's a little on the plump side but very pretty, in my opinion. I'm sure Papa took pity on her when she told him about her desperate financial situation since the loss of her husband. She has three married children who have scattered themselves all about the country.

I would love to see the apartment house again where you and Luke have set up house with your many little charges. I admire you, you know. It took much courage and heaps of faith for you to leave the comforts of Sandy Shores two and a half years ago. I wonder if the Lord will ever call me to do something similar. Oh, how I long to know His will.

Now I've bored you to tears with my ramblings...oh, bother! Please write soon and tell me how things are going for you and Luke at the orphanage. I'm anxious for the day when I can pay you another visit in New York. You always whet my appetite for adventure with your wonderful stories. And it goes without saying that I'm longing to visit my newest nephew, precious Lucas James. At almost seven months of age, he must be learning new things every day!

The weather was quite horrid last week but has since warmed up considerably, turning the snowman Jesse built a few days ago into a withering, pitiable lump with a red scarf and top hat.

Your loving sister,

"Abs"

PS: How could I forget? During our last ladies' union meeting in the church basement, some mean so-and-so tossed a rock through the window with a piece of paper tied to it. Do you know what was on the paper? A picture of a gravestone with my name inscribed on it. Can you imagine? Well, since nothing further ever came of it, I've completely put it out of my head, and I hope Gabe has, as well.

K

Noah stretched out on his side, making the broken springs of his mattress squeak, and stared across the tiny room. In the murky darkness, he identified the straight-backed side chair with his clothes draped over it, looking like some kind of creepy, malformed animal. Upriver at the loading docks, a train whistle sounded, alerting riders and drivers of its midnight arrival. Noah could hear the huff of the engine, and he imagined the smoke rising to meet the stars. Normally, he paid no heed to incoming trains, despite their rumbling, rattling effects on his uncle's small, clapboard house. But, tonight, as a gentle breeze whistled around the house's exterior, a restless spirit overtook him, and his senses were as alert as if it were midday.

The events of the day replayed themselves in his mind a dozen times or more, from his hustling Toby out of bed that morning so he could rustle up some breakfast before going to the barbershop, to the unimpressive manner in which he'd straightened up their little five-room house, shoving dirt under the sofa instead of sweeping it into a dustpan, then haphazardly swishing yesterday's dirty dishes in cold water, running a rag over them, and calling them clean. With the chores behind him, he'd dropped an overly exuberant Toby at his aunt and uncle's place so that he and Uncle Delbert could set off on their fishing excursion, their hopes high for catching the "big one." As it turned out, they'd come home with a bucketful of medium-sized bluegills and a small bass. It occurred to Noah that he, not his uncle, should have been the one devoting his Saturday to Toby, but the prep work at Donald Clayton's house had taken precedence.

These musings set off a whole new string of ponderous thoughts, all centered on the conversation he'd had with Donald Clayton after he'd asked to see Noah's boat design—and on his unexpected suggestion of a proposition.

Noah didn't have the foggiest notion what that proposition might entail, but one thing he did know: if it involved his having to fork over any of his own money, he had none to spare, all thanks to Suzanna, Carl Dunbar, and Tom Grayson, whom he'd long considered his best friend. No matter how long or often he thought about it, he couldn't fathom how he'd been duped. As if it had happened just yesterday, he recalled the entire, sordid mess, right down to the last detail: how he'd returned early from an appointment with a client, made a detour to his home to pick up some paperwork he'd forgotten that morning, and stopped in his bedroom, only to find his wife tangled up in his partner's arms. Both had been naked from the waist up and making fast work of the rest of their clothing. Revolted and enraged, Noah must have stared gape-mouthed in the doorway for all of ten seconds before he'd finally reacted by shouting words he'd never uttered and hurling everything he could get his hands on toward the adulterous pair—from a Tiffany table lamp to a lead crystal paperweight to a spindle-backed chair—and then advancing on Tom with every intention of killing him.

Somehow, though, Tom had escaped the room just in time, seizing his shirt off the bedpost and leaving his belt and shoes behind, red-hot fear glistening in his eyes as he hoofed it out of the room. In the meantime, Suzanna had screamed, grabbed her own clothing, and scuttled into the adjoining room, slamming the door behind her and locking it. In retrospect, she'd saved her own skin by disappearing, Noah realized. In his state of mind, he might well have killed her instead of Grayson. In fact, he'd been about to break down the door when Toby's wee voice had stopped him.

"Why are you and Mama fighting?" he'd asked, his head tilted to one side, a frown pasted on his freckled face.

Just like that, Noah had lowered his arm, made an about-face, and tried to cool his boiling blood. She'd had the nerve to carry on with Tom with her son in the house?

"I thought you were at your grandma's house today."

The lad had shrugged. "She brung me home early. Why'd Uncle Tom leave without sayin' g'bye to me?" He'd given the room a hasty perusal, his mouth sagging at the corners. "How come you broke the lamp?"

"You—you saw Uncle Tom?" Noah had asked him, trying to conceal his rage.

"Yeah. He runned past me. What's Mama doin' in that other room?"

"She…." He'd grasped for the right words, making an enormous effort not to blurt out the truth—that he'd caught her romping with his best friend. Not that Toby would have understood, anyway.

Suddenly, the door had opened, and his wife had stepped out, having donned her dress and smoothed her hair. "Oh, you're home," she'd said with nonchalance, lightly tapping Toby on his shoulder as she passed him on her way over to the bureau.

"You didn't know he was home?" Noah had asked, appalled at her neglect. Oh, how he'd wanted to throttle her on the spot. Thankfully, his son's presence had forced him to control his temper, no doubt the reason Suzanna had picked that precise moment to reenter the room.

She'd turned, her skirts flaring, and settled her back against the tall, walnut chest, her chin jutting out, her blue eyes as cold as ice, as if she hadn't a thing to repent of; as if she blamed *him* for catching her committing fornication. "I didn't hear him come in." She'd sniffed and studied her perfectly manicured fingernails. "Mother should have informed me she was dropping him off an hour earlier than expected."

Noah had glared at her, as if to burn holes through her head with his eyes, and had heaved breaths so heavy that his lungs had nearly exploded, all the while keeping the soles of his feet glued in one spot because of Toby's presence in the room.

The train's piercing whistle and powerful chugging drew Noah out of his reverie. With a good deal of irritation, he flipped to his other side, wincing when a spring poked him in his upper thigh. Why must things be so tipped in Suzanna's favor, as they were? *She* was living the high life; Tom was running *his* business, living in *his* house, and sleeping in *his* comfortable bed, for crying out loud!

Somewhat ashamed of his self-pity, Noah thought of Toby. Of course, the boy had suffered the most, having discovered firsthand the pain of rejection. "Why'd you have t' go and get d'vorced?" he often asked. "Maybe you should tell Mama you're sorry so we can move back home."

Having no one else to blame, Toby laid the responsibility on Noah's shoulders. "Your mama and me, well, we're not going to be living together again, and we decided it'd be best all around if you stayed with me," Noah would respond.

How did one go about explaining to a six-year-old that his mother loved him, but in a very shallow, meaningless way, and only when it didn't present her with an inconvenience? Rarely a day had gone by that Suzanna hadn't carted him off to her mother's house, complaining of fatigue or undue stress—which were ridiculous claims, considering she carried no responsibilities around their rambling house other than to tell the household staff what to do.

Through his window, Noah could see the full moon shining down on a tugboat moving up the river, probably heading for the loading dock. In the winter, barges broke up the ice, making way for ship traffic, and only in the deadliest of storms did cargo boats come to a halt.

My life is a deadly storm, he mused halfheartedly, *halted by the winds of disaster and mistrust.* Even God seemed far off these days—unreachable, unresponsive, even uncaring. Noah groaned at the notion of dragging himself to church in the morning. What would it hurt to miss one Sunday? Nothing. After several minutes of tossing about, Noah finally floated into a semi-restful state of sleep.

Chapter Seven

The bell above the door of the Whatnot rang, alerting Abbie to incoming customers. She peeked around a stack of canvas-covered trunks at the back of the store to see Silas and Wilma Halstead saunter in. A chipper couple in their late sixties, the Halsteads came in like clockwork on the first Monday of every month to stock up on canned goods, sugar and flour, dried fruits, tea and coffee, and anything else Silas could talk Wilma into putting on the counter.

Rita James was standing closest to the door, arranging perfume bottles on a glass shelf. She greeted the Halsteads, and they looked downright surprised to see someone other than Jacob Kane wearing a work apron embroidered with "Kane's Whatnot."

Abbie stepped into view, brushing her dusty hands on the front of her sky-blue skirt. Although the store aprons were practical, they reminded her of gunnysacks with ties in the back, so she usually opted to have a soiled dress or skirt by day's end, instead. "Well, good morning, you two. Have you met Mrs. Rita James, our newest employee? Mrs. James, meet Silas and Wilma Halstead. They live on a farm out on

Comstock Street. Mrs. James just started working for us this past weekend."

"Please, call me Rita," she said, extending her hand to Wilma and then to Silas. "I'm so happy to meet both of you."

Wilma Halstead, ever bubbling over with friendliness and good cheer, gave a wide, toothy grin. "Well, now, 'bout time Jacob hired another clerk for the store—and a pretty one, at that. Abbie here's been busier than a bee in a hive since Hannah Grace had that new baby."

Rita smiled and brushed several strands of graying hair off her temple, tucking them behind her ear. "And I'm delighted I could step in to lend a hand. As soon as I saw that 'Help Wanted' sign in the store window, I hurried inside. Mr. Kane was kind enough to hire me almost on the spot. I can't tell you how grateful I am."

Silas Halstead nodded, then gave a hasty glance over his shoulder. "Speaking of the store window, I heard Shamus Rogan sent some fellow by the name of Carson bounding straight through the storefront in that last bad storm we had. Must have come as quite a shock, Miss Abbie, his busting through the window like that."

"I should say it did," Abbie exclaimed, allowing the events of that day to replay in her mind—as well as the days immediately following, when Noah Carson had replaced the window and made other repairs. She'd meant to tell him yesterday in church about all the compliments she'd received on his fine work, but she hadn't seen him, and Toby hadn't come to Sunday school. As with any child who was absent from Sunday school, Abbie intended to pay him a visit to let him know how much she'd missed him—that is, unless Jesse walked him to the store after school, in which case she could tell him then. Secretly, though, she hoped for the former scenario, as she had an awful hankering to lay eyes on Noah Carson again, no matter the impropriety of such thinking. For at least the tenth time, she reminded herself that he was divorced.

"I'd like to think Judge Bowers's decision to lock up Mr. Rogan for a time will teach that hooligan a lesson, but I've got my serious doubts," Wilma remarked, dragging Abbie's mind back to the moment.

"Yes, well, we'd all like to think that, wouldn't we?" Rita answered in Abbie's place.

The foursome let that thought dangle for a bit before Wilma switched topics. "Say, how is that newest addition to the family? RoseAnn, is it?"

Abbie smiled. "Yes, and she's wonderful, not to mention pretty as a princess, thank you very much."

"Well, I don't doubt that," Silas said with a gleam in his eye. "Pretty looks just seem to run in the Kane family. And, believe me, I recognize a pretty woman when I see one." His eyes twinkled with mischievous merriment as he nudged his wife in the side. "Picked me the prettiest flower in the garden some forty years ago."

Wilma blushed and huffed at the same time, then gave her husband a brisk rap on the arm. "Oh, pshh. You behave yourself, old man."

"Oh, Mr. Halstead, that's so sweet," Abbie crooned.

"Yep, it was the spring of the year, and the daffodils were in full bloom, but she outshone 'em all."

"Don't listen to him, ladies. He's wantin' something, for sure," Wilma said, turning the man around and pointing him in the proper direction. "Now, come on, Mr. Halstead. We have a long list to fill, and time's a'wastin'."

"You got licorice drops on that list?" Silas asked his wife as they set off down the middle aisle. Over her head, he winked at Abbie and Rita.

Wilma glanced back at precisely the same time. "Didn't I tell you? It's always something with him."

Abbie giggled at the pair. "If you want any peace, you best give him what he wants, Mrs. Halstead."

"You tell her, Abbie Ann," Silas said, his eyes gleaming. "In fact, why don't you go scoop me up a pound of those licorice drops and leave them on the counter?"

The couple disappeared around the corner, Wilma murmuring something indiscernible.

Rita's quiet laughter blended with Abbie's. "Are they always like that?" she asked.

"Oh, my, yes. Have been for as long as I've known them."

Rita stared off after them, her eyes glistening. "Even in their banter, their love clearly shines through."

Abbie reflected on Rita's observation as she gazed out the shiny, new window. Melting snow had created standing puddles in the middle of Water Street, making its name more appropriate than ever. "If I ever marry, I hope to be half as happy. Of course, I've always said I don't need a man to be fulfilled. The Lord is all we need to be complete and truly content."

"I'll second that, Abbie," Rita said as she resumed arranging perfumes on the shelf. She sighed, and her weighty tone made Abbie question what sort of marriage she'd had before her husband's passing.

K

"Easy does it," Noah said, as he and three other men set the seven-foot-wide framed pane in the opening he'd prepared. Don Clayton stood to the side to watch the proceedings. After a bit of maneuvering and adjusting, they fitted the window in place, and Noah expelled a sigh of relief to see that it matched the opening. Yes, there would be a bit of additional adjustments necessary to make the casing perfectly square, and then the obligatory trim work to ensure it blended architecturally with the other windows. But the worst was over, and it gave him a sense of satisfaction to know he'd measured accurately. Once they'd secured the window, the men stood back to admire their work and marvel at the picturesque view of the lake below, already thawing in spots from the milder temperatures of the past few days.

"This should make the missus mighty happy," Don said, stepping forward to run a hand along the smooth frame.

"It sure brightens the room up, Don," Delbert said. "That was a fine idea you had to open up this space."

"You can give Esther the credit for that. She's always coming up with ideas, and most of them cost me a good deal of money. This one was worth it, though." He pitched a glance at Noah, then looked through the window, his gaze dropping down to the beach below. "I'm envisioning a shiny, new schooner down there," he said with a bob of his head. "Docked next to my little sloop. A sleek, fast lady."

"Oh?" Noah's uncle shot Don a curious look, crossing his arms and tucking his hands under his armpits. "You getting yourself another boat, are you?"

"That's my hope. Been thinking about that regatta the yacht club sponsors. I'd sure like to win it this year."

"Humph. You and a lot of others. That's a tough race, traversing the rough waters of Lake Michigan from Saugatuck to Sandy Shores. The course is only twenty-six miles, but a body never knows what he'll find when he sets sail on the Big Lake."

All the men but Noah stood gazing out the window. Noah bent down to retrieve his hammer and some nails, keeping one ear tuned to the conversation. He was still curious about Don's intentions and thinking about his remark last Saturday about wanting to make him a proposition.

"Is Rikkers building it for you?" Ray Buford asked, his voice cracking with excitement. Ray was a strapping, sandy-haired young man who'd dropped out of high school to help support his family. Noah liked his enthusiasm and his indomitable spirit. Since coming to work for his uncle in September, Noah had never heard the boy utter a negative word or show an inkling of laziness. He could see why his uncle had hired him.

"I haven't determined that yet," Don responded. "I want a quality vessel, one that'll skim the surface like a speedy water bug. When was the last time a Rikkers boat won the regatta?"

Delbert stroked his whiskered chin. "Can't say I recall. Been a while, I'd guess."

"Exactly. Rikkers builds fine schooners, but they're designed more for hauling cargo, not racing."

"You gonna have somebody from Chicago build it, then?" asked Harold Weaver, a bulky man about Delbert's age who'd been working in the company for the past ten or so years.

"No, it'd be hard to keep an eye on the project if I did that. I'm actually considering someone local for the job: a noted shipbuilder."

"Who would that be, if it ain't Rikkers?" Harold asked.

As if a lightbulb had just turned on inside his skull, Delbert cast a hasty glance down at Noah. Noah held his gaze for a few seconds before letting go of his hammer and nails and plunging his hand into his toolbox, as if searching for a piece of gold. He would thank Don later for the discomfiting moment. If he ever were to consider building a boat for Don, he'd want to discuss it with his uncle first. After all, Delbert had stuck his neck out for Noah, providing him with a place to stay and a steady job. He deserved Noah's utmost gratitude and allegiance.

"'Fraid I'm not at liberty to discuss names right now," Don said, shifting his weight, his eyes fixed out the window.

A collective sigh arose, followed by a reflective quiet, each man seemingly lost in his own thoughts.

Noah cleared his throat. "You fellows won't mind if I finish my job here, will you? I sure appreciate your coming out to help lift that critter into place." He nodded at the massive window perched nicely in its frame.

That started everyone moving, including Don.

"You want me to hang around and lend a hand?" Delbert asked.

"No, I can manage the finish work. Besides, you best get back out to Stickney Ridge. Last I heard, you were installing the windows in those two lakeside cottages at the top of the dune. I'm sure you want to finish them before the weather takes another turn on us."

"You got that right," his uncle harrumphed. "Old Charlie and Ben can't navigate those roads up there at all when they're snow-covered and slippery."

"Well, let's hope the worst of winter is behind us," Harold said, taking off his hat to sweep a hand through his thinning hair, then plopping it back in place. "That last storm was a doozy."

"Yeah, and made worse by that drunken dolt, Rogan, running Noah straight into the Whatnot," said Delbert.

Noah would have liked to forget about that, but every time he turned around, it seemed someone wanted to talk about it, which only made him think more and more about Miss Kane and that pretty face of hers. And, now, he had his own son madder than a dog at him for making him skip her Sunday school class, not to mention Aunt Julia, who'd marched straight over to his place yesterday afternoon to give him a good-sized slice of her mind, saying the least he could have done would have been to call and let her know that Toby needed a ride. "He needs constancy in his life right now, Noah," she'd said, her chin jutting like it used to do when he was a kid and she had to scold him for one reason or another. As a boy, he'd spent many a summer with his childless aunt and uncle, who often had treated him more like a son than his own parents had, his father working at the boatworks company by day and carousing by night, his mother spending most of her time in bed, sick with one ailment or another. A weak heart eventually took her life when she was only in her late thirties. Of course, he'd always had a hunch that his father's neglect had lent to her early death. She'd lost her will to fight.

"Well, at least he's gettin' his just rewards now," young Ray remarked. "And who knows? He might change his ways when Judge Bowers lets him out."

"Ha! Or not," Harold said with a chuckle, slapping the boy on the shoulder. "A man don't change overnight, 'ceptin' if he's got the will for it, son. Somethin' tells me it's gonna take more 'n a month o' jail time to turn that feller around."

They were still murmuring to each other as they made their ways to the garden room and bundled up with their winter gear. Noah heard them tramp across the room, say their good-byes to Donald Clayton, and open and close the side door. Next, he heard Don's footsteps moving about the kitchen, a cabinet door opening and closing, a faucet running, and an attempt at whistling a tune, which, to Noah's ears, sounded off-key. Noah crouched down to fish through his toolbox for his measuring tape. When he found it, he hooked the end of it to the bottom of the window frame and measured its length, extending two inches beyond the casing to allow for a longer sill. He wanted no surprises when mitering and fitting the moldings, beginning with the sill and following with the head and side casings. Because all the windows in the house had Victorian corner blocks, he'd had to do quite a lot of shopping around to find suitable matches for the new one. They weren't identical, but they were so close that no one would know the difference. Of course, to be sure, he'd obtained the Claytons' approval before purchasing them.

He fitted the sill against the window, then took a pencil from behind his ear to mark the forty-five-degree angle at which the corner would need to be mitered.

"How 'bout a nice, cold glass of water?" Don said as he entered the room. "Far as I know, you haven't had a break since you got here."

Noah laid down the piece of trim and turned. "Sure, thanks," he said, accepting the glass Don offered him and raising it to his lips. He took several swallows of the clear, refreshing liquid, avoiding eye contact with Don, even though he knew full well the man's gaze focused on his every gulp.

"I hope you weren't put out with me earlier when I remarked about hiring someone local to build me a new boat."

Noah had been, but he'd since cooled down. He lowered the glass and looked Don in the eye. "You should know that I've committed to helping my uncle in his business. He's thinking about adding on to his building, so I've been working with Peter Sinclair on the finance end of things. This wouldn't be a good time for me to pull up stakes, especially since Uncle Delbert's like a father to me."

Don arched an eyebrow. "You have quite a head on your shoulders, you know that? Not only are you skilled in what you do, but you also have a keen business sense. And you're loyal, to boot. I admire that in a man." He angled his head and bit down on the corner of his lip, his gray eyes narrowed. "I take it you've figured out by now I want to hire you to build that boat."

Noah gave a wry chuckle and swallowed the knot in his throat, along with the rest of his water. "It's an untested design, Don, nothing more."

"Ah, but you said yourself you'd guarantee its speed; that you'd built enough boats in your young life to know it'd be a winner."

"I don't think I put it in quite those terms."

"But that's what you meant to say, isn't it?"

"I may have said something similar, but—"

"As for your uncle's business, Delbert has a good handle on it, wouldn't you say? And a good team of workers. He'll make do without you for a while."

He had him there. As a matter of fact, Noah's uncle had hired him out of the goodness of his heart—not because he'd been desperate for the help. Rather, it was Noah who had been the desperate one, needing to get out of Guilford.

Noah sucked in a deep breath and released it in a long sigh, straightening his shoulders. "You want me to build you a boat," he stated with matter-of-factness.

Don nodded, his mouth curving into the slightest smile. "Specifically, the one you designed."

"Why me? You don't know anything about me, or my work, for that matter."

"I know enough. Your being Del's nephew already puts you in good standing, as far as I'm concerned. I know you spent many a summer here growing up. I learned from talking to Del you're a smart, fast learner, that you know a thing or two about racing boats, and that you've earned yourself more than a dozen trophies."

"When in the world did he tell you all that?"

"After church yesterday. We talked briefly in the foyer."

"I've not seen you at that church before."

Don's eyes twinkled. "I've not seen you, either. Must be, we attend on opposite weeks."

Noah rubbed the back of his neck and looked at his feet. The beginnings of a hole in his right sock revealed a portion of his big toe. Blast if he didn't need to pay a visit to Kane's Whatnot for some new socks.

"Don't be thinking your uncle divulged anything private—beyond what you've already told me, anyway. He did, however, tell me you know a great deal about the ship-building business. Said you had yourself a fine reputation in Guilford."

"*Had* being the definitive word."

"Hear you learned a great deal from your father," Don added, breezing right over his counter remark, "but then, you already told me that on Saturday. 'Course, in Del's eyes, you've far surpassed his brother-in-law in skill, know-how, and gumption."

Noah couldn't help the scoffing noise he made. "My father is far more skilled than I, but, if you'll recall, I also said that he wasted a good deal of his pennies and potential on booze." He shook his head, then wiped several beads of sweat from his brow. His chest knotted uncomfortably. "He might have made something of himself if he'd…. But what am I saying? I'm not much better than he, when you consider the mess I've already made of my life, my being divorced and all."

What was he saying, indeed? Donald Clayton had a way of making him go off at the mouth without even trying. If he were limber enough, he'd give himself a good kick in the rear for making himself so vulnerable.

With his throat gone dry, Noah wished he hadn't drained his water glass so fast. "Thanks," he said, handing off the empty tumbler to Don. With a hasty glance at the unfinished window, he shifted his weight. "I should get back to work."

"I can offer you a good sum for your labor, son." Noah went stone-still. "I have a nice-sized, empty warehouse up on First Street, not two blocks from your place. Until last fall, I'd been renting it out for boat storage, but the folks using it moved out of state, so there it sits, unused. It'd make a fine workspace, with giant double doors and nothing but rafters overhead." Noah's stomach rolled over. He couldn't believe the offer sat on the table like a neatly folded napkin just waiting to be unfurled.

"I don't have a single tool—"

"I have a line of credit a mile long. I'll issue you permission to use it in purchasing every tool and supply you need for getting the job done, not to mention pay you a generous hourly wage. We can discuss what you consider fair."

Fair would be reclaiming Guilford Shipbuilding Company, but Noah didn't see that happening anytime soon. This *would* be the next best thing. Over Don's shoulder, late-morning sunlight slanted through the shiny, new pane, striking an oak ceiling beam. Dark shadows hovered in one sunless corner, where two brocade wingback chairs sat on either side of a low table displaying a neat stack of leather-bound books and a tall vase of dried flowers. In the massive, stone fireplace to the right, a fire crackled.

Don removed a cigar from his front pocket, lit it, and took a couple of deep, almost soothing, drags while studying Noah's face, the smoke lifting between them in a lazy, circular fashion. Noah had never been one for smoking, but his beloved, deceased grandfather's fondness for cigars had endeared to him the aroma of quality tobacco. He breathed its heady scent, casually wondering what it would be like to have the kind of money Donald Clayton had—the sort that not only allowed one to purchase the world's finest Cuban cigars but also permitted one to pay top dollar for a custom-designed boat for which the sole purpose was feeding an obsession with winning an annual regatta. Actually, Noah himself had been well on his way to amassing great wealth before Suzanna and Tom had stepped in to steal his dream.

"What shall it profit a man, if he shall gain the whole world, and lose his own soul?"

Out of nowhere, the Scripture verse bounded across his brain. He tried to recall its source and determined it must have come from a recent sermon he'd heard at the Third Street Church a few Sundays back. He usually only half listened to the reverend's messages, so why had this particular verse implanted itself in his memory? And why did it stir an uneasy feeling in the pit of his stomach?

"So, what do you say?" Don asked. "You interested?"

Was he! And yet, he had so many things to consider—his commitment to Uncle Delbert, for one thing, and the need to make time for Toby, which would be difficult during such an undertaking. Noah knew himself. Once he started working on a boat—not to mention one he'd designed himself and dreamed of building for two years—it consumed his every waking moment. "I'll have to think on it," he said, as firmly as he could.

"How much time do you need?"

Looking past Don, he focused his gaze on the yet unfinished window project. "For one thing, I have a job to complete here. I can't think much beyond that right now."

"I understand. Well, can you estimate how long it would take you to build this design of yours, if you were to take on the job, that is?"

Noah swept a hand across his brow. "Can't say for sure. Three months, probably; four, tops. I'd have to order the sails out of Chicago almost immediately. I can do the rigging myself, though. The only other thing I'd order would be the hardware." He could hardly believe how fast the words poured from his mouth. Had he lost his mind?

"So, you'd build the thing completely unassisted?"

"I might need to hire someone to help me bend the ribs and apply the planking, but that'd be it."

"I can pay another hand, if you need it."

Again, Noah wished for something to wet his dry throat. "You're determined, aren't you?"

Don's crooked grin put him in mind of a crafty fox. "You could say that. I've had my share of losses. 'Course, I'd want you to skipper it—if you wouldn't mind, I mean."

Noah's heart thudded like a cement pendulum. "Me? But I thought you—"

"Oh, don't worry, I'll be on board, but I'd rather take orders from the expert. Remember, I want to win this year, and I presume you'll feel the same, seeing as you'd be captaining your own boat."

"*Your* boat, sir."

"Well, you know what I mean. It's your design. It could mean a big break for you, son, if we won this race. Might be just the ticket for getting you back on your feet in the shipbuilding business."

The man drove a hard bargain. A good, God-fearing Christian would say, "Let me pray about this matter and seek the Lord's direction before I make a decision." But, at the moment, Noah didn't consider himself to be much of a God-fearing man. If anything, he'd become quite the cynic. Life had thrown him some pretty hard punches, making him question just how much God truly cared about his life.

"When would you want me to start?" Noah heard himself ask.

Again, that guileful grin lit Don's ruddy face. "Soon as you wrap up this job. Say, next week?"

That soon? "I'd have to purchase all my supplies ahead of time. The lumber, a saw, sandpaper...."

"I already have a saw and a four-horsepower electro-vapor engine to drive it, if that helps."

Impressive. Noah tried to contain his eagerness. "I'd also need—"

"Like I said, I'll make it known at the hardware and lumber company that you'll be using my line of credit. You get whatever you need."

Noah almost pinched himself to see if he was dreaming. The whole thing seemed too surreal for words.

The two stood there eyeing each other, Don looking hopeful, Noah nonplussed. It still made no sense why Donald Clayton would place so much trust in him.

"Do we have a deal?" Don extended his hand.

Noah stared at it for several seconds and nearly thrust his own hand forward, but then he came to his senses.

"I need to talk to my uncle first."

Don chuckled and dropped his hand. "You're a good man, you know that, son? Well, all right, then, I'll let you finish here." He took a couple of slow drags of his cigar before turning to leave. At the doorway, he paused and looked back. "You do fine work, young man. The window looks grand."

"Thank you, sir."

"You let me know when you've had that talk with your uncle."

"Yes, sir, I will."

Don disappeared to the kitchen, and Noah soon heard him resume his off-key whistling.

Chapter Eight

As it turned out, Jesse didn't walk Toby to the store that day, because Jesse hadn't gone to school. According to Abbie's father, the poor thing had a bad case of the sniffles. It was nothing too serious, but Hannah, ever the doting mother, wanted to keep an eye on him, and she'd forced him to stay in bed to avoid spreading his illness to little Alex and RoseAnn.

Abbie pulled her collar tight against her throat as she made her way up Harbor Street in the direction of the small, blue clapboard house she'd passed on many occasions on her way to the Highland Park beach. She gazed out at the frigid waters and saw a barge carrying coal moving slowly up the channel. A horse and buggy whizzed by, followed by a few horsemen, and the disappearance of the sun on the distant horizon sent a chill racing clear to her bones, despite the long, wool wrap and high-top boots she was wearing. More snow had fallen that day—enough to stick to the roofs and roads, but not enough to make navigating impossible. Since then, though, the clouds had cleared.

As she came upon the Carson residence, Abbie detected some movement inside, based on a shadow that flitted past a front window. The propriety of rapping on the front door of a divorced man's home came into question, but it was his son she intended to visit, so she figured that should make it all right. Still, she couldn't deny the hint of excitement stirring in her veins at the notion of seeing Noah Carson again, nor could she deny the lump forming at the back of her throat. *Pure foolishness*, she berated herself.

Gingerly, she climbed the icy steps and gave a quiet knock with a gloved hand. When no one came to the door, she dared peek through the glass but saw no one about. She did see a good amount of clutter, though—pots and pans piled atop a little cookstove, an array of clothing draped across every available chair, and books and papers scattered hither and yon. Swallowing hard, she rapped again, this time with a little more force. That's when he emerged from a back room, taller and broader than she remembered, finger-combing his hair as he crossed the room. A slight beard shadowed his square-set jaw. Suddenly, she wanted to run. What in heaven's name had she been thinking? She turned on her heel, intending to jump off the porch and make a beeline for the nearest tree to hide behind, but in her rash move, she lost her footing on the slippery porch and went down, landing on her rump—hard—at the precise moment the front door opened.

"What in the—?" Noah stared at her momentarily, then quickly crouched down. "Are you all right?" he asked, giving her a thorough looking over, his mouth gaping in apparent shock to find her on his step—in a sprawled-out position, no less, with one boot pointing northwest, the other south.

If it hadn't been so awfully cold, Abbie probably would have broken into a sweat from sheer embarrassment. "I...I'm fine, thank you," she sputtered. This was mostly true, except for the pang in her hind end. Good thing her wool wrap and countless petticoats had helped cushion her fall. Her first awkward attempt to stand on her own failed when her heel slipped out from under her, landing her flat on her rear again.

"Here." Noah gently took hold of her arm and lifted her as effortlessly as if she weighed little more than a feather. "Sorry, I should have salted this porch."

Upright, Abbie glanced at her booted feet, now firmly planted side by side, then over his shoulder into the room beyond, and then up at the side of the house, where icicles hung from the eaves like crystal daggers—anywhere but into his eyes! Suddenly remembering the purpose of her visit, she thrust her hands deep into her coat pockets, having forgotten which one held the piece of paper on which she'd scrawled that week's Bible memory verse for Toby. Unfortunately, her gloved fingers did not produce so much as a spare piece of lint. Now she could add mortification to her growing list of unpleasant emotions.

"Looking for something?" Noah asked, watching her plunge her hands back into her pockets.

"I...yes, but...oh, humph." Her breaths came out in wispy, white clouds. "I must have dropped it when I pulled out my gloves."

Leaning against the doorframe, Noah arched his brows at her, which, she discovered upon finally looking him full in the face, were dark and thick, making his blue eyes appear shaded and almost mysterious.

"And what exactly did you have in those pockets of yours?"

"A paper."

"A paper?"

"Yes, I—I missed Toby in Sunday school yesterday, and I wanted to bring him the Bible memory verse we learned. I trust he wasn't ill."

"No, he's fine."

"Well, I'm very glad to hear that. I assume you must have been under the weather, then."

They stood nose to chest for five seconds before he answered. "Actually, I'm quite fine, as well, but I do thank you for your deep concern for me." He grinned like a stroked cat.

Abbie felt her foolish heart beat a little too eagerly. "You're...welcome," she said, detesting the lame sound of her voice. She snapped her shoulders back and regained her focus. "I'm challenging the children to learn a verse each week."

"Good idea. I'm sure Toby will benefit from that."

"Of course, he'll need your help to accomplish it."

His expression dulled a shade. "Oh."

"You do have a Bible, right?"

"Yeah, somewhere."

"Well, you'll have to find it, Mr. Carson. It's Psalm 56:11: *'In God have I put my trust: I will not be afraid what man can do unto me.'*" She met his eyes directly. "Shouldn't you write it down?"

"Psalm 56:11, you said?"

"Precisely."

"I'll remember." He raised one eyebrow while shifting his weight. "So, you still on that story about Noah and his ark? You had my boy quite intrigued with that yarn."

"No, actually, we talked about Daniel yesterday."

"Oh, yeah, that guy who was thrown into the fiery furnace."

"No, you're thinking of Shadrach, Meshach, and Abednego. They were friends of Daniel's who were persecuted for their unwavering faith in God and their refusal to bow down to the king. Daniel, you'll recall, was hurled into a den of lions sometime later. All were miraculously rescued by God, of course."

"Of course." Noah scratched his head and grinned sheepishly. "I'm afraid I don't have all those fairy tales—er, Bible stories—straight in my head."

Abbie shivered at his statement. "Is that what you think, Mr. Carson? That the Bible is full of fairy tales? I trust you're not teaching that erroneous belief to your son."

"You want to come in, by the way?" He stepped aside and gave a sweep of his hand, ignoring her remark. "You'll have to excuse the mess. I intend to—"

"Oh, no, I wouldn't—couldn't…. Is Toby about? That's really the reason I stopped by—to see him." She tried to see around his broad physique.

"Well, now, you've hurt my feelings." His chuckle reeked of sarcasm. He shook his head. "'Fraid not. My aunt Julia took him for the night. She does that on occasion."

"Oh, how nice for him, and her. Well…." What a fine note to end on. "I should be on my way, then. Please tell Toby how much I missed him in Sunday school yesterday, and that I hope to see him next week. You *will* bring him next Sunday, won't you?"

"Either his aunt or I will drop him off."

Knowing she was sticking her nose where it didn't belong, Abbie ventured on. "A child is more inclined to follow the Word of God when he sees his parents live it out."

"Is that right? Well, in case you hadn't noticed, there's only one of us around."

"I…yes, I know…so, all the more reason why you need to set the example."

There went those thick brows again, arching like upside-down Vs. "You're not preaching at me, are you, Miss Kane?"

"I wouldn't presume to tell you what to do, Mr. Carson, but a boy of Toby's age should have every opportunity to develop a relationship with our Lord and Savior, and I can't imagine you'd want to rob him of it." She let a span of three seconds pass between them. "Would you, Mr. Carson?"

"You're a persistent little mite, aren't you?" My, but his eyes were striking. She lowered her gaze and noticed his stocking feet, a big toe poking through the left one. Mother of mercy! He may as well have been shirtless, for all the commotion that toe created in the center of her stomach.

She raised her gaze but focused it on the picture hanging slightly askew on the wall. "I'm sorry if I've bothered you," she murmured, starting to turn. "I'll say good night, now."

"Wait." Noah snagged her sleeve and looked out at the road. "Where's your rig?"

"I don't have one."

"So, you walked here?"

"Of course."

He glanced at the clock on the wall behind him. "It's after seven o'clock. I'll drive you home."

"But that's completely unnecessary. I enjoy walking," she protested, even as he stepped into his boots sitting next to the door and snatched his coat off a nearby hook.

"I'm sure you do, but on a cold night such as this, and with it growing dark, I couldn't in good conscience let you set off alone."

"I don't need—"

"Please don't argue, Miss Kane." He threw on his coat and snuffed out a candle on the table under the front window.

"I prefer to walk, Mr. Carson."

He issued her another short-lived smile. "And I prefer to drive you."

It took only a second for him to close the door behind him then loop his arm for her taking. She merely stared at it.

"Hold on to my arm, Miss Kane. You've already displayed your incompetence with steps."

"*Icy* steps," she corrected him.

He raised his chin and waited. She took his arm.

～K～

The nip in the air ran clear to the bone, but the sky was showing its first few stars and an emerging moon, no indications of more snow. Miss Kane had stood motionless in the doorway of the shed, hugging herself, while Noah had hitched Ruby Sue to the wagon, the mare grunting in protest at having to leave the warmth of her stall after he'd already bedded her down with fresh straw and her daily portion of oats and grain. And he didn't blame her one bit. He'd been about to settle in, himself, do some more tinkering with his boat design and start a preliminary list of necessary materials, provided he wound up reaching an agreement with Donald Clayton...until *she'd* come along. Now, he'd be lucky if he could concentrate. He'd forgotten how slender a frame she had, and yet how...hmm, well-proportioned. Even under that long, wool wrap of hers, he pictured her perfect figure, and, for some reason, the whole thing put him in a cross mood.

He didn't need some little brunette with snappy, chocolate-brown eyes clouding his mind, especially one already claimed by the bank president's son.

And then, there was the matter of that Bible verse she'd recited: "*In God have I put my trust: I will not be afraid what man can do unto me.*" He'd committed it to memory immediately, perhaps because it spoke to the deepest recesses of his mind.

Fairy tales? Is that how he perceived a good share of the Bible? His mother would certainly roll over in her grave if she knew he often doubted God's very existence. She'd done her best in her short life to tell him how much God loved him. Unfortunately, his father had worked just as hard at undoing her words and making him believe the opposite. He sometimes wondered where he'd be now if he'd chosen early on to grasp hold of his mother's convictions—but, then, look where those convictions had landed her. What kind of loving God would send such a beautiful young woman to an early grave, forcing her to leave behind a son and hope he'd find a way to survive his father's brutal taunts and raves? Yes, the man had taught him the boatbuilding craft, but if memory served Noah correctly, nothing he'd ever said or done had earned him a single word of praise from his father. If anything, the man had taken great pleasure in deriding his son. Not even when he and Tom Grayson had built their boatworks business to its highest peak in sales and work orders had Gerald Carson uttered one word of affirmation.

With Ruby Sue hitched to the wagon, Noah lent Miss Kane a hand in stepping up to the front seat. "Sorry if you're not accustomed to old rigs. I bought this off a farmer when I first got here. I've been meaning to replace it." *If I ever get ahead*, he almost added.

"I couldn't tell you one thing about Papa's rig," she stated. "I enjoy walking everywhere I go."

"So you said." He supposed she had to figure out some way of expelling all that pent-up energy. He grinned to himself as he helped her up, noting how little effort it took. While she situated herself in the seat, he went around to the other side and jumped up next to her, the seat springs squeaking under his weight. "All set?" he asked. She nodded, so he took up the reins, gave them a snap, and clicked his tongue at Ruby Sue. On cue, the horse whinnied and set off toward town, puffs of steam exiting her nostrils. A rough spot in the road jostled the wagon, making his passenger bump against him. She quickly righted herself—muddled by his touch, was she?—and inched as far away as possible. He turned his face away to hide another slow smile.

As soon as he could keep a straight face, he turned back to Abbie. "So, you make your beau walk all about town with you?"

"Excuse me?" When she looked at him, the wind caught a lock of her hair and whipped it around. She fought to smooth it down and tuck it behind her ear.

"Peter Sinclair. He is your beau, isn't he?"

For the life of him, he couldn't figure out why it took her so blamed long to come up with a simple answer to his simple question. She opened her mouth and closed it twice before finally conceding, "Yes, he is. In fact, we've been courting for some nine months."

"Is that right? Well, then, you'll be engaged soon, no doubt."

This set off another prolonged silence before she finally said, "Perhaps."

Noah chuckled. "Perhaps? Now, there's a definitive answer."

"Anyway, as to your other question, he prefers to drive his rig," Abbie hurriedly explained. "He lives on the east side of town, so it does make sense for him to ride to work. I'm not opposed to riding, Mr. Carson. It's just that I love to walk. It's fine exercise, and it clears the lungs. Did you know several doctors have recently conducted health studies about the benefits of walking?"

"Is that right?" A barge blew its shrill horn on its way upriver, and Noah waited for the sound to die down before continuing. "I prefer chopping wood, myself. Anyway, you must have been running late the other morning, because I swear I saw your father drop you off at the Whatnot."

"Oh, that. Well, a small incident occurred at my last W.C.T.U. meeting, and Gabe—uh, Sheriff Devlin—insisted I ride, not walk, until things calmed down."

"Incident? W.C.T.U.? I don't think I'm following you." Noah clicked Ruby Sue into a little faster gate.

"The Woman's Christian Temperance Union." Abbie looked at him, and the moon's rays glanced off her brilliant, brown eyes. "I'm surprised you haven't heard about it. Around Sandy Shores, news travels lightning-quick. At any rate, right in the middle of our union meeting one Tuesday night, someone sent a rock sailing through the church basement window with a note attached. It wasn't much of a note, just a poorly scribbled rendering of a gravestone with my name inscribed on it. Silly, really."

A sense of unease started to build in Noah's chest. "I wouldn't call that silly, Miss Kane. You've obviously got somebody in a pucker. You're not very good at heeding instructions, are you, walking to my place in the dark? I'm surprised your father allowed it."

"My father knows by now that I can make up my own mind. I'm a grown woman, Mr. Carson."

"I can see that." He assessed her carefully, his eyes lingering perhaps longer than necessary. "And a trifle bullheaded, I'd say." She pursed her lips, which only proved his point.

"And it wasn't after dark, either, just approaching it," she put in. She did like to be right, he could see that quite plainly.

To ease the tension, Noah said, "I didn't know Sandy Shores had a woman's temperance chapter. I've only heard bits and pieces about the organization."

Her slender shoulders straightened like an ironing board beneath her heavy coat. "Before you decide to pass judgment, Mr. Carson, let me assure you, we are not radicals."

He let go a sudden spurt of unexpected laughter. "So, you sensed that coming, did you?" Up ahead, a wagon pulled out into the road, prompting him to pull back on the reins. Ruby Sue slowed her pace, and the clip-clop of her hooves changed to a trotting rhythm.

Miss Kane relaxed her shoulders, allowing a minuscule smile to light her face—and what a transformation it made. Abbie Ann Kane was more than attractive. Striking, lovely, and exquisite were hardly sufficient to sum her up. "You wouldn't be the first to think it," she said, holding on to her hat as a sudden breeze came off the river.

Noah decided to allow one tiny piece of information to leak out. "My old man's a tried and true drunkard. I don't have much use for strong brew, myself, so best wishes in trying to ban it."

She gave a slow nod and seemed to be digesting his revelation. "I'm sorry about your father," she said after a moment. "It must have been hard for you growing up, especially since you mentioned losing your mother at such an early age."

He'd forgotten about letting that slip. "Don't need anyone's sympathy."

That ended that, for the time being. As they rounded the corner onto Water Street, boisterous music coming from several of the town's saloons prompted him to ask, "Does the sheriff think one of the tavern owners might be responsible for the incident with the rock?"

"I assume he does, but I don't think he's determined it for sure."

"Why would the perpetrator single you out, do you suppose?"

"Well, for one thing, I'm the chapter president—and probably the most vocal."

"I guess that would do it."

K

Abbie couldn't believe Noah Carson had insisted on driving her home. Why, it was a distance of only about five blocks, and Peter hadn't offered to drive her to the Plooster farm two days ago, a good five-mile jaunt! They bounced along in the wagon, Abbie doing the majority of it, even as she tried with all her might to stay steady. Goodness gracious! She could have sworn her side of the seat had several missing springs as she tipped, tilted, and swayed, falling against Noah's rock-solid shoulder when he took the bend onto Water Street. With some effort, she managed to pull herself upright when he'd completed the turn.

"Sorry about the rough ride. Toby usually jumps behind me and sits on a hay bale, which makes for a smoother trip, all said. This ol' tin and wood trap is a road hazard, and it wasn't helped by that collision I had with your storefront. The wheels are out of alignment now, and I believe the impact broke a few springs."

Abbie risked stealing a glance at him as he spoke, noting how the starry sky and bright moon lit up his profile. A peculiar flutter raced across her stomach like a whole band of butterflies. *For goodness' sake, what's gotten into me, viewing a divorced man with curiosity? Lord, forgive me.* "The judge ought to have made Shamus Rogan buy you a brand-new rig," she said, forcing calm into her voice. "His wife tells me he has plenty of money, but he's such a cheapskate that he keeps it locked up in the bank, dishing out just enough when she needs to purchase food and supplies for the family."

"He did order him to pay for the repairs, such as they were. Jeb Warner said he fixed it up as best he could, but he muttered something like, 'You can't make a mink coat out of a squirrel's hide.' I had to agree with him."

Abbie had a million questions on the tip of her tongue, none of which she dared ask, especially since they were irrelevant to the subject at hand. *Why are you divorced? Where is Toby's mother? Doesn't she miss him dearly? What made you leave Connecticut? What did you do before you started working for your uncle?* "Well, at least you weren't out the repairs, then," she said through chattering teeth.

If he noticed her chill, he didn't let on. "Won't be long and that stinkin' coot will be back on the streets, rumming it up again."

"Yes, it's quite disheartening to think about. He has a very sweet wife, if you ask me. I feel downright sorry for her and the children."

"How many kids do they have?"

"Three, I believe. The youngest is maybe eight or nine, and the oldest is around fifteen. All girls. I intend to pay them a visit one day soon."

Abbie felt the intensity of his gaze on her face as they rattled along, and, out of the corner of her eye, she watched his arms bounce with every bump, nearly brushing against her. "Oh, yeah? For any particular reason?"

She shrugged and shivered, pulling her wrap closed at her neck. "I want to take them some covered dishes and see how they're managing. I'm sure they don't have any money for food, what with Mr. Rogan sitting in jail. Like I said, he's very stingy, doling out just enough to keep the lot of them from starving. According to Arlena, he makes a decent wage."

"That dolt. What a worthless—"

Deafening piano music coming from Charley's Saloon drowned out the remainder of Noah's words. Moments later, the saloon door blew open, and an ox of a fellow flung somebody out on his posterior, his skinny frame hitting the ground like a scruffy rag doll, a string of expletives such as Abbie had never heard rolling off his tongue. The ox yelled at him to go home and sober up, then slammed the door shut.

"Oh, forevermore!" Abbie spat out. "Have you ever heard such language?"

"Actually, yes."

Without forethought, she rose to her feet and pointed a gloved finger at the prone man. "You shouldn't say such words, mister. Have you no compunction? No self-reproach?"

"What are you doing?" Noah hissed, snagging her by the sleeve for the second time that night and giving her a good yank.

She went down with a plop, but she wasn't finished yet. "You should go home to your family, mister," she persisted, turning around in her seat. And as they passed the dazed, glassy-eyed character, she craned her neck and wagged a finger. "You're wasting your hard-earned money on poison, do you know that?"

With great effort, the man raised his head and called out, "Shhhut up, you li'l hussy, an' m-m-min' yer own business."

"I am minding my business. I'm—"

"Shh, Miss Kane. You're causing more commotion than all the taverns put together," Noah cautioned her.

She turned back around and folded her arms across her chest with a dramatic sigh of exasperation. "You see? That's what I'm talking about. These men work for a living but spend all their money—and time—in the saloons, leaving little for their families."

"I understand that, but your screaming at them won't solve anything."

"I wasn't screaming!" Immediately, she clapped a gloved hand over her mouth. "Was I?" she muttered through the fabric. Sudden shame for the way she'd treated the drunkard made her flush.

Noah slanted her a crooked grin, then set his gaze back on the road. "You are a passionate soul, aren't you, Miss Kane?"

Abbie cleared her throat and straightened her posture. "I have strong convictions, if that's what you mean."

At the precise moment when Noah opened his mouth again, an object whizzed between their heads, bounced off the back of the seat, and landed on the floor of the rig with a loud clunk.

Chapter Nine

W hat in blue blazes?" Noah whirled around, then looked down and found himself staring at a brown beer bottle with a piece of paper sticking out of its narrow neck. Before reaching behind Abbie to get it, he scanned the peppering of people walking the street, most of them minding their own business, if he guessed right. Nowhere did he see anything he would call suspicious. The music coming from the saloons kept up its toe-tapping beat. Instinct told him to look up and back, and that's when he spotted someone's head poking out of an upper-story window. What kind of person opened his window on a frigid, March night? Due to a streetlight's glare, he couldn't make out whether the figure was male or female, young or old; he knew only that the shadow of a person momentarily hovered in the opening before disappearing back inside.

"What in the world just happened?" Abbie squawked.

"Does somebody live up there?"

"What? Where?"

"There." He pointed at the two-story structure behind them. Abbie quickly craned her neck and squinted.

"I couldn't begin to tell you if anyone lives above Erv Baxter's establishment. He might keep ladies up there, for all I know." She let her gaze fall to the floor behind her seat. "What is that, anyway?"

"A bottle—of the beer variety, to be exact."

"Oh, for goodness' sake, how did that wind up in the back of your wagon?"

He raised his eyebrows at her. Was it really possible she could be so naïve? "Someone threw it, dear lady."

Her striking, brown eyes popped with firecracker intensity. "My stars! Why?"

Noah snapped Ruby Sue into a faster canter, then stretched his arm behind the seat, skimming Abbie's shoulder in the process, and snatched the bottle off the floor before it rolled out of reach. "I think we're about to find out."

With one hand, he managed the reins, and, with the other, he removed the paper from the bottle and unfolded it, narrowing his eyes to decipher the messy scrawl.

"What does it say?" Abbie asked, leaning into him, her tone impatient but, at the same time, distinctly wary.

"I can't make it out while I'm driving."

"Here, let me." She snatched the paper out of his hand like a hawk stealing an egg from a bird's nest, fast and purposefully. Now it was his turn to lean over her shoulder.

As they bumped along, she put the paper close to her face, tilted back so that the moon's glow would illuminate it. The handwriting was messy and the spelling atrocious, but she was able to make out, "'You best w-w-watch'—does that say 'watch'?—'your...step, Abbie Kane'—whoever it is spelled my name wrong—'and...sty'? Oh, 'stay out of people's business. You got…enemies'? Oh, for mercy's sake. What is this nonsense? It's ridiculous!"

She balled up the paper in her glove and prepared to hurl it through the air, but Noah caught her by the arm. "Don't. That's evidence." Her arm was still in the air, so he reached up and seized the paper, stuffing it deep into his left coat pocket.

"Evidence?"

She had to be kidding. "This is your street, correct?"

"Yes. Turn right. Our house is at the top of the hill. What do you mean by 'evidence'?"

After making the turn onto Third Street, Noah pulled back on Ruby Sue's reins, brought her to a stop at the side of the road, and turned to look at the woman with the all-too-innocent, large, brown eyes.

"Why are we stopping?" Abbie asked. He noticed that her straight, white teeth had set to chattering, but now was not the time for worrying about that.

Sucking in a frosty breath of air, he thrust his head forward until their noses nearly touched. She inched as far to the right as possible, and he inched right along with her. "Are you serious, young lady?"

"Am I serious? What is that supposed to mean?"

"It means, I am trying to figure out if you are daft or just plain stubborn as a goat." Her mouth dropped open. "That note is another threat on your life, Miss Kane, and you'd best start taking it seriously."

"You can't be serious, Mr. Carson. Why, if you look at this man's, er, person's, penmanship, it's—it's nearly illegible."

"So?"

"So, *he's* the daft one. He can't even spell, for goodness' sake. He's probably upset with my involvement in the W.C.T.U. and thinks these outlandish threats are going to make me abandon my responsibilities. Why doesn't he just face me with his complaints instead of sending me idiotic notes?"

"Because you can't reason with somebody like him. We're going to the sheriff's office."

"Both of us? Now?"

"Yes, on both counts. If you'll recall, that bottle landed in my rig. A couple of inches further in either direction, and one of us would have been injured. In fact, that was probably the bum's heartfelt hope."

"Oh." Abbie's pouty mouth sagged further. "I see what you mean. I'm sorry for the trouble I've caused you."

He straightened, slightly sorry himself for his outburst, but not sorry enough to apologize. "You haven't caused me any trouble."

"But you're angry with me."

"No, I'm not angry with *you*. I'm merely enraged by the situation."

"Gabe's probably not on duty."

"Doesn't matter. We're filing a report with whoever is. You can't dismiss this thing as some kind of hoax, and the sooner you accept that, the better off you'll be."

"You *are* angry."

Rather than argue with her, Noah took two long, measured breaths to regain his bearings, then directed Ruby Sue to turn the rig around, clicking his tongue to urge her forward.

All went temporarily still, save for the crunching sound of Ruby Sue's hooves on the snow-covered road and the squeaking of the rig's front wheel, until Abbie cleared her throat. Through her chattering teeth came a croaky whisper. "Grandmother and Papa will wonder where I am."

Sympathy for her plight brought Noah close to an apology, but he held out. "We'll call your father when we get to the sheriff's office."

"I appreciate that."

Well, at least the impact of his words had finally sunk in. Either that, or she'd decided to stew in silence. On impulse, he reached down and felt for the woolen blanket he kept stored under the seat and quickly produced it. "Here. Put this around you."

She sniffed and took the blanket, stretching it across her lap. "Thank you."

What might have happened if he'd not driven her home tonight? The question produced a shudder. "You're welcome," he returned.

K

The note in the bottle should have done the trick—put the fear of the Almighty in that little lady's bosom. If not, he'd have to come up with something else, which, of course, he was fully capable of doing. Shee-ooot, that was half the fun. Spittle collected at the back of his throat, and he expelled a wad on the cement floor, then gave way to a devilish cackle. He'd teach that girl a lesson yet—teach her to keep her nose out o' his and everyone else's business. Sure-shootin', he would. Why, doing a job on her would make a lot of men—and even a few ladies—in this town downright pleased as pigs on a picnic.

Abbie Ann Kane wasn't doing this town no favors, and he meant to see to it that she saw the light, one way or another. It just irked him no end that she had to be related to that blasted sheriff.

K

Noah held open the double doors to Sandy Shores City Hall so that Abbie could enter ahead of him. As she passed him, she was struck by this tall, daunting man who was pleasant and genial one minute, downright cranky the next. She couldn't believe she had to make a return visit to Gabe's office, this time with him, because of some groundless threats to her well-being. Heavens to Betsy! What a fine predicament and an utter inconvenience.

The dimly lit office seemed unusually quiet, with the regular staff, such as Nathanial Brayton, the city treasurer, and Kitty Oakes, Gabe's secretary, having gone home for the day, and with a number of other desks sitting vacant. At a cluttered desk at the far end of the room sat Randall Cling, one of Gabe's deputies, with his ear to a telephone, engaged in conversation—something about a bull getting out of its pasture and stomping across the neighbor's backyard. At the first sight of Abbie and Noah, he waved and motioned them inside. Abbie offered a weak smile in response and advanced to the counter; Noah came up beside her and immediately set to drumming his fingers on the gritty, pockmarked countertop.

While Randall spoke into the receiver, a hallway door opened, and her brother-in-law emerged in full uniform. "Well, look who's here."

"Gabe, you're on duty."

"I work nights every other Monday. So, what's my favorite sister-in-law doing in my office at this hour?" He always called Abbie his favorite when Maggie Rose wasn't around, and Maggie reported he referred to *her* as his favorite in Abbie's absence. It was a little game Gabe enjoyed playing with the two of them. "And what brings you with her, Mr. Carson—or did the two of you arrive separately? That old scoundrel Shamus Rogan's got another ten or so days in here, in case you were curious," he offered, giving neither of them a chance to answer his questions. "Not that I wouldn't mind tacking on a few more months for bad behavior, mind you. All that fellow's done since he got in here is moan and complain about the sleeping conditions, the damp, cold cell, how dark it is down there, and the meals, which aren't bad, considering Mrs. Terry up the road prepares them in her kitchen for a meager wage, and mostly from the kindness of her heart. Under every plate, she tapes a special Bible verse. Don't know if the prisoners ever read it, but it's her prayer they do. Of course, she leaves out one important feature at each meal, and that's ale, which Rogan claims he can't live without. I tell him now is as good a time as any to lay off the sauce and start living like normal folks, but his response to that is, 'Soon's I step foot out of this rat's hole, I'm headin' me straight for Willie's up on Waverly, Dan's Pub on Madison, or Charley's Saloon or Erv's Place downtown; don't make no never mind to me which joint I choose, s'long as they gots plenty of grog flowin'.' He's a pain in the hindquarters, if you ask me." Gabe scrunched his nose in disgust. "I tell him, seems to me he'd want to go home to his wife and daughters, being as he hasn't seen them in a while, but he just scoffs and says, 'They'll get the pleasure of seein' me soon enough.'"

Gabe finally closed his mouth and stared at the pair, his eyes roving to Noah, who kept finger-tapping and shifting from one boot to the other. And big boots they were, too, Abbie noticed when she looked at her own in contrast.

"Well, sorry for my rambling, there." Gabe scratched the side of his nose. "I believe I asked if the two of you came in at separate times and never gave you a chance to answer. So, did you? Come in separately, that is?"

"No, sir, we came in together," Noah clarified, even though Abbie had her mouth open, ready to speak. "I happened to be driving Miss Kane to her house, when, halfway up Water Street, in front of Erv's Place, to be exact, a beer bottle with a note inside landed in the back of my rig. Abbie had just told me about that rock-throwing incident at her last woman's union meeting, so I was suspicious." He produced the dark, long-necked container and plunked it on the counter. Next, he fished out the note from his coat pocket and tossed it on the counter, as well.

Gabe frowned and picked up the paper, his frown deepening as he studied it in silence. Without a word, he turned and went to a file cabinet across the room, pulled open a drawer, and grabbed a piece of paper from inside a folder. Abbie recognized it as the sketch of the tombstone with her name scribbled on it. He returned to the counter with both notes in hand and laid them side by side on the countertop.

"What do you think? Same handwriting?" His question seemed directed mostly at Noah.

Abbie leaned in to get a better view. When Noah refused to budge, she pressed against his muscular frame—so close, in fact, she smelled his woodsy scent, making her wonder if he'd been hauling in fire logs before she'd dropped in on him earlier that evening.

"Her name is definitely written with the same hand, no doubt about it," Noah mumbled.

"I'd have to agree," Gabe said. He picked up the notes for a more careful study, turning them over to check for clues on the backs, even raising the most recent one to his nose for a sniff. "Smells like nicotine. It's somebody who smokes, or at least hangs around folks who do. Did either of you get a sense of what direction it was thrown from?"

"No, but I did see someone poking his or her head out an upper-story window of Erv's Place. Couldn't make out the face, though," Noah said.

"There're some hotel rooms up there," Gabe said, frowning pensively.

"There are?" Abbie asked. "Actual hotel rooms?"

"Well...." Gabe and Noah Carson exchanged knowing glances. "Let's just say they're not the sort of rooms your average traveler would rent for a night, not when he can go up the street to the Culver House Hotel or the Sherman House or take a room at one of the other well-established, uh, respected, hotels in town."

Abbie swallowed a lump and straightened, clinking her boots together. "Ed Baxter wouldn't be keeping ladies of the night up there, would he, Gabe?"

"Not that I'm aware of, Abs. The most I can tell you is that Baxter runs a rather seamy business—and I gathered that from folks I've talked to along the way."

"Well, why don't you arrest him, then?"

"I would if I could bring up charges that would stick, but no one's filed any formal complaints, and I don't have an ounce of proof to back up my suspicions about him. You can't arrest somebody for operating a questionable establishment."

"He threatened me...and the other union ladies," Abbie reminded him. "That ought to count for something."

"By telling you not to come back, or he'd make you plenty sorry? That's a feeble, undefined threat, honey, and it proves nothing, insofar as these notes are concerned."

"Have you ever seen his John Hancock on anything?" Noah asked.

Gabe shook his head. "Nope, but I can change that easy enough. I'll go in there for lunch tomorrow and study that menu he posts on that big blackboard. I'm fairly sure he adds and takes away from it weekly, as he's forever tweaking the menu when Bart Koster drops off the daily catch of fresh fish or Bill Talsama brings in a side of beef or a wagonload of chickens."

Abbie quaked. "You'd go in there to eat, Gabe? What about your reputation?"

Gabe chortled. "I'm not too worried about what folks think, Abbie. They know I'm doing my job, which often requires me to go to less than desirable places." He leaned over the counter and tweaked her nose. She hated when he did that, as it always made her feel like a child. "And, speaking of reputations, how do you think yours fared, darling sister, when you and your union ladies marched into Erv's Place during the busiest time of day?"

"That was entirely different, and you know it. We went in to sing hymns, pray, and kindly ask the patrons to think about their families and the way they were spending their money."

"Ah. And do you think it's helped?" Gabe asked. "If you ask me, this town's saloons are going about business as usual."

Her neck stiffened. "Which is precisely why the union intends to continue on its course."

Gabe tipped his chin down and slanted his face at her. "What course is that, young lady?"

She raised her chin and stretched to her full height, a mere five feet four inches, and said, "Why, continue our hymn sings and prayer meetings, of course."

"Conducted in the church basement, I would hope."

"It is our belief that visiting the saloons themselves proves most effective."

Gabe and Noah emitted a duet of heavy sighs. "Abbie, not only is that improper, it's also irresponsible, in light of the latest events," Gabe said. He held up the menacing notes—more like stuck them under her nose, giving her a good whiff of their nicotine smell. "Do you want to put other women in danger? Because that's exactly what you'll be doing if you move forward with this—this crazy plan of yours."

"Crazy? Gabriel Devlin, I never took you for a narrow-minded thinker. And, for your information, visiting the saloons was not my idea, but rather a tactic employed by the organization at large, begun by Frances Willard, who served as president from 1879 through 1898. She adopted the watchwords *Agitate, Educate, Legislate,* and the union adheres closely to those principles. How do you propose we agitate the public unless we make our voices heard, Gabe? And how do we educate without promoting awareness, which ultimately results in changing laws?"

Gabe sighed again, even more deeply this time. "And would this Willard woman have approved of continuing with this approach if she knew about threats to the organization?" he asked. Noah propped his elbow on the counter and leaned in for her answer, obviously enjoying the exchange, if his Cheshire-cat grin were any indication. Abbie had the uncanny urge to stomp on his big toe with all her might.

"There have been no threats to the union," she argued. "They've been directed at me, and I personally think they're hogwash, pardon my language."

"Excuse me, madam," Noah put in, leaning closer. "If that bottle had smacked either of us on the head, it hardly would have been hogwash."

Well, all right, he did have a point there. Abbie pursed her lips and folded her arms across her chest. Beads of perspiration wetted her forehead, and she silently stewed about how warm Gabe kept his office. In the stove across the room, she could see the flames flickering through the grate.

"What say you cancel your next union meeting, Abbie?" Gabe ventured.

"What?" she spouted, unfolding her arms and dropping her hands on the counter.

"Just hear me out," Gabe said with uplifted hands. "Two incidents, no matter how much like hogwash they seem, are two too many, in my book. I suggest you cease meeting...." She opened her mouth to argue, but he reached across and pressed two fingers to her lips, hushing her on the spot. "...until this thing blows over. That's all I'm asking, Abbie Ann. If you receive no more threats, you can reconvene, and we'll go from there. Might be, you've just riled somebody, and giving him a chance to cool off will fix matters."

"I don't know," she said, crossing her arms again and relaxing her stance, her lips sagging in a pout. "I'd have to discuss it with the others."

Gabe narrowed his eyes with a mix of concern and determination. "Actually, you wouldn't have to discuss it with anybody."

"Why?"

"Because, as the city's chief law enforcement agent, I am hereby ordering the union to desist meeting until further notice."

Abbie gasped. "Gabriel, you can't do that...can you?"

Beside her, Noah chuckled quietly. "I think he can pretty much do as he pleases, madam."

She turned and gave the man an unrighteous glare, wondering at that moment how she ever could have found him attractive. "You stay out of this."

His eyebrows shot up, and his lips clamped shut and curled under, no doubt hiding another one of those impish smiles.

Gabe shattered the mounting tension with a gentler tone. "Listen, Abs, it's for the best. It doesn't have to be permanent, mind you." He lifted the gate on the counter and walked through to the other side, putting an arm around her shoulder. "How 'bout you go home and sleep on it? Things will look clearer to you in the morning. In the meantime, I'll call your father and let him know you're on your way home."

She allowed him to walk her toward the door, Noah following after. Perhaps it did make sense in the end. This whole situation would right itself in no time, and the union could resume its meetings, moving forward with its mission to *Agitate, Educate, Legislate*. As for finding a suitable house to convert into a sanctuary for abused women, she could continue the search on her own. Why, she would put her telephone to good use and have her "meetings" with individual ladies over the phone wires. No way could Gabe ban her from doing that!

She stopped at the door. "May I walk home from here—alone?"

"No!" both men bellowed in unison.

"Well, you don't have to yell about it." She turned and headed for the door, and as Noah caught up to snag hold of her arm and help her down the steps, a tiny ripple of mirth moved through her at the two men's apparent impression that she was helpless.

Chapter Ten

Noah's uncle looked up from his workbench, a pencil stuck behind an ear, one hand trained on a long board, the other holding a saw, as he prepared to cut the wood at its measured angle. "Morning, son," he said in his usual, genial manner. He had a pleasant way about him—always had, as far back as Noah could remember. And he dressed neat as a pin, too, his thin mustache always trimmed meticulously, his gray hair always carefully combed. Even on the hottest days of summer, when most people dressed casually in as few layers as propriety would permit, Uncle Delbert wore a long-sleeved shirt buttoned clear to the collar.

"G'morning, Uncle Del. Did Toby behave himself at your place last night?"

"He always does. Little stinker beat me twice at checkers, though. He went to bed without argument and woke up this morning without complaint, even gobbled down a whole slew of scrambled eggs, bacon, and fried potatoes. Boy won't need to eat again until tomorrow."

Noah laughed. "He'll be famished by noon."

"You're probably right," Delbert returned with a chortle. "When I left the house, Julia was gettin' him ready for school.

You have a good evening?" He stopped sawing for a moment to hear Noah's response.

Noah set his lunch pail on a shelf and shrugged out of his coat as he recalled the rather harrowing night. "Uh, let's just say it was plenty interesting," he said, hanging his coat on a nail by the door.

This comment provoked a curious expression from Delbert. He set down his saw, leaned back against his workbench, and folded his arms across his chest. "Care to elaborate?"

Noah moved over to his workbench. "You ever hear about an incident that happened not long ago in the basement of the Third Street Church...involving Abbie Ann Kane? Happened during a meeting of the Woman's Christian Temperance Union." He poked haphazardly through a drawer of assorted screwdrivers and hammers, glancing up at Delbert to see if he'd heard the question.

Delbert scratched his head. "Can't say that I did. Julia's not involved in that group, although I think she's interested in joining it at some point, if ever she can find a little more time. That woman's already up to her eyebrows in activities— teaching piano lessons, volunteering at the library, and taking meals to the elderly. What sort of incident was it?"

Noah proceeded to tell him about the episode with the rock and the sinister note, then related what had transpired just last night in front of Erv's Place while he was driving Abbie home, concluding with their visit to the sheriff's office.

"That little woman has a feisty side to her," Noah said at the end of his account. "Sheriff Devlin may be her brother-in-law, but she didn't take too kindly to his orders."

"Every one of Jacob Kane's daughters has that lively spirit about 'er," Delbert said. "They're all different, as far as looks go, but, Lord have mercy, they sure are similar when it comes to spunk. I'd have to say Abbie takes the overall prize, though. That said, I'm glad nothing more serious came of it, like that bottle hitting one of you—or somebody else on the street, for that matter. Obviously, somebody's got a bone to pick with Miss Abbie."

"Try to tell her that. She's a fearless little thing."

Delbert laughed and rubbed his cheek. "I seem to remember that girl riding a pony all over town when she was about this high." He held his hand about three feet above the floor. "I believe Jacob gave her the critter for her seventh or eighth birthday. Kept it stabled at the livery. Bright and early of a summer morning, she'd march down the sidewalk to the livery and, not ten minutes later, be sittin' atop that prancin' horse, ridin' down Water Street like she was the Queen of England herself. Truth be told, she being the baby of the three, I do think Jacob's always had a softer spot for her than the other two—not that he loved them any less, mind you, but she was the last child he and Hattie had before she died of a lung ailment. I'm thinking he must've felt Abbie was the most cheated for losing her mama at such a young age, so he did take to spoiling her, on occasion."

The door opened, ushering in several more employees. For most of them, the workday started at eight, but Noah liked to get an earlier start whenever possible, especially on mornings when he didn't have to drive Toby to school. No matter what time he arrived, though, Uncle Delbert nearly always got there ahead of the rest. Delbert greeted each worker with a wave and a smile, then turned his attention back to his nephew. "Well, I'm glad you're safe, son. I sure hope Abbie Kane heeds Sheriff Devlin's orders. I'd swear she's a younger version of my Julia, full of gumption and grit. If I didn't know better, I'd say they were related."

Noah nodded and grinned. "From what I know of Miss Kane, I'd have to agree."

Delbert slapped him on the shoulder. "Hey, what say we head over to the Sherman House for a cup of coffee before you go out to Don Clayton's place? We haven't had ourselves a good talk in a long while."

"Umm, sure." If Noah's hunch was right, Uncle Delbert wanted to discuss Donald Clayton's boatbuilding proposal. He, of course, hadn't had the chance to tell his uncle about it, but he had a feeling Clayton himself had mentioned it to him. Well, he'd made up his mind that if Delbert was wary of the idea, he would turn down Don's offer. After all, he practically owed his life to Delbert and Julia Huizenga, and the last thing he wanted to do was disappoint them or give them the impression he didn't appreciate all they'd done for Toby and him.

The Sherman House was a first-rate, three-story hotel situated on the corner of Harbor Drive and Water Street, with a restaurant on the ground level. Not many folks went to the restaurant, though, unless they were hotel guests, as the menu items were on the pricier side. Of course, there'd been a time when Noah wouldn't have thought twice about paying an exorbitant price for a meal, but, lately, he'd been trying to cut costs whenever possible.

"Let's sit next to the window," Delbert suggested when they arrived, leading the way to a table across the room that offered a good view of the river. A barge hauling gravel eased slowly upstream. A half mile or so northeast, an incoming train whistled to announce its arrival, and on a very busy

Harbor Street, men whizzed past on horseback and horse-pulled wagons, no doubt making their ways to work.

No sooner had the two seated themselves than a wait-ress arrived at their table, her neatly plaited, white hair pulled back into a tight bun, an immaculate, white apron tied around her plump waist. "Good morning, gentlemen. How can I be of service?"

Uncle Delbert motioned to Noah. "How 'bout some breakfast, son? My treat, of course."

"No, thanks, I already ate. Just some coffee would suit me fine."

"All right," Delbert said, looking at the woman. "Two cof-fees, then."

As proper as you please, she gave a brisk nod, turned, and headed for the kitchen, her long skirts swishing as she moved across the thick, wool carpeting.

Noah fiddled with the corner of his cloth napkin and wondered what to do with his hands, suddenly aware of an odd sort of discomfort swirling around in his gut.

"I should probably tell you about—" Noah blurted out.

"So, I understand Don Clayton has—" Delbert said, almost simultaneously.

Both stopped and waited for the other. "You first," Noah said.

"No, you," Delbert insisted.

Noah swallowed an uncomfortable knot. "This feels a bit awkward."

"Well, it shouldn't, Noah. You've always been like a son to me, and I wouldn't want anything to change that."

"Nor would I."

"So, then, tell me what's on your mind, particularly where Don Clayton's concerned. I have an idea, but I'd like to hear what you have to say on the matter."

Reassured, Noah proceeded. "So, then, you know he's asked me to build him a boat—a fast one that'll up his chances in winning the annual Yacht Club Regatta?"

"He hinted at it, yes. Think he was sort of feeling me out. So, this boat—you'd build it from scratch? And would it be the one you designed yourself, the flat-bottomed schooner?"

"Yes, sir, that's the one. But, I…I don't know."

His uncle leaned forward. "What do you mean, you don't know? This is—" Their waitress returned with a tray carrying two mugs and a steaming pot of coffee. Uncle Delbert hushed while she carefully set the mugs down and poured the black brew into both of them.

"Would either of you care for a dot of cream or a dab of sugar?" she asked.

"Just black for me," Noah replied.

"Same," Delbert said, his tone touching on impatience.

"Very well. Please let me know if I can be of further assistance to either of you."

"Yes, yes. Thank you."

Turning on her heel, she headed off to a tableful of new customers.

"Now, then…." Delbert assumed his forward sitting position, his hands clasped on the table, his expression eager. "Why would you hesitate to take Don up on this offer? He'd be paying you good money, I assume."

Noah wrapped one hand around the hot mug, letting it warm his cold fingers. He glanced out the window at the barge still moving up the river and another just entering the channel. Slowly, his eyes trailed a path back to his uncle's kind face. "We haven't talked details yet, he and I, but I'd have to put in hours on end to build the boat I designed. I don't know how I'd manage that and also see to Toby's care. Besides, you were good enough to give me a job at the company, and I wouldn't want to make it appear as if I don't appreciate all you've done for me."

Delbert's eyes were caring as he leaned in closer, the steam from his coffee rising to touch his chin. "Listen, son. Your coming to work for me has been a blessing, indeed, but I don't expect you to keep working at the shop out of a sense of obligation. You've been a fine worker, a quick study, if you will, but I have a strong suspicion building windows isn't your life's dream." He winked. "As for Toby, he's managed fine up till now, and I wouldn't think you'd have to spend a lot more time working at this boat venture than you do putting in hours for me."

Noah considered that. Boatbuilding consumed him, filled him with fervor to the point of obsession. Could he pace himself to finish the boat in the allotted amount of time without neglecting his son?

"This has been rough going on Toby—the divorce and all. He misses his mama, even though she hasn't sent so much as one word by telephone or mail to ask after him. I'm not sure I can build a boat and still see to his emotional well-being. I'm already not the best at it. I know how I get when I'm up to my eyeballs in a project. It's probably part of the reason my marriage fell apart. My wife and partner had an affair right under my nose, and I didn't have the brains to take my eyes off my work long enough to realize it." He picked up his mug and took a sip of the hot liquid, then shook his head. "I'm blinder than a bat at noontime."

A faint smile appeared on Delbert's mouth, making his thin mustache quiver at the ends. "Don't be so hard on yourself, Noah."

A big freighter sounded its blaring horn as it headed for the docks. Both men gave it half a glance, allowing a moment to pass between them. Loud laughter coming from the other side of the restaurant presented yet another distraction.

Delbert picked up his mug for the first time and took a couple of swigs. Then, setting it back down on the table, he slid a finger along its rim, as if studying it for imperfections. After a moment, he asked, "How much have you prayed about this, if you don't mind my asking? Have you sought God's direction? You know, it's very possible He led you to Michigan for a specific purpose, and if you ask Him about it, He's likely to reveal it to you. All in His good time, of course."

Pray? Noah barely knew the meaning of the word. He knew God from a distance, but to actually speak to Him in an intimate way seemed awkward and contrived. "I'm not much for praying, Uncle Del."

Rather than chastise Noah with a judgmental frown, Delbert merely smiled. "Well, at least you're brave enough to admit it." He lifted his mug to his lips again, so Noah followed suit.

"What did you mean by that, anyway—the part about God leading me to Michigan for a purpose?"

Tilting his head, his uncle considered his question. "Romans 8:28 tells us that if we trust the Lord in all matters, things have a way of working out for our good. I'm paraphrasing, mind you, but that's the gist of it. Even this divorce, as ugly and painful as it's been for you and Toby, can have a good ending. It's amazing how God can take the worst of situations and somehow turn them around so it looks like they were almost meant to happen. 'Course, He hates sin, no question about that. But He won't condemn a contrite spirit. Matter of fact, He's always on the lookout for surrendered hearts." Delbert steepled his hands, holding his fingertips to his chin. "Maybe, you'll even meet another woman someday who'll be able to help you pick up the pieces."

Without warning, an image of Abbie Ann Kane's face flashed across his mind's eye. Quick as lightning, he pushed it right back out again. He didn't need that pretty little live wire cluttering up his thoughts. "I can't imagine ever trusting another woman again, to tell you the truth."

"Not now, you can't, but someday, perhaps. And what's to say your meeting up with Don Clayton wasn't providential? It's possible this boatbuilding dream of yours hasn't met its end, after all. Yes, it's true your partner stole your business right out from under you—and with the help of your wife, no less—but that's no indication you cannot rebuild, or that God doesn't have some amazing plan up His sleeve. He's full of surprises, you know."

Uncle Delbert always did speak about the Lord in practical terms, like He was sitting close by, an unseen guest at their table. It fascinated Noah, the way he made God seem so personal. Why, he almost envied his uncle for it. His mind recaptured flashes of his childhood: his mother's telling him that God sent His Son, Jesus, to die for his sins, and his trying to make sense of that concept. His drunken father would enter the room and lambaste her for putting such wild notions in his head, and she'd cower in the fear that a hand might come out and smack her across the face.

Noah had no idea how his father had become such a useless drunk. *His* father, Noah's grandpa, had been a gentle man. And, of course, Aunt Julia, his father's sister, was cut from the same fabric; her personality, while somewhat severe at times, still rang true of love and goodness. How could a man with the same blood as Aunt Julia's running through his veins turn so evil? Noah thought about bringing the matter before Uncle Delbert, but the business of the boat resurfaced instead.

"Don Clayton said he owns some empty building up on First Street, about a block from my place—er, rather, your place," he said.

Delbert smiled. "It's your place for as long as you and Toby want to stay there, son." He'd always referred to him as *son*, and something about the way he said it never failed to give his heart a tiny surge of weightlessness. "I know the building he's referring to. It's an old warehouse. You could easily convert it into a fine workshop."

"That's what he told me."

Silence prevailed between them for the next few moments as they sipped their coffees, but plenty of noise was around them—folks conversing at other tables, horses' hooves clip-clopping up and down Harbor Drive, and the Interurban's brakes squealing as the car came to a halt on Water Street.

Finally, Delbert spoke. "I think you should build this boat for Don. He's a good man, a little on the voracious side, perhaps, and darned avid about winning everything he attempts, but a man with solid values and a good heart. He'll be fair with you; of that you can be certain. His giving you this opportunity to build a boat of your own design is, well, sort of like a gift dropping out of the sky and landing flat in your lap, wouldn't you say? As for Toby, we'll see to it he's well taken care of, no worries there."

"But I can't continue to ask Aunt Julia to look after him. You said yourself she's one busy woman."

"Well, just the same, things will work out. Remember the Scripture verse I just told you about. Another one I like is Psalm 56:11, which begins, 'In God have I put my trust.' Perhaps you need to start doing more of that, son."

Noah couldn't believe it. That was the memory verse Abbie had given him, the one he hadn't yet had a chance to teach to Toby. What were the chances that, of all the verses in the Bible, his uncle would mention the precise one she had chosen for her six-year-old Sunday school students to learn? Was it coincidence, or divine providence?

"I...I know you're probably right. I'll definitely keep it in mind." Noah finished off what remained of his coffee and set the mug down with a bit too much zeal. Next, he drew in a deep breath, then blew it out as he pushed back in his chair and stood up. "You've really helped me sort through this matter, Uncle Del. Thanks for the coffee and the dose of wisdom."

Delbert lifted silver eyebrows over his twinkling eyes as he pressed his palms to the table and stood, his chair sliding backward against the thick carpet. "So...what's your inclination about this boatbuilding proposition?"

"Well." Noah paused, faced his uncle, and blurted out his thoughts. "I think I'm inclined to take Don Clayton up on his offer, as long as you'll allow me to return to my job afterward. I don't think I could manage both at the same time."

Uncle Delbert fished in his pocket and tossed a couple of coins on the table. "Well, of course you couldn't. I'd not expect you to try. And, you know, I'll always hold open a job for you—my favorite nephew."

"Your *only* nephew," Noah said, finding a grin.

As they left the restaurant, Delbert asked, "You going out to Don's place now?"

"Yes, after I load up a few more tools. Then I have a quick errand to run."

"Oh?"

"I have to make a stop at Kane's Whatnot. My socks have spawned some holes, so it seems I need some new ones."

"Your aunt's a good darner," Uncle Delbert said as they stepped out into the menacingly cold March air. "I'm sure she wouldn't mind repairing your socks. Matter of fact, she enjoys sittin' next to the fireplace in her chair with that needle and whatever needs mending. She tells me it forces her to take time to think and pray."

They started up the sidewalk, bucking the chilly winds coming off the river. Noah yanked his wool collar closer to his throat. "Thanks, but I think my socks are worn beyond the repairing point, Uncle Del. Besides, I'd just as soon get some new ones."

"Well, there's nothing like a fine, new pair of wool socks," Delbert said, and Noah could have sworn he *heard* the grin in his voice. "You might want to ask Miss Abbie for some assistance in picking out a quality pair."

Chapter Eleven

Kane's Whatnot had only a handful of customers when Noah walked through the door at five after nine, causing the bell above it to jangle more loudly than he'd wanted. The blasted gadget made it impossible to enter a public establishment unannounced. A harried-looking woman with two youngsters practically tied to her arms gave him a cursory nod, which he returned.

As was his habit, he glanced at the window he'd installed, running a hand over the smooth sill and side casing closest to him, silently admiring his work. Dropping his hand, he turned and headed up an aisle, subconsciously scanning his surroundings for one petite brunette with a spark in her coal-black eyes, a quirky sense of humor, and a mulish spirit. Not seeing her, he felt the strangest sense of disappointment come over him, which struck him as utterly absurd. Good grief, most of the time, he didn't even like her!

A rippling sound had him whirling on his heel, as if he'd been caught thinking aloud. From behind a curtain, an attractive woman he'd not seen before emerged. Apparently, she was a clerk, since she wore an apron bearing the store's name. At the sight of Noah, a pleasant smile burst onto her mouth, giving her a youthful look, even though she was probably in her late forties or early fifties. He never had been a good judge of age.

"Well, hullo there, sir. Anything I can help you with?"

"Umm, just a pair of socks, is all."

She smiled, making her olive-toned cheeks, dappled with a light sprinkling of freckles, almost touch the wisps of silver hair that had come loose from her bun and were suspended in slight curls around her face. When Jacob Kane hired a new clerk, he at least saw to it she measured up in looks to his daughters— not that Noah had met the other two Kane sisters, but he figured them to be beauties, from what he'd heard.

"Socks, huh? Well, those we have," the woman said. "Are you familiar with our store, Mr...?"

"Carson. Noah Carson. And, yes, I am." He followed her toward the back of the store, weaving around barrels of wheat flour, sugar, and coffee. The aromas were a mixture of homespun goodness—everything from wood to leather to bunches of dusty, dried flowers hanging upside down from ceiling hooks. Noah ducked to avoid hitting a spray of daisies.

Suddenly, the woman halted right in the middle of an aisle and spun around on her high-heeled boots, making her skirts flare out. There were no socks in sight. "Wait a minute. Did you say Noah Carson?"

He arched one eyebrow. "I did." She had yet to divulge her name.

"Well, I declare! Mr. Carson!" she exclaimed, round-eyed and flummoxed. "You're the one who drove straight through the window in that awful storm."

"That seems to be my only claim to fame around here," he said, feeling the beginnings of a smile.

"Well, it was quite something, you know, that storm, and then Mr. Rogan's ramming straight into you."

"More like, he swerved, forcing me to turn into the store to avoid a head-on collision. Afraid it was an impulsive move on my part. I'm mighty glad there weren't any injuries."

"Yes, praise the Lord for that. A head-on collision could have proved even more devastating. I've a feeling the Lord had His eye out for you and your young son. I've heard all about you, you know."

Now, there was an interesting tidbit. "You have?"

"Oh, my, yes." She put a hand to her throat, and he noted they weren't getting any closer to the socks. "Abbie Ann talks a blue streak about you—your son, I should say. Toby, is it? I saw him on one occasion when he walked here after school with Jesse. My, he's a handsome boy. You must be so proud."

"I am. Very. Uh, maybe you could just point me to the socks?"

"Oh, of course! Right this way."

The bell above the door sounded again, and Noah looked back to see a young man and woman, neither of whom he recognized.

"I'll be right with you," the clerk called to them. The couple nodded and moseyed to a display table housing a number of windup clocks.

Turning her attention back to Noah, she extended a hand and smiled up at him. "I'm Rita James, by the way. You did a lovely job on repairing the window. Several people have commented on how nice it looks."

He took her hand and found it pleasantly warm. Smiling back, he said, "Well, that's always good to know. It's nice meeting you, Miss James."

"Oh, it's *Mrs.*, but, please, call me Rita. I'm not actually married, anyway. Well, technically, I suppose I am, but I'm a widow, you see."

"Oh. So sorry."

"No, it's fine, thanks. At any rate, I insist everyone call me by my Christian name. It's much less formal, don't you think?"

He wasn't accustomed to calling women by their first names, even though he longed to know Miss Kane well enough to do so. Would she ever think of him as Noah, or would it always be Mr. Carson?

Rita glanced at the door when yet another customer entered. "Well, now we're getting busy, aren't we? I do hope Abbie Ann returns shortly."

"Ah, where is she?" he asked in as casual a manner as he could muster.

"She's across the street at Pat's Eatery, that brand-spankin'-new restaurant, having some breakfast with that beau of hers, Mr. Sinclair."

Unwarranted irritation at that piece of news made Noah pull at his collar.

"Have you tried the food there yet?" Rita prattled on. "I understand it's quite tasty."

"No, I can't say I have, but maybe I'll do that…after I get my socks."

"Socks!" She snapped her fingers. "Yes, of course. Right this way, Mr. Carson." She set off again, so he followed her.

"Noah, please."

She gave a slight toss of the head and smiled. "Noah, then." At the end of the aisle, she stopped and pointed at a shelf on the far wall. "There're your socks, Noah. As you can see, we've got quite a selection—heavy wool or cotton, plain colors with striped toes, or beautiful Scotch or English designs in browns, olives, grays, cardinals, wines, or black. Most are eighty cents a pair, some less, some a few cents more. Take your pick."

"Ma'am?" a customer called from two aisles over. "Could you give us some assistance?"

"Yes, I'll be right there," she replied. She looked at Noah and sighed. "I'm grateful for this new job, but it surely keeps me busy."

He would imagine it did, especially if she stopped to talk to everybody who came through the door. "You go on, now," he said. "And it was nice meeting you."

Her cheeks grew two pink dots in them. "Oh, well, the pleasure was all mine, of course. I'll tell Abbie Ann she just missed you. Or perhaps you can tell her yourself; that is, if you still plan to walk over to Pat's Eatery."

Noah's stomach grumbled at the thought of food. At the Sherman House, he'd told Uncle Delbert he'd already eaten, but the truth was, all he had left in his kitchen was a partial loaf of bread and a few miscellaneous items, and he'd gone for a slice of bread that morning and called it good. Tonight, after work, he'd head for the meat market. He wasn't much of a cook, and Toby complained almost incessantly about his meals, but at least he knew enough to keep them from starving. A platter of bacon and eggs sounded mighty fine about now. Shoot, he might even run into Peter Sinclair and ask him about the status of his uncle's business loan.

While he was at it, he could also ask him what he planned to do to keep his little lady friend under lock and key.

Abbie pushed her food around on her plate, not hungry in the least but taking small bites, anyway, to appease Peter. He may have plenty of money, but he certainly didn't sanction wasting it. It irked her how he always made a point to wipe his plate clean and half scolded her when she didn't do the same. Well, he could rebuke her all he wanted, but it wouldn't do a bit of good. A jittery stomach equaled no appetite. Gabe had stopped by the house early that morning, and his words still held her in their grip: "You need to be on the alert, Abbie Ann," he'd said from the doorway, with a solemn look on his face that'd had Grandmother Kane chewing her bottom lip and fidgeting with her skirt. "Do not take these incidents lightly. Someone's mighty agitated with you right now, and until we figure out who it is, and what's got 'im so riled up, you cannot let your guard down. Understand?" She'd nodded, wishing this entire thing would go away, baffled that anyone would want to harm her yet refusing to overreact. Her father had wanted her to stay home, but what were they going to do, lock her up for the rest of her life? "I don't think that's necessary—yet," Gabe had replied, directing the statement mostly to her father and grandmother, as if she'd had no say in the matter.

And, now, she had Peter to contend with, having just told him about last night's threat, delivered in a bottle that had sailed through the air and narrowly missed hitting her and Noah Carson.

Peter frowned, the lines etched deeply in his forehead resembling a snaking, twisting road map. "I still don't understand why you had to walk to his house, Abbie—and at dusk, no less. You barely know that man, for Pete's sake, not to mention you are my girl. Going to his house wasn't proper, by any means."

Abbie didn't know what to make of his possessive claim on her. After all, they were not even betrothed yet. "Well, it wasn't after dark when I set out, and I didn't go to see him; I went to see his son, who, I found out upon arriving, wasn't there."

"So, what kept you from turning straight around and heading home?"

"I told you, Mr. Carson wouldn't allow me to go. He insisted on driving me, which, in retrospect, was a good thing, wouldn't you agree?"

Peter huffed a loud breath, obviously perturbed by the whole chain of events. "In retrospect, it would have been altogether better if you hadn't gone there at all. Confound it, Abbie, didn't you hear a word your brother-in-law said? You're supposed to be riding places, not walking."

"I noticed you didn't have any interest in driving me out to the Plooster farm the other day. If you are so concerned for my safety, why didn't you insist on taking me?"

Peter shifted in his chair. "That was before this latest incident. I may have reconsidered, had I known you might be in actual danger. From now on, I don't want you walking anywhere at night, and especially not to Noah Carson's place. As I said, that's not even proper, considering we're courting."

"Absolutely nothing untoward took place, I can assure you."

"I didn't say it did, but you should know, I still don't approve. Moreover, if you had just gone straight home after work, nothing would have happened."

Abbie pressed her lips together, then proceeded to push her eggs into her fried potatoes, patting them down with her fork while trying to tamp down her growing annoyance. With her free hand, she picked up her glass of water and took two hasty swallows.

Over her glass, her eyes met Peter's. He reached across the table and gave her arm a gentle squeeze, his expression softening. "I'm sorry if it seems I'm being harsh, Abbie," he said, his voice suddenly gone gentle. "I don't want us to argue."

She set down her glass and nodded.

"It's this ladies' club, you know. That's what all these notes are stemming from, I'm certain of it."

"It's not a club," she insisted. "It's a national women's organization."

"All right, then." Peter cleared his throat and lowered his voice. "This organization…seems a bit too reactionary and political, if you ask me. This business of entering saloons to pray and sing choruses to a bunch of boozing men…well, it's just downright unseemly, in my eyes. Good grief, if we want to talk about untoward behavior—"

"Which *we* do not," Abbie interrupted him. "And besides, what we do as a group is completely accepted behavior by the organization. We remain orderly and respectful at all times."

Peter cleared his throat some more. "From what I understand, you and Ervin Baxter got into quite a row the night you marched into his place. I would not call that orderly."

"Didn't you just say you don't want us to argue?" Abbie picked up her napkin and wiped her mouth. *Lord, please forgive my beastly short temper.*

"We're not arguing. We're discussing."

She closed her eyes for scant seconds and inhaled slowly. "You and I simply don't agree on my involvement with the W.C.T.U., and, perhaps, we never will."

"It does seem to be a point of contention."

"Morning, you two." The low-timbered voice sliced into their exchange like a newly sharpened knife.

Peter's jaw dropped, and he pushed his chair back and stood up. "Well, hello there, Noah. Your ears must have been ringing; Abbie, here, was just telling me about the encounter you two had with a beer bottle. I was telling her that if she'd just stayed home, as would have been appropriate, nothing would have happened. I'm sure you agree."

Abbie remained glued to her seat, unable to believe Noah's sudden appearance. "Morning, Miss Kane," he said with a subtle nod, then turned to Peter. "Maybe so, but then, it was probably bound to happen at some point—another episode, that is—so it's good she wasn't alone, don't you think? At least now she'll know to be on her guard."

After that, the men had a staring contest of sorts, with Peter finally conceding, "I suppose you do raise a good point." The staring kept up. "Would you care to join us?" Peter asked at last, gesturing to an empty chair at the table.

"Well, thanks, don't mind if I do," Noah said, lowering himself into the chair without hesitation. Peter sat down again with less enthusiasm. Abbie couldn't help watching Noah unbutton his work-worn wool coat and pull his big arms out of the sleeves, then drape it over the back of his chair. He cast a lazy smile at the young waitress, who hastened to his side, then glanced at Abbie's partially eaten plate of food and Peter's empty one. "Just coffee, please." When she walked away, he nodded at Abbie's plate. "You going to eat that?"

She blinked twice, looked down at her plate and its creative arrangement of food, and shook her head.

For a span of five seconds, no one moved or uttered a word. It occurred to Abbie then that he meant to dive into her unfinished breakfast. She glimpsed Peter's tightly drawn expression, noting that his top button looked ready to pop. He adjusted his necktie, his eyes darting from Abbie to Noah and then back to Abbie.

"Would you…would you like my—?" Abbie stammered.

"Are you offering? Well, in that case, thank you very much." Noah reached across the table and pulled her plate in front of him, then picked up his fork and placed his napkin on his lap.

Peter nearly scowled in disbelief as Noah dug in to Abbie's cold eggs, and a tiny ripple of amusement bubbled up in Abbie's chest. Well, now, here was a side to Noah Carson she'd not yet seen—a rather slapdash, audacious, unpredictable side.

And she quite liked it.

⁓ *K* ⁓

Noah couldn't believe his own nerve in taking Abbie's plate, but what was the sense in paying for a full breakfast when he might just as well eat one the kitchen staff would have given to the neighborhood dogs? Besides, he enjoyed seeing the shock of his spontaneous action on both Abbie Ann's and Peter Sinclair's faces. He chewed and swallowed while the pair looked on, Abbie with a mostly hidden smile, Peter Sinclair with complete bewilderment. Noah had intruded on their private conversation, after all, which he wouldn't exactly have termed peaceful, considering Abbie Ann's exasperated expression and Peter Sinclair's irritated one.

He decided to astonish them further. "So," he said between bites, "how's your backside, Miss Kane?"

Peter wheezed sharply and leaned forward. "What did you just say?"

Noah took a swig from the coffee mug the waitress had placed in front of him. "She didn't tell you?" he asked, setting the mug back down. "She knocked on my door last night and then promptly fell on my porch. I opened my door, and there she was, sprawled out like a bear rug—and helpless to get up, too. Are you all right?" This last part he directed at Abbie, who looked ready to kick him.

"Perfectly fine, thank you very much."

Peter's brow crimped. "You didn't tell me that part, Abbie. What else did you leave out?"

"What? Nothing. Oh, for crying in a bucket, I have to get to work. You two enjoy your little conversation." She pushed back from the table, and both men leaped to their feet, but Noah beat Sinclair to the punch in pulling out her chair.

"I'll walk you over," Peter offered.

"It's just across the street. I think I can manage."

"Then, I'll pick you up after work."

"I won't be there," she said, fastening her coat's final button and wrapping a colorful scarf around her neck. "Papa's relieving me at one thirty so I can run an important errand."

"An important errand? But I thought you weren't to be going anywhere alone," Peter said.

Up went her hand. "Hannah's accompanying me, and she's very responsible."

"And your brother-in-law and father approve of this?" Noah asked.

"We're going in broad daylight."

Before either of them could offer an objection, Abbie blew Peter a kiss and gave Noah a perfunctory glance before making her way across the crowded room, her long, wine-colored, cashmere coat flaring at the back, her boots clicking as she walked.

Noah chuckled and said under his breath, "That lady's a little fireball."

Peter Sinclair must have heard him, for he pinched the skin between his eyebrows and muttered back, "Don't I know it."

For a span of two minutes, the men sat in a sort of oddly companionable silence, Noah scraping Abbie Ann's plate of every last crumb, Peter finishing off his coffee.

"You want to step over to my office and finish the paper-work on that bank loan for Delbert?" Peter finally said. "Once you've done that, we can switch the money into his account. It should take only a few minutes."

"Let's do it," Noah said, wiping his chin with his napkin and standing up. He glanced down at his clean plate. "I think I owe you a breakfast."

"You owe me nothing," Peter said, standing so that they faced each other—not quite eyeball-to-eyeball, though, as Noah stood a few inches taller. "Fact is, I probably owe you."

"How's that?"

Peter looked past him, probably casting his gaze at Kane's Whatnot across the street. "You may well have saved my soon-to-be fiancée's life. Like you said, it was good that she wasn't alone when that beer bottle incident occurred."

Noah's neck grew prickly warm. This blasted wool shirt collar! He pulled at it, then picked up his coat and threw it over his arm, shoving in his chair.

"Aren't you going to put that on?" Peter asked, nodding at Noah's work jacket as he buttoned up his perfectly tailored, handsome mackintosh and donned his nutria-fur crusher hat.

"It's only a block or so to the bank. I'll carry it."

For one brief moment, they stood, unmoving, Peter shooting Noah a defiant glare, which Noah read as an undeclared challenge to stay away from Abbie Ann Kane.

"Shall we?" he asked, thrusting out his arm in invitation for Peter to go before him. The fellow walked briskly to the door, followed by a full and happy Noah.

Chapter Twelve

O h, it's wonderful to be out and about, minus two squealing little ones demanding every second of my attention. I do hope they won't be too much for Mrs. Garvey to handle."

Abbie pulled her eyes off the road to glance over at Hannah, relaxing her hold on the reins now that they had set themselves on a straight jaunt to the Rogan residence. Bessie, the Kane family's trusty horse, perked up her ears and sniffed the fresh air expectantly as she trotted along, pulling the small buckboard and its two passengers.

"It will be a good trial run for Mrs. Garvey. It's so convenient, her living right next door and all. I'm glad she's so eager to watch the kids, Hannah. And, may I say, I'm eager for you to come back to the Whatnot? Everyone misses you. Will you have regrets about leaving the children for a few hours at a time?"

Hannah let out a gentle burst of laughter. "Make no mistake, my darling sister, I love being a mother to RoseAnn, Alex, and Jesse. In fact, I do believe motherhood is my calling in life. But, to be a good mother, I also need to separate myself from the children, on occasion, if for no other reason than to refresh my tired mind and body. Working at the Whatnot for a few hours a day will do that."

Abbie shook her head. "Working for refreshment? It sounds like an oxymoron, if you ask me, Hannah. I get plain tired working in that store."

"That's because your passions don't lie in the retail business, Abs. I simply adore running that lovely, little establishment, and, of course, I love seeing the customers, filling orders, listening to folks' endless woes, tallying figures, balancing the books, ordering inventory, stacking shelves…. And, with Mrs. James's joining us, things should be much easier for the three of us…well, four, counting Papa, even though he rarely works the store, what with his growing insurance business."

"He's been working a bit more since Rita joined the staff. I suppose he wants to be sure I don't lead her astray."

"Oh, you're a silly duck, Abbie. You're perfectly capable of training her."

"Well, whatever the reason, he's been helping more often, though that will probably cease once you return."

Abbie adjusted her position on the hard seat and rubbed her chilly nose. Heading straight east, they rode past thick groves of oak, maple, and ash on either side of Grant Street, the trees' branches as dry as skeleton bones. Stout little houses sat in neat rows on both sides of the street, some with sheds in back for their horses and chickens. The sky was clear, the sun sparkling, but the air held a bite. About seven blocks north, one of the many creeks leading into the Grand River flowed westward, eventually dipping into the cold waters of Lake Michigan.

"How did it happen that you and I came out to be so different, Hannah? I wish I could be more like you and

Maggie—deliberate, domestic, yet with business smarts, settled into a career, and heading exactly where you know God desires you to go."

"You don't know how often I wish to be more like you, darling sister, so full of grit and zeal. I love your plucky spirit, that enthusiasm for venturing into uncharted territory. And make no mistake, you are living within God's will as long as you daily commit your ways to Him and ask for guidance. I don't know if I've told you how proud I am of you—your involvement in the W.C.T.U., your love for those comical Plooster sisters, your eagerness for teaching six-year-olds every Sunday morning, and your genuine selflessness to work additional hours at the Whatnot so I can spend time with RoseAnn and Alex. Why, just your deep desire to help Arlena Rogan says a great deal about your character. Not many would venture into others' lives for fear of putting their noses where they didn't belong, but you, my dear, have no apprehension whatsoever."

Abbie chuckled. "Naturally, the fact that Shamus Rogan's sitting in a jail cell right now erases my worries about visiting the family. Otherwise, I don't think I'd be so brave. It also helps that you agreed to come with me. Of course, Gabe would've had a fit if I'd driven out here alone and something had happened. I'm still surprised he consented to your coming along."

Hannah turned full around in her seat and gave someone a wave. Confused, Abbie cranked her neck around. "Why are you waving? Who's back there?"

"Can you see that man on horseback trailing us about a block away?"

Abbie swung around again, squinting into the low-lying sun. "Yes, but who is it?"

"You didn't really think Gabe would allow us to drive out here completely unattended, did you?"

"Is that Gabe?"

"No, it's one of his deputies, Gus Van Der Voort. He intends to hang back just to keep an eye on things, but don't pay him any heed. He's just there to make sure no one noticed you leaving town."

"Tst." Abbie frowned and turned back around. "I hate that Gabe's paying him to do that. It makes me feel like a regular nuisance."

"Don't be silly. Someone is plenty irritated with you, for some ridiculous reason, and Gabe is not about to take any chances with your life—or mine. Be thankful he's concerned for your welfare."

"Oh, I am, I am, but I can't help being embarrassed by all the attention. I enjoy my independence, and it suddenly feels like it's been stolen out from under me."

"I'm sure it will all smooth out in due time. Be patient, Abs, and let Gabe continue with his investigation. So far, he has little to go on."

"Well, perhaps nothing more will transpire, giving him even less, which would be a good thing."

"I know Gabe, and, believe me, he won't rest until he finds the perpetrator—even if that fellow stops making threats."

"I talked to some of the union women by phone from the Whatnot this very morning," Abbie said. "All of them agreed we should remain in contact, particularly with regard to finding a suitable house for our women's shelter. Gertie Pridmore suggested I contact Donald Clayton to see if he has any empty houses floating around, but I hate to ask him. I think the Lord will provide the house at just the right time, don't you? And it will probably come about when we least expect it."

Hannah nodded in agreement. "Speaking of Donald Clayton, were you aware Noah Carson is building a racing boat for him?"

Abbie's heart gave a start. "I had no idea he built boats."

"Apparently so. Mr. Clayton spoke to Gabe about it this morning when he stopped by his office on other business. When Gabe called to tell me a deputy would be following us out to the Rogans' house, he mentioned that Mr. Clayton and Mr. Carson had come to some sort of agreement this morning out at the Clayton house. You do know Mr. Carson's been doing some work out there, don't you, installing a big window?"

"I heard about that, yes. I wonder how Mr. Carson wound up in the window business with his uncle, if he is such a proficient boatbuilder."

"I don't know. Why don't you ask him sometime?"

"Oh, Peter would love that. He's already worried that something improper is going on between us."

"Really? Hmm. And is there?" Hannah asked, pinning Abbie with a stare.

A spurt of laughter pealed out of her. "Absolutely not! I think he's sinfully handsome, of course, but he's divorced and has a son, which puts him in an untouchable box, as far as I'm concerned."

"Have you learned the circumstances surrounding his divorce?"

"No, and I don't care to," she fibbed.

"Of course, you don't." Hannah sounded less than convinced.

Bessie neighed, and Abbie snapped the reins, encouraging her into a faster gait.

The Rogans' house was nothing more than an unkempt, square structure with a sagging roof and broken-down front steps. A large piece of canvas covered a side window, and the front door sported a large indentation near the bottom, resembling a mark the toe of a boot might have made. Out back, a row of skirts, petticoats, and the like hung from a line, swaying in the crisp breeze. A mangy, black mutt emerged from under the rickety porch and gave a low growl when they pulled into the drive but soon began wagging his tail in a friendly fashion. Abbie looped the reins over the brake lever and took a long, deep breath, letting it out before looking at Hannah. "Are you ready?"

Hannah nodded. "I am just as eager as you are to determine what we can do for this family before Shamus Rogan gets out of jail. Let's go knock on the door."

The dog approached them immediately, raising its head to sniff the aroma from the large platters of food they carried. Grandmother Kane had sent along dried pork and beef, two fresh loaves of bread, a meatloaf still warm from the oven, and a covered dish of roasted vegetables. In the back of the wagon were more items—potatoes, carrots, jars of preserved fruits and pickles, and assorted jams and jellies. The family ought to live well for at least the next few weeks, Abbie figured.

Climbing the front steps reminded Abbie of the fall she'd taken the previous night on Noah Carson's landing. Thankfully, this morning's sun had done a good job of melting the snow and ice, and it helped that no snow had fallen, of late.

After about the third knock, the door opened a crack, revealing a pair of wide, brown eyes at Abbie's waist level. "Yes?" came the wee voice.

"Hello, there. I'm Abbie Ann Kane, and this is my sister, Hannah Grace Devlin."

"I know who you are," the child said, her death grip on the door indicating she had no intention of opening it further. This had to be the youngest of the three, Abbie thought. She wished she knew the girls' names, but she barely knew Arlena, let alone her daughters. "Yer the ones what run that Whatnot store. My ma goes in there fer supplies."

"Yes, indeed. Is she about?" Abbie tried to see beyond the one-inch opening in the door, but to no avail.

"She ain't doin' so good right now."

Alarm bells sounded in Abbie's head. "How do you mean?"

"She gots a fever."

"May we come in?" Hannah asked, her voice a gentle whisper of assurance.

Through the tiny opening, Abbie was finally able to make out some movement inside—another of the sisters?—and also get a strong whiff of some putrid odor. It was the smell of untended sickness.

"Please, we've brought you some food and supplies, and we want to see your mother. She may need to see a doctor."

"I don't know..." she said, clearly beginning to waver, if one went by her tone, which stirred hope in Abbie's heart. The slit in the door widened a couple of inches, revealing a soiled face and a freckled nose, though the freckles may have just been more dirt. Two loosely plaited braids hung down the girl's scrawny shoulders.

"What're you wantin'?" Suddenly, the door slammed shut, and Abbie and Hannah whirled at hearing a harsh-sounding female voice. Standing by the side of the house, an older girl (who looked more like a boy, Abbie thought) in a long, plaid shirt, torn overalls, and a hat pulled low over her intense, steel-gray eyes held a shotgun at the ready.

"Drop that gun, boy," said yet another voice—Gus Van Der Voort. Momentary relief gave way to a resurgence of fear as Abbie saw the girl swivel and point her gun directly at Gus.

"First, I ain't a boy, and second, you drop yers, fella."

"'Fraid I can't do that, miss." Gus kept his voice steady and his aim fixed. "I'm the law, and I mean to keep peace, even at the expense of shooting that gun straight out of your hands, if I have to. Don't make me do that, though, as I'm not the best aim, and it's possible I might hit that spot between your eyebrows, instead."

Intense worry trickled up and down Abbie's spine, yet she knew the importance of not letting her emotions get the better of her. A fleeting glance at Hannah told her she felt the same.

"What's your name, young lady?" the deputy asked. "And why you got that gun aimed, anyway? There's no one here intending you harm."

"Somebody's got to stand watch."

"You mean 'cause your pa's in prison? Has anybody been creatin' any problems for you? 'Cause, if they have, you need to come forward with it so we can help you. There's no reason you should be living in fear."

The rifle slipped a few inches, but the girl quickly regained her focus, shifting her stance and crimping her brow in confusion. "Ain't been nobody botherin' us," she replied. Abbie hoped the crack in her voice indicated a weakening of her resolve.

"Put the gun down, then, all right? No need to be pointin' it. These ladies are here to help you."

"Your sister tells us your mama's sick," Abbie put in, her own voice a bit wobbly. "We'd like to go inside and see what we can do to help. Would you let us check on her?"

For several seconds, neither Gus nor the girl wavered, Gus straddling his horse, the girl standing with her legs apart, her face a picture of determination. Eerie silence filled the air, broken intermittently by the mangy dog's whining on the porch.

"Please put the gun down, young lady," Gus said firmly.

"Yes, please," urged Hannah.

"How does a batch of fresh-baked sugar cookies sound to you?" Abbie thought to ask the girl. "Our grandmother baked them just this morning."

That finally got her attention, and Abbie caught a better glimpse of her eyes, shimmering in the corners with dampness. The poor thing was as frightened as a cornered fox. Wary, for sure, but also probably fatigued, she surrendered her gun to the ground. Quicker than a blink, Gus slid down from his saddle and gave an audible sigh as he advanced slowly toward the girl. She cowered against the front of the house, not five feet away from Abbie and Hannah, shielding her face with her arms, as if she expected a good lashing.

"I'm not goin' to hurt you," Gus assured her. "You were defending your property. No law against that. I just didn't want to see you or these young ladies hurt by any foolish moves. You understand." She gave a slow nod as he bent to retrieve her weapon. "Now, how about we go inside and check on your mama?"

The girl nodded again, and Abbie and Hannah heaved long-held breaths. As they prepared to enter, something prompted Abbie to glance at the house next door, where she thought she saw a pair of eyes watching from a side window.

K

An old, white dog with black spots came to meet Noah at the door of DeBoer's Hardware Store and sniffed his boots before plodding back to the rug where he'd been lying. The afternoon sun cast its rays through the dirty, front window and onto the dusty, marred floor, which looked like it hadn't seen a broom in a month.

"What can I do for you?" asked a middle-aged man with a paunchy, apron-covered belly, as he climbed down a wooden ladder missing a rung and leaned it against the wall.

"Just picking up a few supplies," Noah replied, pulling out of his hip pocket a list he'd been working on: pencils, sandpaper, hammer, nails, broom, measuring tape, and several other items. Of course, he could have found all the supplies he would ever need in Uncle Delbert's shop, but he had determined not to borrow from his inventory. Besides, Don Clayton had insisted he purchase everything he needed to complete the job, right down to his morning coffee—and to charge everything to his account. "I'll inform DeBoer and the lumberyard you're coming," he'd told Noah.

"What d'you have on that list? Maybe I can lend you a hand. I'm Alvin DeBoer, by the way. I own this place."

Noah tipped his hat at him. "Noah Carson, sir."

Pulling on a shaggy, graying beard, Alvin slanted his head back and smiled, revealing a wide gap between two yellow front teeth. "Ah, you're the one Don Clayton told me to be expectin'. Hear tell you're buildin' him a fast boat." My, how news got around, thanks to Don Clayton, his new employer. *Well, temporary employer*, he corrected in his head. As of this morning, they'd reached a verbal agreement pertaining to the boat he wanted Noah to build, and while Noah still had some work to finish on the window out at the Claytons' lake house, he was itching to get this new project underway.

"Yes, sir, I am. Well, I'm trusting she'll be fast, anyway."

Alvin chuckled. "That Clayton's always looking for the best of the best. Usually finds it, too. He's a good judge of character, and my hunch is, he's seen somethin' promising in you. Yut, yut," he mused, rubbing his beard. "So, I guess you want to get started on that boat as soon as possible, eh? When you expect to have the thing finished?"

If Noah had learned one thing about Sandy Shores, it was that folks were friendly. He'd just as soon have filled his supply order as fill in Alvin DeBoer on the details of his boat, but patience was the rule of the day. He'd found the same thing at the lumberyard, where Frank Langly, the owner, and a couple of workers who'd helped him select the choicest lumber—spruce, cedar, oak, and mahogany—had asked a slew of questions about the boatbuilding process. As little as he liked wasting even a minute of his time, it had felt mighty fine talking about his obsession, not to mention watching the eyes of his audience light up with genuine interest.

"Don Clayton wants to enter the Sandy Shores Yacht Club Regatta this summer, so I have three months to get the job done."

"Phew!" Alvin scratched his head with a coarse-looking hand. "That sounds like quite a feat, but I imagine by the looks of you, all trim and fit, that you're up to the job. I guess you've had a bit of experience."

Here is where Noah drew the line. He knew the fellow meant well, but he did not intend to divulge his past to a complete stranger, no matter that he'd already done so to Don Clayton. "A bit, yes," Noah said, smoothing out his list of items to purchase. "You think you have all these things in stock?"

Alvin snatched the list from Noah's hand and gave it a hurried perusal, then shot him another toothy grin, this one hinting of pride. "You saw the sign out there, didn't you? 'DeBoer's Has It All!' Yut, yut, I can have all this stuff boxed up for you in no time. You just make yourself at home."

It took Alvin about ten minutes to round up everything, total the bill, and charge it to Don Clayton's account. Noah felt almost like a thief walking out the door with a box filled with merchandise for which he hadn't paid a dime from his own pocket, Alvin waving him out and insisting he return if he had need of anything else. *Well*, he reminded himself, *DeBoer's has it all!*

Sunshine on his shoulder made Noah think about springtime—thawing snow, budding daffodils, blossoming forsythia. As he sucked in a cavernous breath, his spirit leaped at the prospect of holding a plane in his hand again, ripping and curling a long section of spruce—not to fashion a window frame, though, but to fashion a mast. He could imagine the smells of wood and dust and sweat filling the air as he removed a batch of fragrant white oak from a steam box; he could almost taste the satisfaction of nailing ribs over a frame and watching the boat take on its own form, a product of his resourcefulness and skill.

He hefted the box of supplies into the back of his wagon, adjusting a few other items like puzzle pieces to make it fit.

Satisfied, he moved to the front of the wagon, untied the reins from the hitching post, patted Ruby Sue's warm neck, and hauled himself up into the front seat. Up a block and across the street, a cluster of men in conversation prompted him to twist his neck around. The one doing the talking pointed a finger southward; it seemed he was giving directions to someone. It wasn't until that someone turned his head that Noah's stomach seemed to dislodge itself and drop clear to his ankles.

What in tarnation was *he* doing in town?

⌒ℛ⌒

"She's going to need your prompt attention, Doc," Abbie said of Arlena Rogan to Ralston Van Huff, the doctor among the three in Sandy Shores in whom the Kane family had the most confidence. Once upon a time, he'd courted Hannah Grace, but then Gabriel Devlin had ridden into town and stolen her heart right out from under him. No hard feelings remained, though, especially since, shortly thereafter, Ralston had hired a nurse to help at his practice and married her a year later. Abbie never had figured out what Hannah had seen in Ralston, and while the two had been courting, she'd often referred to him as "Stuffy Huffy" for his staid, impeccably proper demeanor, not to mention his utter lack of cleverness. Still, he remained a family friend and a trusted physician.

Ralston raised a questioning brow at Abbie, and his wife, Garnett, stood beside him wringing her hands, her face contorted with worry. "She's burning with fever," Hannah put in. "We left her daughters with instructions as to how to help bring down her fever, but Arlena's clearly not doing well, and she could be starving, by the looks of her. We tried to feed her some chicken broth and urged her to drink some water, but, unfortunately, none of it sat on her stomach for more than five minutes."

"Be forewarned, there's an awful stench in there," Abbie added. "Mostly from her soiled sheets, we believe, which Hannah and I changed. We promptly burned the dirty ones, being that they had holes and tears galore, anyway. I'll take some new ones out there as soon as possible."

"Those children didn't have the first clue of what to do for their mother," Hannah lamented. "They all appear rather uneducated, poor dears."

"She might have a bad case of influenza, since you mentioned the vomiting and high fever," Ralston said, pulling at his goatee, his brows pinched in thought. "Did you detect a rash of any kind?"

"No," Hannah answered, "just pale, paper-thin skin. Her wrists look about the size of my Alex's, although that's probably stretching the truth a bit. She complained of a sour stomach and an awful headache but had no rash that we could see."

Abbie shook her head, her heart sinking fast. "I could just kick myself for not going out there sooner. I wondered why she hadn't come into the Whatnot, especially since she's had more freedom lately, what with Shamus sitting in jail the past few weeks. Here, she's been suffering something terrible with no one to look out for her but those skittish girls. The middle one hardly even showed her face to us, staying holed up in a back room while Hannah and I tended her mother. At least the oldest one showed us where to find the matches so we could burn the sheets, and the youngest brought us a freshly laundered pair."

"You mustn't lay any blame to yourself, Abbie Ann," said Garnett. "Goodness, you have your hands full with the Whatnot and all your other responsibilities."

"I appreciate that," Abbie said, and she truly did, but it still didn't erase her regrets.

"How did you manage to change the sheets?" Garnett asked, her brow still etched with worry lines.

"We worked around her," Hannah explained. "Virginia, the oldest girl, helped lift her so we could get the sheet under her. Poor Arlena was huffing with exhaustion by the time we finished, but she did manage to utter several weak thank-yous while we worked."

"Well." Ralston rubbed his hands together, turned, and snatched his coat from the rack by the door, his expression resolute. "I've heard all I need to hear. I best get out there and have a look. I appreciate you ladies taking the time to check in on the family." He looked to his wife. "I may need to bring her back here, where we can keep a better eye on her, but I'll know more after I've had a chance to evaluate her condition." He then addressed Abbie and Hannah. "I have one patient still recovering from an appendectomy, but he's greatly improved, so between Garnett and me, we should be able to manage Mrs. Rogan. You think those three girls can take care of themselves for a few days?"

Abbie chewed her lower lip and looked over at Hannah. "Perhaps I should bring them to our house. I don't think Grandmother would mind. They're pretty frail-looking, themselves."

Hannah expelled a deep breath. "They do appear to need some added attention, and who better to give it than Grandmother? I'm afraid I can't take the time to go out again, though, Abs. Mrs. Garvey will be expecting me. I'll ask Gus to accompany you back."

"That's not necessary, if Dr. Van Huff is going out there. I'll collect the girls while he's seeing to Arlena. You don't mind if I ride with you, do you, Doc?"

"I wouldn't mind, if it weren't for the fact that I have only a two-seater. If I bring Mrs. Rogan back to the clinic, she'll no doubt be stretched out in the back. Could you drive your own rig and allow me to follow you?" he asked while buttoning his coat. "I'm not certain I can find the Rogans' house on my own. It's been a long while since I was out that way."

"That's actually much better, as we'll need the extra room for bringing back Arlena's girls."

Ralston nodded. "Just let me get my bag."

"And may we stop off at my house first so I can speak to Grandmother before I drop those children on her doorstep?" she asked.

"Good idea," all three said in unison.

Chapter Thirteen

Noah directed Ruby Sue down his aunt and uncle's long driveway, stopped her in the circle drive, leaped off the rig, and looped the reins over a post next to the house before taking the porch steps two at a time. He gave the front door a loud rap. "Aunt Julia, are you home?" He rapped again, louder this time, shifting impatient legs. "Aunt Julia!"

Through clear-as-diamond glass, he saw her coming, her skirts skimming the polished, oak floor, her roundish frame waddling like a mother duck's. At first glimpse of him, she gave the slightest pause, then hurried the rest of the way to the door. He opened it ahead of her. "He's here, Aunt Julia," he said, bursting inside and right past her. Turning on his heel, he looked her straight in the eye. "What is he doing here?" he hissed. "Did you know he was coming?"

"Settle down, Noah. Take a seat."

He clawed eight fingers through his hair and started pacing. "What possessed him to come to Michigan? Did he call you?"

"I assume you're talking about your father, and, yes, he called me."

"Then you knew. Why didn't you tell me, for Pete's sake?"

"I just learned it myself yesterday, that he was coming, that is. Sit down."

Sit down? She expected him to sit when his mind was traveling faster than a freight train? He paced some more. "I don't want him here. The first thing he'll want to do is see Toby, and I'll not allow it. He's a no-good—"

"He's my brother, Noah, and I love him. Not only that... he's changed."

"He hasn't changed. He'll never change. He's a drunk who killed my mother, and I won't tolerate him being in this town. I swear, if he comes near us...."

"Noah." Her sharp tone made his breath stop short. "He may have neglected your mother, but he didn't kill her, honey. She was sick. Yes, he drinks incessantly...drank, rather. He hasn't had as much as a swallow of it in six months."

The news hit Noah like a splash of cold water on the face. "My father hasn't had a drop of booze in six months? I don't believe it. Once a drunk, always a drunk."

"Have you ever known him not to drink for this long a period?"

Noah had to admit he hadn't, but that didn't mean a thing. Drunks often stopped and started, stopped and started. He fidgeted anxiously with his fingers. "It still makes no sense to me why he came here. He knows I don't ever want to see him again, drunk or sober."

Aunt Julia sniffed in that way she often did when she meant to make an important point and wanted to make sure you didn't miss it. "Maybe he has something significant he wants to tell you."

"Haw! The only significant thing he could tell me is that he's been a no-good father all my life, and that he promises to leave Toby and me alone until he breathes his final breath."

Aunt Julia's pursed lips reflected her displeasure at his razor-sharp statement, yet she managed to take a few calming breaths and unclenched them. "Listen, dear. I want you to sit down and try to relax. Let me tell you something." She nestled into the chair next to the fireplace. "Sit," she ordered him again.

"I'll sit, but I won't relax," Noah said, walking across the room and slamming his body into the plush club chair that matched the one his aunt was seated in.

Aunt Julia picked fretfully at her wool skirt, flinging away a few pieces of lint. After a moment, she set her shoulders back, pinned him with her gray-blue eyes, and cleared her throat. "Gerald tells me he's found the Lord."

"What?" Noah gripped the armrests of his chair. Hard. "That's ridiculous. All he's ever done my entire life is put God down. When my mother was alive, he berated her something awful for her beliefs, screamed at her for shoving lies down my throat."

"I know that. But God is in the miracle business, dear, and He can soften the hardest hearts."

"Not hearts of stone."

"Yes, even those."

"Well, I'm not buying it," Noah said, even as he felt his own heart hardening like cement. "It's some kind of trick on his part. He probably wants money, of which I have none to give, and I don't want you or Uncle Del catering to him, either."

"We will do only what we believe the Lord is leading us to do. I've already told him he may have one of our spare rooms for now." Noah opened his mouth to protest, but she hurried to add, "Just as we opened our home and hearts to you when you needed us most."

How could he dispute that? His aunt and uncle were just too doggone generous, and he loved them for it, but it didn't inspire enthusiasm in him about coming eye to eye with his no-good father.

Noah took a few measured breaths, swallowed a lump in his throat, and rubbed the back of his neck. "One of the reasons I left Guilford was to escape him, Aunt Julia. Yes, I also left because I lost my wife, my business, my dignity, my home—shoot, pretty much everything."

"Except for the most important thing of all—your son."

"I was getting to that."

"You're young, Noah. You have plenty of time for starting over; your father, on the other hand, is getting older. You don't want to be shouldered with regret after he's gone."

"Is he dying or something?"

"No, no, not that I know of, but I do know this: he left Guilford for almost the same reason you did: he wanted a new start, a second chance."

"Why'd he have to come here to do that?"

"I suppose he hoped he might reestablish a relationship with you—and Toby. And, of course, Delbert and I are his family. It's always good to start over surrounded by people who love and care about you. Do you think you could at least speak to him? Judge for yourself whether or not he's changed?"

Angered, Noah leaped to his feet. "Speaking of change, this is going to change everything. His being here just makes everything more complicated. Toby and I used to feel free to drop by to see you whenever we could."

"And you still can."

"Not with him here."

"Noah, he's been writing letters to me every week."

That gave him pause. "What about?"

"Oh, how he came to ask the Lord Jesus into his life and his deliverance from alcohol, among other things."

"Hah!" Noah sneered. "Among other things, indeed. Women, you mean?"

"Noah." Aunt Julia folded her hands in her lap and fixed her gaze on him. "Nothing we do or say in life is outside the realm of God's forgiveness."

To avoid meeting her eyes, he walked over to the fireplace, rested an elbow on the mantel, and studied the painting above it, a rendering of the channel with ships leaving and entering Lake Michigan, rays of sunlight casting a silvery glow on the rough whitecaps.

"Sweetheart, I know you considered him a worthless father growing up, and I don't blame you. I will be the first to admit he had little ability when it came to parenting. The effects of alcohol are often brutal, affecting relationships, jobs, and home life. Your precious mother suffered greatly under his cruelty, but you must know he lives with deep regrets for the way he treated her."

Out of the cuckoo clock popped an irksome bird, announcing the four o'clock hour from his wooden perch. Noah waited for the thing to silence itself before muttering, "He *should* have regrets. He sent Mama to the grave entirely too young."

"I know you'd like to believe that, dear, but it isn't quite so. Your mother was frail long before the day she married Gerald. There are other things I could tell you, if—"

"I need to fetch Toby, Aunt Julia. He'll be waiting in the schoolyard." The truth was, Noah didn't want to hear any further justification of the way his father had treated his mother or him, and he certainly had no wish to hear about his mother's obvious infirmities. It would only intensify his sadness over losing her all those years ago.

A look of consternation flitted across Aunt Julia's face, followed by an expression of calm resignation. "Of course, you do. Speaking of Toby, hasn't he been walking with that Devlin boy to the Whatnot most nights?"

"Often, yes, and then Jesse walks him home at six o'clock. But I told Toby before he spent the night with you that I'd pick him up for a change and take him out for some supper. We rarely do that, so he's probably looking forward to it."

Aunt Julia smiled. "Well, isn't that nice? You two have a lovely supper, then. Where will you take him?"

"I'm not sure. Maybe that new place across the street from the Whatnot, Pat's Eatery." He thought about how good Abbie's unfinished plate of food had tasted that morning and wondered what the supper menu looked like. Of course, he also thought about Abbie herself, but his persistent irritation about his father forced his thoughts elsewhere.

He approached his aunt's chair and leaned down to kiss her rosy cheek. "I love you, Aunt Julia. I'm sorry if I reacted harshly. I'm just…." He couldn't even finish the sentence, seeing as any word he reached for fell far short when it came to expressing his feelings.

"I know, dear," she replied with a lengthy sigh. "It will all work out."

Noah smiled grimly, then plunked his wool cap on his head on his way out the door.

In the wagon, he directed Ruby Sue down the long drive and out into the street. As they made the turn, a man crossed the street, somewhat hunched and with a familiar gait.

"Noah," the man said when they made eye contact.

But Noah pretended he neither saw nor heard him as he slapped Ruby Sue into a gallop up Clinton Avenue.

⟋ 𝒦 ⟋

Abbie marched the three Rogan girls briskly up Water Street, even though the middle one, Fiona, longed to lag behind, and the eldest, Virginia, walked several steps ahead. Holding the hand of the youngest, Margaret, Abbie sensed a hovering tension. "This will be fun," she said, trying to keep things light. "I love going into the Whatnot after closing time. It's so quiet and peaceful but also quite cluttered. I actually enjoy putting things back to rights, though. Mrs. James probably locked up about fifteen minutes ago, so she'll be busy counting the cash box and trying to get the place back in order. When customers come in, they often pick up various items, carry them around, and then change their minds, laying the items where they don't belong. Sometimes, we'll find a pair of children's knee pants on top of a milk can, or a neatly folded handkerchief lying in the hardware department. Last week, I found an ice chipper among the men's underwear."

This actually drew a giggle from Virginia, who paused long enough to let the rest of them catch up. They passed the bank, and Abbie purposely avoided looking inside for fear of catching Peter's eye. She did not have time to explain her plan to take the girls to the Whatnot for a couple of new dresses. Besides, Grandmother had given strict orders that they weren't to loiter, since she'd have supper on the table within the hour. As expected, Helena Kane had shifted right into her take-charge mode as soon as she'd learned of the Rogan girls' plight and the plan for them to stay with the Kanes for a few days, until Arlena felt well enough to return home. Ralston's earlier conjecture had been right—she had influenza, her worst symptoms being a fever and severe dehydration. He believed a few good days of recuperation would do wonders for her. Of course, Arlena had resisted being taken from her house, arguing that she didn't want to be a burden to anyone. Between Abbie, Ralston, and her own daughters convincing her it was for the best, though, she'd finally given in.

After the bank, they passed Curly's Barber Shop, followed by Tim's Bicycle Repair and then Pat's Eatery. "We'll cross here," she said, pointing to the Whatnot. Though the Closed sign hung in the window, a few remaining customers still moved about inside.

"Miss Kane!"

Abbie whirled around, stopping the girls in their tracks before crossing. Little Toby Carson came rushing up to her, his father tagging close behind.

"Well, looky here," she said, bending down to tweak Toby's freckled nose. "I missed you at Sunday school. Did your papa tell you?"

"Yes, and he learned me the Bible verse you gived him whilst we ate ar beef soup an' sandwiches."

"Did he, now?" Something about that revelation made her heart quiver with pleasure. She straightened and looked up into Noah Carson's sea-blue eyes, their glimmer reflecting the draining sunlight. Her stomach took a foolish leap. Quickly setting her gaze back on Toby, she asked, "Can you recite it for me?"

His brows furrowed as he poked a finger into his cheek, making it dimple. "I can try." He swallowed and looked to his father for support. "Umm…I will trust God and make sure not to be scared of what men can do to me?" He looked hopefully at his father, then at Abbie. "Did I do it good?"

Noah gave a hearty chuckle. "Well…what do you say, Miss Kane?"

Though the recitation fell far short of perfect, it certainly passed muster with her. "Excellent, that's what I say, Mr. Carson." She patted the boy's cheek, then gave his ear a gentle tug. "You are one clever boy."

Toby beamed, after which he let his eyes rove to the girl grasping tightly to Abbie's gloved hand. "Who's she?"

"Well, for goodness' sake, allow me to introduce you. These are the Rogan girls—Margaret, Fiona, and Virginia. Girls, meet Toby Carson and his father, Mr. Carson." It occurred to her then that the lad might wonder if Shamus Rogan was their father, and she uttered a silent prayer that if he did, he wouldn't bring up the accident. If he'd made the connection, however, it didn't show up in his eyes.

The girls nodded at Toby but remained aloof; or, perhaps, shy and wary better described their deportment. At Noah's tilted face and raised eyebrows, Abbie explained that the girls would be staying with the Kanes for a few days, until their mother had a chance to recover from her illness.

He nodded, his mouth slightly open. "Ah, so that explains the errand you and your sister had to run earlier today."

It both pleased and surprised her that he remembered. "Yes."

He paused, dipped his chin, then set his probing eyes on her. "And did all go well on your drive there and back?"

She caught his hidden meaning. "Yes, thanks. All went fine and dandy."

While Toby watched Margaret with great interest and Virginia and Fiona grew restless, Abbie shifted her weight and blew out a breath. "Well, very nice to see you both. We need to get going; we have some purchases to make at the Whatnot."

"You're not walking back to your place after you finish at the Whatnot, are you? I mean, it'll probably be dark by the time you finish." The man's cerulean eyes crinkled in the corners, one thick, intriguing brow arching higher than the other.

Abbie tried to hold back a smile but failed. "Don't worry, Mr. Carson. My father plans to drive us all home. He's just closing up at the insurance office now."

His eyebrows evened out. "That's good, then." He gave each girl a final glance and put a hand around Toby's shoulder, pulling him to his side. "You ladies enjoy your shopping." To Abbie, he added, "I'll talk to you later."

"Oh. Yes, fine. Good-bye, Mr. Carson...and Toby."

A brief smile lit his square-set face. "Call me Noah."

"I—" A missed heartbeat made her breath catch in her throat. "All right."

Brisk air coming off the river had her suddenly hurrying the girls across the street. "Was that your beau?" Margaret asked in so high-pitched a voice that a horse half a block over raised its head and snorted.

Mother of mercy! What if Mr. Carson—*Noah*, rather—had heard? Abbie ushered the youngster along, but she glanced back and waved her free hand, anyway.

Sleep did not come easily for Noah that night. Lately, it never did, but now it posed a bigger problem than usual. First, he had the boat to think about, his head swimming with several slight adjustments he planned to make to the design. The blamed thing never did quite satisfy him. And, now that he was actually preparing to build it, the drawing had to be perfect in every way.

Second, Abbie's pretty face kept popping into his mind. Much as he hated to admit it, he was attracted to her, which was altogether brainless, considering Peter Sinclair's disclosure that he planned to make her his fiancée. Apparently, he'd earned Jacob Kane's approval, and no wonder. The man had it all—wealth, respect, a solid career, not to mention rock-solid faith. Noah should know. He'd sat under his tutelage and listened to him spout off one Bible verse after another in the men's Sunday school class. The only Bible verse that he could conjure was the one Abbie wanted Toby to learn. He recalled sitting in Pat's Eatery, going over it again and again with him, only to have him botch it when he recited it to Abbie; and yet, she'd had a look of sheer pleasure and pride on her face while she'd listened. Something about that girl—the compassion in her eyes for those Rogan girls, for example—stirred dormant feelings in his heart, and the realization irked him to the core. He had no time for another female in his life, nor did he desire one. And yet....

Then, there was the matter of his father's arrival in Sandy Shores. They'd made eye contact. Shoot! His father had acknowledged him in the driveway, spoken his name, as if he actually expected a warm greeting in return. Well, he could greet him until the moon fell out of the sky, as far as Noah was concerned. The nerve he had, waltzing into Sandy Shores after Noah had just started putting his life back together.

The next thing he knew, Suzanna would be showing her face. Just what he needed.

At that asinine thought, Noah rolled over on his side, pulling his blanket with him, and muttered a cuss before falling into a restless sleep.

Chapter Fourteen

W ho did Abbie Ann Kane think she was, marching through town with the Rogan girls like she
knew best what they needed, and all's she had to
do was wave her pretty hand and make it happen? Sure, he'd
scared the little twit into closing down her ladies' meetings—
leastways, that was the buzz in the taverns. But hadn't he
hinted in his notes she was to mind her own business, as well,
which included staying clear of folks' families and their affairs?
Women like her needed takin' care of, and he didn't mean in no
tender-lovin' way, neither. Why, all she needed to do was stir up
the women of this town, and, next thing he knew, there'd be no
saloons for buyin' booze, not to mention no trampish women
struttin' their wares. Far as he was concerned, that little Kane
lady was the main cause for worry in these parts. Oh, there'd
been other presidents of that ladies' temperance club, but not
till young Abbie Kane took office had the group gotten so bold
about proclaimin' their beliefs. Before he knew it, they'd be
standin' in election lines, what with that suffrage movement
stirring up every state in the union. The whole country was
startin' to lean toward closing down saloons, and mostly due to
women who didn't know their proper place in society.

Well, somebody ought to do something about shutting these women up, and it had to start somewhere. May as well be right here in Sandy Shores, Michigan.

He'd lay low for a while, make her and that stinkin' brother-in-law of hers, Sheriff Devlin, think the threats had ended. Might be, she'd even grow so sure of herself as to start up those stupid meetings again.

He'd teach her, though—he sure-shootin' would. He'd show her who was boss, and she'd bow to him before it was over, too.

Overheated just from thinking about it, he wiped the sweat from his brow and took another slow drag of his cigarette.

K

With his window work at Donald Clayton's house complete and Esther Clayton singing his praises for the light and the view the new window provided, Noah had started putting all his energies into building the boat, first taking two full days to sweep out the unused storage building Don had provided for him and clear it of cobwebs and debris. The place would serve him well with its wide-open space. Beams stretched from wall to wall for support, but there was no finished ceiling, which allowed plenty of room for boatbuilding. A big stove situated on a far wall supplied some warmth, even though most of it seeped out through the cracks in the walls. Oh, well. Before he knew it, warmer weather would move in, and then he'd be too hot. Thankfully, the place offered plenty of windows for cross ventilation.

With the building finally cleaned to his liking, he'd been tweaking his drawings, tacking several pieces of paper to the marred tabletop on which he worked, and eyeballing the pictures from various angles, tipping his head one way and then another, as if in doing so he'd find a brand-new perspective. Soon, perhaps as early as Monday, he'd start nailing down the long sheets of cedar to stretch across the floor, a good forty or more feet in length. He could almost smell their fresh-milled aroma now. Once he'd secured the boards in place, he'd be able to start the lofting process, fairing up the boat to make sure it had a smooth, even shape—no bumps or lumps. He'd measure, mark, and tack down a black rubber batten, then create a full-scale design of the boat, a side profile, and a fore-and-aft diagram of all the cross sections. He'd put a series of dots on the floor and connect them with the batten while looking for bulges and imperfections in the design. If he found any, it would be easy to correct them by changing the curve, even if by only one-sixteenth of an inch, before he made the mold.

Today was Saturday, so Toby was with him. He sat on the floor near the stove, playing with some toy wooden boats Abbie had given him from the Whatnot. He made throaty, little noises and talked under his breath, his imagination taking him to faraway places. Noah lifted his head to watch him for a moment, feeling a smile emerge on his lips. He had more love for his son than for anything else on earth, including boatbuilding, but he still felt inadequate when it came to raising him. He should be playing with him outside, maybe tossing a ball back and forth, not keeping him cooped up in this warehouse while he worked on a boat. Still, he figured this was better than leaving him at home to manage on his own.

So far, he'd had the good fortune not to run into his father, by planning his visits to his aunt and uncle's house around Gerald's work schedule. Not surprisingly, because of his years of experience in a shipyard, his father had landed a job at Rikkers Shipbuilding in Mill Point on his second day in Sandy Shores. Aunt Julia had told Noah that Gerald planned to get a place of his own once he had his feet on solid ground. "Naturally, I told him no need to hurry," she'd said over a hot stove yesterday, stirring a pot of her famous spicy chili con carne. Noah had been standing in the kitchen doorway, his mouth watering at the aroma. But she wasn't going to win him over with her cooking. "I don't want him showing his face around us. I hope you told him that."

"I told him you were still hurting over the affairs of your past and needed time to process his unexpected arrival in town. I said he should be patient."

"Why'd you tell him that?" Noah had groused. "No amount of time is going to change the fact I don't want to see him, Aunt Julia."

"We'll see," she'd said in return, wiping her brow with the corner of her apron. "He's different, Noah. You ought to at least allow Toby to see him."

"That's exactly what I don't want to happen. About the time Toby gets used to his grandfather being around, he'll up and skip town, or he'll go on one of his drunken binges and embarrass the lot of us. He'll discover himself in a jail cell, right alongside Shamus Rogan. Can you imagine the talk around town when folks discover there's another drunk living here who'll give Shamus a run for his money? That's just what Sandy Shores' citizens need—one more pie-eyed rabble-rouser.

"Well, he says he's quit, and I believe him. He has a whole new countenance about him. I'm not saying he'll never fall off the wagon again, but the longer a person goes without drinking, the stronger he becomes in the battle. I'm praying he'll remain strong, and you should be doing the same. Regardless of your feelings on the matter, Noah, he's still your father. Have you at least told Toby he's in town?"

"Not yet."

"Well, perhaps you ought to do that before he runs into him all on his own."

"I don't know how that would happen, seeing as I've been keeping a close eye on him."

"Except for the days when Jesse Devlin walks him home from school."

He'd been giving her words serious consideration ever since and even now mulled them over while watching his son push his two toy boats on the fresh-swept floor, which still couldn't be called clean, considering the dust particles drifting around the room, glistening like fine snow in the rays of sunshine coming through the west window.

"Do you think much about where we used to live, son?" he asked, breaking the silence.

Toby's humming stopped for a moment, and he looked pensive. "Want to watch my boats crash into each other?" he asked by way of a response. Without giving Noah a chance to answer, he set the wooden toys as far away from each other as his arms could reach, then made them zoom across the bumpy, cement floor in opposite directions, causing a head-on collision, complete with sound effects.

Noah pushed back from the table he'd been working at, the stool's wobbly legs protesting with a loud screech. Toby kept his eyes down, replaying the clash of the boats, this time making them weave in and out and around each other before finally meeting head-on again.

He squatted down beside his son, resting his elbows on his bent knees. The boy kept up his play, feigning oblivion, Noah could tell. He should have given Toby a better explanation for why they were leaving Connecticut than, "We're going for a long visit to Michigan, and your mama's not coming." Noah realized he looked like the bad guy, from Toby's viewpoint. But, at the time, it had been all he could manage, with his anger and the pain of betrayal threatening his sanity and preventing him from going into further detail. How would he have explained divorce to a five-year-old, anyway? Moreover, how did he now explain to him his mother's utter lack of interest in picking up the telephone to check on him or even dropping him a friendly note? Suzanna's mother had at least done as much, writing five or six times—nothing newsy, just a few lines to say how much she missed her grandson and asking Noah to tell him. Of course, he hadn't mentioned it to Toby, for what possible good could come from reminding him of the very people who had sought to destroy his father's livelihood, standing behind their faithless daughter and Noah's double-crossing partner? Ellen Dunbar may not have participated directly in the deception, but she also had not mustered the courage to step in and speak up when she found out what was going on.

"I'm sorry we don't talk more, son. Is there anything you'd like to ask me now?"

"Nope," the boy said, turning his back to Noah as he scooted his boats in another direction. The seat of his trousers could use a good brushing off, Noah saw.

He decided to persist. "You remember much about Grandpa Carson?"

His eyes still on his play, Toby said, "He took me down to the big ships sometimes."

"He took me, as well, when I was your age." *When he wasn't drunk as a skunk and calling me every rotten name in the book.* "We used to walk out on the long docks. Pa would pull out this contraption called a telescope and slide the tube out as long as it would go, then let me look through it and try to spot ships on the horizon."

"Uncle Delbert's got one of those. He showed me how it worked when we went fishin'."

"Did he? I didn't know that." A stab of guilt sliced Noah in the side for not being the first to show him using his own telescope, the one tucked away in a velvet-lined case somewhere in his father's storage shed. Suddenly, he wondered what had happened to all the things he'd left stored there. Had his father sold the old homestead and left all his belongings to the new owners? Strange how he hadn't thought about that till now. Somehow, Noah had to find out without confronting him. He wondered if Aunt Julia knew.

"Yeah," Toby went on. "I sawed a fish jump when I was lookin' through that thing."

"*Saw.*"

"Saw," he said, still pushing the boats around. Noah watched in silence, sitting back to take some of the pressure off his heels and put it on the balls of his feet, instead. He cleared his throat. "Do you miss your grandpa?"

"Just Grandpa Carson. Not Grandpa Dunbar, though. He's a mean ol' cuss."

"Where'd you learn a word like that, *cuss*? It's not exactly proper." *Accurate, though.*

"I dunno. I think from you. I heard you say lotsa words. I tried one of 'em once, but Aunt Julia scolded me awful."

Noah felt that place between his brows pull into a tight crinkle as his gut did a little flip. "Oh, blast. I'm sorry about that." He was careful never to take the Lord's name in vain, but he wasn't entirely innocent of using slang.

Toby paused his play and threw Noah a curious look. "Can I say blast?"

"I…well, I guess you can, although you never quite know with Aunt Julia. Best not, just to stay on the safe side."

Toby bit down on the corner of his lip, his freckled nose wrinkling. "Yeah, you're prolly right."

Noah chewed his lower lip to keep from smiling. "So, there's something I need to tell you about Grandpa Carson."

Toby ran the boats around the side of the stove, crawling on his knees and gathering more dust on his pants. "What?"

Noah swallowed, surprised by how hard this was to spit out, yet knowing Aunt Julia was right. The boy deserved to know. "He's here. In Sandy Shores."

The news gave the boy a reason to spin his body around. "Grandpa Carson's here?" He dropped his boats, plopped himself into a seated position and folded his legs in front of him, sweeping several wisps of blond hair out of his eyes, a silent reminder that he needed another haircut. Noah could have sworn the kid's hair grew faster than a dandelion in May. "Really? What's he doin' here? Is he goin' t' live with us?"

"What? No, no. He's…right now, he's just staying with Uncle Del and Aunt Julia. He's your aunt's brother, you know."

"I know. She tol' me once. When we goin' t' see him?"

Noah fished for the right words. "I don't want to see him just yet." *Or ever.*

"'Cause you don't like him?" Toby's bluntness unnerved him.

"I guess you could say that. We don't—we've never gotten along very well."

"I know." For a six-year-old, Toby sure looked like a little man sitting there with his frown firmly in place, three straight lines etched across his forehead, his crystalline, blue eyes looking like little pools of wisdom.

"He's—um, well, a—"

"A drunk? Like that guy what runned us off the road?"

Noah sucked in a breath that went clear to his toes, then slowly let it out, shaking his head and rubbing the back of his neck. *Foolish me for thinking I could get anything past Toby Carson,* he thought. Apparently, six-year-old minds were a lot smarter than he realized. "Yeah. Like him."

"Aunt Julia says you gots t' forgive everybody, even that guy."

"She said that, huh? Well…." But he had nothing to add. Forgiveness was a realm he didn't visit often.

"She says it's the only way t' find peace with God…or somethin' like that."

"You're a smart little whippersnapper for recalling her words, you know that?"

Toby shrugged one shoulder and tipped his head at a slight angle. "Yeah, I know. I think it jus' comes natural."

Noah tossed back his head and laughed, then reached up to tousle the boy's silky hair, wanting to forget the words his aunt had said to Toby yet chewing on them just the same. "You know I love you, don't you?"

This made Toby's chin drop a notch and his cheeks flush. "Yeah, I guess." He swiveled and went for his toy boats again, marking the end of their conversation.

K

Abbie and Jesse Devlin's bodies bounced against each other on the wagon seat as she directed Bessie to make the turn off Franklin Avenue onto South First Street. "I think Mr. Clayton's warehouse is at the corner of Lafayette and First, which is just one more block. He told me yesterday that Noah, er, Mr. Carson, would be working on the boat today. I presume Toby will be with him, wouldn't you think? It being Saturday and all. How are the muffins doing? Are they still warm?" Her jittery stomach had set her mouth to chattering a mile a minute, and she wondered if Jesse noticed.

In his lap, Jesse held a basket wrapped in several layers of towels. He gazed up at her. "You don't want me to check, do you?"

"No, no, of course not. I just wondered if you could feel the warmth coming through the bottom of the basket."

"No, not really, but it doesn't matter. Grandmother's corn muffins are just as good cold as warm."

"That's true enough, I suppose."

"Why'd you say we're delivering these muffins to the Carsons, again?"

Why, indeed? "I thought it would be a nice gesture, a way to thank Mr. Carson for seeing to my safety that night the bottle landed in the back of his wagon and barely missed his head. Little Toby is in my Sunday school class, and I always like to pay calls on my students." Of course, there was her ulterior motive—wanting to look upon the face of Noah Carson—which was purely childish on her part. Wouldn't Peter have a conniption if he knew of her errand? Well, at least he couldn't accuse her of unseemly behavior this time, seeing as she'd brought Jesse along for safety's sake—and propriety's.

"Oh." Jesse remained quiet for all of fifteen seconds. "Do you visit all your Sunday school kids, then?"

"Yes, as regularly as possible." Which wasn't all that often, really, considering all her other duties. The last student she'd paid a call on had been Frankie Hesselbart, after learning he had a bad case of chicken pox, and that had been a good three months ago. She pressed her lips together and tried to tamp down her doubts about making yet another unexpected visit to the Carsons, praying in all earnestness that Toby would be present this time. Otherwise, whatever would Mr. Carson think? He probably already considered her quite a pest.

"So, you said he's building a boat for Mr. Clayton?" Jesse asked as they jostled along, the warehouse coming into view. When Abbie saw Noah's rig parked out by the road, she could have sworn her stomach flipped completely over.

"Yes, that's what I'm told. Mr. Clayton claims it will be a fine one, too; good enough to earn him a blue ribbon in the regatta this summer…or a plaque…or a trophy. Gracious, I'm not sure what the prize amounts to. Perhaps it's money." There she went again, rattling on mindlessly. "Anyway, I figured you might be interested in seeing what progress he's made to this point."

"Would I! I love watching the boats come in, so to actually see how a person builds one…well, man!" Jesse exclaimed. "It's gonna be fantastic."

"The truth is, we're barging in on him today, and I can't guarantee he'll appreciate the interruption."

"Are you serious? Soon as he gets a whiff of Grandmother's muffins, he'll be asking you to drop over every Saturday."

And there went her skittish stomach again, this time spinning fast cartwheels. "Ha! That seems a bit far-fetched." She directed Bessie to make the turn onto Lafayette, then to enter the narrow drive in front of the tall, clapboard structure with several windows on the side and wide double doors in the front with one step leading up to them. Setting the brake in place, she jumped down, ducked her head under Bessie's strong neck, and looped the reins over a nearby tree branch. Stealing a breath for courage, she stepped up to the doors and prepared to knock.

Chapter Fifteen

Noah had been about to wrap things up for the day and tell Toby to put away the hammer he'd been using in his pretend building project, which he'd begun after tiring of the toy boats. Using several scraps of wood, Toby would stack them as high as possible, then knock them over into a heap with a hammer, only to start all over again. The explosion of sound every time the wood tumbled to the floor had made it difficult for Noah to concentrate. Hearing footsteps outside, followed by a gentle knock on the door, came as a great relief.

"Enter at your own risk," he called, fully expecting to see Don Clayton or, perhaps, Uncle Del, but certainly not the lovely Abbie Ann Kane and her nephew, Jesse Devlin. Jesse stood beside Abbie in the doorway, holding a bundle in his arms, which Noah imagined to be the source of the delectable aroma wafting toward him. He slid off his stool in too much of a hurry and stumbled over one of Toby's wooden toys, turning his ankle and nearly going down but quickly righting himself by grabbing hold of the back of the stool.

"Oh!" Abbie exclaimed, cupping her open mouth with her hand, her eyeballs as wide as a rabbit's. "Are you all right?"

"Right as rain," he fibbed, longing to rub his aching ankle as he limped toward the door, wishing he'd not removed his boots earlier.

"You're not trying to reenact what I did on your icy porch, I hope?"

"Naw." Somewhere deep down, he found his laugh. "'Fraid that graceful move of yours would be hard to duplicate, although I probably came close." Abbie giggled beneath her gloved hand, and he found himself tempted to pull it down so he could catch a glimpse of her full smile.

"So, how did you—? What are you—?" he stammered, looking from her to Jesse before rewording his scrambled sentence. "To whom do I owe this—honor?" He scratched his temple.

"Would you believe Don Clayton?" Abbie said in a timid voice. "He told me yesterday you'd be here."

Noah ran a hand through his hair, suddenly realizing how awful he must look in his holey, denim pants and grubby, flannel shirt, not to mention his unwashed, straggly hair. It was Saturday, after all, and the last person he'd expected to run into was this pretty little woman. She suddenly laughed, and the sound fairly floated to the rafters. "Don't look so worried. We're not staying," she assured him.

"No, please come in." Noah pushed the door shut behind them, and, for the next few moments, they all stared at one another, until Abbie's eyes drifted downward to Noah's feet. "I see you're wearing your new stockings," she said, her voice bright. "Rita told me you stopped by the other morning. The navy stripes are quite becoming."

Noah shook his head at Jesse and started to relax, collect his bearings. "Can't a man buy a few pairs of socks in this town without word getting out?"

Jesse grinned. "That's about the truth of it, Mr. Carson. Everybody knows everybody in Sandy Shores."

"I'm beginning to believe that."

By now, Toby had come to stand at Jesse's side, all eyes for the taller boy and what he held in his arms. "What's you got in there?" he asked, tilting his blond head inquisitively at the towel-covered package. "It smells better than anything my pa makes."

"I was thinking the same," Noah said. "And wondering what the occasion is for your dropping in. Surely not my irresistible looks."

At that, Abbie actually blushed, which he found interesting. "Well, we…." She looked to her nephew as if she'd suddenly forgotten her own name.

"She wants to thank you for protectin' her that night the bottle came flying past your heads," Jesse answered.

"I wouldn't say I actually prot—"

"And for taking her to my pa's office to report it. And—"

"That's pretty much it," Abbie cut in. "Like I said, we don't intend to stay. We just wanted to drop off a little something my grandmother baked."

Man, she had an alluring face, as much as Noah hated noticing. "Not you?" He feigned disappointment.

"She doesn't bake. She doesn't cook, either," Jesse freely offered.

"Jesse Devlin." Abbie poked the boy in the side with her elbow. "Stop telling on me." She looked up at Noah with a sheepish expression. "It's not that I can't cook, mind you."

"Sure, she can cook, but she burns everything," Jesse said.

"Jesse." She turned and gave him a playful slap on the arm.

The boy's eyes twinkled with mischief. "She sets a good table, though."

"Would you stop?"

Noah crossed his arms and cocked his head at the pair, chuckling aloud at their repartee. Another woman who didn't cook. Suzanna would sooner starve than lift a finger in the kitchen, but that was because she'd come from privileged stock and couldn't understand why not everyone had hired help. Noah had a feeling that, where Abbie Kane was concerned, she simply didn't have the time to spend in the kitchen. Domestic chores probably bored her practically to tears. What on earth was Peter Sinclair doing with a woman like her? Indeed, what man in his right mind would be drawn to her—never mind her olive skin, jet-black tresses, charcoal eyes, well-proportioned curves, and perfect face? *What man, indeed?*

"Can we see what's in the basket?" Toby asked with clear impatience. As Jesse started peeling back several towels, Toby stood on tiptoe to watch, and Noah couldn't help feeling rather curious, himself.

At Toby and Noah's request, Abbie and Jesse stayed to help partake of the muffins, sitting picnic-style on the floor in a sort of circle because there were no chairs in the place except for a single stool. Jesse situated himself across from Abbie and next to Noah, and Toby snuggled close to her side.

She'd intended to make her delivery, offer a few words of friendly greeting, and then take her leave with Jesse; but, well, the invitation had come off sounding quite sincere, and

Toby was her Sunday school student, after all. So, she and Jesse had removed their coats and kicked off their boots, which were now positioned by the door. Abbie's were next to Noah's, as if they belonged together.

Abbie nibbled her second muffin, raking the crumbs that fell into a neat little pile in the lap of her blue, linen skirt. She would have reached for a third if Noah had, but she restrained herself. Then, too, she had to save her appetite for dinner with Peter that evening, and three muffins would have crossed the limit. Still, Grandmother Kane made the best cornbread cakes this side of the equator, so rich, sweet, and moist. *I must remember to ask her for the recipe—someday. Perhaps. If I wake up some morning with a bent for domesticity, that is.* Poor Helena Kane had done the best she could to teach her granddaughters everything there was to know about managing a household, and she'd succeeded with two of the three, not an altogether bad record.

The four of them kept the conversation light, with Jesse and Toby doing most of the talking, until Noah asked, "So, how are those Rogan girls faring, including their mother? Are they still staying with you—the girls, that is?"

"No, they've returned to their home," Abbie replied. "Arlena Rogan is much improved but still quite weak. Dr. Van Huff and his wife, Garnett, managed to nurse her back to health, for which I am so thankful. I heard that Gabe's unlocking Shamus Rogan's jail cell first thing Monday morning, though, and, frankly, I hate to see that scoundrel go back to his family. I'm worried what will transpire between him and Arlena. I simply don't trust him one jot."

"Maybe his time in jail will have reformed him," Noah said. "Given him time to reevaluate where he's headed."

"It's a nice thought, anyway."

"But you're not too hopeful."

"Folks familiar with Shamus know a few weeks in jail can't cure what ails him. He's so mean, he'd make a lion look like a kitten."

"Well, here's one good thing: I did receive the money for my rig repairs. Sheriff said that was one stipulation of his getting out of jail. The bank took care of the transaction. So, that's something."

"Yes, that's something, and Papa got money for damages done to the store. Also, Dr. Van Huff talked to the girls about cooperating to complete the household chores, hinting they were to do the best they could to keep their father happy. I sat right there and listened as he gave his little spiel, and I hope it made an impression. I know it impressed me. Stuffy Huffy's certainly mellowed over the years."

Noah arched one eyebrow and popped the last of his muffin between his lips, wiping his mouth with the back of his hand. My, but she wished she hadn't noticed the lovely shape of his lips. "Is that what you call the doctor?"

"Oh, never to his face."

"It's a nickname she gave him when he used to court my mom," Jesse put in. "I heard all about it."

Abbie nodded at Jesse. "Yes, he had a stodgy self-importance about him that used to drive me to distraction. I knew from the start he was wrong for Hannah. Good gracious, he rarely even smiled in those days, and he certainly never laughed, that I can recall. He'd have considered it irreverent, I think. Not that he's bubbling over with hilarity now, but back then, he had no sense of humor."

"Prolly because he didn't think Aunt Abbie's jokes were that funny...and, well, they mostly aren't."

"Say," Abbie said, reaching over to yank on the toe of Jesse's stocking. "You'd best mind your manners, young man, or I'll start rattling off a few jokes right here and now."

"No-o-o-o." He gave a perilous groan and clutched his chest. "Don't let her, Mr. Carson."

Noah's chortle had a rugged, raspy quality that Abbie found appealing. "I think I could do with a joke or two, actually," he said, his brilliant, blue eyes catching her gaze, his mouth curved into a most charming grin. "Especially after talk about that varmint, Shamus Rogan. Do you have any up that puffy, yellow sleeve of yours?"

"Oh, mercy, I don't know. I think I've exhausted most of them." Abbie thought for a moment. "Wait. I did hear one the other day in the Whatnot from Gertie Pridmore, the librarian. She came in for supplies, and, as usual, she and I exchanged jokes. The one I told she'd heard before, so it didn't earn the laughter I'd hoped for, but hers was rather good. Let's see if I can recall it." She corralled her thoughts, trying to reel in each detail—a feat made more difficult when she discovered Noah staring intently at her, which rattled her nearly to the point of numbness.

Meanwhile, Jesse rolled his eyes and heaved an exaggerated sigh. "You're asking for it, Mr. Carson."

"I'm armed and ready," Noah said, chuckling.

"Okay, okay, I think I have it," Abbie said, clapping her hands together and sucking in a long, deep breath of wood-scented air. "And this one is especially funny because I just finished teaching my Sunday school class about Noah's ark—and, of course, your name is in the joke." Young Toby, still nestled close to her, had grown quiet. She licked her lips, noting that the grin on Noah's face had not wavered.

He raised his eyebrows. "Well, that alone should give it some added humor, then."

"Of course." She glanced down at Toby to find his eyes growing heavier by the second but decided not to disturb him. He probably wouldn't appreciate the joke, anyway. She forged ahead. "One Sunday morning, a preacher finished his sermon and announced he would preach about Noah and the ark the following week. He gave the Bible reference and told his congregation to read the passage ahead of time.

"Well, a couple of boys noticed something interesting about the placement of the story in the Bible, so, one day that week, they slipped into the church and glued two pages of the preacher's pulpit Bible together.

"The next Sunday, the preacher got up to read his text, and this is what he read: 'Noah took unto himself a wife,' he began, 'and she was'—he turned the page to continue—'three hundred cubits long, fifty cubits wide, and thirty cubits high.'"

She couldn't help her sudden spurt of wild laughter. But she sobered when Toby slumped against her, having fallen asleep, Jesse scratched his head and frowned, and Noah merely raised his brows a fraction higher.

"What? You didn't think that was funny?"

"That was it?" Noah asked. "That was your joke?"

"I warned you," Jesse said.

"Oh, bosh, you two are pathetic." At that, she brushed every last muffin crumb off her skirt and onto the floor. "You just don't appreciate good humor. Everyone knows me as a good jokester."

"Is that right?" Noah said as he and Jesse exchanged knowing glances. "I guess it did have one funny part," he said, stretching out his legs and leaning back on the palms of his hands.

"Which part was that?" Jesse asked.

"The part when your aunt nearly burst her buttons laughing at her own joke."

Now they decided to laugh. *Well, this is just grand,* Abbie thought, *winding up the butt of the joke.* Still, if it had gotten them laughing, then she'd succeeded. Since they were in a jovial mood, she decided to toss out another. "A farmer boy accidentally overturned his wagonload of corn. The farmer who lived nearby heard the noise and rushed right over.

"'Hey!' the farmer yelled. 'Don't worry about it. It's suppertime now. Come on over and eat with us, and I'll help you with the wagon later.'

"'That's mighty nice of you, sir, but I don't think my pa would like that very much,' the farmer boy said.

"'Aw, come on, now,' the farmer insisted. 'You have to eat, don't you? We'll get back to the wagon soon enough.'

"'Well, all right, then,' the farmer boy finally agreed. 'But Pa ain't goin' to like it, I tell ya.'

"After a hearty dinner, the farmer boy thanked his host. 'That was real good, but I better get back to my wagon now. I know Pa's goin' to be real upset with me.'

"'Oh, nonsense,' the farmer said with a smile. 'I'll explain it to him. Where is he, by the way?'

"'Under the wagon,'" her audience said in unison.

"How did you know?" Abbie pouted.

There went Jesse and Noah, grinning at each other again. "It was just slightly predictable, Aunt Abbie."

"It was not the least bit predictable," she insisted. "*I didn't get it the first time.*"

At that, both fellows spewed hearty batches of laughter, and, this time, Abbie joined them.

The three sparred back and forth for the next half hour, each taking a turn at telling a joke, none of which was one speck funnier than her original ones had been, but still they laughed. All except for Toby, that is, who managed to sleep right through the racket.

When their laughter had died down, Abbie decided to broach another topic.

"Can you tell us about the boat you're building for Mr. Clayton?"

"Yeah, tell us!" Jesse urged him, repositioning himself on the floor as if preparing for a long stay.

By now, Toby's slumber had given rise to light snoring. *The poor thing's probably been here all day*, Abbie thought as she eased his head into her lap.

Noah looked over, and she thought she detected some warmth spring to his eyes. "I take it Don told you, then—that he'd hired me."

Abbie swept a few pieces of hair out of her eyes, then began sifting Toby's feathery hair through her fingers. "Actually, I heard it from my sister, Hannah, who heard it from her husband, Gabe, who heard it from Mr. Clayton."

Noah arched one thick eyebrow and lowered his chin at Jesse. "See what I mean, Jess? Can't get a thing past the people of Sandy Shores. Who needs a daily newspaper?"

Jesse laughed, and Abbie could see that Noah had won himself an adoring fan. Jesse looked around the large room. "You gonna build it right in here?"

"Yep. Right over there, in fact." Noah pointed to the east end of the building. "See those rafters up there? They're plenty sturdy enough to support the winch."

"The witch?" Jesse asked, his oval eyes going round.

Noah gave a hearty laugh, and the sound warmed Abbie clear to her chilly toes. "No, not witch, *winch*. It's like a vise, a giant clamp with jaws closed by a lever. I'll need it for holding sections of the boat."

Jesse nodded and frowned pensively. "Oh." He looked over at the planks of wood stacked neatly against a far wall. "I guess that's your boat over there."

Another jovial chuckle from Noah. "You got it. You want to see how she'll look when she's complete?"

"Have you got a picture?"

"Not exactly, but a rendering. You know what a rendering is?"

"Is it like a drawing?"

"Yep. It's over there at my workbench. It'll give you an idea of the finished product." He glanced down at Toby, still slumped against Abbie.

"I'll sit right here and listen," she whispered when he lifted his gaze to meet hers.

"You sure?"

She nodded, not wanting to disturb the sleeping boy.

For the next half hour or so, Noah explained every inch and angle of his boat design to Jesse, patiently answering his every question. "What's keel config—configuration?" "Where's the hull?" "What's fairing up a boat?" "What's lofting?" "How long will it take to build it?" Abbie listened from her position on the floor, where she continued combing her fingers through

Toby's hair. The truth was, there was no place on earth she would rather have been than here, with this little guy nestled against her, totally relaxed and trusting; with Jesse, her beloved nephew, ever anxious to learn new things; and with Noah Carson, a man she still barely knew but found more fascinating every time they met. The patient, even tenor of his voice as he explained boatbuilding to Jesse, the graceful movement of his muscles as he bent over the drawing table with a pencil to point out a particular area of his design—these things made her mind travel down paths she'd never ventured when she thought about Peter Sinclair. Even his passion for boatbuilding intrigued her, and she found herself caught up in his discussion about the process and filled with desire to watch the project progress from start to finish. Still, she'd meant to stay only a couple of minutes, and there was the matter of needing to take Jesse home before heading back to the Kane residence to ready herself for her outing with Peter.

"Why does it have to have a flat bottom?" Jesse inquired, his small frame nearly sprawled over the blueprint, brushing against Noah's broad chest as he reached out to point to a particular spot on the design.

"Jesse, that's probably about enough questions for Mr. Carson," Abbie called out. "You'll wear him out with all the asking, and, besides, I should get you back home."

"The flat bottom's so she'll glide along the water's surface without making so much as a ripple," Noah said, both of them ignoring her comment.

"Really? I'd like to see that. When you gonna start building it?"

"As early as Monday, I hope. And I already placed an order for the hardware and sails. There are certain things you just have to rely on the experts to make when you're building a boat."

"Where'd you learn to build boats, anyway?"

A minor pause ensued, and Noah's eyes darted over Jesse's head and connected with hers. In them, Abbie read the slightest bit of discomfiture. Wanting to ease it, she said, "Jesse, it's probably best we take our leave. As I started to say before, we've used up enough of Mr. Carson's time." She hated to do it, but she removed herself from beneath Toby, looking around the room for something, anything, to use as a pillow for his head. Noah guessed her aim and tossed her his coat, which had been draped over his stool. Upon seizing it, Abbie caught the musky, woodsy scent of him. She almost brought the coat to her nose for a deep whiff but caught herself in time, instead folding it in half and placing it under Toby's sunny-colored head. The boy's eyes didn't open so much as a slit.

"I've built boats all my life, actually," Abbie heard Noah say to Jesse.

"You mean, when you lived in Connecticut?"

To her surprise, he answered in the next beat. "Yep, owned my own boatworks company." She found her ears tuning in with great interest as she left the dozing boy on the floor and walked across the room to retrieve Jesse's and her coats. She handed Jesse his and slipped into her own. After buttoning it up, she realized that she probably looked a sight in her stocking feet. Of course, no one appeared to notice, so what difference did it make? With unveiled interest, she gazed over Jesse's shoulder at the drawings, having only imagined how they looked from listening to Noah's patient explanations. Seeing them firsthand on stiff, manila chart paper, though, gave her a new appreciation for Noah's talent; the way the penciled lines, drawn with precision and clear detail, nearly made the boat come to life. She imagined it skimming the water's surface, gliding over waves, tipping and tilting, its sails snapping in the wind.

"Why'd you quit building boats at your company?" Jesse asked, ever the curious child.

Noah quirked an eyebrow at Jesse and, with a slanted grin, ruffled the lad's dark head of thick hair. "I'm afraid that's where things get a bit complicated."

"Oh." Instinct must have told Jesse not to press him. Although only eleven, he possessed a level of maturity surpassing most others his age, probably due to all he'd experienced as a youngster. He was orphaned at around six years of age, jumping one train after another and literally running for his life, until he'd wound up in the arms of Sheriff Gabriel Devlin in Holland, Michigan, later to be adopted by him and his new bride, Hannah. Still, a tiny piece of Abbie wished the boy had persisted with his questions. Why, indeed, had Noah Carson left his boatbuilding company to start over at his uncle's window and door business? And what of his former wife, Toby's mother? Didn't she long to see her son? And then, there was the matter of his father, whom he'd said was an alcoholic. Did they ever speak or exchange mail? Surely, young Toby had family who dearly missed him.

Abbie chanced a discreet glance at Noah. Their gazes met and held for mere seconds, she being the first to tear her eyes away, prodding Jesse to put on his coat and hat. "Thank you for sparing the time to tell my nephew about your boat design, Mr., er, Noah. I found it very interesting, myself."

He laughed, and the pleasant sound set her heart in fast motion. Gracious, but she had a bad case of, well, something quite indefinable. A crush, perhaps? "I should be the one doing the thanking. Your unexpected visit was a pure pleasure." Noah glanced at Toby. "It would have come as a great pleasure to him, too, if he hadn't been so tuckered out."

"He still takes naps, I see," she said.

"Occasionally, yes. I started him out early today."

This prompted Abbie to say something she hadn't seen coming. "You can always send him over to the Whatnot, you know. I love his company."

Her excited heart beat faster still as he leaned his body forward, tipping his chin down so that their faces came within inches of each other. "Really? Do you know how much Toby loves that place…and how much he enjoys you?"

"It's probably all those candy sticks," she said with a giggle as they started toward the door. Abbie stepped into her leather, high-top boots and bent over to lace them up, wishing she could find a more ladylike way of going about it.

"Be sure to tell your grandmother how much I enjoyed the muffins," Noah said, standing over her. With his coat buttoned and his hat plopped into place, Jesse opened the door, letting in a gust of cold air.

"Thanks again for showing me your boat plans, Mr. Carson," he said.

"You're quite welcome, young man. Come back anytime and check my progress."

"Are you serious?"

"As a dead loon," he answered with a chuckle.

"Man!" Jesse murmured, stretching out the word. "Thanks!" Then, "I'll go get the rig turned around, Aunt Abbie."

"Good idea," she said from her awkward, stooped-over position, finishing off one boot before moving to the next. She was thankful when Jesse closed the door.

"Here, allow me," Noah said, abruptly getting down on one knee and stealing the laces from her hand. Their eyes locked for one disquieting moment while she remained bent, frozen, and not because her back developed a crick, either, but because the cloudless blue of his eyes had purely mesmerized her. "These things can present a challenge," he said.

"I'll be glad when I can go back to wearing my leather-soled slip-ons."

"And I look forward to being able to roll up the cuffs of my cotton shirts."

"Yes, that will be nice, indeed." She could only envision the muscular arms beneath those sleeves. Why, his shoulders alone were about as broad as a bull's, she noted, probably exaggerated by that loose-fitting, partially tucked in flannel shirt he wore. To her dismay, she discovered herself making a comparison between Noah's sturdy physique and Peter's lean and lanky frame, Noah's relaxed, casual attire and Peter's perfectly groomed appearance. Why, even on a hot, summer night, no matter that he'd need to blot his perspiring forehead with a handkerchief, Peter wouldn't dream of rolling up his shirtsleeves. Even if he tried, the stiff, starched fabric would no doubt prevent it.

They looked at each other. They looked at the sleeping boy. Outside, Bessie neighed, and a light breeze whiffled past the door.

"You want to stand up?" Noah asked, breaking the silence.

"Excuse me?"

"Stand up, please? Your skirts are in the way."

"Oh! Yes, of course." Abbie got to her feet so fast that the blood rushed from her head, making her go temporarily dizzy. "Thank you for your help." She easily could have reached out and run her fingers through his gleaming, chestnut hair. *Foolish notion.* What she needed was a good, hard smack across the face to snap her out of this quixotic mood.

Noah made fast work of lacing her boot, then stood and put a hand on the doorknob, where it lingered while he looked at her with those intense, blue eyes. With his free hand, he reached up and gently touched the tip of her nose. The gesture, innocent as it may have been, sent her head to spinning. "I had a good time with you today. I wonder what Sinclair would say about that."

She swallowed a hard lump. "Sinclair?"

"Are you going to tell him you stopped by to see me?"

"*We* stopped by to see you—Jesse and I. Remember? And my purpose in coming was to deliver the muffins, a sort of thanks offering. By the way, I do appreciate your insisting to drive me home that night, even though I may not have shown it at the time."

"I've pretty much figured you for the kind of woman who sometimes acts—and speaks—before thinking. Not till later do the regrets start piling up."

"You think you know me, don't you?" Abbie challenged him, riled by his impudence. She stuck out her chin a fraction, even as her heart thumped against the wall of her chest like a pesky woodpecker. Noah's steady gaze into her eyes did little to settle her nerves.

He chuckled down deep. "I'm beginning to, yes."

For the life of her, she couldn't keep her thoughts in a straight row nor figure out a decent retort. Her voice felt clogged, so she cleared her throat. "I best get Jesse home."

"You still haven't answered my question," he said, his hand motionless on the doorknob.

"What question?" She focused her eyes on a few stray muffin crumbs that clung to his shirtfront.

"Are you going to tell Sinclair you came here?"

Her forehead wrinkled with annoyance. "I don't know. Maybe. Perhaps. It isn't as if anything unseemly took place, so what should it matter?"

If he would only stop gazing down at her, his warm breath grazing her face, she would push forward, insist he open the door. But, instead, he held her prisoner. "Oh, it doesn't matter at all. Unless...."

Noah let go of the door handle and gently grasped her arm just above the elbow, and the heat penetrated right through her thick sleeve. He took one fateful step closer and lowered his head. Her heart thrummed in wild, sporadic beats, and she should have pulled away, but for reasons she couldn't fathom, she stood still, as if rooted to the spot. *Lord, have mercy, what is happening?* Their lips touched, and everything in her went still—everything but her racing heart, that is. Noah's grip on her arm tightened, and the angle of his head deepened as he seemed to be exploring the texture of her lips. The sensation did not begin to compare to that of Peter's kisses—no, not one smidgeon. In fact, it was nothing short of exquisite the way Noah made it last—and last—and last, as if time itself had lost the ability to tick away, second by second.

Outside, the breeze kicked up, and the sound of another horse startled them apart. Still, he gripped her arm, his eyes traversing her face. "...unless I kissed you, I was about to say." He looked her square in the face, his eyes glinting. "Now, would that be considered unseemly, Miss Kane?"

His question made her come to her senses, and she stepped back, forcing him to drop his hand. "Was that a trick, Mr. Carson? Because, if it was, I don't consider it the least bit humorous."

He slanted his head at her and grinned. "More like a test."

"A test." She had no idea what he meant, and her woman's intuition told her not to question him on it. The fact that she'd enjoyed the kiss rankled her clear to her booted toes. Peter would be mortified, indeed, to learn of what she'd done. *Mortified? Outraged* better described how he'd feel. And there was no way in the world she would tell him about it. Anger at herself for succumbing to temptation and guilt for betraying Peter merged in a most unpleasant recipe for ruination. Goodness gracious, she'd just kissed a divorced man—and enjoyed it! *Lord, forgive me.* "Good day, Mr. Carson. Rest assured, this...this kiss...was a onetime occurrence."

"Absolutely. I told you, it was a test."

She longed like nobody's business to know what he meant, but utter urgency to escape him kept her from asking. With his hand controlling the doorknob again, she could do little but wait for him to turn it. "Give my regards to Sinclair," Noah said, his voice a blend of gruffness and amusement.

Abbie straightened her shoulders. "I may do that—over dinner tonight." His intense scrutiny made normal breathing beyond difficult.

"Tonight, huh?"

"Would you mind opening the door?"

One corner of his mouth twisted upward as he pinned her with his blue gaze. "Not at all. You have a pleasant dinner." His words hinted at smugness.

"I'm certain I will." Hers came off sounding hollow and insincere.

Out front, Jesse gave a friendly greeting to someone whose voice she didn't recognize. There was nothing unusual about that, though, considering Sandy Shores' growing population.

Noah opened the door and peered out, then stepped back inside and slammed the door. "What in the Sam Hill is he doing here?" he muttered, running a hand through his already mussed hair and opening the door a crack to take another look.

In the blink of an eye, the atmosphere changed from titillating to repugnant, in Abbie's opinion. The tallish man talking to Jesse looked pleasant enough to her, despite his ruddy complexion and somewhat ragged attire; his soiled, brown coat, weathered trousers, and worn boots looked like they'd seen better days. He wore a wool cap on his head, from which wisps of grayish-white hair stuck out on all sides, and his goatee matched his hair.

"Who is he?" Abbie whispered to Noah, then looked over to see his jaw tensed in apparent anger. When she repeated the question, he frowned with ice-cold fury while sucking in a loud breath.

"My no-good, boozer father, that's who."

Chapter Sixteen

"Who do you think you are, coming here uninvited?" Noah asked in a hissing voice. He longed to bellow at the top of his lungs, yet didn't want to awaken his son. "You're not welcome here. I should think you would know that by now, being as I haven't come looking for you."

"I can understand your anger. I would expect it."

"What?" he growled through his teeth. "You didn't understand me as a kid, and you sure as horse dung don't understand me now. Why did you have to come to Sandy Shores, anyway? Don't you know you were one of the reasons I left Guilford—you and Suzanna and the whole lot of them? I came here to start over, and I was making a fine go of it. How do you expect me to continue with you here? I don't want to wake up every morning asking myself if our paths are going to cross, and thinking up ways to avoid you."

Movement outside caught his eye, and he glanced out the window to watch Abbie take up the reins and direct her horse onto the road, her posture straight as an arrow, Jesse slouching next to her. Noah hated that he hadn't even given her a decent good-bye, nor taken a moment to explain the kiss—not that he'd have had a good explanation for it. Heck, even he didn't know what had possessed him to initiate it. The "test" had been merely for his benefit, to see if he still had an ounce of desire left in him to start up something with another woman. It turned out he did, and that bothered him plenty.

"You don't have to worry about that, son."

His father's words promptly brought him back to the issue at hand. "Don't call me son. You never did before; there's no reason to start now."

The man removed his cap to run four fingers through his thinning hair, his goatee making his face appear even longer. His shoulders, once square and firm, were now curved with age, giving him the appearance of a man much older than his fifty-four years. Without a doubt, the booze had done it to him. His gray eyes sparked with indefinable emotion as he dropped his gaze to the floor, turned his cap in his hands, and exhaled a heavy sigh.

"All right, then, Noah. I'll try to stay out of your way as much as possible, but…." His eyes flitted around the room and came to rest on his sleeping grandson, curled in a tight ball, his downy head buried in the folds of Noah's coat.

"And don't get any ideas about trying to push yourself on Toby. He's had enough heartbreak to last him a lifetime."

The man blinked hard and swallowed, his Adam's apple bobbing like a cork on a wavy sea. "Yes, he has, no question about that. He'll come through it, though, just as you have." He looked up into Noah's face, for he was a few inches shorter than his son, and it struck Noah then that he could easily take the fellow down. The thought scared him to his bones. He needed to get a grip, but how?

"In God have I put my trust: I will not be afraid what man can do unto me." Out of nowhere, Toby's memory verse punched him square in the gut. He gave it a mental shove, but, like a ball striking a wall, it bounced right back to him. The verse prompted him to take a few measured breaths. He rubbed the back of his neck, where the muscles had bound into a hard knot. After a moment of agitated silence, he asked, "What do you want from me?"

"I was hoping for a second chance."

Noah opened his mouth to protest, but his father put a hand on his arm. The last time he recalled his father's touch, it hadn't been gentle. He quickly recoiled, stuffing his hands deep into the pockets of his pants and shifting his weight to one side.

"Hear me out, okay? Just this once," his father said.

Noah looked at the floor. "Make it snappy, then."

"Your aunt may have told you I gave my heart to the Lord."

"She mentioned something about it, but I don't believe it."

"That's your prerogative, of course. I suppose only time will prove to you that it's true. I'm changed, Noah, and all I can say is that God is responsible. My sheer desire is to surrender to His plans for my life."

A scoffing sound passed Noah's lips. "A little late for that, wouldn't you say?"

"I've made a mess of things; I'll be the first to admit it," Gerald said, seemingly undaunted by his son's derision. "Denying God all those years, berating your mother for her faith...but I would like to tell you how God—"

"Don't mention my mother. I don't even want to hear your excuses."

"I did love her, Noah, as much as you don't want to believe it. But I failed her. She had so many health issues I couldn't deal with. And then, the miscarriages…it was too much for either of us. As the years went by—"

"Wait." The blood in Noah's veins felt like it had turned to ice. "What do you mean, miscarriages?"

Gerald's face went as pale as a plaster wall, and his shoulders fell into an even deeper slump. "I thought you knew. I thought she would have told—"

"She never told me anything about any miscarriages. You're lying. If it were true, Aunt Julia would have said something." It took every ounce of mental strength not to pull the man up by the front of his coat.

"It was before you were born. Julia probably figured you knew. Your mother, she fell into a well of deep, deep sadness after all those losses, and, I guess, in a sense, I did, as well. She retreated to her bed, and I to alcohol. When she discovered she was carrying you, it was her eighth pregnancy. The doctor ordered her to remain prone the entire time, and, by some miracle, she managed to carry you all the way to the end. She adored you, you know."

Flabbergasted, Noah could do little but stare wide-eyed and gape-mouthed.

"We, your mother and I, never talked about those miscarriages. I tried many times, but always she screamed at me to stop. Still, I thought she would have told you at some point. You two were so close, and I was…well, she didn't want me in the same room with her."

"You shoved her around, you fool. Of course, she didn't want you around." Fresh anger surged through Noah's body, begging to explode through his pores.

"I was the worst of the worst on booze. Some people turn mellow, but I went mean as a snake. But I'm off the stuff, Noah. I've not had a drop in almost seven months, all glory to God. He's delivered—"

Noah raised his palm to his father's face. "You can leave anytime now. I've heard enough."

"Just one more chance. That's all I ask."

Behind Noah's eyes, the sockets burned like fire. "Leave."

"I hear you're building a boat for some wealthy fellow in town. Del told me. That's great, Noah. You'll build a fine vessel." Once again, his eyes flitted about the room to his sleeping grandson, the high rafters, the stacks of fragrant, cedar boards. "You've got some nice tools, there. You should be set—except for one thing. You'll need some help when it comes time to bend the ribs."

"I'll hire someone."

"I've got plenty of experience, and I come cheap."

Of all the shipbuilders in Sandy Shores, Gerald Carson probably did have the most talent. "I'll make do just fine, thanks," Noah spat out.

"I see. Well, let me know if you have a change of heart." He spun his cap a few times, then plopped it back in place. Again, his gaze drifted to the lad on the floor. "He looks like he's grown a couple inches." Noah met the remark with silence. His father pulled his bent frame as straight as he could but then wound up looking at the floor, scraping the sole of his boot against the rough cement. "I've been in the boat business for more than forty years, Noah. I could help you when I'm not working over at—"

"Good-bye."

Gerald turned and opened the door, then quickly whirled back around. "I'm not asking for much, Noah."

"Wrong. You're asking me to move a mountain, that's what you're asking."

"No," Gerald said in a voice just above a whisper. "I'm asking God to move the mountain."

At that, he turned and headed up the drive. With all his being, Noah wished to slam the door, to throw his fist into the wall, to pick up his boot and watch it sail across the room, maybe do some damage. But he had his napping son to think about, so he closed the door quietly. In his mind, though, he slammed it with a fierceness.

Then, for reasons he couldn't explain, he went to the window and watched the man trudge up the street, shuffling his shabby boots and favoring one leg. Noah gripped his head between both hands and squeezed, as if to try crowding out all the ugly memories.

"*In God have I put my trust: I will not be afraid what man—*"

"Pa?" His son's voice came as a welcome interruption. Toby sat up and wiped the sleep from his eyes. "Where'd Miss Abbie and Jesse go?"

Abbie. Again, the memory of their kiss flooded his clogged thoughts. Oh, he hated that he'd kissed her, hated even more that he'd taken pleasure in it. But what he hated most was that Peter Sinclair had serious plans to put a ring on her finger.

"They're gone for now, son, but you'll see them at church tomorrow." He couldn't allow himself to skip another Sunday and risk Abbie's wrath. On the other hand, the wrathful side of Abbie Ann Kane rather intrigued him.

Blast it all! He had more important things to mull over than that woman and the silly, unplanned, onetime kiss— and the way her lips had melded to his—and her adorable smile and mystifying, black eyes....

Yes, he had more important things to worry about. Avoiding Gerald Carson, for starters.

K

That evening at dinner, Abbie had difficulty keeping up with the conversation. At the last minute, Peter had invited Lester and Jane Emery to join them for dinner at the Haven House on Harbor Drive. They were a couple in their forties with two grown children. Lester worked at Sandy Shores Bank with Peter, having been hired by Peter's father several years ago. While Lester and Peter engaged in business conversation, finding plenty of things to discuss, Abbie and Jane sought to find common ground on which to settle. Jane had two married daughters, one living in New Jersey, her home state, and the other in New York, so Abbie told her about Maggie Rose having traveled to New York City to work at the Sheltering Arms Refuge, only to settle there upon marrying Luke Madison. Jane's father owned a newspaper, so she told her how her brother-in-law, Maggie's husband, had once worked for the *New York World*—that is, until he gave it up in order to devote his energies to caring for lost and orphaned children, which led her straight into Jesse's story and how he'd come to live in Sandy Shores.

"This is a lovely place, isn't it?" Abbie said, lifting her crystal goblet for a sip of cold water.

The woman followed suit, bringing her glass to her lips and swallowing once before setting it daintily back in place. "Yes, quite lovely."

The restaurant served its signature cuisine on the finest china at tables set with white, linen tablecloths and perfectly polished silver. Each table was also illuminated with a brass oil lamp, which lent a romantic ambiance to the already dreamy setting on the sandy banks of Lake Michigan. The land side of the restaurant looked out on towering sand dunes and a sprinkling of summer getaway cottages.

Their waiter had settled them at a corner table next to the wall of windows overlooking the beach, and while Abbie couldn't deny the tranquil backdrop and the lavish atmosphere, with its dimly lit, sparkling chandeliers and plush, Persian carpets, she never had been one for dining extravagantly. Peter knew it, too, yet, here they were, again, spending a fortune on food, when so many in Sandy Shores had so little in their cupboards. Abbie's thoughts drifted to the Rogans, and she imagined the girls flitting around the house, putting things in order, and, she hoped, taking good care of their mother.

Perhaps, after dinner tomorrow, she would take the Interurban to their house to check on their welfare—unless she could convince Peter to drive her. Gabe planned to release Shamus on Monday morning, and she saw tomorrow as one of her final opportunities to visit his family before his return.

"Do you come here often?" Jane inquired, drawing Abbie out of her musings.

Abbie dabbed at her chin with her linen napkin. While Jane Emery had a plain, oval face, she certainly made up for it in her elegant, green cheviot suit with a puff-sleeved jacket, its collar and lapels appliquéd and elaborately embroidered, its waist trimmed with green moiré ribbon. Her rust-colored hair, piled high atop her head with interlacing ribbon identical to that around her waist, lent to a lovely appearance overall. "We've been here a few times," Abbie replied. "Peter enjoys fine dining, but I'm more of a typical eatery girl, if you know what I mean, so we compromise. I also enjoy my grand-mother's cooking, being as I'm not the handiest tool in the kitchen."

This confession produced a hearty laugh from Jane. "Ah, I know what you mean. Before I married Lester, I knew next to nothing about household matters, and, to my mother's dismay, I did not care to. But, don't worry; you will learn kitchen secrets and household skills once you marry."

"Which will be very soon, I hope," said Peter, jumping into the conversation as if he'd been eavesdropping the entire time and paying Lester Emery little heed. He reached over and lifted Abbie's hand from her lap, bringing it to his chest in a gentle squeeze and soaking up her face with his eyes. "Abbie and I have talked a good deal about marriage, haven't we, Abbie? Really, it's just a matter of her setting the date, and, for the life of me, I don't know why she insists on drag-ging her feet."

"Peter." She couldn't have been more mortified. Such an intimate topic, laid out before near strangers—at least, to her. Gracious, she hadn't even accepted his proposal, and now, with Noah's spine-tingling kiss floating around in her memory, why, the mere thought of marrying Peter made her queasy.

"It is a woman's privilege to drag her feet, Mr. Sinclair," Jane said matter-of-factly. "There's the dress to buy, the cater-ing to consider, the guest list to write, the invitations to send… my, making wedding preparations can be an overwhelming task for a lady."

Lester sat back and folded his arms across his lean chest, looking pleased. "And it's a man's privilege to sit by and watch his wife-to-be submerge herself in all those elaborate details. If it had been my choice, which it never is, by the way, I would have marched her over to the justice of the peace twenty-four years ago and gotten those vows out of the way in short order."

"A woman wants a wedding to be about her," Jane said, ignoring her husband's attempt at humor. *She does?* Abbie couldn't quite fathom walking down the center aisle of the Third Street Church with all eyes on her as if she were the queen herself. Yes, her sisters had done it, and, yes, she'd walked ahead of them, but envisioning herself in the bridal gown still seemed like a faraway dream. Moreover, picturing Peter at the front of the church awaiting her arrival felt more like a nightmare. "And if it takes her a month of Sundays—goodness, a year of Sundays—to get ready for her big day, then so be it," Jane finished.

"Well, I've patiently waited for—what is it? Nine months, now? Ten? I suppose I can muster up a bit more staying power." Peter squeezed Abbie's hand even more tightly before releasing it and giving her an adoring, if not somewhat put-on, smile. She returned an ephemeral one and quickly clasped her hands in her lap, wishing upon every star in the sky that their dinners would arrive soon. Why on earth did these fancy restaurants have to take an eternity to bake a potato, cook a piece of chicken, or fry up a steak? She took another sip of water and realized that one or two more would drain her glass. Why couldn't they give each person a bigger goblet?

"So, tell us," Lester Emery said, folding his hands on the table and leaning forward. "What is it you two have in common?"

Luckily, her water went down before he asked the question; otherwise, she might have choked on it. Not that it wasn't a fair question. Why, most people wouldn't think twice about asking it of a couple who'd been courting for several months.

"Oh, yes, tell us," Jane chimed in.

Peter cast Abbie a stranded look, which nearly made her laugh. He couldn't come up with anything, either?

"Well, we certainly do enjoy attending church together," she managed at the last second, before it became obvious how stumped they were.

"Yes!" Peter said with gusto. "We both teach Sunday school; I teach the men, and she, the six-year-olds."

"How wonderful," Jane said. "I teach the twelve-year-old girls at our church." She glanced at her husband with a prideful smile. "Lester is an elder, of course."

Lester smiled back at his wife, then moved his gaze from Peter to Abbie. "She always thinks everything I do is praiseworthy."

Peter smiled and glanced at Abbie, as if expecting her to chime in about all his many fine attributes. Taking the hint, she spouted, "Peter is a brilliant Sunday school teacher. He knows his Bible through and through." Nothing could have been truer. In fact, he often put her to shame with his knowledge of the Scriptures. Why, then, didn't she see him as the perfect catch? He'd told her on several occasions that he loved her, even though she had yet to repeat the words back to him. How did one go about saying those three words to a man for the very first time? They seemed incredibly profound and impossibly transcendent. Saying them meant not turning back, never looking the other way, and never, ever pining over someone else, much less kissing him.

The three of them—Peter, Lester, and Jane—set off on some theological discussion, a question for which, throughout the ages, no one had ever been credited with providing the final answer. As if on cue, their platters of food arrived, and, soon, their attentions turned to their stomachs, all thoughts of solving the age-old question consigned to oblivion.

Chapter Seventeen

O n their drive home that night, Abbie pulled her fur cape tight to her neck. In spite of Peter's buggy having a top and side windows, it was hardly warm, due to its open front, which let in wind that bit clear to her toes. "Cold?" Peter asked.

"Just a bit chilly, is all," she replied, even as she shivered. She reflected on the evening—the satisfying yet overpriced meal, the varied conversations, and the very warm, friendly person who was Jane Emery. Abbie's mention of her involvement in the W.C.T.U. had triggered a definite spark of interest in Jane's emerald eyes. "Oh, I think it's wonderful the way you're speaking out on behalf of women—and all of Sandy Shores, for that matter. Suffrage is a major issue. It's time women earned the right to vote. Why should men make all the decisions regarding our country's future?" She'd shot her husband a pointed look. "Isn't that right, Lester?"

"What? Yes, yes, no reason women shouldn't have that right…someday, perhaps." If only Abbie had had a Brownie Kodak with her at that precise moment to capture Lester Emery's wearisome expression as his eyes darted from his wife to Peter. On the one hand, he wanted to keep the peace with his wife; on the other, he had to consider his reputation in the presence of Peter Sinclair, his boss's nephew.

"And the work you're doing to close down the saloons in this town—why, I daresay, there's one on every corner. What night do you hold your meetings, Abbie? Perhaps I can join your league." Lester had coughed and gone quickly for his water goblet.

"Our bimonthly meetings take place on Tuesday nights," Abbie had said, hauling her mind back to the present when she realized Jane had been sitting there, waiting for a response. She'd decided against mentioning how Gabe had put their meetings on hold for the time being, thinking it might very well dampen Jane's enthusiasm about getting involved. Besides, Abbie envisioned the meetings reconvening in the next few weeks. To appease Gabe, she would go along with his temporary order, but if things continued to remain peaceful, they had no excuse not to resume meeting, and Gabe could hardly argue it. "We discuss a gamut of issues, one, in particular, being our need to secure a house in which to start up a women's shelter."

"A women's shelter?" Jane had asked, dabbing at her chin. "Do tell me more."

And so, Abbie had, explaining that she and several other members of the group were aware of specific women and children in need of protection from the abusive men in their lives. Of course, she did not mention names, particularly those of the Rogans, for it wasn't her intention to soil anyone's reputation, only to get the word out that a real problem existed.

"That's preposterous—a man laying a hand to his wife. Can you even imagine such a thing, Lester?" Jane had asked.

He'd rushed to take another drink of water.

"Can you, Lester?" she'd prodded him.

"It's completely unthinkable, dear."

Satisfied, Jane had given her full attention back to Abbie, allowing her to elaborate on the Woman's Christian Temperance Union's objectives and Abbie's strong personal desire to make a difference for the good of society, specifically for women and children.

"I thought the Emerys were lovely people. I'm glad you thought to invite them," Abbie said into the night as they bumped along up Water Street, the only sounds being that of a distant dog's bark and the clip-clopping hooves of Peter's thoroughbred.

"Yes, lovely," he replied.

When he might have reached out to take her gloved hand, he held to the reins, his eyes never leaving the road. In the full moon's light, Abbie looked at his face and saw a muscle tightening in his jaw. Reflecting further on the night, she realized he'd had little to contribute to the conversation once she and Jane had taken up the topic of the W.C.T.U. Actually, neither man had said much on the subject, now that she thought about it. She wondered if Lester was subjecting Jane to this same silent treatment as they made their way back home.

She decided to test the waters. "Jane certainly did show interest in learning more about the temperance union."

"Yes, didn't she?" This, Peter said in a most disgusted tone. Ah, she'd been right. "And I can't for a minute think why you had to bring it up, knowing as you do my objections to your involvement in that club." He snapped his horse into a faster trot. "I would hope that once we marry—"

"Once we marry?" she shot back. "I haven't even accepted your proposal, Peter. And, while we're on the subject, I resent your bringing it up in the Emerys' presence. Didn't you think it might cause me undue embarrassment?"

Without so much as a second of deliberation, he said, "I thought, perhaps, it might incite a snap decision from you."

"You thought putting me on the spot would persuade me?"

He sighed, pulled in the reins, and made the turn onto Third Street. As usual, thanks to Grandmother Kane, the porch light glowed on the house at the top of the hill. "I'm sorry if you felt uncomfortable. That wasn't my intention. But we're getting off the subject, Abbie Ann. We were speaking about your involvement in this—this ladies' club."

It did no good to remind him that her "ladies' club" was a national organization. Good grief! If he hadn't caught on to that yet, he never would.

"It's more like a calling, Peter. As much as you may not like it, women deserve equal treatment in society. This includes their right to vote, to serve on a jury, and to receive equal pay for equal work. Besides our active fight against the use of all drugs—alcohol, in particular—we promote good nutrition and sanitation, education for the poor, uniform marriage and divorce laws, the eight-hour workday, passive demonstrations, international peace…and the list continues. I have a strong desire in my heart to—"

"I've heard all this countless times, Abigail Ann." Rarely did he use her full name unless he wanted to drive home a specific point, which, she suspected, he intended to do now. "And they are all worthy ambitions, I'm sure. I just don't think the wife of a future bank president ought to be the one presiding over such a cl—an organization."

This notion stumped her. "And why is that? I should think a bank president would welcome his wife's involvement in social organizations."

"Charitable organizations, yes, but a temperance union has too much of a political agenda. Abbie, you know I don't condone the use of harmful substances, but you must remember, I have clients who don't share my views on the subject. Your continued participation in this—this organization could well cost the bank some of our best patrons."

The hairs on the back of her neck stood up, and not because of the chill in the air. "What are you saying, Peter? That you would compromise your principles for the almighty dollar? Because that's what it sounds like to me. Does your uncle share your views with regard to my association with the W.C.T.U.?"

Peter's uncle was like a father to him; he and his wife, Opal, had raised Peter since his parents' death when he was a young boy.

"My uncle?" At the top of the hill, he veered his horse into the Kanes' driveway and yanked on the reins. The animal stopped, neighing and pawing at the ground. Peter set the brake in place, tied the reins around the handle, and leaned back in his seat. His heavy sigh emitted a puffy cloud of steam. Moonlight streamed through the glass windows, alighting on Peter's pleasant yet angular face. "I suppose he feels the same. He's said as much. Of course, he admires you a great deal and would like nothing more than for you to join the family, as would Aunt Opal. But he'd very much like to see you less involved in controversial matters, and, you must admit, the W.C.T.U. is not exactly without debate."

Responding could very well have meant spouting words she would later regret, so Abbie prayed for an overflow of self-control. She bit her lip hard to keep from reacting. How could she possibly marry a man who stifled her passions, let alone one who didn't even come close to understanding what made her tick?

Peter placed an arm around her shoulder and drew her close. Numb with cold and perplexity, she leaned against him without emotion. "I don't want to fight, Abbie," he whispered into her ear, his warm breath brushing her cheek.

"Nor do I," she managed.

He kissed her earlobe where her bonnet didn't quite cover. She allowed it—for now, anyway—her perturbation still swimming circles in her head, her emotions muddled. Next, he traced her jawline with his lips, placing tiny, feather-like kisses an inch or so apart, the effect of which made her heart begin to race—though not because she enjoyed the sensation, she realized. It was because it made her think about another man who'd kissed her that very afternoon.

"I do love you, Abbie Ann," Peter murmured, shutting out the moonlight with his head as his arms fully encircled her body and his mouth descended hungrily to partake of a kiss. He moved his head, fitting his lips against hers in a most prodding, almost desperate, way, kneading the center of her back with his hands and tugging her as close as their winter attire would allow. At the distant edge of her consciousness, Abbie heard a door slam, a dog bark, and two cats send up mewing howls, all of which prompted her back to her senses.

"Peter, I...I'm sorry I cannot return the words," she whispered.

"Will you ever?" he asked, his face set back a mere two inches from her face and his arms still holding her in a tight embrace. Sadly, the taste of Noah's kisses had ruined

Peter's for her—and ruined everyone else's, as far as she was concerned.

Dear Lord, I don't even know where Noah stands with You, and yet I allowed him to kiss me. Whatever is wrong with me? She felt the bite of her own betrayal but couldn't bring herself to tell Peter.

"I think you're a very fine man, but...."

He studied her with such intentness that she had to turn and look at the Kanes' foursquare house with its wraparound porch—anywhere but his eyes. "You think I'm a very fine man, but...? But what, Abbie?"

His horse whinnied and pawed at the ground, distracting him for a moment. Abbie quickly righted herself on the buggy seat to put some space between them.

"I think...perhaps...you hold stronger feelings for me than I for you." There. It hurt her to say it, yet it filled her with relief to have it out in the open.

Silence prevailed for a good minute. She heard his quiet breaths, sensed the urgency in each one. "What can I do?" he finally asked.

She decided to crawl out on a shaky limb. "Would you like to accompany me out to the Rogan place tomorrow?"

His countenance dropped. *Clearly not the answer he wanted to hear,* she observed. He pinched the bridge of his nose. "Haven't you already bent over backwards for that family?"

Her heart actually mourned for his lack of compassion. "Peter, as the men's Sunday school teacher, I would think you'd know we're called to be light in a dark world. Shamus Rogan has made life difficult for Arlena and her girls, and they need encouragement and protection. Do you not see it as our Christian duty to step forward and do our part to foster this family?"

He sighed, his face contorting into a frown. "What I see is a woman who made a poor choice, Abbie. Had she been using her head right from the start, she would not have married an abusive alcoholic."

"So, you're saying it's her own fault that she's found herself in this predicament? I'm sure, early on, she had no idea what lay ahead for her."

"Perhaps not, but now that she has, there's little she or anyone else can do about it, and that's the sad truth of the matter, Christian or not."

"Peter, you should hear yourself. Your solution, then, to the Rogans' situation is to stand back and allow the abuse to continue? That is an injustice of the worst proportion. If everyone took your attitude, no one would be safe."

"Abbie, there are law enforcement officials to handle these types of problems. I don't mean to come off sounding heartless, but if there's abuse going on in the home, then Sheriff Devlin needs to get involved."

"He's investigated the matter, but until Arlena presses charges, there's little he can do. She doesn't open up to Gabe as she does to me."

Since her toes had frozen through her thin leather boots and she no longer felt her fingertips, Abbie put a hand on the door, preparing to exit the rig. First, though, she tilted her head up at Peter. He made no fast move to prevent her from opening the door. "I thank you for the nice dinner tonight. I think I should go inside now, and," she laid her hand on his arm, "I think it would be a good idea if you did not sit with me in church tomorrow."

A tight gasp whistled up his throat. "Are you breaking off our relationship, then?"

She caught her lower lip between her teeth and gave a slow, steady nod. "I'm sorry for any hurt I've caused you."

"Abbie...."

"I'll walk myself to the door."

He sighed and bridged the gap she'd put between them, planting a soft kiss on her cheek. She waited for a sensation of loveliness to sweep her heart into a flutter, but it didn't come.

When she climbed the porch steps, she heard the snap of reins as Peter urged his horse onto the road, and, soon, the clipping of hooves and the squeaking of a wheel faded into silence as the wagon made its way back down the hill toward Water Street.

Chapter Eighteen

Noah noticed three things in church on Sunday morning: one, Abbie Ann had chosen to sit in the row behind the Kane clan with her friends, the Sterlings, smack-dab between their three-year-old twin girls; two, a somber-looking Peter Sinclair sat several rows behind and on the opposite side of the church. Noah couldn't help but wonder what had happened to cause the rift and questioned whether the kiss he'd laid on her lips had played a part. If not, it sure should have.

The third thing he took note of as soon as he and Toby entered the sanctuary was that his father was there, sharing a pew with his aunt and uncle. As chance would have it, in his search for Uncle Delbert and Aunt Julia, Toby discovered his grandfather and begged to go sit with him. Not wanting to make a scene, Noah relented, though not happily. It didn't make sense to hope they would never run into each other, and he supposed refusing his son the right to sit with his own grandpa in church would serve no purpose. So, Toby took off on a run, despite Noah's warning to walk, and rushed into his grandfather's arms, quickly climbing into his lap. Immediately, Gerald Carson angled his head around in search of Noah.

Their eyes met, and Noah gave him a begrudging, unsmiling nod, then walked to his usual pew at the back of the church.

Following the reverend's sermon on forgiveness, which Noah had intentionally blocked out in order to dwell on his boat plans, he stood in the lobby area and waited for Toby. Trouble was, the lad got caught up in talking to one of his little Sunday school friends who'd been sitting in the row in front of him, which meant his plan to duck out immediately afterward had been thwarted. His aunt and uncle were engaged in conversation with another couple, while his father met the reverend, both gesturing with their hands as they talked and even found something to chuckle over. What normal, thinking person would ever have conceived one year ago the drunk, Gerald Carson, carrying on a civil conversation with a preacher? Noah wondered if the preacher had one clue about his father's history.

On either side of him, people poured past, some greeting Noah with a smile, nod, or handshake, others hardly noticing him, evidently eager to get to their Sunday dinners. Peter Sinclair hurried by, unaware of him, as far as Noah could tell. "Peter!" someone called from the opposite end of the foyer. It was Peter's uncle, Roland Withers, president of Sandy Shores Bank and Trust. Weaving his robust body through the crowd, he reached his nephew at the door and said, "Your aunt wants to know if you're bringing Abbie Ann for dinner today." In the open entryway, their voices carried. Of course, it helped that Noah had edged a bit closer, his back to the pair as he pretended to be studying a sign, pinned to a corkboard, that read:

April 20 – 6:00 p.m.
Potluck Dinner in Church Basement
Followed by Missionary Speaker,
Edmund Harding

"No, she's not coming," he answered.

"Oh, that's too bad. The Halsteads are coming over, and Opal was hoping you and Abbie…well, you must be going to her place, then."

"No, I'll be home for dinner," Peter said, lowering his voice.

"Oh? And Abbie?"

"She…has other plans."

The two continued conversing, but their voices were drowned out as a flock of boys, Jesse Devlin among them, raced toward the door, talking in a flurry of excited chatter about getting together a game of baseball later that week. Spring had definitely hit Sandy Shores, if baseball talk was in the air. Noah inched a little closer to Sinclair and Roland Withers, the meddlesome side to him unable to resist eavesdropping. Thankfully, an elderly couple stood between them, blocking Noah's view of Peter's back but not preventing his ears from picking up on his words.

"We had a bit of a tiff last night, having to do with that ladies' club of hers."

"That girl's strong willed," said Peter's uncle with a hint of disdain.

"You've got that right. She's paying a visit to the Rogan family today—asked me to come with her—but I've suggested she's already done her fair share for that woman and her daughters and ought to let Sheriff Devlin conduct an investigation instead of getting involved in the couple's marital disputes. She claims Shamus abuses his wife."

"You're not going out there, I hope?"

Peter shook his head. "I think it's best I stay out of it, and I wish she'd do the same."

"Let Jacob take her, if she insists on going. You have your reputation to uphold. You start sticking your nose in that family's business, and Shamus will move his funds elsewhere."

"My thoughts, exactly."

It was all Noah could do to keep from strangling both of them—and in the house of the Lord, no less. To keep from blowing a gasket, he turned away and went in search of Abbie Ann Kane.

K

Abbie still couldn't believe Noah's insistence on escorting her to the Rogans', and she remained in the dark as to how he'd even gotten wind of her planned excursion. When asked, he refused to enlighten her, saying only that he wouldn't hear of her going alone. Of course, she'd protested, claiming not to need his assistance.

"If you're worried I plan to kiss you again, you can relax," he'd quipped, leaning in close as several churchgoers exited through the double doors, including Katrina, who had given her a light poke in the side as she passed. She'd pretended it had been an accident, but by her mischievous, furtive glance, Abbie knew Katrina had been saying she noticed her talking to Noah.

"That is the last thing on my mind," Abbie had replied, jutting out her chin and trying to sound convincing. "I've already told you, that was a onetime occurrence."

He grinned. "And I didn't argue it, did I?" No; in fact, he'd called it some sort of test, as she recalled, but what he'd been testing, she still had no notion. "What time shall I pick you up?"

"If you insist on taking me, then one o'clock should be sufficient, but I wouldn't mind taking the train. It's just as quick, if not quicker."

"I prefer to pick you up. No need to use public transportation when I have a perfectly good horse that needs the exercise. Old girl gets downright lazy on Sunday afternoons, otherwise."

So, here they were, taking the same route she and Hannah had traversed mere days ago, Noah's broad body bumping against hers as they jostled along in his ramshackle rig, reminding her of the night he'd insisted on driving her home. It seemed he didn't like taking no for an answer. As she'd done that night, she kept her hands tightly clasped in her lap, her shoulders back, and her spine as straight as an arrow. Gray storm clouds loomed overhead, looking like the rain variety, the way they gathered in gloomy puffs of smoke-like mist, moving as though pushed by a fierce locomotive.

"We might be in for a storm," Noah said, as if reading her mind.

"I was thinking the same thing. I suppose we're due for one, after several days in a row of sunshine." He nodded, guiding Ruby Sue to the side of the road to allow another rig to pass. "It would help to melt the last of the snow," she added.

"And make way for the next snowfall. You know there'll probably be another."

"Don't even say it. I'm quite ready for spring, thank you very much."

He chuckled softly, the sound warming her bones. "You said Toby went to Lyle Constant's house for the day?" she asked. "The Constants are a very nice family. I've noticed Lyle and Toby sitting by each other in Sunday school. I think perhaps they might even have the same schoolteacher—Mrs. Wescott, is it?"

He glanced at her. "I'm impressed you'd know that. You do a pretty good job of keeping track of your little charges. You've sure won Toby's heart."

Abbie smiled. "And he mine. He's got the cutest little face and the sweetest personality."

"He takes after his father, of course."

Out of the corner of her eye, she caught his grin and couldn't help but giggle. "Is that so? And what of the former Mrs. Carson?" she quickly asked, bracing herself for his reaction to her boldness. "Does he take after her, as well?"

"In looks, maybe. She is very pretty," he said, surprising her with his matter-of-factness. "But about as sweet as a teaspoon of vinegar."

Fully expecting him to change the subject, she chanced another question. "How long were you married?"

"Just short of seven years," he offered. The news thumped her hard in the chest. Whatever was she doing sharing a wagon seat with a man who'd been married for seven years? "None of them was terribly happy," he added, "with the exception of the first year or so. I was a young buck, infatuated and without much in the way of brains, when I married her. Toby came along early on, so, for that reason, I tried to stick it out with her."

"I'm sorry—about the unhappy part, not your lack of brains."

He chuckled. "You have a way with words, you know that?"

"It's a talent, I suppose," Abbie joked. "So, your unhappiness led to the divorce?"

"That, and her blatant infidelity. Let's just say marriage never did suit her. She's not a one-man sort of woman. Matter of fact, I don't doubt she's already having a hard time of it staying married to her newest fling—my former partner, by the way."

"Oh." His sudden candor shocked her. She wondered if that had been his goal. Blowing out a whistled breath, she decided not to let his words intimidate her. "Does she stay in contact with Toby?"

"Not in the least. She has no interest in mothering him, never has. She took me for all I was worth, except for Toby, the best part of me. I had a lucrative shipbuilding company out East that interested her far more than her son. You might say she was willing to make the trade."

"Oh, my goodness." Unexpected tears welled up in her eyes as a knot that seemed the size of a boulder stuck in her throat. "I can't imagine a woman—a mother—forsaking her child in such a way. How did Toby take that?"

"He used to ask about her a lot more, but I think he's learning to accept that she's a part of his past. It's hard to know what goes on in the head of a six-year-old, you know? Actually, you probably do know better than I when it comes to that sort of thing."

They bumped along, and, for a while, both sat in a kind of uncomfortable silence as Abbie tried to rein in her emotions and let this latest information sink in. Who knew what thoughts he harbored? Did he regret having divulged so much?

A flock of birds soared overhead, squawking to one another as they came to perch in a leafless tree alongside the well-trodden road. "How did you come to own a shipbuilding business?" Abbie ventured to ask.

"I learned the trade from my father, actually. From there, my passion grew. One thing led to another, and I formed a partnership with—a friend."

"Not with your father, the no-good bum who showed up at the warehouse yesterday and at church this morning?" she remarked on impulse.

"No, not my father. I went with my double-crossing friend, instead. 'Course, at the time, I had no idea he had eyes for my wife. As you can see, I like to choose my partners carefully." He gave a bawdy laugh, then angled her a short-lived glance. "You say you saw my father at church?"

"Your aunt reintroduced me to him before the morning service. We sort of met in passing yesterday, you'll recall."

"Sorry that I was in no mood to do the formal honors."

"I understand. I could tell his stopping by didn't give you an overwhelming sense of joy."

"Ha! Now, there's an understatement."

"Hmm, I must say, he seems like a pretty nice bum." She studied him at close range, noting the sudden fixing of his jaw, the way his eyes narrowed on the road ahead, his thick brows crinkling.

He squared his shoulders and looked at her, longer this time, his shapely lips curving into a not-so-warm smile. "He claims to have had some sort of conversion experience. He's been a drunk as far back as I can remember, and I attribute my mother's early passing to the way he treated her."

"That's a pretty harsh thing to say, Noah."

"It is, isn't it? But you didn't live with him," he said, setting his eyes on the road again. They were drawing nearer to the Rogan home, but Abbie felt an urgency to continue the conversation. Who knew if they'd have the opportunity to do so on their ride back to town? By then, Noah may have closed himself up tighter than a drum.

"Don't you believe that God can transform a person from the inside out?"

"Sometimes, maybe…just not a person like Gerald Carson."

"No? Well, maybe you should give your father—and the Lord—a chance to prove you wrong."

His response came in total silence. Still, Abbie pressed on, even as the Rogan house came into full view. "Have you experienced a heart change, Noah? Invited Christ to take control of your life?"

Seconds lapsed, and she practiced patience. "A long time ago, I guess," he finally muttered. "My mother told me about the Lord and helped me pray this little prayer of confession." He chuckled. "I don't think it stuck, though."

When Abbie prepared to speak a word of encouragement, a cloud opened up and started spitting heavy droplets of rain down on them. Noah urged Ruby Sue into a faster gait, after which their conversation all but ended, with the exception of his telling her to cover her head with the blanket he had stored beneath the seat. When they pulled into the drive, he grabbed the covered basket she'd brought along and helped her down from the wagon, and off they set on a run through the rain. On her jaunt up the porch steps, she cast a gaze at the neighbor's house and saw a curtain flutter shut.

Someone had been watching them—again.

K

By Noah's standards, the Rogans lived in utter squalor. If it were true that Shamus held down a decent-paying job and had money to spare in the bank but issued his wife only a paltry allowance on which to barely survive, then he was nothing but a raunchy miser. Of course, Noah already had that pretty well figured out, considering how the fellow had run him off the road in one of his drunken stupors, not to mention the rest of the negative talk he'd heard around town about him.

Arlena Rogan looked about as frail as a newborn calf, and her daughters were mostly reserved—well, with the exception of Virginia. She'd met them at the door with an aimed rifle, which Abbie had coaxed her into surrendering for a thick slice of her grandmother's peanut butter pie. Noah was trying to think what he could surrender in order to earn a piece for himself.

He admired the way Abbie ministered to Arlena Rogan and her girls, showing them unconditional love, speaking kind, cheering words, and helping them finish chores around the house before their father's homecoming: changing bed linens, washing a pile of dishes, and sweeping the floor, all the while coaching them with more patience than he could have mustered on the importance of working together as a team. "You remember how Dr. Van Huff said your mother needs your help in order to regain her strength?" she asked them. They gave ready nods, so she added, "Well, he's right, and with your father getting out of jail tomorrow, there's no telling what to expect. I suggest you all try to be on your best behavior."

To make himself useful, Noah had volunteered to wash the windows, replace a couple of broken ones, and fix the front door, which hung crooked on its hinges. Thankfully, the box he always carried in the back of his wagon was full of all the necessary tools and supplies. Windows and doors he could handle; women and girls, not so much. He listened to their chatter as he worked but refrained from speaking as much as possible.

"Pa's a meanie," young Margaret said from the sink while drying the plate Abbie had handed off to her. "Sometimes he hits Mama."

"Don't tell things like that, Margaret June," Virginia scolded her, taking the dry dish from her sister's hands and stacking it on a cupboard shelf.

"Well, it's true," the middle girl, Fiona, put in, sweeping a pile of dirt into a corner. "Mama don't do nothin' wrong, and he hauls off and punches her."

"Girls," their mother spoke from the living room, where she was reclining on a ragged sofa, covered by a tattered blanket, her face as pale as a summer moon. "Please don't…make trouble."

With all the mental strength he could manage, Noah kept his mouth clamped shut, exchanging glances with Abbie from across the room as he finished washing the last window and she the last dish, he wringing out the dirty washrag and setting it on the cold cement floor, she squeezing out the dishrag and laying it on a hook to dry. He would have liked to stand in the shadows when Shamus Rogan laid a hand to his wife so he could step out, twist his skinny neck, and watch him struggle for breath. No woman deserved maltreatment. Visions of the abuse his mother had suffered at the hands of his father came back with an evil vengeance, as did bits and pieces of the reverend's morning message on forgiveness. Although he'd blocked out most of it, there had been parts he couldn't quite dismiss. Even now, a verse from the book of Matthew, *"But if ye forgive not men their trespasses, neither will your Father forgive your trespasses,"* stuck to him like glue.

Rain was coming down in torrents when he opened the front door to fling the bucket of dirty water out over the yard. He watched as it disappeared in the vast puddles collecting in the drive, wondering what Ruby Sue was thinking when she cast him a weary-eyed look and snorted. *Patient critter,* he thought. It occurred to him that he and Abbie might well be swimming back to town rather than riding. At least, they'd arrive in the same condition as if they'd swum. What he wouldn't do now for a covered rig!

He turned to go back inside when something caught his eye—a movement like someone darting from behind a tree to the side of the house next door; one moment, there, the next, out of sight. He leaned forward as far as he could without completely drenching himself, hoping to catch another glimpse of whatever it was he'd seen—a large dog, a boy, a man, perhaps—or a figment of his imagination. He gave his head a fast shake and reentered the house.

Chapter Nineteen

At four thirty, with the worst of the rain having let up, Noah announced their leave-taking, saying it would be best to head out before the next wave of rain swept through the area. Abbie had to agree, even though it bothered her to have to leave the girls untended—for that's what they were, mere girls, including the mostly helpless Arlena. She worried that when Shamus returned home, her fragile state would anger him, for he would likely expect her to tend him constantly. According to Virginia, it wasn't enough that his daughters were prepared to see to his every need; in his mind, that duty fell solely to the wife. When sober, he could be somewhat reasonable, Virginia explained, but when drunk, the very worst came out in him.

Abbie bit her lip hard and blinked back tears of worry as the rig backed out of the drive. The girls stood in the doorway, their faces long and forlorn, and even Arlena had made it to the door to lift her hand in a wave of gratitude. She knew it was a sin to worry, and that the Bible said to cast your cares on God, but how could she help it when little Fiona was staring back at her with those big, round, mournful eyes?

"Who knows? Maybe jail reformed him," Noah said, trying to encourage her.

She harrumphed. "Wouldn't that be something?"

He leaned into her, giving her a playful jab in the side. "Hey, aren't you the one who lectured me on the way here about how God can transform a person from the inside out?"

She blinked and swallowed. So, he had been listening. "Thank you for the reminder," she said, settling back in the seat and wiping her cheeks as droplets of rain dribbled off the brim of her hat. "And thank you for driving me here today and lending a hand around the house. It was very generous of you. I didn't actually expect you to do that, you know, but I'm thankful you did."

Noah grinned. "You didn't actually expect me to drive you, period," he reminded her. "And you're welcome. I'm truly glad I could help…and glad I insisted on driving you. Sorry about the rain, though."

She looked at him and laughed.

"What?" he asked, his eyebrows raised in innocence.

"That's the first time I've ever heard anyone apologize for the weather. As if we have any control over it!"

He joined her in a hearty chuckle, and their shared mirth made it easier for Abbie to relinquish her worry.

Seeming to know her own way home, Ruby Sue made the turn onto Grant Street with little urging, and as they bumped along, the rain came down a little harder. "If we did have any control over the elements, now would be a good time to call a halt to this cloudburst," Noah said.

She laughed again. "I don't mind getting wet, Noah," she said, meaning it. "And with a name like yours, you shouldn't, either."

He pulled his mouth into an exaggerated frown and groaned. "You're so funny," he said with playful sarcasm. "Do you know how many similar puns I've heard in my lifetime? And here, you thought you had a good one. My name has been the butt of so many pathetic attempts at humor, it's... well, it's not even funny." At that, they laughed again.

"Really? Lots of people have poked fun at your name?"

"Are you kidding? How could they not? My name is Noah, and I build boats. Think about it, Miss Kane."

"You're right!" she exclaimed. "Why haven't I ever thought of it in that light?"

He shook his head in wonder. "Why not, indeed?"

Ruby Sue led the rig straight into a pothole, pitching Abbie into Noah's side. In her endeavor to right herself, Abbie overcompensated and, with the next bump, nearly fell off altogether. Indeed, she might have, had Noah not quickly reached out and pulled her to his side, the strength of his grip impressing her, even as she feared falling.

"You best hang on to my arm," he said. "This old wagon appears to be riding rougher than usual. I think I'll slow her down, even with this rain, if you don't mind."

Abbie sensed a hint of concern in his voice but passed it off. "Like I said, I don't mind a little rain. Besides, we don't have that many blocks to go."

The raindrops continued pelting them, and Abbie found herself nestling closer to Noah just to stay warm.

"So, are you going to tell me why you and Sinclair didn't sit together in church today?" he asked, turning his gaze on her for the briefest instant, his crystal-blue eyes grazing her face as water droplets trickled between them and down his straight nose.

"We...we had a parting of ways," Abbie said, deciding that since he'd freely answered her questions earlier, it was only fair she do the same now.

"Did you wind up telling him you came to see me yesterday?"

"No. Why would I?"

The sound of his laughter must surely have reached inside the houses they passed. "I think you know very well why you might have told him. But, of course, that would have created an even bigger rift between you, right?"

She chose to ignore his remark, and had it not been for the cold air and the rough ride, she might even have slid away from him. "He thinks I ought to drop out of the W.C.T.U."

"That so? What reason does he give?"

She shrugged. "It's not good for public image, or some such thing. The bottom line is, he's worried how my involvement will look to his big-money customers at the bank."

"Sort of shallow, don't you think?"

"Exactly. He hates that I'm so vocal about women's suffrage and prohibition, to be exact. The other issues—locating a home for abused women and children, promoting child labor laws and fair and equal employment, and so on—they don't pose nearly as big a problem to him. But the others? Phew!"

"There is the matter of Sheriff Devlin, Abbie. Your own brother-in-law has told you to back down from the organization."

"Temporarily," she reminded him. "Peter would like me to pull out altogether, as would his uncle."

"His uncle."

"They'd like to turn me into a puppet!" she exclaimed.

He raised an eyebrow impishly. "I can't quite see anyone succeeding at that."

The rain poured down at a slant now, thoroughly drenching both of them. A little rain was fine, but a downpour? Ruby Sue stepped up her clip of her own accord, and Abbie shivered without warning. "Snuggle up," Noah said in an ordering tone.

"I am." She didn't know how she could get much closer to him.

"Here." He thrust a big arm around her and pulled her tight to his side, then reached up and gave the front of her hat a friendly little tug. *This feels lovely*, she nearly said aloud.

"So, you and Sinclair separated, did you?"

She started to respond, but they hit another bump in the road, and she suddenly went into survival mode. Everything happened so fast, and yet in apparent slow motion, that, while she later could barely recall the details of what transpired next, strangely, every second seemed to flash before her eyes in a slow sequence. One moment, she'd been sitting snugly next to Noah, the next, sliding off the wagon seat and spiraling toward the ground. Noah's hand grasped hold of her arm to keep her from falling, but to no avail, as he slipped right along with her. She vaguely heard a scream escape her throat and felt a jab of pain surge through her backside as she landed on something sharp—a rock, perhaps?—then felt the weight of Noah's body knock the wind from her lungs as he landed square on top of her with a thud. The wagon had tipped precariously on its side and covered their bodies like a broken-down shack with a leaky roof. Ruby Sue squealed in fright, dancing and pawing and making a regular racket.

When Abbie dared open her eyes, she was nose to nose with Noah, his breath hot on her face as he stared at her for at least a solid minute before moving, probably trying to process what had just happened. As far as she could tell, she wasn't hurt, save for the sharp object stabbing her posterior and the pressure of Noah's weight on top of her. Thankfully, it seemed they were in a ditch, and the bulk of the wagon's burden straddled the sloped sides above. Without the ditch, they would surely have been crushed. Abbie silently gave thanks to the Lord for His divine protection as Noah scrambled to adjust his weight so they could attempt to slide out. However, the back of his coat had caught on a protruding spring, stopping his progress. "Are you all right?" he asked. He managed to go up on one elbow, giving her much-needed relief.

"I'm—fine—I think," she stammered weakly. "You?"

"Same." He tried to reach behind him to free his coat, but to no avail.

"Here, let me try," Abbie said, looping her arm around his back in an attempt to reach the coat. "It's like a big, rusty spring or something." As it was, they were pinned so tightly together, he couldn't even unbutton his coat to get it off. "I think—I found—no, I can't quite reach it."

"Can you rip it—my coat?"

She tugged but couldn't get a good grip. "No, it's out of my reach." And so, they lay there awkwardly, Noah doing his best to move, but on either side of them was higher ground; in front of them was a stationary piece of the buckboard, blocking their ability to inch forward. At their feet, the rig had fallen, leaving nary a crawl space.

"What do you think happened?" she asked. Rain continued pelting the wagon, and, while their temporary shelter kept their faces dry, water flooded down the sides of the ditch, soaking Abbie's backside. Would her wool coat ever come clean? *But that should be the least of my concerns*, she chided herself. Escaping this pit came first on her list of priorities—that, and getting Noah Carson's body off of her so she could catch a decent breath of air.

"We lost a wheel; came clean off and rolled down that incline. Could be, the fellow at Jeb's Wagon and Wheel Repair didn't fix it properly last month, but I don't know. It shouldn't have fallen off. Besides, because of the age of this rig, I'm obsessive about checking the condition of the wheels and bearings. Inspected them just this morning before church, in fact, and they were all fine." He grunted and winced.

"Are you sure you're not hurt?" Abbie asked.

"No, probably just bruised a little, but you're the one who took the fall first. I'm sorry about this. You don't think you broke anything, do you?"

"Broke anything?"

"Like bones?"

"Oh, no. Just...." But how could she properly tell him where she most hurt?

"What?" His expression, or what she could see of it in their dimly lit, prison-like setting, sagged with worry. "Are you in pain?"

"Uh, I've...landed on something, and my...derrière... does hurt some."

"Well, shoot." In desperation, he pushed at the "roof," which was really the rig's side, in an attempt to hoist it even a fraction, but all he got from his effort was a red face. "It won't budge. Is there anything I can do for you?"

"Yes. Get off me," she jested.

"I'm sorry I can't move. There's just nowhere to go."

"It's all right; don't fret. Someone will come by soon."

To avoid their noses touching, she turned her face to the side. Icy mud oozed down her cheek, but she couldn't even free her hand to wipe it. "Here." Noah turned her face toward him and swabbed off the worst of the mud with the pad of his thumb before it reached her eye.

"Thank you," she whispered, trying to avoid looking at his mouth, even though it aligned perfectly with her vision. How she possibly could have found this moment the least bit enchanting, she did not know, but there it was, and it made her heart thump unexpectedly. Kissing would be completely out of the question, unthinkable, actually, but, my, his eyes did shine with such intensity. Rather than dwell on the idea, though, she took the prudent route and decided to strike up a conversation.

"Oh, I do hate predicaments, don't you? But the challenge of them makes me want to go in search of a humorous side."

"A humorous side? Uh, I think you'd be hard-pressed to find one this time."

"Really? Well, how's this, for starters? Do you realize this is the third falling incident between us? The first was that night when I fell on your front porch; the second, your stumbling over something in the warehouse when Jesse and I came over. What do you think we'll fall into next?"

"I don't know. Love, maybe?"

Her head reeled, and she dared look into his eyes. "What?"

He laughed, and she felt it rumble clear to her spine. "It was just a thought. You said you were looking for something humorous in all of this. Think of it—your falling in love with a divorced man, my falling for a naïve, little wisp of a girl. You don't think that'd be, well, a trifle amusing?"

Her heart tripped. "No. Yes. I have no idea, because it's an absurd notion. And I'm not naïve, either," she tacked on.

"No? How old are you, anyway? Eighteen? Nineteen? You never have told me."

His impression that she was still an adolescent gave her a strong urge to slap him, but then, that would surely confirm her lack of maturity. She huffed in annoyance. "I'll have you know, I'll be twenty-two this year."

"Hmm." He lifted an eyebrow. "All of that." He turned his gaze upward. "So, what do you suppose folks will say to a Sunday school teacher spending time under a wagon with a divorced man?"

"Oh, for goodness' sake, you're a troublemaker, Noah Carson. You don't think they'll print this in the *Sandy Shores Tribune*, do you?"

"Oh, I hope they do. In fact, I'll see to it. That would put an end to it, for sure."

"An end to what?"

"Why, to Sinclair's pursuit of you."

"Besides troublemaker, I can now add conniving scamp."

"Oh, the scandal. Can't you see the headlines now? 'Woman's Christian Temperance Union Leader Caught in Questionable Position under Wagon with Local Shipbuilder.'"

"Oh, my." In spite of herself, she laughed, and he joined in. "It would be completely incorrect, of course, since there is no 'questionable' activity involved."

"Want to bet?"

Just like that, he lowered his face, which didn't have far to go, and planted a warm, moist, toe-curling kiss on her mouth. For the second time, Abbie realized how very much she'd been missing in Peter's dry, stiff, boring kisses. Why, the way Noah's lips fit hers to perfection made her think delicious thoughts—like what it would be like to live out her life with Noah Carson, the shipbuilder, to call Toby her son, to share a cozy little house with them, to walk together to church.... *Church.* That single word brought up the matter of Noah's faith—or, rather, the lack thereof. Why, hadn't he confessed earlier that he didn't truly walk with God? Peter at least did that much. Oh, bother! What on earth was she doing? In her urgency to put a halt to their intimacy, she turned her face away and sputtered at him, "I thought you promised you weren't going to kiss me today."

Breathless, he gave his head a little shake and squinted down at her, his mouth crinkling up at the corners. "Did I actually promise that?"

"Oh, this...this is ridiculous. Help! Somebody!" she screamed at the top of her lungs.

As if God had immediately petitioned His angels to come to her rescue, she heard the rumbling of a wagon at close range.

"Help!" she repeated, screaming with everything she had in her.

"I think all of Sandy Shores has heard you, by now."

Ruby Sue neighed, and someone called out a loud, "Whoa!" They heard the pound of approaching footsteps, along with a chorus of frenzied male voices. Angling her head just so, Abbie was able to peek through a tiny opening, and she saw men's boots, about three or four pairs of them.

"Anybody down there?" someone asked.

"Yes, yes! Help us!" she called out. Then, to Noah, she yelled, "Tell them to help us!"

He slanted her a bemused expression. "I think they got the message."

Chapter Twenty

B oatbuilding took up the better share of Noah's mind, time, and attention in the days to follow. It took a full week to lay down the plywood and carry out the lofting process—making a full-sized drawing of the ship. While many boatbuilders detested this task, due to its sheer tediousness, and sought out ready-made plans, not to mention paid an arm and a leg for the standard-size drawings, Noah enjoyed the practice of transferring the dimensions from the plans to the actual full-sized plywood part he'd need to build the boat. It required drawing a grid on the plywood in twelve-inch increments, assuring its precision using a carpenter's square, and crossing out dimensions from his drawing with his pencil so as not to lose his place in the middle of lofting a part. As each element of the section he lofted began to take shape, he'd stand back at a distance and compare his drawings with the plywood to make sure the full-sized part he'd lofted looked the same, proportion-wise. If it didn't, he'd check his measurements again, then make the necessary corrections. Once he was sure that each full-sized part of the plywood had the same contour as its to-scale equivalent on his drawing, he started cutting out the plywood sections and stacking them in a corner of the warehouse.

The mere task of carrying each piece to the pile, and watching that pile grow, brought a sense of satisfaction as he began to envision the boat taking shape, and he grew anxious to start the assembling process. Of course, much had to be done before he reached the assembling stage—building the cross sections about every two feet down the length of the boat to form the basis of the mold, for one thing. That's what would really define the shape of the hull.

Much to his dismay, and despite his orders for him to stay away, his father had taken to stopping by unannounced to check on Noah's progress. His interest in his son's work was something he'd never showed before, and he continued to offer his assistance. Often, he'd pull up the one and only stool in the place and sit down to watch—like he had the right. Noah made every effort to ignore his presence, particularly when the fellow tried engaging him in conversation. He either didn't "get" that Noah hadn't thrown out the welcome mat, or it made no difference to him that most of their conversations wound up being one-sided, Gerald doing the talking, Noah humming to himself and feigning indifference.

Of course, if Toby happened to be about during his grandfather's visits, he'd often climb into his lap and look on from there. He'd hauled several of his toys over to the warehouse, and, sometimes, he'd talk his grandpa into playing a game of checkers, tossing a rubber ball back and forth, or putting together a puzzle. To Noah's surprise, the man got right down on the floor with the lad to participate in whatever activity he chose. He'd never paid this much attention to Toby in Connecticut, but then, he hadn't been sober for more than a few days at a time, either. As much as Noah hated to admit it, he did appreciate not having to think up things to keep his son entertained when his father was there. Usually, it wasn't an issue, as he mostly worked during the day while Toby was at school, disciplining himself to stop at suppertime. But there were days when, in the middle of an important step, he and Toby would eat a quick bite, then head back to the warehouse. Toby didn't mind doing this, thankfully, as it often meant a later bedtime. Plus, Gerald often stopped by on those evenings.

Abbie Ann never drifted far from his thoughts, and many were the times he'd wander up Water Street at lunchtime for a quick bite at Pat's Eatery, only to come up with some excuse or another to stop by the Whatnot afterward. Sometimes, she was there, and sometimes, not. Since her sister, Hannah, had resumed working at the store a few hours a day, Noah seemed to see less of Abbie and wondered if he shouldn't just show up on the Kanes' doorstep one day and make it known that he'd like to see her again. Whether she felt the same remained unclear, as the last few times he'd run into her, she'd given him the cold shoulder. It was probably because of that kiss under the wagon, which he hadn't exactly planned but also didn't regret for a second. For one thing, it cemented even more a few things in his mind: she definitely interested him, he wanted to see more of her, and the very notion of her spending one more moment courting with Peter Sinclair made his stomach twist into a tangled knot. He'd been encouraged, though, to see that they hadn't shared a church pew for the past few Sundays.

He couldn't believe he'd allowed himself to care for her, particularly since he'd told himself repeatedly over the past months he didn't need another woman to complicate his life—especially not a spitfire like Abbie Kane. He supposed the front-page article in the *Tribune* hadn't helped matters, either, as it left no question that the two of them had been together.

He'd half expected Sinclair to show up at the warehouse for a man-to-man. Had he stopped pursuing Abbie, given up on them without a fight? Somehow, Noah had to find out. Maybe he'd ride out to her place tonight after supper, with Toby, of course, and show off his new, two-seated buggy with an enclosed top. With the advance Don Clayton had given him and what savings he'd managed to put away from his other earnings, he'd decided he could shell out seventy-five dollars for a new rig—one with decent springs, comfortable seats, and four good wheels. Who knew but what his next vehicle might be the motorized version? Those newfangled automobiles were becoming the talk of the town, as manufacturers sought daily to improve quality and increase quantity.

Yes, that is what he'd do—hitch up Ruby Sue to the new rig and ride straight over there, if for no other reason than to thank Helena Kane for those delicious cornbread muffins she'd baked for him several weeks back.

𝒦

"Oh, it is so lovely to walk into the Whatnot and find you behind the cash register again, Miss Hannah," said Gertie Pridmore, placing a few sewing supplies on the counter along with some cans of vegetables, a dustpan, and several mousetraps. "The whole town missed you so much. Don't get me wrong, it's wonderful you've been spending time with that brand-new baby of yours, but we've all been counting down the days till your return."

Hannah started ringing up Gertie's items, smiling all the while. "Well, thank you, Gertie. I have to admit, I missed all of you, as well. I love being a mother to my three precious ones, but running the Whatnot is a great pleasure to me, too."

"You're not hoping to see less of me, I hope, Gertie," Abbie joshed from the front of the store, where she stood stocking shelves. "All right, so I made a couple of blunders in calculating your bills. That's no reason to go all batty and beside yourself over my sister's coming back to the Whatnot."

"Oh, Abbie, you're so silly. Of course, we want to see just as much of you as always, maybe just not behind the cash register," Gertie teased.

It was true. Abbie had botched a couple of Gertie's orders, and a few others', for that matter, but who didn't make the occasional honest mistake? Hannah, that's who—impeccable, particular, perfectionist Hannah. Well, so be it. She, Abbie, wasn't cut out for running the Whatnot, and she'd be the first to admit her joy at welcoming Hannah back to work.

As she reached up to put the last few jars of pickles on a top shelf, she asked Gertie, "Are you coming to our W.C.T.U. meeting tonight?"

"Oh, mercy, yes. I'm ever so glad to see we're resuming them. You've had no more threats, I assume? And the sheriff's granted his approval to reconvene?"

"Yes, although not without argument, right, Hannah?"

"He believes in the organization, of course, but he's hesitant about Abbie playing a key role in light of those awful threats."

"Which have effectively ceased," Abbie put in. "My brother-in-law is an overprotective sort."

"He is only doing his duty, Abbie Ann Kane," Hannah scolded. "You should be glad he's looking out for you."

"Oh, I am, I am, but he needn't worry so. I have all the ladies watching over me like mother hens, as well."

Gertie picked up her cloth bag, full of her purchases, thanked Hannah, and headed toward the door. "Did the sheriff ever determine who might have been behind those suspicious events?" she asked Abbie.

Abbie wiped her dusty hands on her apron and shook her head. "He tried matching up the handwriting from the notes with a few men's around town, particularly Erv Baxter's, but with little success. In questioning him, he said Erv vehemently denied any involvement, saying he'd be a fool to follow through on his previous threat, particularly since others had heard him make it. Besides, he said that while he considers me a nuisance, he doesn't necessarily wish me undue harm." Abbie shrugged. "All I know is, Gabe's agreed to allow us to resume our meetings as long as we keep them to an hour, so as to dismiss before dark."

"That's reasonable," Gertie said.

"And he's ordered us to desist holding prayer vigils in or near the saloons, at least until further notice."

"Good. I don't like those things, anyway. They tend to give me the creeps," Gertie said. "I went more or less out of a sense of duty, and because I knew it meant a great deal to you, but I don't like the way those men, and the women, for that matter, look at us with accusing eyes. Besides, it stinks in those places."

"Gertie, sometimes, we have to go into putrid places in order to spread the message of God's love, but let's not get into a debate about it. Let's just say I am willing to make this compromise, as we can pray during our meetings, I suppose, and in the summer, we can meet in the park for public prayer. Gabe shouldn't find any problem with that. Besides, come summer, I'm sure all of this will have become no more than a distant memory."

Gertie paused at the door. "Let us hope so. I'll see you tonight, then."

That afternoon, the sisters welcomed incoming customers, filled orders, offered assistance, and chatted during the lulls, Hannah catching Abbie up on little Alex's latest tricks, Jesse's excellent marks in school, and young RoseAnn's eating and sleeping habits. They also discussed Abbie's recent break with Peter Sinclair. She didn't love him, she confessed.

"Did Noah Carson play a part in your decision, by any chance?" Hannah asked, settling herself onto a stool behind the counter. They'd decided to take a break from straightening shelves.

"No," Abbie answered in all honesty. "He doesn't profess much of a faith, and I can't abide dating someone lacking love for God. It was more a matter of my not wanting to waste anymore of Peter's time."

"I completely admire you, baby sister. You've grown up on me." Hannah wadded up a piece of paper and tossed it in the wastebasket. "Still, you were trapped under that wagon with Noah Carson for quite some time. Are you going to tell me nothing happened?"

Abbie crooked a finger at her sister, and Hannah bent forward, her face eager. "I'm going to tell you nothing. Period."

In the line of customers coming and going that day was Arlena Rogan. Her daughters were in school, so she entered alone. While she looked stronger and even wore a smile, Abbie couldn't tell if it was genuine or just a front. She questioned her about how things were going, now that her husband had been released from jail, and all too quickly, it seemed, she responded that things had never been better. The girls were fine, she was fine, and Shamus was fine. Everyone was fine.

Except for one thing, Abbie noted: the woman had a bruise on her forehead, albeit mostly covered by the wide brim of her hat, but there it was, nonetheless. When Abbie inquired about it, Arlena touched the spot and promptly produced an answer: while reaching for a can on a top shelf, she'd clumsily allowed it to slip through her fingers, and the thing had tumbled down on her. Of course, neither Abbie nor Hannah bought it, but what could they do beyond praying for protection for the family? Abbie feared something terrible happening before Gabe could make any kind of arrest. Short of clear proof, or Arlena's filing charges against her husband, everyone's hands were painfully tied.

The meeting of the W.C.T.U. went off without a hitch, and to Abbie's great surprise and pleasure, they even welcomed a few new members. Among them was Jane Emery, who brought much to the table, including a lead on a house that might work well as a women's shelter. Situated in the heart of town, the large, two-story structure sat empty next door to the Emerys. The owner had passed away, and her daughter, a Florida resident, wished to either donate it to a worthy cause or sell it at a minimal price. The place would require some work, they were told, but this posed no problem to the ladies, who said they enjoyed a good project. Not only that, but their able-bodied husbands could chip right in, someone chimed, generating a chorus of amens. The matter came up of who would run such a facility, and the consensus was that it would require a compassionate husband and wife team committed to protecting women and children.

Also discussed were plans to provide a lunch for the hard-working teachers of the town, host a spaghetti supper for the elderly, develop a curriculum on nutrition to teach to young mothers, sponsor an auction to raise money for the women's shelter, and write letters of encouragement to the country's servicemen. Promptly at 8:00 p.m., someone made a motion to adjourn the meeting, so Abbie said a closing prayer and dismissed the ladies, reminding them about their next meeting and encouraging them to each bring a friend.

Later, with high hopes and a light step, she set off up Third Street. The sun was just starting to set in the West, a few folks were milling about in front of Jellema Newsstand, and the usual raucous music was coming from Erv's Place, one block over. Fortunately, she did not have to pass the saloon, or she surely would have driven her father's rig. By now, the snow had melted, except in a few spots that always tended to collect high piles of snow that never dissipated totally until early May. She swallowed a fresh breath of brisk air and watched a black squirrel scamper across her path and scurry up a tree, on which she took note of budding branches, and she gave thanks for the changing seasons—particularly the promise of new life brought about by springtime.

Just two blocks from home, a sudden wallop in the center of her back shocked her out of her pleasant reverie. Fortunately, her coat acted as a cushion, so the impact of the golf-ball-sized rock now lying on the road had done her no harm. Rather than set off at a faster pace, she stopped, surveyed her surroundings, and tried to imagine where the rock had come from. Surely, someone had thrown it, for rocks did not fall from trees, but nothing looked amiss. When she should have felt fear, anger came on instead. "Who did that?" she called out, feeling foolish when no response came. Deciding it was just a fluke of nature, she set off again, walking a trifle faster. A dog barked, prompting her to turn at the sound. And that's when she saw the shadow of a man dart from behind a tree and disappear around the corner of a house. The dog's barking escalated, then changed to a frantic-sounding yelp, which was preceded by a sharp, popping sound. Icy-cold chills shot up her spine. Merciful heavens! Was someone following her? The notion spurred her into a jog, her heart tripping as she went. When an approaching wagon pulled up beside her and a male voice called out her name, she nearly jumped straight out of her skin.

"Are you running for any particular reason?" It was Noah Carson, pulling back on Ruby Sue's reins and slanting her one of his endearing, crooked grins as she slowed to a walk, panting heavily. Never had she been so happy to see a familiar face. That it was Noah's only added to her relief. But she wouldn't give away her emotions.

"Just getting my daily exercise," she answered, deciding not to mention the flying rock and then the mysterious man lurking around the neighborhood. The next thing she knew, Noah would be escorting her off to Gabe's office again. No, sirree, this she would keep to herself. "Where's Toby?"

"Boo!" the lad said, jumping up from the floor, a blanket covering his head.

"Whoa! You scared me!" she exclaimed, which wasn't far from fact. "Is that a new rig you're riding in?"

"Indeed, it is," Noah said, looking pleased. "Hop aboard, and we'll take you the rest of the way home."

"Yeah, hop up. We gots two whole seats in this one." In less than a second, Toby leaped to the back, making room for her next to Noah. She probably should have resisted, but in light of what had just transpired, she could not refuse. Tonight, she probably would have accepted a ride from Erv Baxter.

K

He'd sure frightened the little lady. He'd seen red-hot fear in those eyes even from a distance, and the very idea warmed his gut with satisfaction. Oh, she'd wanted him to think of her as fearless, the way she'd hollered out afterward. But the dead calm she got, and that fool dog's incessant barking, had her runnin'! Nothing fearless about her, no sir. Dumb mutt looked ready to attack him, so he'd had to shut him up for good. He didn't like hurting dogs. They were mostly innocent creatures. But that one needed to be silenced, no question.

He hoped she hadn't recognized him, but how could she have, with the sun just starting to set and his hat drawn low on his head, his long coat draped loosely around him to hide his rifle?

In due time, he would reveal himself, and, when he did, he would make it good and clear that he meant business with his threats. He'd thought he'd already done that, but the start-up of those stupid women's meetings exposed her total disregard, not to mention lack of sense. Obviously, she didn't know who she was dealin' with and would need to be taught a lesson.

Something bothered him, though, and he had to give it careful consideration before proceeding. Sandy Shores' newest citizen, Noah Carson, appeared to have a crush on her. He'd hoped the busted wheel might do some serious damage, and it had, of course, but both Noah and Abbie Kane had come out of the incident unscathed. And now, if the fellow wasn't sportin' himself a brand-new rig, actin' all high 'n' mighty and protective, the way he showed up just about the time he meant to throw another stone, this time aiming for the back of the little she-cat's head.

He had time. Plenty of it, matter of fact. Some things just required extra careful planning before comin' to fruition. This might be one of those things.

ᴋ

"How's the boatbuilding coming?" Jacob Kane asked Noah after everyone had taken a seat in the living room later that evening. Abbie looked wary, whether from his unexpected visit or from an unfounded fear that he intended to kiss her again, he didn't know. Of course, he wouldn't kiss her again, especially with Toby looking on. Noah had said they couldn't stay long, since tomorrow was a school day, but Jacob and Helena both insisted they sit at least a few minutes, long enough to have some hot tea and a piece of freshly baked lemon meringue pie. Now, who could resist that, especially with Toby tugging at his sleeve to sit? And it had been his goal, after all, to see Abbie Ann, forget that she looked about as skittish as a cat in a dog kennel and still out of breath with her cup of tea in hand. Why, exactly, had she been running when he'd come upon her? He doubted exercise had been her main motive.

After chewing and swallowing his first bite of pie, he addressed Jacob's question. "Fine, sir. I'm in the lofting process. Won't be long before I'll start bending the ribs. Have to build a steam box before I can do that, though."

Everyone stared at him as if he'd just spoken in some foreign language—well, everyone except for Toby, who'd been living the process with him when he wasn't in school and to whom he'd been explaining things as he went along.

"It must be a complicated endeavor, especially working on your own, as you are," Helena Kane said after taking a sip of tea. Noah's eyes caught and held Abbie's for the briefest second, but she quickly looked down, squared off a piece of pie with her fork, and pushed it around with her fork. Something had happened to set her on edge, but what?

Toby had chosen to sit on the floor at Noah's feet, his plate of pie in his lap as he awkwardly sought a way to eat it without its sliding off. Next to him was a mug of milk, which he eagerly gulped between bites.

"I prefer to work alone, actually. There are certain tasks, like bending the ribs, for example, that go smoother with an extra hand, but it can be mostly a one-man job if you know what you're doing." He looked up at Helena. "Delicious pie, by the way," he said, raising his nearly empty plate. "Is this your own recipe?"

"It came from my grandmother. Please, may we get you another piece? Abbie, get Mr. Carson another piece."

Abbie set her plate and teacup on the tea table and started to rise.

"No, thanks, I'm quite full. But it was delicious." Slowly, Abbie lowered herself back down. He noted that most of her pie sat untouched, and she made no move to finish it.

"So, Miss Kane, I heard the sheriff gave you permission to resume your temperance union meetings," Noah said. "I ran into Lester Emery on the sidewalk this evening, and we talked a while. I met Lester a few weeks ago, doing some business at the bank, by the way. Nice fellow. Anyway, he passed the word along about your meeting; also told me his wife planned to attend."

Abbie sat a little straighter, took up her teacup, and sipped. "Yes, she brought a lot of fine ideas to the table for discussion. I was so pleased to have her join us."

He nodded and sipped his tea, as well, studying her over the rim of his cup. Setting the cup down, he said, "I take it you didn't run into any problems, then. No rocks sailing through windows?"

He didn't think anyone but he noticed the way her spine went stiff as a board.

"Of course not."

"There'd better not have been, or I'll put my foot down about these meetings," Jacob said. *Good for him*, thought Noah. "Abbie knows I'm not thrilled about her starting up the meetings again, but if you haven't yet figured out my Abbie, Mr. Carson, just let me say, she sets her mind to something, and there's no stopping her. May as well be talking to a doorknob."

"Papa!"

"Well…."

Noah couldn't help it. He burst out laughing. "I think I have seen that side to her, sir, and while I'm thinking about it, please call me Noah."

"Fine enough, if you'll call me Jacob."

Abbie's lips pursed into a straight little line. Cute.

"You and Toby must come for Sunday dinner sometime," Helena put in, standing up to gather the empty dishes. Abbie followed suit, taking Toby's plate but not his cup of milk, which he was still working on. She looked at Noah's empty plate, and he winked as he handed it off to her.

"Yes, yes, that's a great idea," Jacob said, giving up his plate and teacup to Helena. "How about this Sunday? I'd love to hear more about your project. We've barely gotten the chance to get acquainted, so Sunday dinner would be perfect for that."

"And we can invite Hannah and Gabe and the family. Oh, and how about Rita James?" Helena suggested.

"Rita?" Jacob asked, a sudden croak developing in his throat. "Well, now we're talking a houseful."

"Oh, bosh. We're used to housefuls. What do you say, Mr. Carson? Would this Sunday work with your schedule?"

Abbie had stayed quiet on the matter. Noah captured her eyes where she stood, looking for a hint of approval. He decided to venture into murky waters. "What about Mr. Sinclair? Will he be joining us?"

Now, she shot him a most unnerving glare.

"Oh, well, Mr. Sinclair...." Helena's voice lowered to a respectful hush. She shook her head from side to side, her brow etched deeply, as if to announce the pope's passing. "He seems to have left the scene."

"I see," Noah said, elation bubbling in his chest. "That's too bad. Well, you can count on Toby and me to be here. Yes, indeed, this Sunday should work perfectly."

Chapter Twenty-one

It took guts to walk into Kane's Whatnot near closing time a few days later, the annoying bell above the door jingling to announce his arrival, but guts he had. With his hat drawn low and his shoulders hunched, he surveyed the place. There she was, standing at the back, assisting an old couple with their order and flapping her tongue about the benefits of exercise or some such nonsense. She glanced up at the sound of the bell, so he quickly ducked behind a display shelf.

"I'll be right with you," she called out.

"No need," he answered, though none too audibly.

With an uncommon sense of audacity, he walked toward the cash register. A few other customers mingled about, but, thankfully, no one paid him any mind. A young squirt not much older than five or six had wandered away from his mother, though, and looked him full in the face. Curling his upper lip at the boy and narrowing his eyes, he bent at the waist and whispered, "What's you lookin' at?"

"That scar you gots on your cheek," the boy replied, undaunted.

Quickly, he plastered his hand across the slash mark, angered with himself for not having covered it with his scarf. "Ain't anybody ever taught you not to stare?"

The boy didn't flinch; he just stared the harder. "Nope."

He made a sneering sound, then moved the rest of the way up to the counter, taking a rumpled piece of paper from his pocket and opening it for a final perusal.

Duz it bother you that sumbody iz watchen you?

Satisfied, he refolded the paper so that the words "To Miss Kane" appeared on the front and laid it under a paperweight next to the cash register. Lifting his gaze to the wall behind the counter, he spotted a work schedule and grinned to himself. The names Jacob, Rita, Hannah, and Abbie were listed vertically with days and hours after them. He took special note of Abbie's times, committing them to memory.

Turning, he observed the boy still watching him through probing eyes.

He issued his coldest possible smile. "Go find your ma, kid."

"She ain't here," he replied.

"Oh. Well, then, go find whoever it is you came in with. Yer a royal pest."

The boy murmured something when he turned his back, but he missed it as he sauntered to the door and then stepped out into the mist-filled, dreary day. Next stop: Erv's Place for some nice, cold beers. Might be, he'd even find himself a warm woman.

K

Abbie locked the door and flipped the OPEN sign around so that it read CLOSED to passersby. At the back of the store, Toby busied himself on the floor with one of the many puzzles kept stored in a toy box in the corner. Many were the children who entered Kane's Whatnot with their parents, only to make a beeline for that toy box Hannah had decided to fill with a bunch of Jesse's old toys. The only stipulation she attached to it was that the children had to return the toys before exiting the store, and for the most part, they, or their parents, abided by the unwritten rule.

Jesse had walked Toby to the store that day with a promise to return later to take him home after he'd finished running the errands his mother had sent him on. Abbie expected him any minute. "I've been so busy, I didn't even have a chance to ask you if you had a good day at school," she said to Toby, stopping at a display table that was in complete disarray from customers digging for just the right item. She sighed and started to set things aright.

"It was okay," he mumbled just loudly enough to carry through the quiet store.

"Just okay?" she asked.

"It was fine, then," he clarified.

She smiled. "I like 'fine' much better than 'okay.' How're you doing on that puzzle?"

"It's almost done, and I didn't need nobody's help this time."

His grammar left much to be desired, but she decided that was for his father to worry about. "That must mean you're growing smarter every day."

"I am!" he declared in all earnestness. "My grandpa says I'm handsome, to boot."

"And he is ever so right about that." Abbie moved away from the table and bent down to straighten several pairs of men's boots, lining them up just so, then fixing the women's boots, as well. Standing, she perused the rest of the store, contenting herself with the fact that it looked quite good after a busy afternoon with a steady flow of customers coming and going. "I'm sure you're happy to have your grandfather living nearby now. You must have missed him before."

"I did, but he's here for good, now. He promised me."

"Well, then, that's something to hold tight to." She hoped the man could be trusted to keep his word. Toby didn't need another disappointment in his young life. From what she'd heard, though, Gerald Carson had made a complete turnabout, abandoning his old life and putting on a new one. Julia Huizenga had said that her brother had undergone what some would term a miraculous deliverance from alcohol, something that didn't often happen in conversion experiences but certainly wasn't to be discounted when it did. Truly, God could do as He pleased, and if that meant reaching down and healing a repentant, contrite man of his alcohol addiction, then so be it. Now, if only Noah would believe it.

Next, Abbie walked over to the counter, stood at the cash register, and prepared to count the day's receipts, a chore she detested but had to do before leaving for the day. She pushed a key to release the drawer and watched it slide open with a zing. When she would have reached inside to draw out the dozens of small sheets, held together with a clip, her eyes meandered to a mysterious piece of paper hidden under a paperweight just to the right of the drawer. Immediately, she saw her name scrawled in that memorable handwriting, broken and slanting in various directions. Her heart thudded wildly against her chest as warm waves of anxiety swept over her. She glanced up to find Toby still playing on the floor. With shaky fingers, she unfurled the wrinkled, smudged paper, slowly at first, but then with a kind of sick eagerness.

She read and reread the single statement, then quickly scanned the store, half expecting to discover an intruder lurking in a dimly lit corner. But, of course, she'd walked up and down each aisle before locking up the front and back doors, so it was foolish to think anyone could possibly be about. There were the stairs leading to the unused second floor, where, at one time, the town library had been located, until the community had raised enough funds to build a small facility on Columbus Avenue. Now, the stairs were blocked off to the public, and she'd not seen anyone approach them.

Her heart throbbing as if she'd just run around the block, she all but fell to the floor in fright when someone rapped on the front door. "Abbie," came the sweetly familiar sound of Noah Carson's voice from the other side. Cool relief washed over her as she gathered her wits and moved out from behind the counter, quickly folding the note and stuffing it into her apron pocket.

"Aw, shoot, that's my pa," said Toby. "I wanted Jesse to walk me home."

Abbie heaved a loaded breath, one part of her delighted at the prospect of seeing Noah, another part wary of her own emotions. She dared not love a man who didn't share her passion for serving Christ. Then, there was another part of her still reeling from the note. What to do about it? Showing it to Noah would surely mean heading straight to Gabe's office, and then everyone and his neighbor's insisting she go into hiding until she reached a ripe, old age. She could not have that. And yet, a dangerous *somebody* meant to frighten the daylights out of her. "Don't worry, sweetheart," she said to Toby, putting on a calm demeanor. "You've plenty of other opportunities to see Jesse. Your pa's probably just anxious to see you."

"Can I keep doin' puzzles till Jesse comes?"

"We'll see what your pa says."

Her heart still beating twice as fast as the second hand on the wall clock, she unlocked the door and opened it to the warm eyes of Noah Carson. "Abbie Ann Kane, what would you say to me courting you?"

"What?" Those were not the first words she'd expected to hear him say.

"Well, I was just thinking that if Sinclair truly isn't in the running anymore, I'd like to be next in line to court you."

She blinked hard. Twice. And then, it happened. Her eyes welled up. What a fine predicament. She actually felt like laughing, but her emotions had run amok, and she hardly knew how to react. He stepped inside and closed the door behind him.

"What's wrong?"

"Pa, can we wait till Jesse gets here?" Toby called across the room.

Noah tilted his head up slightly, but his eyes did not waver from Abbie's face. "Yes, I suppose we can wait."

"Good. He was s'posed to take me home, not you."

"I'm happy to see you, too, son." This he said in jest, while tipping Abbie's chin up with his forefinger and gazing into her eyes. "Tell me what's wrong," he whispered.

"Nothing," she managed, wanting to tell him the truth and yet not. "I'm just—surprised to see you, that's all."

"So surprised that I've put tears in your eyes?" He wiped them dry with the pads of both thumbs, cradling her face with his fingers as he did so. To her dismay, the gesture made her even more weepy-eyed. "You are a beguiling little lady, do you know that?" She folded her lips under and pinched them closed, willing herself to straighten up, and, for heaven's sake, quit caving in to his advances. *Lord, I am so weak when it comes to this man.*

Do not fret so, My child, came a voice in her heart. *I know your heart better than anyone. Trust Me for strength and discernment. Allow Me to work in Noah's heart.*

Yes, Lord. I trust You with all that is in me.

"So? You haven't answered my question." One step closer, and their fronts would touch. He still held her face with tender care. She still felt on the brink of more tears. "Have you and Sinclair parted ways for good?"

"I told you we had."

"And he gave up on you that quickly? He's a fool."

She let a light giggle escape her throat. His thumbs had started a warm caress of her cheekbones, which made her spine tingle. *Lord, if You're going to work in his heart, please do it soon.* With great reluctance, she took a giant step back, forcing his hands to drop to his sides. He'd set her nerves on edge, and then, there was the matter of that note. Frankly, she didn't know which was worse. She started to turn, wanting to hide her rattled emotions.

He took her gently by the arm and turned her back around. "I want to court you, Abbie," he said in little more than a hush. "Do you have any objections?"

She pushed her chin out. "You'll have to talk to my father," she heard herself say.

He reached for her hand and gave it a gentle squeeze. "I can do that. I'll gladly do that. How is Sunday?"

"Sunday is fine, but there's one more thing you'd have to adhere to, and I mean to enforce it, Noah Carson."

"I'll adhere to it if you tell me what it is."

"There'll be no more kissing." This she said with pulled back, determined shoulders.

"No kiss—"

"Take it or leave it," she said.

He took only a second to ponder her edict. "I'll take it."

Her heart did a strange leap of elation, mixed with fear and uncertainty. So many things to consider, so many things to pray about.

Lord, where do I begin?

You begin by trusting, My child. Trust in Me alone.

I shall do my best.

ᘔK

Noah had driven Abbie and Jesse home in his rig about a half hour later, his heart jumping nearly out of his chest for what he'd done and said. It was officially out in the open. He cared about her, and he'd told her so—well, not in so many words, maybe, but she had to know it now that he'd asked to court her and had even agreed to ask her father's permission. "No more kisses, though," she'd reminded him while standing at the cash register, counting and recounting the money she'd taken in that day.

"I don't quite get this no more kissing rule. Doesn't courting allow for kissing?"

"Not necessarily."

298 ⌒ Sharlene MacLaren

"Didn't you and Sinclair kiss while you courted?"

"That was different."

He'd propped an elbow on the counter and leaned closer, certain he presented a distraction from the way she'd furrowed her brow in the cutest fashion and started the process of sorting out her dollar bills all over again. "How so?" he'd asked, breathing against her cheek. At the back of the store, Jesse and Toby had started up a game of checkers and hadn't appeared to be paying them any heed.

"I must guard my heart against you, for one thing," she'd stated with matter-of-factness, "because you don't seem to share my passion for serving the Lord."

She'd had him there, and, amazingly, her candor forced him to look inside himself.

"I'll try to do better," he'd said, meaning it.

"Living a Christian life is not so much a matter of trying, Noah. It's more a matter of trusting."

That had put him in his place, given him something solid to chew on. Clearly, if he meant to win this girl, he had some cleaning up to do beforehand.

"Shall we swing by the warehouse?" he asked Toby on their way back home after dropping off Abbie and Jesse.

"Sure," he said, drawing out the word with a wide yawn.

"We won't stay long. Tomorrow's another school day, and you need your rest."

"I ain't tired," he claimed, even as he yawned again.

"I'm *not* tired," he corrected him.

"Mmm-hmm," the boy said, laying his head against Noah's arm.

A flickering light gleamed in the warehouse window, which was strange, since he distinctly remembered snuffing it out before leaving earlier that day. As they rounded the corner to the front of the building, he noted the double doors standing open and the shadow of someone moving about inside.

"Who's in there?" Toby asked, lifting his head.

"I don't know, son, but I'm about to find out." Noah reined in Ruby Sue and pulled the brake in place. "You stay here for a minute, okay?"

"'Kay."

Approaching the open doors, he heard someone whistling a familiar tune—"Amazing Grace," to be exact. What he discovered brought relief—at least, no one had burglarized him—but also aggravation. He gave Toby two thumbs up, then motioned for him to jump down from the rig. Stepping inside the large room, he cleared his throat. "What are you doing here?"

Gerald Carson looked up with a start. "Oh, hi there, son. How does she look?" He gestured downward.

"You built a steam box. It looks good. But who asked you to do it?"

"Well, obviously, no one, but I thought you could use the help. I saw you were ready to start bending the ribs, so I thought I'd save you some labor by building the box. When do you want to start the bending?"

"I didn't ask for your help."

"That's true, but bending takes two strong men. You got another one in mind?"

"Not one with experience. But don't you have your own job to do?"

"I'll take off a day."

"You just started working there."

"I'll make up my time with them. The boss is pretty flexible."

"Nice boss."

"I sort of told him about your needing my help. He's agreeable."

He could have reminded him he hadn't asked for it, but that didn't seem to matter to him. *Stubborn loon.*

After accepting a bear hug from his grandfather, Toby walked over to inspect the long box that would emit the steam for bending the white oak ribs. They'd go in as hard as dry bones and come out looking like wet noodles. He'd made the box out of large-diameter metal piping, plugging one end with a wooden stopper. The other end remained open but, on the day of steaming, would have a cloth cover to hold in the steam. Supporting it at the open end were wooden legs and, at the closed end, a hot water boiler, from which steam would rise and fill the pipe.

"I'd planned on building it out of plywood, but the metal piping was a good idea," Noah said.

"I've seen it both ways. I think the tubing holds the steam better and can withstand the higher temperature. My opinion, anyway."

"You should know." When he might have used a begrudging tone, he chose not to. After all, his father was a master craftsman when it came to boatbuilding, never mind that he'd wasted years of talent and money on his drunken binges.

"As you can see, I've completed the cedar cross sections, the mold is all ready, and the notches cut in the stringers," Noah commented, gazing at his creation thus far.

"And with the board-boxes in and the gunwale on, all you need are those bent ribs," Gerald concluded.

There was a round of quiet musing as all three of them walked around the boat mold. Noah stooped to pick up a bit of debris from his day's labor and carried it to the wastebasket. "I'd like to do a bit of cleanup around here before starting the process."

"You always were an organized kid," Gerald said. Another pause ensued. "What about bright and early Monday morning? I can get here ahead of you and fire up the boiler while you get your boy ready and off to school. It should be at a nice sizzle by the time you arrive."

Noah thought about his proposition. It had been years since he'd worked alongside his father. Shoot, he'd been a mere boy, already passionate about learning the craft, and he'd learned, in spite of his father's constant criticism. He hadn't thought he'd ever see the day when they'd work side by side again, nor had he wished for it—and he'd be darned if he was ready for it yet, not with those harsh, trenchant reprimands still echoing in the recesses of his mind.

Gerald must have sensed his hesitation. "I'm different now, son. Besides God working on my wretched life—and He still has a long ways to go, let me tell you—I've also mellowed over the years. The booze wreaked havoc with my body, and I'm paying the price now, but I thank God my savage temper has all but vanished. I give God the credit, of course."

A long, jagged sigh came out of Noah. He'd told his father not to call him son but figured it was a bit petty to keep reminding him. "I don't know what you want from me," he said, kicking a small block of wood across the floor like it was a pebble.

"I'm not asking anything from you, except that second chance I mentioned earlier."

"Humph." Noah sucked in a cavernous breath. "I guess... we can take things a day at a time. But that's all I can offer for now."

"Hey," his father said, putting a hand to his shoulder. Noah winced but didn't wrench away. "That's enough for me. It's plenty, actually."

Noah found another small piece of wood and gave it a shove with the toe of his boot. "Monday, then."

"I'll be here."

Chapter Twenty-two

Grandmother Kane had invited Noah's aunt and uncle at the last minute to Sunday dinner, which also meant including Gerald Carson. Abbie was pleased to see him and anxious to make his further acquaintance. He was such a jovial, kind-spirited soul, in her opinion, and not at all the gruff, irascible man Noah had made him out to be. Of course, she'd heard only bits and pieces about Noah's upbringing, and she knew, albeit not firsthand, how drunkenness could affect a household. If Noah's childhood held tragic memories, then she completely understood why viewing his father in a different light since he'd accepted Christ could prove difficult. One didn't simply start trusting another individual overnight if he'd been hurt by him countless times. She watched them interact and sensed Noah's discomfort, wishing she could ease it but realizing God alone could do that. As she moved around the table with a pitcher, filling each glass with water, her eyes often met Noah's, and she simply couldn't help it—her heart leaped with indescribable joy. Today, he planned to ask her father for permission to court her. Had she met the man she would love for the rest of her life? She couldn't recall ever having this same giddiness with Peter.

The Kane house fairly buzzed with conversation. In one corner, Rita James and Julia Huizenga were having a tête-à-tête, laughing every so often about one thing or another. The more Abbie had gotten to know Rita, the more she loved her. The men—Delbert Huizenga, Gerald Carson, Gabe, Noah, and her father—had gathered by the fireplace. They were discussing Noah's boat project and the rib bending he'd do the following day. It sounded like a momentous event, and had she not been scheduled to work at the Whatnot, she would have liked to watch the process herself. In the kitchen, Grandmother Kane scurried about, claiming to have everything under control, as she began dishing food onto serving platters. Amid the hubbub, the children ran helter-skelter through every room, circling through the kitchen, the parlor, and the dining and living rooms, into the main-floor bedroom and the adjoining bathroom, and then back through the kitchen. Alex bellowed with joy at all the commotion until Hannah, with baby RoseAnn in her arms, put a stop to things, telling the children to go upstairs and play in the large office area, where Grandmother Kane kept a toy box full of goodies. Off they scampered, the boy-man Jesse herding them in the right direction. Dear Jesse had reached that awkward, in-between stage where one part of him probably longed to stand with the men and listen in on their grown-up talk while another part still wished to linger in the world of innocence and play.

Although the day called for lightness and gaiety, Abbie could not swallow down the heavy lump that seemed to have lodged itself permanently between her chest and stomach, made worse every time she remembered the note she'd found next to the cash register a few days ago and had yet to mention to anyone. The memory of the man she'd seen lurking in the shadows on her walk back home from the W.C.T.U. meeting—and of the barking dog that had mysteriously quieted after a popping noise—hardly helped matters. She told herself that one more incident would be enough to send her straight to Gabe's office—oh, the inconvenience of it—and so she prayed even more earnestly for no more such occurrences.

Wise matriarch that she was, Grandmother Kane strategically placed all the adults around the expansive, oak table, making sure to pair off Noah and Abbie, Hannah and Gabe, Delbert and Julia, and Rita and Jacob. She seated Gerald Carson on Jacob's other side. Of course, Grandmother Kane took the spot closest to the kitchen; and the children, along with poor Jesse as supervisor, sat at a table in the next room. Oblivious to everything, baby RoseAnn slept peacefully on a blanket on the floor behind Hannah.

After Jacob led the lively bunch in a prayer of thanks for friends, family, and food, folks started passing a bowl heaped with mashed potatoes, a steaming gravy boat, a platter piled with a sumptuous beef roast, a tureen of green beans, a basket of Grandmother Kane's subtly sweet dinner rolls, and, of course, a crock of her famous applesauce, flavored with cinnamon. Conversation topics ran the gamut, and laughter abounded for the duration of the meal. Every so often, Noah pressed his knee against Abbie's under the table, setting her heart into a frenzied rhythm. At one point, when everyone else seemed deeply engaged in conversation, he took a sip of water, then leaned close to Abbie and whispered, "Let's hope your father stays in a happy mood."

She stifled a giggle by pressing her napkin to her mouth.

Later on, he leaned even closer and boldly spoke into her ear, "Tell me again about this no kissing rule."

Quickly, she found his shoe and stomped on it, not hard enough, though, considering the thickness of the leather. He chuckled so hard that several people looked at him to see what they'd missed. Abbie held her breath, thankful when all he did was nod at them and take another swig from his water goblet. He was turning out to be such a rascal.

K

With a delicious dinner under their belts, as well as a delectable, chocolate cake, which had topped off the meal, the women gathered in the kitchen to make fast work of the dishes. Soon thereafter, folks began their leave-takings, Gabe and Hannah heading out the door first, a kicking, screaming Alex in Gabe's arms, apparently in need of a nap or a spanking—Noah couldn't tell which—with Uncle Delbert, Aunt Julia, and his father following close behind. Rita James lingered, absorbed in quiet conversation with Jacob by the fireplace. Noah kept a discreet eye on them, looking for the right opportunity to grab Jacob's attention, but by the look of things, Rita had captured it completely, and Noah wasn't sure he'd be stealing him away anytime soon.

Helena Kane put on a fine spread, and he could see she lived for entertaining. He wished now, with his stomach all in jitters, that he hadn't eaten so much. He wanted to get this talk with Jacob out of the way, the sooner, the better. The house was blissfully quiet now, like the peaceful calm after a thunderstorm, and when Abbie finally emerged from the kitchen, Noah gestured by way of a tilt of his head for her to follow him out to the porch. With permission, Toby had stayed upstairs and, according to Jesse, had found several toys to keep him occupied.

It was a fine, spring day with a nip in the air, to be sure, but sunny and pleasant. Abbie had nabbed a cape from the coat tree by the door, and she swung it over her shoulders. Noah felt the deepest longing to pull her to his side, but he gripped the porch railing, instead. Together, they looked out over the yard at the burgeoning forsythia, blooming marigolds, and buds ripe on the trees, yearning, it seemed, to break out of their shells and sprout blossoms.

"Look, a robin—my first of the season!" Abbie exclaimed, pointing a slender finger at the orange-bellied bird pecking at the dirt.

He nodded, smiling. "Have you ever gone sailing?" he asked, quite out of the blue.

She glanced up at him, her deep-brown eyes sparkling with interest. "I have, and I loved it. But it's not something I've had much chance to do, being as Papa's never taken up the hobby. Peter took me out once, with someone else skippering. He doesn't know much about the sport."

"I'll take you sometime."

"Would you? I'd love that. Where would you get the boat?"

"I'm building one, remember?"

"Oh! You mean…you'd take me out in that one?"

"Yep. It's Donald's boat, but he's already told me I'll be free to borrow it anytime it's not in use."

"Gracious, that would be an honor."

He bumped against her in a playful fashion, almost dizzy to be standing so close to her, especially since he was still somewhat exhilarated from having disclosed his feelings for her. He hadn't planned to fall in love—had fought it, even— but there it was, bright and shining like a new silver dollar.

Abbie was dressed in dazzling yellow today, a frothy, puffy-sleeved getup with a high neck and fancy buttons going down the front, cinched at her small waist with a matching sash. She looked like a fresh-hatched yellow chick, save for her glistening, black hair, pushed away from her temples with two elegant combs. He didn't think she'd appreciate his drawing that comparison, though, so he kept it to himself.

"I have my doubts about getting your father's attention today."

"Really? Why?"

Surely, she knew. "Don't tell me you haven't noticed he has eyes for Rita James."

Her head snapped back and her eyes went as round as boulders. "What?"

He laughed louder than intended, but her look of utter astonishment had him so amused, he couldn't help it. "You're kidding, right? You haven't been talking about it with your grandmother or Hannah?" She shook her head, a dazed expression now replacing her look of surprise. "I can't believe it. I thought women were always the first ones to pick up on these things."

"But it's impossible," she murmured. "Papa's never pursued another woman."

"Well, perhaps he just hasn't met one who interested him—until now."

She stood there in stunned silence. "Do you really think…?"

He chuckled and bumped against her again. "Yes, I really think. Who knows? There could be two budding romances in the Kane family."

At this, she went pink in the face.

He finally got his moment with Jacob, having waited nearly an hour for Rita to take her leave. When she did, Jacob walked her out to the porch and down the path to her waiting horse and buggy parked at the side of the house, returning five minutes later with a light step and a whistle to accompany it. That's when he spotted Noah and Abbie on the porch swing, Toby seated between them. "Well, I didn't even see you there," he said, his face a little flushed as he climbed the steps.

"Hello, Papa," Abbie said, grinning and swinging her feet like a carefree child.

"Hello, yourself," he said, pulling open the door.

"Mr. Kane," Noah said, jumping up.

He paused. "Yes?"

"May I...have a minute of your time?"

Jacob looked from him to Abbie, then to Toby, as if the boy would have a clue what he wanted. "Of course, of course. Goodness, like I said, I didn't even know you were still about. Forgive my manners."

"It wasn't a problem, sir."

"Well, come in, then."

For courage, Noah shot Abbie a hopeful glance. But all he got back was a bemused smile and a shrug of the shoulders.

K

So, it was official. Abbie was courting Noah Carson, or vice versa. Grandmother Kane hummed loudly in the kitchen the next morning, her usual rattling around rising clear to the rafters. "He is much better for her than Peter Sinclair, don't you think?" Abbie heard her say to her father.

Quickly, Abbie slid off the cushioned bench in front of her dressing table, got down on her knees, and pressed her ear to the floor register. "I'd say he's a fine gentleman, Mother. We must pray the two of them don't put the cart before the horse, though. He lacks Peter's spiritual depth."

"That will come," Grandmother said. "I've been on my knees in prayer about it, and I have a feeling the Lord has some great things stored up for those two. Don't you worry; your Abbie has a fine head on her shoulders. She'll not be doing any of this cart-before-the-horse business."

"I know you're right."

"Peter's always been a fine man, but he doesn't...well, light Abbie's fire."

Grandmother! Abbie sat up and stared at the register. Had she heard her correctly?

"So, you're the expert, are you, Mother?" She heard the crinkling of a newspaper and the scraping of a utensil on a plate.

"I remember exactly how your father used to make me feel." The sound of running water made Abbie picture her grandmother standing at the sink and gazing out the window at Ambrose and Norma Barton's driveway, perhaps in a dreamlike state, as she prepared the dishwater. "My, but he had a way of making my heart pitter-patter."

"After all these years, you still think about that?"

"Don't you with Hattie?"

"I suppose...to a degree...but—"

"Ah! I knew it!" Grandmother exclaimed. "Your heart beats for another someone, Jacob Edward Kane...one Rita James, perhaps?"

Abbie dared not breathe for fear of missing her father's response. In fact, she held back even her urge to swallow. *Answer, Papa*, she mentally implored him.

"I suppose it's possible," he muttered after a pause, then folded his newspaper, Abbie assumed, from the crinkling sound she heard. She pictured her father setting his paper down, draining his cup of coffee, and preparing to stand up. And she wasn't far off—next, she heard the clink of cup to saucer and the scrape of chair legs on linoleum.

"Well, it's about time you found someone, Jacob."

"You don't object, then?"

"Oh, my London stars, you're a grown man; you don't require my approval. But if you did—just *if* you did—then, I'd have to say I highly approve."

He chuckled. "Well, that's good, then. Even at the ripe, old age of forty-seven, I have to admit, your opinion still matters greatly."

"Mercy! You think forty-seven is old? Now, how do you suppose that makes me feel, Jacob? It seems like yesterday I gave birth to you."

More chuckling. "What do you suppose the girls will think about all of this?"

"Well." Grandmother paused, and Abbie pictured her wiping off the table. "I suppose you'll have to find that out for yourself."

"Yes, I guess you're right. Speaking of daughters, I wonder if that youngest one is ready to set off for work soon. I plan to spend an hour or two over at Don Clayton's warehouse watching Noah and Gerald Carson bend ribs for this boat he's building, and I don't want to miss the start of the process."

Abbie scrambled up from the floor, gave herself one last hurried glance in the mirror, and straightened the rumpled collar of her blue, floral-patterned, Chelsea cloth shirtwaist before tucking her blouse into her beige skirt. She touched a hand to her hair, which had decided to be somewhat unmanageable that morning, forcing her to pull the whole mess up into a topknot. She threw a blue ribbon around her bun and let the ends of it dangle down the sides. "Oh, piffle!" she mumbled. "I'm only going to work." Of course, the slimmest chance of seeing Noah that day prompted her to primp a second longer in front of the mirror.

"Abbie!" her father called from the foot of the stairs. "Are you coming down soon?"

"Coming, Papa!" she returned, glancing at her unmade bed. Grandmother Kane would have a fit, of course, but what could she do? She yanked her comforter haphazardly over the wrinkled sheets and scurried out the door.

Assembled at the warehouse to watch the rib-bending procedure were Donald Clayton, Uncle Delbert, Gabe, Jesse, and Jacob. According to Gabe, Jesse's incessant begging the night before had worn him down to the point of allowing him to miss the first hour or so of school. One would have thought they'd all come to watch an event comparable to the Wright Brothers' first flight, the way they all stood around in a semicircle, looking on with insatiable interest, Jesse shooting off a dozen questions before they even got things underway. "How long does the wood have to cook in there?" "How many degrees is it inside that tube?" "What makes the wood bend?" And on it went. While they worked, either Noah or his father patiently answered him: "About an hour," "Around two hundred," "The heat." Of course, they elaborated some, but the way he kept pitching out questions didn't leave much time for going into detail. The boy had a thirst for knowledge, no doubt about it.

As promised, Gerald had arrived well before Noah, firing up the boiler so that every window in the warehouse had fogged over by the time he got there. In addition, several one-inch-thick white oak boards were already steaming in the box. With gloves on, Noah removed the rag from the end of the pipe, stood back and waited for the rippling clouds of fragrant steam to clear, and then reached in and pulled out a long, white board as limp as a string bean. He held one end while his father took the other, and they quickly fitted it across the boat from gunwale to gunwale, setting it into the notches they'd prepared. Then, standing on opposite sides of the boat, they trimmed off the length with handsaws before nailing the board into the stringers, bending it down with their knees.

With the first rib done, they repeated the process, flopping one board down after another over the mold, every eight inches along the cross sections, until it became routine: fit, hammer, trim off, hammer. The more they worked, the more the boat took shape, albeit looking more like a long, white skeleton than a real boat.

"Here comes another hot one," his father announced in a raspy voice about three-quarters of the way through the job. Gerald Carson worked with swift precision, exposing his skill to everyone present, and, for the first time that Noah could recall, he sensed an undeniable oneness with his father as they toiled together, matching motions and movements in perfect time, finishing ribs at precisely the same second. Every so often, they'd share a look of satisfaction as they paused to inspect their work, bending, squatting, caressing the fair line from every which angle, starboard side to port side. "She's fair, all right," Gerald would say. "Yut, she's fair. You did good, son. You did real good."

And that was another thing. He couldn't remember the last time his father had paid him a compliment. Matter of fact, he had to think hard to remember any such occasion. Maybe today marked the first.

The entire process took a few hours. Jesse reluctantly left for school before they finished, happy that he'd gotten to watch for an hour or so. Gabe went with him, saying he had a deputy filling in for him, and Jacob excused himself soon after, heading to an appointment with an insurance client. That left Noah, Donald, Uncle Del, and his father. The four of them talked boats in general while Noah started sweeping up sawdust and the stubs from the ends of the wood they'd trimmed. From there, the discussion moved to the regatta.

"I'd expect you to lend your hand at the sail," Don said to Noah's father. "I want an experienced crew aboard."

"Me?" Gerald said. "I'm more a builder than a sailor, sir."

"But a man who knows ships as you do knows the inner workings," Don argued. "You'll sail with us. Besides, it's only right, your being Noah's father and all."

Noah kept his gaze pointed downward, sweeping up every stray splinter of wood and particle of sawdust his broom could find. He felt his father's eyes on him. "In that case," Gerald said in low tones, "it'd be my honor, sir."

Noah swallowed a hard lump and sent a silent prayer heavenward. *Lord, I admit I'm afraid to trust that man. Yes, it was great working with him today, feeling a connection, but what if everything he's said has been a lie? What if he's living a lie right before my eyes? How can I know for sure he won't break Toby's heart, or mine, for that matter, by disappearing tomorrow on another one of his drunken binges?*

How the inner voice materialized in his head, he could not say, but it did, clearly and incisively: ***Do not place your trust in mere man, My son. Place it in Me alone. Humans fail, but in My Word, I promise that I will never leave you or forsake you. You must learn to let go of your past hurts—look beyond them—and find healing for your wounded soul. My grace, My love, and My forgiveness are sufficient for you.***

Not since his mother's passing those many years ago had he felt so close to allowing a tear to fall.

Chapter Twenty-three

The final week of April produced showers aplenty, which, of course, fed the flowers and other foliage. Tiny leaves of vibrant green sprouted on every tree, and the grass started filling in folks' yards. Before long, they'd be out there with their T-handled, side-wheel mowers and sickles, cutting down weeds and trimming their lawns. On dry days, Sandy Shores' citizens started coming out of their winter caves, raking yards, planting seeds and bulbs in gardens, waving greetings to passersby, engaging in sidewalk conversations, and trading their winter coats for lightweight capes, sweaters, and wraps. It was a celebration, of sorts, the arrival of spring, with its promise of new life and fresh beginnings.

To the rhythm of the pelting rain on the roof of Kane's Whatnot, Abbie stacked shelves and racks with a new shipment of spring apparel. Jesse had the day off from school, so he had come to the store to help, bringing along his dog, Dusty, who quickly found a place to park his brown and white body and doze, raising his head to the occasional customer but then settling back into his comfortable, curled-up position.

To Abbie's great relief, there'd been no more mysterious occurrences with strangers darting from behind trees on her walks to and from the W.C.T.U. meetings, so she'd begun to believe that what she'd experienced that night had been nothing more than a coincidence—someone out walking, perhaps, taking a shortcut to his house by tramping through a neighbor's backyard. That didn't explain the rock that had hit her square in the back, the popping noise she'd heard, followed by the yelping sound the dog had made, or the eerie note she'd found beside her cash register. But the fact that nothing further had transpired gave her a sense of safety. Of course, Gabe's not knowing about the last few incidents had made him soften his demand that she be ever watchful. As much as he didn't like it, she'd resumed walking to and from work, enjoying the crisp, morning air and the sights and smells of springtime. And with the ever-lengthening days, she had no need to walk in the dark, which only boosted her confidence.

Noah was still courting her, but until he made a firmer commitment to Christ, she was determined to keep it low-key and to continue enforcing her "no kissing" decree, despite her growing feelings for him. Besides, having only recently severed her romantic ties to Peter, she didn't think it prudent to immediately make public her newfound interest in Noah Carson. For that reason, to his great dismay, she didn't allow him to share a pew with her at church on Sunday mornings. She also wasn't quite sure what folks would think about her being courted by a divorced man, even though her father had agreed to the arrangement, provided they didn't rush into anything and promised to pray about their relationship. Thus, their "courting" consisted mainly of Noah's dropping in at the Whatnot and waiting for the customers to clear out so he could have a few minutes of her time before heading back to the warehouse to work on his boat. They laughed and joked a great deal during those impromptu visits but also took up some serious topics, she telling him about her earnest desire to witness the closing of several saloons around town, he talking about his near obsession for opening his own boatworks; she sharing her excitement over the donated house for the women's shelter, which the ladies had dubbed Hope House, he elaborating a bit more on his painful upbringing.

With each newly exposed layer of their inner cores came a more intimate understanding of each other and a more deeply rooted friendship. Just three months ago, she would not have dreamed of ending her courtship with Peter, only to abruptly begin one with another man for whom she had feelings—feelings she still didn't know if she had a right to entertain.

Arlena Rogan had stopped by the store on a few occasions, but always when the store was abuzz with customers, leaving them little opportunity to visit. "I truly need to go visit Arlena again, and most assuredly when Shamus is nowhere around," Abbie had told Noah a couple of days ago.

"I'll take you," he'd offered, leaning against the counter, where she'd strewn the day's receipts so she could total her sales. As usual, his nearness had ruffled her nerves. "And I promise, no more loose wheels." The very mention of their last trip, which had included their getting stranded under his wagon—and a few stolen kisses—had made her cheeks go warm. She would have liked to fan her face, but then he would have known for sure the effect he had on her.

"I'd appreciate that—your taking me back there again. I constantly worry about Arlena and her girls."

"Hmm. Doesn't the Bible command us not to worry?"

He'd had her there. "You are absolutely right. Let me rephrase. I am deeply concerned for their well-being."

He'd chuckled. "You should have stuck with worried."

Abbie had seen little of Peter Sinclair in the past weeks, but it wasn't that she'd been avoiding him; their paths did not cross except at church, and he usually made a point to scurry off after the service, especially if she made a move to greet him. And she couldn't blame him one bit. After all, she'd been the one who had broken off their relationship, and she was sure she'd damaged his ego, though apparently to no great degree, as Katrina Sterling had told her she'd seen him talking to Charity Keeton in the church lobby. Charity was the daughter of the owner of Keeton Supply, a large manufacturing company in town, and it had sounded like Peter was inviting her to a concert in Muskegon.

The door rattled open, drawing Abbie out of her reverie, and, to her great joy, she saw Katrina herself enter, armed with dripping umbrella yet looking as fair as a summer day. She rushed toward Katrina and gave her a hug. Jesse emerged long enough to say hello and inquire after his best friend, Katrina's younger brother, Billy B. She told him she had dropped her twins off at her mother's house, where he was helping to entertain them while she ran errands, but that he'd probably be happy to play later, provided the rain let up.

"Whatever are you doing out in this wretched weather, Katrina?" Abbie asked after the small talk ended and Jesse returned to the back of the store to continue stocking shelves.

"Well, one needs supplies, regardless of the weather, and, besides, I just had to see you. It's been a while, except for when I saw you on Sunday, I guess. But you and I have not had much time to talk, and those girls of mine keep me running from morning till night."

"I don't know how you do it, Kat—keep your house in tip-top shape, keep your children and husband healthy and happy, keep that farm of yours operating smoothly, and still find time to come to town with your youngsters in tow. Not only that, but you always seem to have a glow about you, and especially today. What is your secret?"

"My secret? First of all, Micah and I are madly in love, which makes even daily housekeeping less mundane."

Abbie giggled. "Your being in love is no secret. A person would have to be blind not to see the way you and Micah ogle each other across a crowded room."

"Oh, my, is it that obvious?" Katrina leaned in close, laying a hand on Abbie's arm, and whispered, "There is another reason for my glow, dear friend. Do you want to hear it?" Abbie's heart skipped. She was always game for sharing a secret with her best friend, and she gave a fast nod. "I'm with child," Katrina said.

"No! Really?" Abbie squealed, then quickly clamped a hand over her mouth to hide her excitement when another customer, Frieda Marshall, walked through the door with three children behind her, all of whom made a beeline for the toy box at the back of the store, stopping first to pat Dusty's head.

"I'll be right with you, Mrs. Marshall," Abbie called.

The woman glanced up and smiled. "I plan to do a little looking around first. You two keep talking and don't mind me." She moved down a side aisle and out of sight.

"When are you due to have the baby—or should I say babies?"

"You bite your tongue, young lady," Katrina scolded her. "I think another set of twins would send me over the edge."

"Not you. You're so organized and relaxed about every-thing. I don't have a domestic bone in my body."

"Of course, you do, silly girl. It's just that you haven't had to put it to use yet. But you will. When the time comes for you to marry and start a family, God will provide you with all the strength, energy, and wisdom you need. Besides, you have enough wit to laugh at what life brings you. You'll make a fine wife and mother someday." With her hand still resting on Abbie's arm, she lowered her voice again. "And, speaking of being a wife, how are you and that handsome Mr. Carson getting on?"

Despite Katrina's being her best friend, she still felt a blush creep up her neck.

"Oh, Kat, I can't allow myself to love him just yet. Not with his lack of complete commitment to the Lord. He still harbors resentment toward his father, and he's as much as admitted that he doesn't walk as closely to God as he ought. And then, there's the matter of his being divorced."

"Well, I suppose we all err from time to time in our walks with God, sweetie. It's a daily challenge not to put our self-ish desires in front of Him, so, if you're waiting for Noah to be perfect in his faith, then you have a lifelong wait ahead of you. Growing up in the Lord comes with practicing God's presence, praying, and studying His Word, and when one is only a young Christian, it sometimes takes a while to see real progress. Our job, my dear, is to pray the Lord will soften his heart and give him a true appetite for God's Word. As for his being divorced, if you can't get beyond it, then you best end your friendship with him before it develops any further."

When Abbie sucked in a breath and prepared to respond, Katrina shushed her with a gentle squeeze. "*But*, first, you must bear in mind that forgiveness may be something you yourself need to explore. Divorce is a terrible thing—a gross injustice for the children involved and a deep disappointment to our heavenly Father—but it's not the unpardonable sin. It seems to me you need to first seek God's divine guidance, and then you need to listen to your heart and hear what it's telling you."

Abbie blinked hard and stared at her friend, who never failed to speak the truth in love to her. "I do believe you missed your calling, Katrina Sterling. Them thar are preacher's words," she said with a Southern drawl.

Hannah arrived mid-afternoon, around the time Jesse left to visit Billy B. The sun was beginning to show its face after a two-hour rainfall, and the sisters exchanged friendly prattle, Abbie speaking of Katrina's visit and the exciting news of her pregnancy, Hannah talking about RoseAnn's sniffles and Alex's fall from a chair, which resulted in a good-sized goose egg. After that, they talked in hushed voices about the secret courtship of their father and Rita. "When do you think he's going to talk to us about it?" Hannah asked. "And do you think he'll call us all together as a family, or will he talk to us separately?"

"I haven't a clue," Abbie said. "I picture Papa being quite embarrassed."

"I know, I know." Hannah covered a giggle when a customer walked past. Leaning closer, she whispered, "I can't imagine how he'll go about it, but I wish he'd make it snappy. Maybe he'll make Rita break it to us. Tee-hee. Wouldn't that be funny! Maggie seems to think they'll marry in no time, based on what I've written to her."

"I wouldn't doubt it. I've been watching Rita extra closely these days. She's awestruck, you know," Abbie said.

"And Papa's just as bad. They ogle each other across the store as if they're the only ones around. And here, they think no one's the wiser."

"Wouldn't Papa be surprised to know I eavesdropped on his conversation with Grandmother this morning?"

"Does he not know that we girls used that floor register for listening in on more adult conversations than the sky has clouds? And to think that you're still at it, Abbie Ann." They shared more quiet laughter as Abbie put on her cape and retrieved her umbrella from the hook where she'd hung it that morning to dry.

"Have you plans to see Noah this weekend?"

"Actually, he's invited me to go for a walk with him down by the water this Saturday evening, provided the weather doesn't turn bad. Afterward, he's suggested we go to Marie's Ice Cream Parlor. Marie's just opened for the season, have you heard? They say folks swarmed the place last Friday night, even though it was only fifty-four degrees outside."

"What folks won't do for an ice cream cone! Ever since its introduction at the St. Louis World's Fair, people seem not to care how long they have to stand in line to get one—myself included!"

Abbie buttoned her cape to the neck. "One can never have too many of those tasty creations, it's true." She hooked her umbrella over her arm and put her hand on the door-knob. But before she opened the door, she gave a half turn and looked one last time at Hannah, suddenly contemplative. "It will be our first time to appear in public as a couple since I broke off my relationship with Peter. What do you suppose people will think?"

"Abigail Ann, since when do you care what people think? You are the outspoken president of the local, sometimes controversial, W.C.T.U. You don't seem to care what folks say on that matter, and yet you concern yourself with how they'll feel about your taking a stroll with a man I daresay most know nothing about? Here's what's important, dear heart: as long as you've prayed about this newfound friendship you and Noah Carson have formed, then all you need to think about is how and where the Lord will lead you."

"Well, now you sound like Katrina. I think you've both missed your callings."

"Our callings?" Hannah wrinkled her nose.

"Never mind, sister dear." Abbie heard herself giggle as she opened the door and stepped out into the brisk, spring air. "Have a lovely afternoon. As for me, I'm off to the library for a good book. Gertie told me a few new titles have arrived." She closed the door behind her and set off up Water Street toward Fifth, enjoying the sun on her shoulders and the fresh scent of spring. Along the way, she passed several friends, stopping to talk to a few and merely waving at others.

Halfway up Water Street, she passed Erv's Place on the opposite side of the street at precisely the same time the proprietor himself stepped out onto the sidewalk, a cigarette hanging from his slack mouth, his mammoth gut sagging, and his suspenders doing a poor job of holding his pants at his waistline. He watched her with cold, eagle-like eyes. Knowing it was the Christian thing to do, she waved and said, "Good afternoon, Mr. Baxter. I hope you're enjoying the wonderful sunshine after all that rain."

He made a feeble attempt at a smile, but it came off more like a smirk. He tipped his hat at her, but, of course, no words of greeting accompanied the gesture. Undaunted, she kept her smile in place and continued on her way.

⟨*K*⟩

He liked watching her comings and goings, loved that she hadn't a clue about his vigilant eye. Little wench had grown awfully confident these days. One could even say careless. He knew she thought the danger had passed, because he'd made sure not to pull any more pranks, thereby giving the impression that all was well. But all wasn't well, not in his book. Oh, she and her little ladies' group may have backed off temporarily from their campaign to close the saloons, but that wouldn't last, he was sure, not with efforts rising up all over the country to close down beer and whiskey establishments. Prohibition, they called it, and it was mostly pious, self-righteous women leading the pack.

Women need to learn their place in society, he repeated in his head as he watched her stop at the corner of Water and Fifth streets to look both ways. Their place was at home, keeping a tidy house, preparing meals, raising the young'uns, and seeing to their husbands' wants and needs. After a noisy rig rumbled by, she crossed the street, then headed north. Probably going to the library to jaw with Gertie Pridmore. Well, he could just hole up on a park bench and wait for her to come back out.

He didn't mind waiting. He had all the time in the world. He inhaled the last of his cigarette and tossed it on the ground, wrenching the life out of it with the sole of his shoe.

Fact was, he liked watching her—liked the sense of power it gave him and how it made him feel almost invisible.

K

Noah mopped his damp brow with his sleeve and stopped to inspect his work. The planking had begun, meaning the steam box was running almost daily now, heating up the warehouse and steaming the windows. Today's rainfall certainly hadn't diminished the room's humidity any. The scent of the steamed, six-inch-wide cedar boards filled the room, mingling with the smells of sawdust and sweat. He had a regular routine going: steam a plank, glue it down and screw it in place, then overlap it with the next. Once he finished the planking—perhaps as early as tomorrow—he could proceed with caulking between the planks and filling the screw holes with wooden plugs. After that, he'd start fairing her up with a hand plane before sanding her down from one end to the other, leaning, stretching, twisting, running a hand over her frame, then eyeballing her surface, checking for bulges or imperfections. Any he found would need to be reworked until perfect. In his sober moments, his father used to say, "A boat that's fair is a thing of beauty." That single statement had stuck with him over the years, turning him into a regular fussbudget.

Checking his pocket watch for the time, he sighed at the hour, laid down his tool, and began cleaning up for the day. Since there'd been no school that day, Aunt Julia had offered to take Toby off Noah's hands, saying she needed a "helper" in the kitchen. Toby had leaped with joy, knowing that helping in the kitchen also meant testing cake batter and licking icing from spoons.

It was time to pick him up, but a part of Noah hoped the boy might be either taking a late nap or playing in another room when he got there, as he wanted to spend a few minutes talking to his aunt. His other hope was that his father wouldn't be there.

He wasn't disappointed. Aunt Julia was in her sewing room, working on a quilt, and she told him Uncle Del and his father had taken Toby down to the pier to fish and watch the boats come in, two of Toby's favorite activities. They would surely return within the hour, she assured him.

From the kitchen, the delightful smells of fresh-baked goodies floated through the house. He couldn't quite identify each one, but he guessed a cake and, perhaps, a batch of cookies or a tray of fudge. His mouth watered at the possibilities. Julia Huizenga loved to bake, and her rather full-bodied frame indicated she also liked to partake of the fruits of her efforts.

Aunt Julia laid down her work and swiveled in her chair, sweeping a few loose strands of gray hair off her forehead to study him with intentness. "Want to sit a spell and tell me how that boat of yours is coming? Are you managing to stay on schedule?"

He leaned against the doorframe and folded his arms. A glistening shaft of light shone through the window, casting a warm glow on the shiny, wood floor and glancing off Noah's dull work boots. Since the sun had made an appearance, the temperature had climbed all the way to sixty degrees, and before Noah had left the warehouse, he'd opened the windows to clear the humidity, thankful for the gentle breezes that would make fast work of it.

"I'll stand, for now. The boat's coming along fine, right on schedule, actually. You're making a quilt, are you?" He eyeballed her colorful handiwork.

She glanced down at the mass of fabric on her sewing table. "It's for the benefit auction in May, sponsored by the W.C.T.U. The proceeds will go to the women's shelter they're hoping to open later this fall. Isn't that wonderful?"

"Mmm-hmm. Abbie's been telling me about some lady down South who decided to donate a house to their cause. It's something, all right. Apparently, it's in need of a few repairs, but it's in good structural shape. If they can round up enough volunteers, they figure it won't take much more than a few months of labor. I plan to donate some of my spare time to work on it."

"As do Del and Gerald." She cleared her throat. "I'm sure Abbie will appreciate your help." He caught the slight inflection in her tone, along with the mischievous twinkle in her eye. "She's a lovely girl, that Abbie. A fine catch, if you ask me."

A fine catch, indeed, but whether he would ever manage to fully win her over remained to be seen. So far, she'd managed to make him toe the line with regard to her kissing ban. He reminded himself that, one year ago, he'd been a married man—unhappy, to be sure, but married. Chances were mighty good he didn't deserve one so fine as Abbie Ann Kane. If he were smart and considerate, he would stop this courting business. Some days it seemed downright selfish on his part.

"I'd have to agree, Aunt Julia, but I actually came here to talk to you about something else entirely."

"I figured you did. In fact, I'm pretty sure I can tell you what it is you want to discuss." She folded her hands in her lap, biting down on her lower lip before continuing. "Gerald told me he let slip the news of your mother's miscarriages. He thought you knew."

Doggone if she didn't read him like a book. Now, he did choose to lower himself into the only other chair in the room, a small wingback that had seen better days. Suddenly, his shoulders felt weighted as he blew out a heavy breath.

"Why in the world didn't you ever tell me about them? I had no idea."

"I'm sorry, honey. I just...never found the right opportunity, I guess. In the back of my mind, I thought, perhaps, your mama might have told you, and that bringing up the matter would only remind you of the pain she suffered. I know how very much you clung to her and how dreadful it was for you when she passed. Such a young, impressionable lad you were, and so alone. I want you to know that our hearts broke for you, Del's and mine.

"And then, there were those times I thought, perchance, you didn't know, and I should have checked, but I just didn't. I think now, if I had told you, it might've helped you see things a little clearer."

Noah raised his eyebrows thoughtfully as she paused before continuing.

"I'm not making any excuses for my brother, Noah, but I do have to say he felt the losses of those babies as much as your mama did. She always thought her pain was greater—and maybe it was, I don't know. All I know is that most of the time, your father was helpless to say or do anything right for her. For about a year, I'd say, she literally took to her bed in a horribly depressed state of mind. I even came and stayed with her and Gerald for a time, thinking my presence might lend a bit of comfort and stability to the situation, but neither of them was consolable, and both had started to retreat to their own little corners. If your mother wasn't crying a river of tears, she was ranting at Gerald. Yes, your mother ranted, but it was all that medication the doctor put her on, and I do believe it made her moods and thoughts somewhat irrational.

"Those were trying times for both of them, terribly so. I'd say it was about that time your father started drinking. While your mother drank the medication the doctor had prescribed to dull her emotional state, your father took up his own bottle. Looking back, I wonder what the doctor gave her—some sort of sedative, I'm sure. Whatever it was, she came to depend on it as much as your father depended on his booze.

"In time, she became with child again, perhaps for the sixth or seventh time. I've lost track, myself, of the number of miscarriages she actually had, and I'm not sure she or your father even knew. The doctor ordered her to bed for the duration, but he didn't take away that awful medicine. That was her lifeblood; it kept her sane and intact—physically, emotionally, and mentally, I suppose.

"Still, you can't imagine how hard Del and I prayed that this particular pregnancy would take, and that if it did, the baby would not suffer any repercussions from all that liquid drug traversing your mama's veins. Praise the Lord, you came out perfect as a brand-new, shiny watch, everything in fine working order. Del and I always thought God had preserved your life for a very special reason. I still believe He has wondrous and mighty things planned for you."

She emitted a loud sigh, then furrowed her brow in thought. Noah's own emotions teetered precariously as he silently took everything in, and he didn't notice how tightly his hands gripped his knees, his fingers squeezing so hard that they nearly stopped the blood flow to his lower legs.

Clearing her throat, Aunt Julia went on. "It wasn't long after your birth that your mother began crawling out of her deep, dark hole. As she started finding purpose and meaning, diving into motherhood like she was born for it, she somehow managed to stop taking that hideous drug, but the effects of it had weakened her—her heart, in particular. I'm sorry to say she never did fully regain her strength and energy, but what she did do was start investigating God and His generous, faithful, and patient dealings with her. Soon, she started reading her Bible and praying, and the next thing we knew, she'd found a little church not many blocks from your house and started attending regularly. Shortly thereafter, she gave her heart to Jesus. Del and I so hoped that Gerald would follow suit, but, instead, he did the opposite. He fell deeper into the throes of alcoholism, and, as you know, continued in that state for many years, distancing himself the more from Sarah and you and failing miserably at fatherhood."

She shook her head as tears pooled in her eyes. "Many were the lectures I delivered in those days, but his ears were all but deaf to me. That's why Delbert and I were so adamant about your spending several weeks each summer with us. Somehow, we had to get you out of that environment so you could see the joy that could be found beyond your wretched world."

For the second time in a long, long while, he felt close to tears, but since it wouldn't do for a grown man to cry, he hurriedly swallowed them back. "And I thank you for that, Auntie." The childhood endearment slipped out quite by accident. "I have scores of happy memories of summers gone by, thanks to you and Uncle Del. I suppose you're more like parents to me than my own father."

"It doesn't always have to be that way, you know, not that we don't love that you view us in that light. I just believe the Lord can and wants to heal the rift between you and your father."

What was he supposed to say to that? For a change, he couldn't refute her claim.

Chapter Twenty-four

Did your father ever tell you how he came to know the Lord, Noah?" Aunt Julia asked, her glistening eyes still focused intently on him.

He released his firm grip on his knees and clenched the armrests of his chair, instead. "I can't say that he did." And he wasn't sure he wanted to hear about it, either, seeing that his emotions already felt raw and spent.

"I should probably let him tell you," she said, then paused and put an index finger to her chin, "but I don't think he'll mind if I go ahead." She fell silent for another moment, apparently gathering the details in a straight little row. "He tells me that his estrangement from you started wearing on his conscience something fierce, and that when your marriage crumbled and you set off with Toby, he thought he'd lost you forever. He started evaluating his life, wondering how he'd ever let it reach such a low point. He said that shortly after you came to Michigan, he went down on his knees and cried out to God, asking Him to prove His existence. Well, a picture of that little church your mama and you used to attend started to materialize in his head, and he pulled himself up and walked the four or five blocks to that white, clapboard building with the steeple and the stained glass windows."

Noah visualized it himself, surprised at the dampness gathering at the corners of his eyes.

"It just so happened that the preacher was there, dusting the pews, when your father walked into that little sanctuary—not the same preacher you and your mama would remember, though." She shook her head and chortled. "Your father said he was a young whippersnapper. Anyway, Gerald said he talked at great length with the preacher, telling him his entire life story. He listened with patience and kindness and then did a most amazing thing."

At that point, Aunt Julia choked up, and so many tears rolled down her cheeks in a steady succession that she had to wipe them with her sleeve. Noah fished for a handkerchief to aid her but came up short. Great—what was he going to use if he started blubbering? Not since boyhood had he truly cried, and he didn't intend to start today, no matter how touching Aunt Julia's story ended up.

She sniffed and looked at Noah with watery eyes. "Mercy! I'm a mess, and I haven't even gotten out the best part yet." Clearing her craggy throat, she went on. "The preacher walked to the front of the church, where a big Bible rested on the podium."

"I remember that Bible!" Noah declared. "I always thought of it as the perfect size for a giant."

She smiled and dabbed at her wet cheeks, this time with a discarded patch of fabric lying next to her Singer treadle sewing machine. "From that Bible, he pulled out an envelope that contained a folded piece of paper. It was a letter, Noah—a letter your mother had sent to a Reverend Newville."

"Rev. Newville...I have a faint recollection of the man. He had muttonchops that wiggled when he got to talking real fast and a belly so round he couldn't button his jacket front. What was the letter about? And what in the world was it doing in the church Bible?"

"Well, I didn't read the letter, myself, and I can't tell you exactly how it came to be in the Bible. The current preacher believes that Rev. Newville put it there for a specific reason, being full of faith that God would one day direct just the right person to read it, which, of course, wound up being the young man now shepherding that little church. Another remarkable twist to this story is that he'd found the letter only a week or so before your father went to the church and met him."

She shifted in her seat, flattening out a wrinkle in her skirt and appearing to have reined in her emotions. "Your father has the letter tucked away for safekeeping, so, I suppose, if you want to know its contents, you'll have to ask to see it. I do know, though, that that letter was the defining moment, as Gerald puts it, when he became convinced of God's eternal existence. After that, he said, he fell to his knees in repentance."

For several seconds, Noah simply stared at his shoes, awed by the depth and breadth of the story. He was anxious now to see the letter, although leery of asking his father if he could. If Gerald hadn't shared it with his own sister, perhaps he wouldn't want his son to read it, either.

"Are you going to ask him to show it to you?" There she went, reading his mind again.

"Yes," he said. "Not sure exactly when, but I will talk to him about it."

"Good. That's good. I'm sure you'll find the perfect time."

Noah stood up and stretched his taut muscles, then walked across the room to give his aunt a hug. "You are a special lady, you know that?"

"Oh, pish-posh! Nothing special about me, save for the Lord's making me His child."

He could have cited many reasons beyond that one why she was special, but the sound of the front door sweeping open and his son's excited chatter interrupted his thoughts.

"Pa, are you here?" Toby's voice rang through the house.

Noah winked at his aunt and stepped out into the hallway. "Back here, son."

"Pa, I caught a fish!" The boy sailed across the expanse and flew into his arms. Noah caught him and spun him around, for some reason loving him more in this moment than he'd ever thought possible. It would seem that Aunt Julia's account had turned him into a regular bowl of sentimental mush. Over his boy's blond head, he locked eyes with his father for a few seconds, then quickly averted his gaze, setting Toby back down and tousling his silky hair.

"How big a fish did you catch?"

"This big!" Toby spread his arms wide, putting Noah in mind of a baby eagle's wingspan, his lively blue eyes dancing with pure joy. Another glance at his father showed Noah the fish's true size as the man held his two index fingers about six inches apart.

All Noah could do was smile and shake his head.

⌒K⌒

My favorite baby sister,

I trust you are doing well. I have enjoyed reading your letters but fear I've been remiss in writing back as often as I should. Will you forgive me? Life here continues at its usual hectic, sometimes out-of-control state, but it is still blessedly sweet. I miss all of you so very much, especially as I look forward to fall, followed by the holiday season's approach. (It's only May, and already I picture Grandmother cooking fudge over the stove and taking a fresh batch of peanut butter delights out of the oven.) But I also love my husband, my children, and the home we've established for the precious, needy street urchins, so I must say I'm perfectly content. It is a blissful thing to know you're living in the center of God's will, doing His work.

And, guess what else? I adore city life! I suppose you could say I have acclimated myself to the point of wondering if we will ever leave this place. To be sure, there is much despair in a big city, but I have come to love the clamor and clutter of New York! Not that I am not excited beyond words about coming home to Sandy Shores for Christmas—goodness, no! In fact, I shall arrive there with bells on my boots—and I shall make Luke and all the children wear them, too!

Furthermore, I can't wait to meet this Rita James person. Has Papa had "the talk" with you yet regarding his feelings for her? It does seem like somebody ought to just tell him we all know and approve, that he may as well give up the façade. But, wait! I can just hear you now. You'll be saying, "What? And spoil the fun? I want to watch Papa squirm a little bit." Am I right, sister dear?

On to more serious matters…is it true that you have ended things with Peter Sinclair and are now courting with the divorced man you mentioned in one of your earlier letters to me? Oh, my precious sister, do be careful with your heart. I don't want this man to break it in two. Have you learned the reasons for his divorce, and do they seem plausible to you? And what of his spiritual state? You don't want to become involved with someone who does not share your heart for serving Christ. Does he have anything to say about your involvement with the W.C.T.U.? You know how very much that work means to you. This is where I think Peter stifled you. (Peter's a dear man, by the way, but he was not a good match for you. I can say that now that you've parted ways.) But getting back to this other fellow—I believe you told me his name is Noah—do not allow him to suppress your passions. Of course, I don't know him at all, so I have no idea if he would do that. I'm just asking you to approach this relationship with utmost care and sincere prayer for guidance.

Abbie laid down Maggie's letter, having already read it a couple of times over, and picked up her hairbrush to freshen up her hairdo before Noah picked her up for their Saturday night walk. It certainly did seem to her that she'd been hearing a lot of "preaching" lately—first, from Katrina on the matter of forgiveness and trusting God to give Noah a soft heart for Him; next, from Hannah, regarding not worrying so much about what people said about her friendship with Noah but more about what the Lord had to say; and, now, from Maggie, who cautioned her to ask God for guidance and steer clear of anyone who would stifle her passionate side. It was enough to make her head swim.

The sound of her father's patient plodding up the stairs caused her head to turn. "Papa, is that you?"

"It is. Are you presentable?"

"Of course, come in." She heard him round the corner at the top of the stairs and advance across the wide expanse on his way to her room, which she'd once shared with her sisters.

Her father appeared in the doorway, smelling like spice, spiffed up in fancy trousers, and wearing a dress shirt and necktie. "My goodness, look how handsome you are!" she exclaimed.

He looked down at himself. "Me?"

"No, that gentleman behind you. Of course, you, silly." She jumped up from her dressing bench and went to give him a hug. He welcomed her embrace, returning it with a gentle squeeze.

Setting her back from him, he gave her a quick perusal. "You look lovely, yourself. Going out with Noah, I take it?"

"It's just a little walk, that's all."

He lifted his bearded chin, freshly trimmed, she noted. "Ah. I trust you're taking things slow and easy with that young man."

"You know I am, Papa." She had half a mind to ask if he was doing the same with Rita James, but he had yet to tell her they were courting. "What do you think about my keeping company with a divorced man? Do you think it's scandalous?"

"Scandalous would be cavorting with a married man, honey."

"But divorce is a rare thing, and it's wrong, not to mention the fact that folks tend to look down on those who can't hold their marriages together."

"Indeed, they do, but I'm a big believer in redemption. Remember, God sent His Son into a broken, imperfect world to save broken people. Yes, He desires that the sacred institution of marriage be a covenant relationship that's held intact, but it takes two people to do that, and, from what I know of the situation, Noah's wife held no respect for God's laws, going so far as to defile the marriage bed."

"He told you that?"

"He did."

"He told me, as well," she confessed somberly. "So, in his case, divorce was acceptable in God's eyes?"

"I would never say He views it as acceptable, but, again, it goes back to redemption, this matter of forgiveness and God's grace, immeasurable and unfathomable, but nonetheless real."

Abbie nodded, looking at the matter in somewhat of a new light—an emboldened, glimmering light. Dare she hope?

In an unexpected motion, her father moved over to her bed and sat down on the edge. She decided to join him, the springs of the ancient mattress squeaking when she plopped down. Picking at a loose thread on his trousers, he went on, "He also told me a bit about his upbringing and the resentment he holds toward his father. I told him what I just told you—there is redemption for our transgressions, a means for forgiveness and reconciliation. Truly, while we conversed, I sensed the Lord at work in his life. I also questioned him on his faith."

Her heart skipped. "And what did he say?"

Her father turned to her with a smile and touched a finger to her nose. "He said that he was a work in progress, and I thought to myself, *Well, aren't we all?* I admired his honesty. Now, he could have given me a better answer; he might have said, 'I am right in the center of God's will, sir. I try to live a holy, righteous life and daily seek God for direction. I read my Bible daily and pray without ceasing.'"

"Papa." She nudged him in the side. "You jest."

"Well, that would have been the answer I'd have preferred. What proper father wouldn't? But because he didn't try to bluff his way into my good graces, I thought him worthy of my trust. Now, that doesn't mean I would endorse your marrying him yet, only that I think the man deserves a chance to prove himself."

He tilted his face at her, his brow crumpling. "Of course, there is the matter of his son. Were you ever to fall in love with Noah, you would have to love his boy as if he were your own."

Abbie thought about that for all of three seconds, then laughed. "I've fallen hard for that child already, Papa. From the first time I saw him peering through the Whatnot's broken front window back in February, I lost my heart to him."

Her father rubbed his beard and grinned. "I guess I've observed that."

A few seconds of silence stretched between them. She pulled back her shoulders, sucked in a deep breath, and decided to switch topics. "Well, are you going to tell me where you're off to, all dressed up in your Sunday best? I'm not missing a church meeting, am I?"

"No, no. I'm…going to a concert in Grand Rapids tonight. Taking the Interurban."

"No! A concert? That sounds wonderful. Are you…umm, taking anyone with you?"

"Well, as a matter of fact, I'm taking…." He paused and, of all things, blushed. Sweet Papa. "You'll probably never believe it," he said.

"Why don't you try me?" Her heart bubbled with excitement, but she kept her manner calm and controlled.

Suddenly, he put his hands on his knees and pushed himself up. "Rita James," he declared, as if it took a great deal of courage to say her name.

"Rita! Well, isn't that nice," she said from the bed. "She's such a pleasant person, and she fits in so perfectly at the Whatnot, don't you think?"

"Yes, I believe she does." He stared at her for several seconds, looking stumped. "You don't seem overly surprised."

Abbie stood up and walked over to her mirror, where she hastily adjusted the silver broach at her throat, feigning nonchalance. "Why should I be? Rita's wonderful. You'd be crazy not to give her a second look, Papa. I'm very glad to hear you're taking her away for the evening. I'm sure she's lonely after the loss of her husband."

"Turns out he wasn't a very good man. When he died of a lung disease, she didn't grieve long, sad to say. Apparently, she lived in fear of him and, in fact, visited Dr. Van Huff on more than one occasion for severe cuts and abrasions. Swore him to secrecy, though, because she was too afraid to report the abuse."

Outright anger at the news flared in Abbie's chest. "That's awful. She's never mentioned any of that to Hannah or me."

"Ridiculous as it sounds, she harbors guilt, somehow thinking she herself is to blame for not being a good enough wife. Can you imagine?"

"Then he manipulated her into thinking it. No woman should have to endure physical abuse. Can you see why the W.C.T.U. is eager to get this women's shelter up and running? If more women knew they had a safe place to run to, they might be more apt to press charges against their abusive husbands."

"I believe you're right, daughter. Now more than ever."

"Well, enough of that. I think if anyone can turn Rita's thinking around, it's you." Moving away from the mirror, she stood on tiptoe and kissed his whiskered cheek. "I'm happy for you and Rita, Papa."

His eyes glistened at the corners as he let out a lengthy sigh. "Well, one down and two to go. What do you think your sisters will say about this—this new relationship?"

His fretful expression nearly made her giggle. Instead, she put on a serious demeanor and straightened his bow tie with both hands. "I suppose you'll have to find that out for yourself."

"Huh. That's exactly what your grandmother said."

"Did she, now?"

Downstairs, a knock sounded on the front door. *Noah?* Abbie's stomach did its usual somersault, and she gave a little jolt. A glance at the mantel clock on her dresser told her it was five o'clock on the dot.

Papa raised an eyebrow. "Sounds like your gentleman is here."

She didn't correct his choice of words. Smiling up at him, she responded, "And your lady is probably sitting at home on pins and needles."

His beard waggled when he chuckled.

Chapter Twenty-five

Brisk air bit at their noses as they walked along the water's edge. The white-capped waves that rushed in to kiss the sandy beach just missed their feet as Noah gave Abbie a gentle nudge to veer them away from the waves' icy fingers. Despite the cool air, the weather was definitely acting in their favor, presenting them with waning sunlight that sparkled on the water. The sun promised to set in an array of colors, judging by the way the cirrus clouds had spread their slender, pink tentacles across the azure sky.

So far, the two had talked about Jacob and Rita's courtship, Abbie's most recent visit with the Plooster sisters, Toby's latest fishing expedition, the upcoming auction the W.C.T.U. ladies were sponsoring, and Noah's boatbuilding project. Along the way, they met a number of people Abbie knew. They stopped to talk with a few of them, Abbie introducing Noah as her friend and answering inquiries about what he did for a living and how her family was. Most were exceptionally cordial; as for the few who were simply polite, Noah surmised they were wondering what had happened to Peter Sinclair. But, of course, Abbie never mentioned her former beau.

Their sides brushed together as they walked, and he'd have liked to take one of her hands in his, but she kept them either clasped or tucked inside her coat pockets. Clearly, she meant to stay at a safe distance. He found this amusing, considering they'd already shared some pretty meaningful kisses, the memory of which still lingered in his mind like the sunlight on the beach.

"Have you seen much of your father since the Sunday you both came for dinner?" she asked.

Noah kicked a piece of driftwood toward the water, where several white gulls were pecking at the sand, and they scattered. "He often stops by to check on things after he finishes his workday. He loves boats as much as I do. Sometimes, he lends a hand with whatever I'm doing. 'Course, he wants to see Toby, too. The two of them have formed a pretty tight bond since he moved here."

"That's good, right?" she asked.

He gave her a slanted glance and grinned. "Yeah, it's good. I guess."

"You don't sound convinced."

"Truth be told, it's a little startling to me that my father's coming around doesn't bother me as much as it used to. When he first came to Sandy Shores, I wanted to punch him square in the gut. I thought he had nerve invading my privacy, as if I had some kind of claim on this town. Lately, though, it's like I'm getting to know him for the first time in my life. I don't know. He's definitely...different." It was true, much as he hated admitting it. "And you are the first person who's heard me utter those words," he confessed, giving her a playful jab in the side with his elbow. "So, you better keep 'em to yourself."

"I'm honored you'd let me in on your secret, and I swear it's safe with me," Abbie said, grinning up at him. My, but she had a sparkling smile. And those chocolate eyes! He drank them in for as long as she held his gaze.

"It's an answer to prayer, of course. I hope you know that."

He pondered that notion and scratched the side of his nose, which was nearly numb with cold. "My aunt's told me she's praying for me, and for the situation."

"I've been praying for you, as well."

They locked eyes again, and his heart thumped against his chest. "Really? Now, who's honored?"

They stopped for a minute to look out over the expanse of water, the red lighthouse at the end of the pier standing tall and regal against the horizon. In the distance, a barge could be seen moving closer to the shore, carrying a load of coal, perhaps, or maybe some essential parts for one of the manufacturers in town.

"Want to head back?"

She looked at him again with those magical, brown eyes, her cheeks and nose glowing with a pinkish cast. "I'm ready whenever you are."

Placing his hands on her slender shoulders, he gently turned her in the opposite direction. She giggled, and the rippling sound turned him to mush. What was he going to do with himself? "Want to stop by the warehouse on the way to Marie's and see the boat?"

"You mean it?"

"Of course."

"I would love to see your progress. Jesse tells me how nice it looks whenever he walks Toby there after school."

"It's high time you saw it for yourself, then. Matter of fact, you ought to make a habit of it."

There went that cute, little chortle again, and blast if he wasn't getting used to it.

K

Well, didn't they make an admirable pair strolling up Harbor Street at dusk, her long hair flying like a black skirt torn to ribbons? He could just imagine Carson's hand itching to run his fingers through it. Might be, he even wished to wrap his arm around that tiny waist of hers, covered up now by that wool coat. Dash it all if he didn't have the same longings! He'd been watching her for so long now that she'd started to appeal to his base, if not depraved, instincts. Perhaps, before he *did* away with her, he'd *have* his way with her. He sniggered at his own notion, his throat going dry just thinking about it.

He puffed his cigarette, watching the twosome from behind a parked horse and wagon, humored by their utter obliviousness that he'd been following them from a distance, stopping when they stopped and resuming his walk when they did theirs. When they'd turned around to retrace their steps, he'd had to duck behind some tall, dried dune grass and put his back to them. Fools never spotted him, never grew the least bit suspicious of his presence on the other side of Harbor Street, so engrossed were they in each other. He belched up the beer he'd drunk an hour ago, grimacing at its sour taste. Booze always tasted better going down than coming up, he decided, dropping his cigarette where he stood and letting it burn itself out in the sand.

He'd figured Carson for being smarter than a donkey's rear, but he guessed he was wrong.

K

"It looks like a boat!" Abbie exclaimed after Noah opened the door to the warehouse and allowed her to step in ahead of him. "It's magnificent. So, you've already removed it from its mold, I see. When will you turn it over to start working on the inside? What's Mr. Clayton saying? I bet he's growing anxious for you to finish it." She rushed ahead of him to get a closer look, leaving her violet scent behind, immediately running her hand along the upturned underside of the boat. He hung back to watch, thrilled by her questions and her sheer enthusiasm. "I don't see any lumps or bumps," she said, walking around the entire boat to admire it from every angle. "That means she's fair, right? See, I was listening when you told me that part."

Her sweet candor made him toss back his head and laugh. "She's fair, all right." He wasn't just talking about the boat, though.

To his surprise, she threw off her coffee-colored, velveteen coat and let it drop to the floor. Although he'd shut down the wood-burning stove earlier, the room had stayed comfortably warm with the windows shut and locked. It appeared she intended to make herself at home.

For the first time, he got a good look at her floral-print skirt and puffy-sleeved shirtwaist with the high neck, a pinkish concoction that made her cheeks glow like a just-picked apple. Good grief, she was pretty! She bent over to look underneath the boat, touching it, inspecting it, and seeming to revel in seeing it firsthand. He couldn't recall Suzanna's ever coming to his boatworks to ooh and aah over his efforts unless his partner was about. In retrospect, he realized that the few times she'd dropped in at his boatshed, it had been to ogle Tom Grayson. Man, he'd been a fool. Somehow, though, the animosity he'd felt for the two of them had started to fade some weeks ago, almost turning into gratitude for having been rescued from the situation. He couldn't pinpoint when he'd started viewing the matter in this light, but the reality was he didn't possess nearly the same bitterness he once had, always reminding himself that he had legal claim to Toby, and they did not.

He and Abbie stayed at the warehouse a full hour, keeping up a steady conversation. Abbie had made a cushion of her coat, leaning her slender back against a beam in the center of the room and facing the boat. She'd kicked off her boots so that her toes peeked out from the hem of her skirt, wiggling in the cutest fashion. Noah sat a foot or so away from her, his legs stretched out and crossed at the ankles. At the end of the hour, he began to think that Marie's Ice Cream Parlor might close before they ever got there, but he had no desire to bring it up to Abbie.

She wanted to know the steps he'd followed to get the boat to its current stage and what remained to be done. He explained the necessity of having good, tight joints, sealing the craft up for waterproofing, building the seats of cypress, fastening the center posts, nailing in the keel, placing the beams of the deck in place, and getting the cockpit ready so the coaming could take place. Lastly, he would paint the boat, attach the sails, install the table, cabinetry, cushioned benches, and brass hardware, and generally make the boat sail worthy. She listened with intense interest, if the brightness of her eyes and the pensive tilt of her head were any indication.

"Are you going to finish it in time for the regatta?"

"I'd better, or Donald Clayton will have my hide—or demand his money back, at the very least."

"He wouldn't. He's too nice a man."

"He's determined to win this race."

"Are you confident he will?" she asked, her graceful hands clasped and nearly hidden in the folds of her flowery skirt. Strands of charcoal hair fell around her temples, beckoning him to brush them behind her delicate ears, yet he restrained himself.

"Fairly confident, but there's always the chance I may have miscalculated something, even though I've worked and reworked this design in my head and on paper for almost two years, now."

"You watch. It'll skim across the water like butter on a hot skillet."

He laughed. "Now, there's a picture. I hope you're right."

"You've built sailboats all your life?"

"Started by watching my father. He's a master builder, always has been; even in a drunken daze, he could loft a boat. Never have been able to figure that one out. I guess he was born with a gift."

"And you inherited it."

He shrugged, weary of talking about himself. "Did you inherit your mother's looks?"

She took the unexpected question in stride. "Folks say so. She was Italian. When I look at photos of her, it's rather eerie. I feel as though I'm looking at my own reflection."

"Ah. Then, she was beautiful."

She ignored the implied compliment. "I wish I'd known her, but she died just before my second birthday."

"That must have been hard for you and your sisters."

"Hardest on Hannah, I suppose; as the oldest, she probably knew Mother the best, and, thus, missed her the most. But Grandmother quickly stepped in, helped us adjust, and made life as normal for us as possible. I don't remember ever feeling especially deprived. Don't get me wrong; there are times I miss her deeply, even though I don't remember her. Does that make sense?"

"Perfect sense," Noah said. The wind had picked up, whistling through the trees and prompting him to think it best to drive her to Marie's and back to her house afterward rather than finish out their walk. Low-burning gas lamps lit the darkening room. A thumping sound outside impelled him to glance at the door.

"Does Toby miss his mother?"

"He hardly ever asks about her anymore." Mild concern over the strange noise made him wonder if he ought to check it out, but since Abbie hadn't appeared to notice it, he decided not to jump the gun. Most likely, the wind had blown down a small limb, which he could tend to later.

They kept up their conversation, she asking about Suzanna, he not holding back any details. On many levels, it felt downright good to express his feelings, as well as to tell her how little he dwelt on his anger these days.

"I hope you know that's another answer to prayer," she said with a warm smile.

He gave a slow nod. "I agree."

A look of relief washed over her face. "You do?"

"What else could I attribute it to? I came into Sandy Shores an angry, confused, wounded man, but as the days have passed, I've felt myself sort of slipping out of that skin and into something new and fresh. I pulled out my Bible a few days ago and actually started studying it, and that's something I haven't felt like doing for a long while."

Her eyes fairly sparkled with delight, and he had the strongest urge to lean forward and kiss their lids. To combat the urge, he quickly stood up, stretched out his arms to her, and said, "Come on, you. It's time we head for Marie's, but in my rig."

"You know," she said, taking his hands and allowing him to help her up, "as much as I love walking, the idea of riding suddenly appeals to me." She brushed at her skirts while he bent to retrieve her coat. When he stood up, their eyes locked and held. "This has been a most enjoyable night, Mr. Carson."

He smiled and held up her coat. Turning her back to him, she pushed her arms through the sleeves. He couldn't resist. He leaned close to her ear, brushing her lobe with his mouth. "And it's not even over yet."

"Oh...."

He gently took her by the shoulders and turned her back around. Looking down, he judged he had to be at least seven or eight inches taller than she. "I'm not exactly sure what's happening with my heart, but it sure acts strange whenever I'm around you."

Her dark, sculpted eyebrows arched with pretend concern. "That sounds serious. Perhaps you should pay a visit to Stuffy Huffy."

He shook his head twice. "I doubt Stuffy would have a cure for me."

"No?" She released a nervous half laugh, half sigh. "Ah, well, that could be a problem."

"Or not." He leaned down to close the distance between them, his mouth coming within a mere inch of hers before he stopped. "I'm about to do away with your mandate, Miss Kane, so if you're of a mind to object, you best speak now."

"I…I can't think of a single objection, Mr. Carson."

The sound of his heartbeat seemed magnified to the point that he thought she might hear it, or, at least, see it pulsing in his neck, which was where her eyes had decided to settle.

Slowly closing the distance between their mouths, he pressed his lips to hers, melding, molding, and tasting. This kiss differed from the others in that he knew her better now; it wasn't as much a kiss of exploration and discovery as it was a kiss of confirmation and commitment. Yes, commitment. Whether he wanted to come clean yet or not, his heart and soul had slipped off a cliff and fallen into a deep hole that he couldn't escape. He hadn't meant to walk so close to the edge, but she'd captured him and pulled him to it. And the mystery of it all was that she had no idea she'd done it. Enchanting described her—that, and tender, intelligent, passionate, funny, intriguing—and soft. The kiss was nothing short of lush and dense, her fingers spread across his back like stars and planets, his hands slowly caressing the permissible spots—her ribs, her waist, her back, her hair, and the nape of her neck. When, at last, they drew back from each other, their breaths heated each other's faces, their eyes wide and wondering, their lips unsmiling.

"Does this qualify me to share a pew with you tomorrow morning?" he asked her.

She blinked. "I would consider that a strong possibility."

K

He followed them on foot as they made their way to Marie's Ice Cream Parlor in Carson's shiny, new rig, sitting about as close to each other as two folded dollar bills and staying that way until he made the turn onto Water Street, at which time Abbie scooted to the other side of the seat, no doubt trying to avoid sparking gossip. Now, leaning against a lamppost across the street, he sneered and spat on the sidewalk, his need for a drink making him crankier than a crab on a hook. Who did she think she was fooling, anyway? He knew her for who she was—a meddlesome, troublemaking, intruding sow. Add to that hot-blooded man-chaser! Mere weeks ago, she'd been courting with the banker; now, she'd moved on to the rugged boatbuilder. He'd watched through the window as they'd kissed just after the fallen branch had narrowly missed his head when the wind had taken it down, making him nearly wet himself. Thankfully, that Carson fellow hadn't come out to investigate, or he'd have had to make a run for it.

He grew bored of waiting for them to come back out and decided he'd had enough for one night. He'd walk across the street and up the block to Erv's Place for a bottle of whiskey. After watching her tonight, he needed some shots of the hard stuff to help even out his feverish temper. Besides, he had to plan his strategy. Hopefully, Angus Clemens would be waiting for him.

Chapter Twenty-six

They did share a church pew that Sunday, and the next Sunday after that, and, soon, it became clear to most that Abbie Ann Kane and Noah Carson had become an item. What folks thought about their courtship, Abbie couldn't say—with the exception of Miss Ida Sprig, that is, who always tended to look down on blossoming love, her spinsterhood having turned her into somewhat of a sour biddy. Whenever they passed her in the church lobby, despite Abbie's warm, albeit forced, greeting, the prudish woman never failed to turn up her nose at them disapprovingly.

"Why does she always wear such a frown?" Noah had whispered in Abbie's ear one Sunday when they had walked past the woman at the top of the stairs, where she usually parked herself. "You couldn't have been any friendlier to her just now, and yet, she barely managed a hello."

Abbie had giggled. "That's Miss Ida Sprig, and anyone who knows her swears she eats lemons for every meal." They'd found their usual pew, the one that may as well have had the name Kane etched into each end, Toby plopping his body between them and giving the appearance that they were a family. Abbie's father, grandmother, and the entire Devlin family squeezed into the pew, as well.

The earliest signs of summer marched on the scene in a parade of vibrant colors and marvelous scents, trees looking cavalier with their fresh, young leaves, forsythias blooming in rich yellows, and magnolias blossoming, then dropping their flowers within a week or so to make way for green sprouts. Multihued tulips stood in proud, straight lines in front of houses and in flower boxes. Everything about the season made Abbie's heart sing and swell. The best part was, no more bizarre incidents had occurred to cloud her mind and spirits, and even Gabe had slackened his search for the culprit who'd threatened her that winter. With nothing to go on but a few misspelled words scrawled on scraps of paper, he had high hopes that whoever had been behind the ill-intentioned messages and drawings had given up his quest. She'd avoided telling him, and anyone else, for that matter, about the other mysterious occurrences. Not even Noah had a clue.

The W.C.T.U. meetings went on without incident, and Abbie figured, perhaps, the additional hours of daylight discouraged the offender from harassing them. Discussion about the tactic of storming local saloons with hymns and prayers had reemerged at the last meeting with arguments on both sides, some members thinking it unwise in light of the rock-throwing incident and the apparent danger to Abbie, others saying they shouldn't let a bully influence their actions. Abbie tended to side with the latter group but had kept her opinion to herself, acting as a disinterested moderator and letting the discussion run its course. After a time, Gertie Pridmore had made a motion to table it until their next meeting, and to pray about it in the meantime. The motion had been seconded and voted on in the affirmative.

With that matter settled, at least for the moment, they'd moved on to the next topic: the upcoming auction to benefit Hope House. The various committees had reported their progress regarding plans for the auction, and Abbie had deemed everything in order. Now, all that remained was to pray for a good turnout, and that enough funds would come in to cover the expenses of replacing the roof, painting the interior and exterior, installing new front and back doors with decent locks, and making other minor improvements. On top of that, they needed a good number of volunteers to carry out these jobs. Noah had already said he'd be available.

Dear, sweet Noah. Abbie tried to remember what life had been like without him, so accustomed had she grown to seeing him often—not daily, but often. *I'll see him tonight*, she thought to herself with delight; Grandmother Kane had invited Rita James and Noah and Toby to dinner. Adding to Abbie's excitement was that she would be preparing the meal—with Grandmother's help, of course. On the menu were baked marmalade pork chops, mashed potatoes and gravy, Grandmother Kane's home-canned green beans, fresh-baked bread, and applesauce cake. Abbie had already baked the bread and the cake, and they'd turned out dandily, if she did say so herself. She would be the first to admit she had few culinary skills, despite Grandmother Kane's tireless efforts to teach her, but, lo and behold, this growing relationship with Noah had somehow given her new motivation to learn.

She'd allowed Noah a few more kisses, but none as passionate as the one in the warehouse. Yes, Noah had shown a deeper commitment to grow in his faith, but she had to discern whether he wanted this for himself or for the purpose of securing a place in her heart. The latter simply would not do, so she patiently waited for more evidence of the former.

With her morning hours at the Whatnot completed, she and Jesse decided to take a walk to the loading dock to watch the ships come in. They hadn't done so for some time, even though they both loved to walk and talk. She could have sworn her nephew had grown a foot in the last year, not to mention a few shoe sizes, and, to top matters off, his voice had gone croaky and inconsistent, low one day, an octave higher the next. Someday, he'd be too busy to take walks with her, so whenever he suggested one, she leaped at the chance. Waving good-bye to Rita, who had already jumped headlong into the job of assisting a customer with her long list of needs, they headed out the door and up Water Street, Dusty at their heels, his nose to the ground, and his tail wagging with glee.

After two solid days of rain, the sun had risen that morning in a cloudless, sapphire sky, lending promise to the weekend. They chatted about the warmth of its rays on their shoulders and their surprising lack of need for sweaters and capes. "Such a lovely day!" Abbie said as they walked along, passing stores and shops and peeking through open doors to wave at proprietors if they happened to be looking their way.

"Yeah. I'm gettin' up a game of baseball with Billy B and some other kids later today. I'm pretty good with a bat, did you know that?"

"You are? Well, I'm going to have to come to the field and watch you hit one over the fence."

"There isn't a fence. It's just a big field out behind Varner's Feed Store."

"Oh. Well, then, I'll come watch you hit it out of the field, how's that?"

He grinned and bent down to pick up a couple of flat pebbles, stuffing them into the pocket of his trousers. "Won't be long an' school will be out."

"Are you getting excited for summer?"

"Yeah. 'Cept I'll prolly get bored after the first month."

"I can't even imagine that! I never once got bored in the summer, that I can recall. Why, there's swimming at the beach, jumping on the sand dunes, fishing at the pier, boating on the lake—and, of course, working at the infamous Kane's Whatnot." She gave him a nudge in the side with her elbow.

Jesse laughed. The train sounded its whistle, close, shrill, and piercing, its brakes shrieking on the tracks. "Hey, the train's comin' in. Let's go see who's gettin' off."

"Race you there!" Abbie picked up her skirts and set off at a run toward the depot before she'd even finished the phrase.

"No fair; you didn't say, 'On your mark!'" he hollered, his footsteps pounding at her back, Dusty's barking louder than the train whistle itself as he ran ahead.

They arrived completely breathless, Jesse beating Abbie by a hair's breadth. Both of them bent over, laughing, then sought out a bench on which to rest. Reaching one, they plopped into it, Abbie stretching out her legs and crossing her ankles, her pointy-toed boots peeking out from the hem of her navy skirt. Dusty found a place to sit, his tongue hanging nearly to the ground. She patted the trusty mutt's head, then mopped her perspiring brow. Truly, she must have looked a sight.

"Well, that was fun," Jesse said, panting louder than his dog. "And did you see how I beat you, even though you had the advantage?" He folded his arms over his narrow chest.

"And did you see how I slowed down for you, my dear nephew, because you're younger, and because I thought it would be good for your self-esteem to come out the winner?"

"Pfff, hogwash!" He poked her in the side. "I beat you, fair and square. By the way, you run like a girl," he added.

"Then it wasn't fair and square, after all," she shot back satirically.

Their banter continued as they sought to catch their breaths and watched the conductor begin welcoming customers off the train. She had no idea why folks found it so fascinating to observe incoming travelers disembark, but, without fail, they gathered in droves, some to reunite with loved ones, others just to witness the activity. Mothers brought their young children so they could see the monstrous locomotive and hear it whir with power and steam. Men converged at the station docks, smoking their pipes and cigars, palavering with their cronies over politics and making conjectures about next year's presidential election. Some spoke of things more closely affecting them—their homes, families, crops, or businesses. Little tykes squealed and ran across the docks, their mothers scrambling to keep up, fearful of their falling off the platform.

With a mixture of mild interest and plain nosiness, Abbie wondered where all these travelers hailed from, and what had drawn them to her fair city. Of course, some she recognized as longtime customers of the Whatnot, returning after perhaps visiting family or conducting business, but others she had no recollection of having seen before. She observed many folks receiving a welcoming hug or a friendly handshake; other people stepped down with nary a soul waiting for them. She had the strongest urge to approach these people and give them a hearty Sandy Shores welcome.

The passengers who disembarked included young and old; well-dressed and shabbily attired; some in hats, some bareheaded; some with a child in their arms, some carrying satchels that looked even more cumbersome than the wriggling youngsters. One thing they all had in common, though, was an air of fatigue and relief. Abbie knew firsthand from visiting Maggie and Luke just how exhausting a train ride could be, especially if it went on for hours. The quarters were always cramped and smoke-filled, and one was occasionally stuck sitting next to a smelly drunkard, which had been her cross to bear on her last train ride East.

When it appeared that the train had been emptied of most of its passengers, she turned to Jesse. "Want to finish our walk?"

"Sure."

As they stood up, Abbie's eye caught sight of a pair of women, a mother and daughter, she surmised, daintily descending the stairs, each with a parasol over an arm. They wore flowery hats and the finest of clothing, imported silk, from the looks of it. Behind them, a dark-skinned man who looked to be their steward, if the older woman's commanding tone was any indication, carried two valises, two capes, and a large box. Like an expert juggler, he somehow managed his load with apparent ease. The women brushed themselves off and simultaneously grimaced, as if the trip had somehow tarnished them for life. While they stood there and glanced about, looking as helpless as two lost children, their assistant did his duty of hailing a cab, which, in Sandy Shores, meant alerting old Bob Haskell, who parked across the street in his rusty rig with his swayback horse, to deliver someone to his or her destination. On his rig, a painted notice advertised his services:

TAxi RidEs:
MiLe or Less=10¢. 5-MiLe LiMiT.
(HoRse is OLd)

When old Bob didn't budge from his spot across the road, no matter how hard the fellow waved at him, Abbie decided to get involved. "Come on," she said to Jesse. He followed after her, seeming to instinctively know her aim.

Approaching the ladies, who were murmuring quietly with their backs to her, she said, "I don't mean to interfere, but are you in need of assistance?"

They both whirled around, and that's when Abbie saw how lovely they were, the older woman sophisticated and elegant, even in light of her powdered-over wrinkles, the younger, small-boned and fair of skin, perhaps on the pale side and looking overfatigued, blond wisps of hair escaping her hat and falling around her exquisite, oval face.

The older woman produced the tiniest hint of a smile, while the younger merely granted Abbie a brief survey, her pretty lips set in a pout and refusing to turn up. Undaunted, Abbie put on her friendliest face. "Were you needing a ride?" she rephrased.

"Oh, yes! Yes, indeed," the older lady said. Then, pointing a kid-gloved fingertip across the road and frowning, she asked, "Is that the only taxi you have in this town?"

"I'm sorry to say it is."

At this point, their steward angled a curious look at Abbie. "He ain't movin', miss. There somethin' wrong with him?"

She chortled. "He's sleeping." Then, to the old fellow perched on his rig with his legs propped up and his hat pulled low on his head to shield his eyes, she gave a holler. "Mr. Haskell, you have customers!"

Just like that, he came to life, stomping his feet on the floor and pushing his hat off his forehead. "I'm a'comin'," he shot back, getting his old mare in gear.

"What's your destination?" Abbie asked, directing her question to the two women.

"Our destination?" the older one asked.

"With whom are you staying? I might know them, as my family owns the general store in town." She produced a light-hearted laugh. "We know just about everybody around here. I could probably direct—"

"Really? Do you happen to know—?" The young woman started to ask something, but the one Abbie presumed to be her mother quickly put a hand on her arm to squelch the rest of her question.

"We simply need to find the Culver House Hotel."

"Oh, of course, the Culver House. It's just a few blocks east." By now, Bob Haskell had reined in his horse, and he issued a toothless grin from his high perch. "These ladies need a ride to the Culver House, Mr. Haskell," Abbie told him.

"Culver House it is." He tipped his shabby hat at her and the ladies, then sent dust in every direction when he leaped off the rig to tend to their luggage.

"Kindly help him, Jeffries," the younger one said to the steward.

"Yes, ma'am." In an instant, the dark-skinned fellow jumped to Bob Haskell's aid, then helped the ladies aboard.

Abbie and Jesse watched while Bob Haskell scrambled back to his seat and prepared to set off. Then, putting the ladies out of their minds, she and Jesse resumed their chatter. She was glad she'd wrapped up the end pieces of the bread she'd baked last night and stuffed them in her skirt pockets. The quacking ducks swimming near the loading docks sounded hungry.

K

Noah's steps felt light as he made his way west on Water Street after having picked up a box of imported candy at Caneparo's Sweet Shop. He wasn't sure what Helena Kane or Abbie had planned for dessert that night, but who could turn up a nose at a box of assorted Italian chocolates? He tucked the box under his arm and smiled to himself. *Abbie Ann Carson.* He'd been testing the sound in his mind for a few weeks now and liked the ring of it, not that he'd even come close to asking Abbie to marry him. Shoot, he'd only just admitted to himself that he loved her. That seemed enough for now.

There was something else new on the horizon: he'd started the practice of praying about this newfound love he had for Abbie, about his hopes for restarting a boatworks, and about God's plan for his life and what that might look like. Most recently, he'd ventured to ask God to soften his hard edges where his father was concerned, and to begin a healing work in that relationship. To his surprise, when his father had stopped by yesterday after his workday and offered to lend a hand with the sanding, he'd been glad to see him. *Glad.* Now, there was a miracle. As for asking him to show him the letter Aunt Julia had told him about, he'd not yet gotten up the nerve. Curious as he was to read it, something told him doing so would dredge up unwelcome emotions.

"Hello, Noah!" a voice called from across the street. He waved and called back a greeting to Chuck Rycenga, a man around his age with a wife and family whom he'd met in Peter Sinclair's Sunday school class a few weeks ago. And that was another thing—not long ago, the Bible had started coming to life for him. At first, he'd started reading it out of a sense of duty; after all, Abbie wanted him to. Next, he'd read it out of curiosity. He'd start reading a story about the life of one of the patriarchs in the Old Testament, and, soon, he'd discover he'd devoured all of Genesis, Exodus, and Leviticus. Not only that, but he'd also started soaking up Sinclair's words, actually looking forward to his class. The man did know his Bible, and despite Noah's having stolen his girl, Peter still welcomed him to the men's circle. *Maybe that's what true forgiveness looks like*, he mused. Naturally, it helped that he had found someone else with whom to share a pew—some pretty girl, though not as lovely as Abbie, seemed to have taken Abbie's place. Noah was glad for the guy.

Horseback riders, horse-drawn rigs, the occasional motorcar, which looked completely out of place, and pedestrians peppered the street. A street cleaner with an apron tied around his neck and waist diligently scooped up manure and tossed it into his little wagon, dodging traffic as he worked. From the west, the one and only taxi driver in town rambled up the street in his rusty, run-down contraption with a pathetic, swayback horse pulling it. His two passengers—two fancily dressed women with wide-brimmed, floral hats and lacy parasols—made quite a contrast.

He set his gaze back on the sidewalk and his next stop, Kane's Whatnot. Yes, he had plans to see Abbie tonight, but with Toby in tow. Alone, he felt much freer to put on a flirty front with her. After popping in on her—if, indeed, she'd gone to work that morning—he'd head back over to Aunt Julia's to retrieve his son. Then, he'd go to the warehouse and put in a few more hours of work before he and Toby cleaned up and went to the Kane home for a seven o'clock dinner.

He wasn't prepared to run into Shamus Rogan on the sidewalk. Noah's steps momentarily faltered, and his body went about as stiff as a log when they actually eyeballed each other. Oh, he'd seen Shamus from a distance, but never at close range, and the man had never once apologized for running him off the road last February.

At first, it seemed they would pass each other with no more than a nod, but then, Noah decided to greet him. Another outright miracle, as two months ago, he'd just as soon have plastered him in the nose, particularly in light of what he knew about his physical abuse of Arlena.

"Shamus Rogan, right?" Noah asked.

The fellow stopped and turned his whiskery face. "And yer Carson, the one I runned into. I see you got yerself a new rig."

The man evidently felt no remorse for his deed. And how would he know about the new rig? "'Fraid I was forced to. Thing never did line up right after I went through the window of Kane's Whatnot. The wheel came off while I was driving it some weeks ago."

"You don't say. Must've been a piece o' junk, huh? Di'n't you buy it used off o' Enoch Sprock?"

"How would you know that?"

The man threw back his head and laughed, but not in a friendly way. He rubbed his jaw, and that's when Noah noticed a long, jagged scar, partially hidden by his unshaven face. "Sandy Shores has quite a grapevine, Carson. All y' gotta do is come into Erv's one o' these afternoons, sip on some brew, and do some jawin' with us. Y' learn a lot that way."

"Is that so? Well, I prefer to avoid the drinking joints, thanks."

Shamus pulled back his head and looked down his hooked nose at him. "She got to you, eh?"

"Pardon?"

"That little saloon hater you been hangin' out with, Abbie Kane."

Noah held his temper even though he had the strongest urge to make mincemeat of Shamus Rogan's innards. *Lord, help me not to create a scene in the middle of the sidewalk*, he silently prayed on the spot.

Move on. Forget about him. Good advice. But, before Noah could follow it, he had to ask, "How're your wife and girls doing? She got awful sick when you were in jail, but I'm sure you heard that through the grapevine."

"Pfff." Shamus spat a big wad of tobacco juice on the sidewalk and sneered. "Blame woman's always lookin' for sympathy. If that Kane girl hadn't of interfered, the whole thing woulda blowed over in a few days. She's a nosy li'l cuss, that girl."

Noah's feelers went up. Why all the bitterness toward Abbie? "That Kane girl, as you put it, is a caring, compassionate woman." Another loud sneer and spit. "And, excuse me for reminding you, but Dr. Van Huff had to place your wife in his infirmary and feed her lots of liquids. If Abbie and her sister hadn't gone out there that day, she might well have died."

Shamus rubbed the ugly scar along his jaw and huffed. "Well, Arlena's livin' an' breathin' now, ain't she, and none the worse."

"That may be so, Rogan, but now that you're out of jail, there're some of us still worried Arlena and your girls aren't getting the best of care, if you know what I mean." He leaned close and tilted his head down at the measly monster. "I just thought you should know we're concerned and aware, that's all." He made a point to emphasize each word with careful enunciation.

Shamus's upper lip shot up in the corner, and his glare burned like ice, his alcohol-tinged breath polluting the air. For all of seven or eight seconds, not another word passed between them, and Noah could have sworn he detected the slightest hint of unease pass over Shamus's expression, even though it vanished in a flash.

"This world would be a better place if folks'd mind their own business," Shamus finally said.

Noah boldly met Shamus's eyes, lifting one eyebrow higher than the other. "Or, if men would learn that women deserved the utmost respect."

Shamus's upper lip contorted again, and his mouth morphed into a cynical, ice-laden smile. "I s'pose your father taught you that little tidbit, eh? Speakin' of, I hear tell he used to go heavy on the drink hisself."

Reacting without forethought, Noah grabbed the man by the front of his shirt with both hands and lifted him slightly off the ground so that their faces came within inches of each other, the box of candy hitting the sidewalk with a plunk. "'Used to' being the definitive words, Rogan. My father's a changed man." He couldn't believe how quickly he'd come to his defense. "You'd do well to start changing your ways, as well, 'fore you wind up in a cold, lonely grave."

He slowly set him back down, released his shirtfront, and brushed it off in a perfunctory manner before bending to retrieve his candy box. Then, looking down at the dirty-faced man, he issued a warning: "I'd advise you to mind your manners. If anything happens to your wife or kids, you better believe the sheriff will know exactly where to point his finger."

He dared to snicker. "Ain't nothin' happenin' to my wife and kids, Carson." At that, he straightened himself as best he could and sauntered on. Noah watched until he disappeared through the front door of Erv's Place.

Noah collected his composure and headed for his aunt and uncle's place to get Toby, his mind a whir of troubling thoughts, all of them centered on Shamus Rogan.

Chapter Twenty-seven

Abbie and Jesse's walk took them to the top of Five Mile Hill for a gander out over the lake on the west side and the town of Mill Point three miles to the east. Surrounded by sand dunes and a sprinkling of summer cottages, Jesse and Abbie covered about every topic they could think of, from school to Jesse's friends, from his baby sister RoseAnn and his little brother Alex to his Sunday school teacher, Mr. Metzger, a kind grandfather figure who still related well to young boys and their struggles.

"You think you're gonna marry Noah Carson?" Jesse asked on their descent. They'd spent a good half hour at the top of the hill, enjoying the view. Jesse was a mature young man for his eleven years, but Abbie hadn't expected that question to come out of his mouth.

"Jesse Devlin, what would make you ask that?"

"You got eyes for each other, Aunt Abs. Everyone sees it, and I know you're courtin'."

"What do you know about courting?"

"I know it's something I ain't lookin' forward to."

This made her laugh till her sides hurt. Jesse joined in, and for the next few seconds, all they did was chuckle.

When they finally composed themselves, Jesse said, "Toby sure wants his pa to marry you."

"Really? How do you know that?"

"He told me. We have these little man-to-man talks on the way home from school, you know."

"Man-to-man, huh?"

"Yeah. He told me he never sees his mama and doesn't care if he ever does. But he would like one, and he outright told me he wished it could be you."

Her heart grew suddenly warm. "That's very sweet. He's a dear, dear boy, and I have to say, if I ever had a son, I'd want him to be just like Toby—with a brother just like you, of course."

"Of course." Jesse kicked a rusted tin cup on the ground, and sand went flying. "Want to stop and see Noah's boat?"

"I saw it not long ago."

"Let's stop and see it again. Please?"

"Without an invitation?" Her heart soared at the thought, but she had to get home to help Grandmother Kane clean the house and make preparations for the evening meal. "I wouldn't want to interrupt his work. And besides, it's Saturday. He may not even be there."

"Let's check, anyway."

She hesitated, then threw caution to the wind. "All right, let's!"

K

Noah decided to put his run-in with Shamus Rogan out of mind for now, at least until he had a chance to ask Abbie if she'd ever had an unpleasant encounter with him. Aside from her occasional visits with Arlena, he didn't think she'd ever actually spoken to Shamus. Still, the man seemed to hold some kind of grudge against her, and if it weren't for the fact that he'd been sitting in a cell both when the rock had flown through the church window and when the beer bottle had landed in his rig, he might well have suspected him of doing the deeds.

Something didn't quite sit well with him, though, and he wished he could put his finger on it.

He had begun the interior work on Don Clayton's boat, the bottom varnished and dried and, he hoped, waterproofed. Of course, putting her out to sea would be the test, not that he had reason to worry, considering all the putty and coats of varnish he'd used. With the help of his father and Uncle Delbert, he'd gently flipped her over and set her on wooden stanchions so he could laminate her center backbone and construct and put the bilgeboards in place. Now, she lay there, waiting for her creator to start framing up the deck beams, nail down the cedar planking, and, once more, commence with the planing, sanding, and fairing process. When he'd finished planking the deck, he'd stretch the canvas over it, which would require more muscle and hands than he had, so his father had readily volunteered to help. Rocky as things still were between them, Noah was beginning to think there just could be a tiny ray of hope for reconciliation.

Humming while he worked, Noah smiled as he thought about Toby, who'd insisted he wanted to stay at Aunt Julia's a little longer—at least, until the cookies had come out of the oven and he'd played one more game of checkers with Uncle Del and his grandpa. "I'll walk him back later, if you don't mind," Noah's father had said over the top of his newspaper. "Haven't seen her in two days, after all." He'd made it sound like he had some sort of kinship to Clayton's boat, and, maybe, he did. It did seem to be the common thread that kept trying to knit their lives together. That, and Toby.

Early afternoon sun rays streaming through the open windows cast their golden hue across the room, glancing off the walls and producing a natural light that was ideal for detail work. A light breeze caught the unlatched door and made it bump against the frame. Outside, a chorus of birds sang in harmony while squeaky wagons passed by, horses' hooves clip-clopped on the road, and the Interurban whizzed along on its steel tracks, all indicators of a busy Saturday of errand running.

Noah was standing inside the boat and drilling a hole, with sweat dripping off his brow, when the door creaked. Thinking it was just the wind, he ignored the sound. But then, the sound of swishing skirts followed.

He swung around just as a woman with her back to him closed and latched the door, a woman wearing a pale-blue, foamy, silken gown and a flowery hat to match. What in the name of—? The drill slipped from his fingers, hitting the floor of the boat with a loud thud. Instant bile gathered in his mouth as he stared and swallowed.

She turned to face him, her blue eyes wary. "Hello, Noah," she said in a feathery tone that had once captivated him but now made his stomach boil with rage. Blond wisps of hair curled around her china-doll face.

"Suzanna." For a moment, he could do nothing but catch his breath. "What...do you think you're doing here?" He stepped out of the boat but stayed glued to that spot, the shock at seeing her in *his* boatshed swelling his veins almost to the point of bursting them wide open.

As if she belonged there with him, she pulled off her hat, releasing the rest of her yellow curls, and looked for a place to lay it. Finding nowhere suitable, she chose to hold it as she approached him slowly, falteringly. "Are you just a tiny bit happy to see me?" she asked, holding up her thumb and index finger a half inch apart and squinting.

"No!"

She winced. "I know you're angry with me, Noah, and you've every right to be."

"You're not welcome here, Suzanna. I have no idea what even possessed you to come." She stepped closer. "And stay away from me," he ordered her, laying one hand on his boat to steady himself and putting the other up in a halting gesture.

She laughed, and it all came back to him like a bad dream—the way she'd manipulated him right from the start, charmed him into courting her while they were yet in high school, mostly because she'd known her father wouldn't approve, because she loved a challenge, and because boys intrigued her. "You aren't scared of me, are you? Goodness, you're as pale as if you've just seen a ghost."

He quickly gathered his wits, not in the least wanting her to think she held one ounce of influence over him. No, if anything, it was taking every bit of his willpower not to walk over and strangle her. *Lord, give me strength. Let me not say or do anything I'll have to pay for later.*

"You didn't answer my question. What are you doing here?" he said through gritted teeth.

"Mother and I wanted to see Toby." She took another step closer.

"Your mother? She's here, too?"

"Yes, we're staying at the—oh, what is it?—the Culver House, yes. Apparently, it's the nicest hotel in these parts, but it's still a bit under par, if you ask me."

Everything was under par, according to Suzanna—even he. "I don't want you seeing Toby. It'll only confuse him. He's finally beginning to adjust to your being out of his life."

One more step. "He's my son, Noah, and I'd like to make amends with him…and you."

"What? It's impossible. Besides, you've remarried, remember?"

She lifted her left hand, and he saw that her ring finger was bare. "Not for much longer, I'm afraid."

That sort of set him back. "Already? You haven't even been married a year. What did you do, run after the first pair of pants that came along?" The statement was probably uncalled for, but he couldn't resist saying it.

She looked only slightly wounded. "No, nothing like that. I…it's complicated." Her attempt at laughter fell flat, and she gave her wrist a flick. "It never worked from the start, Noah. I don't know why I married him."

"Greed?" he asked, arching an eyebrow.

"I suppose. Oh, bosh, I was a fool, and I know that now. Do you think you could find it in you to forgive me?"

"I already have," he heard himself say. She let out a heavy sigh, as if he'd just told her he would give her the moon if she wanted it. "But if you're asking me if there's a chance for us as a couple," he felt a cold smile emerge on his lips, "I'd have to say, not until God parts the waters of Lake Michigan so we can walk to Wisconsin, not until the planets rearrange themselves, not until a horse's rear switches places with its head, not until—"

"Oh, all right, you've made your point," she said, shushing him, close enough now to put a hand on his arm. He pulled it away faster than a bolt of lightning.

"You've got to be crazy, Suzanna. You've done nothing but waste valuable time in coming here—and dragging your mother along, no less."

"She misses her grandson."

"Then she should have come alone. She was always good to Toby, but you? You never did have the faintest idea how to be a mother, and I'd say it's about a 99.9 percent chance you still don't have the knack."

"We never should have had a child so young."

"Twenty-two is not considered young, Suzanna. The truth is, *you* shouldn't have had a child." She didn't argue the fact, just stared at him with those glossy, blue eyes. Eyes that had no effect on him whatsoever.

"I still would like to see him." She looked around the room. "I was hoping he might be here."

"Oh, that would have been dandy, your just waltzing in and giving me no time to prepare him. Don't do that to him, Suzanna. Besides, you have no legal right to see him."

"I'm aware of that, and I don't intend to fight you on it. I just—"

"Well, that's good, because you'd be fighting a losing battle. You may have a bulldog for a father, but I'm a lot smarter now. This time, I'd hire the best lawyer in the country, no matter what the cost, and he'd make Carl Dunbar look like a slab of meat on a chopping block."

She cleared her throat. "I just told you, I have no intention of fighting for custody, or even visitation. I—Mother and I—would merely like to see him."

Noah allowed himself a deep swallow. "I'd prefer you got on the next train out of here. You have to think of the boy's well-being, Suzanna, especially since he's just recently been able to put you out of his mind."

Deep lines disrupted her perfect brow. "How do you know he has?"

He sneered. "Easy. He hasn't asked about you in weeks."

"That doesn't mean he hasn't thought about me or his grandparents."

"It doesn't mean he *has*, either."

She ignored him and turned her attention to the shop, giving it a complete scan, her perfectly sculpted face looking less youthful than the last time he'd seen her. It was almost pallid, now that he allowed himself a closer look. And another thing—she had not one ounce of fat on her frame. Not that she'd ever been heavy, just fuller. Today, she looked all bones.

"I see you're back at it. You always were an ardent boatbuilder. Learned the trade from your father, drunken skunk that he was. I heard he's reformed and living in Sandy Shores."

"You heard right."

She nodded and swatted at a fly. "My guess is, you'll have a business up and running here in no time. And I've no doubt you'll be every bit as successful here as you were in Guilford. Tom hasn't done well, you know. When you left, the business fell apart. Folks were asking for your expertise, your level of skill, but Tom couldn't deliver. He's lost several accounts and has gained only a few this year. He had to let go Bill Noble, Hiram Jennings, and Joseph Getty for lack of funds to pay them. It's turned him into a ball of nerves."

He could have told her that would happen. Unfortunately for Tom, Noah had been the more talented of the two. His skill came from an inbred aptitude passed down from his father, and Tom lacked that ingrained, deep-seated passion. Noah had wondered how long it would take before the business started crumbling. At one time, he'd looked forward to its demise, but the news actually saddened him.

"Add to that his complete lack of love for me...you might say I only compounded his problems tenfold."

Noah shrugged to feign indifference, even though there was a twinge of regret that, at only twenty-eight, Suzanna had already failed at two marriages. "There's not a thing I can do for you, Suzanna." He certainly had no intention of involving himself in her tangled web.

Actual tears formed in the corners of her eyes, which threw him for a loop. Suzanna was nothing if she wasn't hard as steel. Tears? He tried to determine if they were genuine. She laid a hand on his arm and stepped an inch closer. "Please," she choked. "May I...see my son?"

"I can't—"

The door creaked open, accompanied by familiar laughter. Noah spun on his heel, and the laughter stilled. Bright beams of sunlight on the newcomers' backs blinded him to their expressions, but Jesse and Abbie's silhouettes in the doorway could not have been more distinct.

"Oh," Abbie said. "We didn't mean.... We'll just be going."

"No, no, come in," Noah quickly countered, leaving Suzanna's side to walk across the room, seeing their faces clearly now.

If ever confusion had filled a room, it was now. Jesse's mouth had sagged open, and his eyes went blank as he gave Suzanna a quick perusal. Abbie looked stricken, and before Noah could say anything, she made an about-turn and started pushing Jesse out the door.

Noah ran to reach her and caught her by the arm. "Wait. Please." She wrangled out of his grasp.

"It's you," Suzanna said, coming over. "You're the girl from the train station. You—oh! Well!" Realization dawned in her eyes as she looked back and forth from Noah to Abbie.

"You've met?" he asked.

"Not officially, no." Suzanna extended her hand. "I'm Noah's wife...er, former wife, I should clarify."

"Yes, you should," Noah said, his irritation obvious.

"Toby's mother," she made sure to tack on.

Without a bit of dithering, Abbie took her hand and they shared a two-second handshake. "Hello, I'm Abbie Ann Kane, and this is my nephew, Jesse Devlin," she said, giving him a nudge in the side. He did the polite thing and stuck out his hand, as well, but Noah read a certain anger in his eyes—the kind that wells up when protective mode kicks in. He admired him for it.

Awkward silence engulfed the four of them for a moment. "Well, I should be going," Suzanna finally said, to Noah's great relief.

"No need," Abbie said. "You two finish your conversation." Again, she turned and started steering Jesse away. The two set off almost at a sprint.

"Abbie, wait!" Noah left Suzanna in the doorway and ran after them, nabbing Abbie by the arm. "Jesse," he said. "May I have a moment with Abbie?"

The boy narrowed his eyes and arched an eyebrow. "It's fine," Abbie said. "You go ahead, and I'll catch up."

"All right, but I'll walk slow."

Jesse set off, and they both watched until he hit Lafayette Street. "I swear to you, I had no idea she was coming to town," Noah said, turning her at the shoulders and forcing her to face him. "She wants to see Toby."

"Then you should let her."

"What?"

She lifted her gaze and looked him in the eyes. "She's his mother, Noah. She has a right to see her son."

"I have legal custody of him. She gave up those rights."

"Toby deserves to see her. You shouldn't deny him the opportunity."

"I...." He hadn't expected such a prompt, decisive response. "What if he doesn't want to see her?"

"You'll have to ask him, I guess. How long will she be staying?"

"I don't know."

"I see." She breathed deeply. Glancing up Lafayette Street, Noah saw Jesse stopped along the road, his arms folded, waiting. So much for his walking slowly. "I don't want you to come to supper tonight," Abbie said quietly.

"What? Why?" His heart thudded hard, and he squeezed her upper arms. "But your grandmother invited me."

Her chin jutted out. "Well, I'm uninviting you. You have matters to tend to, Noah, and, frankly, I...."

"You what?"

"I...can't keep up this friendship."

"What do you mean, friendship? We have more than just friendship between us, Abbie Ann, and you know it."

She sniffed, pulled back her shoulders, and went as solemn-faced as a priest giving the last rites. "You are a divorced man, Noah, with a son, no less."

"I'm sorry I carry that badge of dishonor."

"And a mother who wants to see him. If you and I were to continue this—this friendship, and if it were to progress… into…."

"Love?" he whispered, raising her chin with his index finger.

She ignored the word. "Then she would always be there, in the shadows."

"And we would deal with it."

"You would deal with it, perhaps, but I'm not sure I could. It would mean a lifetime of her coming in and out of our lives. It's just—it's not going to work, Noah. I'm sorry if I…I don't know…led you to believe…."

"What? Listen to yourself, Abbie." He clutched her arms the tighter, wanting to shake some sense into her. "We need to talk more about this. It's just…." He glanced at the open door. At least Suzanna had had the common courtesy to give them some privacy. "Now is not a very good time. Please let me come to supper tonight, and we can talk things over."

"No. As I said before, it's not going to work. I've been praying about this, and I just haven't received a clear sense from God about us." Looking over at the warehouse, she added, "And this…well, this sort of cinches it for me." For the second time, she wriggled out of his grip.

"Abbie, this needs more discussion. Don't do this."

She gave him one last look before turning away, her eyes glinting with determination. "It's for the best, Noah."

She started walking. "It isn't for the best, Abbie, and just what are you going to tell your grandmother and your father when I don't show up?"

She paused but failed to turn around. "The truth."

Jesse ran back to meet her, and the two started walking up Lafayette together. Turning slowly, Noah reluctantly headed back toward the warehouse. He looked down and kicked a good-sized rock clear across the yard, watching it bounce off a tree trunk. Suzanna appeared in the doorway, her arms folded. "Is she mad?"

"I wouldn't call it mad."

"Humph. She's mad. Sorry to have caused a rift between you."

It was the first time he'd ever heard an apology roll off her tongue, but it hardly made him feel better. "I want you to go now. My father's bringing Toby over, and they could be here any minute. I don't want you around when he gets here."

She hesitated a moment, her eyes brimming with tears. "I understand." She bit her plump lower lip. "Would you at least talk to him, ask him if he wants to see me? And his Grandma Dunbar? As I said, we're staying at the Culver House."

"I'll think about it, but I can't make any promises. He's had a lot of disappointments in his life."

She dropped her chin and seemed to be studying the pointy toe of her shoe. "And I'm to blame for them."

"Not all of them," he said, meaning it. "Looking back, I wasn't the best husband. I realize I spent more hours than I should have at the boatworks."

"I'd like a chance...." She choked and coughed, and, for a second, he thought he was going to have to give her a hearty slap on the back. "A chance to see him again." More tears gathered in her blue eyes, but they failed to move him much. Rather, a sort of numbness overtook him. Abbie still filled the front of his mind.

Chapter Twenty-eight

A wagonload of new merchandise arrived at the Whatnot on Monday, keeping Abbie, Hannah, and Rita occupied the entire morning. While sorting through crates to decide what to shelve and what to store away, Hannah and Rita chattered nonstop. Abbie's spirits weren't quite as chipper, though, and she figured they could tell; listening to their prattle did help her to keep her mind off her own affairs. Several times, either Hannah or Rita tried to draw her out of her quiet shell, but she continually resisted baring her broken heart to them. Oh, for certain, they knew her morose mood involved Noah; in fact, who at the Third Street Church didn't? For a number of Sundays, Noah and Toby Carson had been fixtures in the Kane family pew, but yesterday, the two had conspicuously sat on the opposite side of the church. And, after the service, when Noah had tried to greet Abbie in the lobby, Toby at his side, she'd spoken only to Toby, wishing him a good week and promising to see him next week at Sunday school. Whether it was just her imagination or not, it did seem as if people walked slowly past them, their ears tuned to try to catch what they might be saying to each other.

Customers came and went the entire morning, stepping over boxes stacked in the middles of the aisles and accepting the women's apologies for the clutter. Abbie, Hannah, and Rita took turns tallying up folks' items at the cash register, then going back to the business of putting the store to rights. Papa came in mid-morning to check on their progress, making special eyes at Rita, which, Abbie knew, he thought no one else noticed. In some ways, it provoked a wave of jealousy in the deepest parts of her core; it wasn't that she didn't love Rita and accept her with wholehearted eagerness, but she sometimes felt almost invisible to her father these days. Since having "the talk" with each of his daughters about his newfound love for Rita—yes, he'd identified it as love— he'd let down his guard around Rita, and everyone else in town, for that matter, even going so far as to hold her hand in church. With the tiniest degree of chagrin, Abbie realized that he well could be the next Kane to marry, a thought that produced in her a rather lopsided reaction—joy for his well-deserved happiness, a twinge of sadness that the Kane family dynamics would change in a dramatic way. She and her sisters had always been the most important women in their father's eyes, but now, another woman had taken that spot. *Rightfully so, of course*, Abbie had mused several times, but the acknowledgment hadn't relieved her melancholy mood.

While her father helped sort through the new inventory, claiming he could take a longer than usual break from working at the insurance office due to a canceled appointment, Gabe strolled into the Whatnot. The appearance of his uniform, club, and holstered gun always gave Abbie pause, but she recognized their importance to his charge to uphold the law. He wore a jovial expression as he removed his police hat and greeted everyone, then purposefully stepped over several boxes to reach his wife and plant a kiss on her rose-hued cheek. Hannah never had been successful at hiding her blush of joy when Gabe entered a room, and this time was no exception.

"What are you doing here?" she asked him. "Have you come to whisk me away?"

"If only I could, but by the look of things, you'll be busy here for the next month. Actually, I came to see Abbie."

"Me?" Abbie said, pointing a finger at herself. "Are you planning to arrest me? What are the charges? Just let me say right off, I didn't do it."

Everyone chortled. "Don't listen to her, Gabe. She's been a little troublemaker for as long as I've known her. Lock her up till she comes to her senses," Hannah teased.

Gabe laughed, but his serious side came out when he said, straight-faced, "Can you step outside with me for a second, Abbie?"

"I was just kidding, Gabe," Hannah said. Yet when Gabe did not respond with a friendly retort, but merely held the door open for Abbie, the room went as somber as a funeral parlor.

The sunny, blue skies of the past few days had disappeared, giving way to gray clouds that only made Gabe's sudden soberness all the more unnerving.

"What's wrong?" Abbie asked.

He sat down on the bench in front of the Whatnot and motioned for her to join him. "Probably nothing at all, but I want to ask you something."

"Ask away." She folded her hands and set them in the folds of her purple, flowered skirt. A mild breeze feathered her face. Water Street was buzzing with traffic, and the

Interurban train whizzed past them, forcing Gabe to hold his question until the noise had lessened.

"Have you ever had any contact with Shamus Rogan?"

"Shamus Rogan? No, none at all. Why do you ask?"

"Noah paid me a visit first thing this morning. He's a little concerned."

Just the mention of her beloved's name made her heart skip two full beats. "What did he have to say?"

"Well, he ran into Shamus in town on Saturday. The fellow seems to have a beef with you, said you ought not to have interfered in his family. He called you a 'saloon hater' and a 'nosy, little cuss.'"

Abbie snickered to herself. "Well, at least he has me pegged."

He ignored that. "I went out to see Arlena Rogan afterward, just to check on things and see if I could get anything out of her. I didn't see any signs of abuse, but something seemed a little off to me. Couldn't quite put my finger on it."

Abbie's spine went as straight as a stick. "Arlena has a knack for hiding her marks. She's been perfecting the façade all her married days. Were her girls at school?"

"She said Virginia had stayed home. Had a bad case of influenza, but that the other girls went to school. I asked if she'd seen the doctor, and she hemmed and hawed a bit before changing her tune, saying it was more likely just a cold. I stepped inside, uninvited, and asked to see Virginia for myself, but when I opened her door, she wasn't there. That's when Arlena broke down and said she'd run off, claiming her father had hurt her badly and she couldn't take it anymore."

"In what way had he hurt her?"

"I couldn't get it out of Arlena, but I have a sick feeling about it."

Rather than pursue his suspicions, she said, "Virginia's not capable of taking care of herself. If she's wounded in some way, then we have to find her."

"I agree. I brought Arlena back with me. She's at the jail now, and she's completely bewildered, crying and spewing about what's going to happen to her and her girls. I promised her we'd fetch the other two at school. I'm heading over to Don Clayton's house to see if he might have a temporary place for them to hole up—maybe in one of his cottages. We could probably keep her and the girls safe, for now, but in the meantime, I'm putting out a warrant for Shamus's arrest. I don't want him going near those young women—or you, for that matter. My guess is, he's in hiding, because none of the saloon proprietors has seen him since Saturday night, and he didn't report to work today, either."

"The auction's tonight, so I'll be at the community hall all afternoon to help set things up," Abbie said. "I'll stop by your office at noon to see if I can offer some comfort to Arlena before I go to the hall."

Gabe nodded. "Good. Thanks for doing that. But keep your eyes peeled the whole time you're out and about, you hear?"

"I will."

He stared straight ahead, lost in thought, then asked, "You haven't encountered any more strange occurrences of late, have you?"

"No, none," she said, even as her conscience pricked her hard. She'd kept the secret long enough. "Well, there was this one time, quite a while back, when I sensed someone might be following me. I was on my way home from a W.C.T.U. meeting and something hit me in the back. When I turned around, I saw someone dart across a yard and disappear behind a house." She frowned. "As I recall, a dog kept barking, until I heard a loud, popping sound."

Gabe looked away. "That may have been around the same time Grant Farmer reported his dog had been shot with a .22."

She gasped. "You don't think…?"

"I don't know what to think."

She pondered that for a second, trying to remain calm. "Well, if someone had wanted to harm me, he could have just as well shot me as the dog. Maybe he shot the dog in self-defense."

"It's possible."

She pressed her lips together to the point of pain before releasing them with a loud sigh. "There was just one other little thing."

Gabe's eyes narrowed into dark slits. "Abbie Ann…."

"I found a silly, little note next to the cash register one day." She kept her voice light. "It was one of those days the school was closed, because I recall Toby's being at the store while Jesse ran some errands for Hannah."

"What did the note say?"

"Hmm, let me think, now." Of course, she could remember every detail. "Oh, yes—something like, did it bother me to know someone was following me? It was plain ridiculous."

"That is not ridiculous!" Gabe bellowed, causing a few folks to turn and gawk at him as they passed. He swallowed and breathed, swallowed and breathed. "You should have brought it straight to me," he said with a lowered voice. "Tell me you at least kept the note."

Abbie looked down at her hands. "It's in my top dresser drawer."

He sighed. "Good. I'll stop by your house and get it later." He put his hands on his knees, preparing to stand. "You're not keeping anything else from me, are you?"

"No. I promise. You don't think it's Shamus Rogan who's been sending the notes and following me, do you?"

"Well, it's feasible he shot the dog, I suppose, and also left the note at the store, but the other things happened while he was sitting in a jail cell. What I need to do is compare the handwriting on the notes, then somehow try to get a sample of his penmanship."

"Maybe Arlena can provide you with that."

"I already asked her, being that I had enough reason to be suspicious, but she claimed not to have anything lying around with his writing on it. 'Course, I'm not prepared to believe that. Was anyone else in the store the day you found that note by the cash register?"

"Oh, yes, oodles!" Her shoulders dropped in a slump. "But I couldn't tell you who, for sure—except Toby, of course."

"I'll try asking him a couple of simple questions. You never know; he may have seen something unusual."

Abbie pinched the bridge of her nose. "Did anyone ever visit Shamus while he was incarcerated?"

"Good question. Not that I'm aware of, but I'll ask my deputies. Someone could very well have come in during my off hours. We can't keep our prisoners from receiving visitors—unless they're being held for some heinous crime."

The Whatnot's door opened with a jingle, and Hannah popped her head out. "Are you abusing my baby sister in any way? I heard you raise your voice to her a bit ago, Gabriel Devlin. My father sent me out here to check on things."

He chuckled. "Blood runs thick in the Kane family. Believe me, I wouldn't dare tangle with any of you. To do so would be reckless."

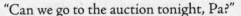

"Can we go to the auction tonight, Pa?"

Noah had been sanding the life out of his boat's interior, his mind darting in a million directions. Abbie was still foremost on his mind, followed by Suzanna and her mother and the question of whether to tell Toby they were in town, and, of course, his relationship with his father, who intended to come to the warehouse today after work to help stretch the canvas over the deck to make the deck watertight, definitely a two-man job.

"You bet we can, son."

"What's an auction?"

He grinned. "It's an event at which you'll find lots of items for sale, with a man standing up front trying to get you to buy them, but you have to make bids and outbid everyone else who wants to buy the same items."

"Are you gonna buy anything?"

"Only if I see something there I can't manage to live without."

"Like a toy for me? Do you think they'll have toys?"

"There may be toys there."

"I'm goin' t' look for toys."

I'm going to look for Abbie. "You do that."

His father showed up at four o'clock, bearing a basket of food prepared by Aunt Julia and smiling cheerfully. That was something Noah had had to work at getting accustomed to—his father's smile. Truly, his inner joy did not stay put. It seeped through his very pores and came out in the form of kindness, laughter, generosity, and smiles galore. For the longest time, Noah had thought it all an act, but he couldn't imagine how or why a drunk would do that. What would be his motivation? Clearly, a change had taken place in Gerald Carson's soul, and the more Noah knew him, the more he believed the miracle.

They sat down to a picnic dinner, of sorts, and talked about a number of mundane things.

"Whatever happened to all my trophies and the stuff I had in storage in Guilford?" Noah decided to ask.

"Everything's all right there in my shed, your stuff and mine, just waiting for someone to pick it up. I'm planning to move to my own place soon, so I'll no doubt be making a trip back East to retrieve my things. Naturally, I'll fetch everything of yours, as well. I got a call from a real estate man out there who says he has someone interested in buying my place."

Noah thought about the old homestead and waited for a sense of regret to come over him about its being sold, but none came. "That's great. I hope it sells."

He had the urge to tell his father about Suzanna's coming to Sandy Shores, but with Toby sitting right there, chomping on his bologna sandwich, he couldn't figure out a way to do it.

The subject of the auction came up. "Are you goin' to it, Grandpa?" Toby asked.

"Nope." Gerald wiped a smear of mustard off his whiskery cheek. "Around seven thirty, I'm to meet some folks who have a house for rent. They're goin' to show me through it, and if the price is right, I'll move in."

"Hot dog! When you move in, I can prolly spend a night with you. Right?"

The two men eyeballed each other over their mugs of cider, his father's eyes looking hopeful. "We'll have to see," Noah said. "Where's this house located?"

"Over in Mill Point, half a mile from the boatworks. I'll be able to walk to work. 'Course, the Interurban makes it convenient to travel back and forth between the two towns."

"You could get a rig."

"Or walk."

"I noticed you have a bit of a limp."

"I'm embarrassed to say I acquired that after a knee injury. Fell off a barstool in one of my stupors. The pain in my joint serves to remind me of how God rescued me from myself."

They finished their suppers in comfortable silence. When it was time to clean up, Gerald lifted the lid of the picnic basket, reached inside, and produced an apple-sized rubber ball. "Well, would you looky here."

"Whoa!" came Toby's gasp of wonder. "Where'd you get that?"

"Some little fairy must have stuck it under our sandwiches." His mischievous eyes made Noah laugh.

"Why don't you take it outside and bounce it against the wall, son?" Noah suggested.

"Could I?" Toby squealed.

At his father's nod, the boy sailed out the door, giving Noah the perfect opportunity to unravel an interesting story for his father.

Chapter Twenty-nine

I t's about time you showed up! I'm starvin' here, and yer takin' yer sweet time to bring me some victuals."

"Oh, stop yer bellyachin'. I had to scope out stuff in town 'fore I could get back to rustle somethin' up. What's wrong with you that you couldn'ta fixed yer own self somethin' t' eat? Stove's right there."

"I don't know nothin' 'bout cookin'. That's always been Arlena's job. You find out where the sheriff done took her?"

"Far's I know, she's still at the jail. One of the deputies picked up your two young'uns."

"Pfff. Maybe he'll make the lot of 'em sit there and rot in a cell fer a month, like he did me."

"Shut up. Yer gettin' off track."

"You figure out where Virginia went off to?"

"She ain't nowhere t' be seen. You shoulda done a better job o' beatin' 'er up, you donkey's rear. You do know she's prob'ly goin' to go straight to the sheriff and tell 'im she overheard ar plan."

"That's why I had to leave. Don't worry, though. Ain't no one goin' to come lookin' here. 'Sides, I put the fear of the

Almighty in that girl, told her I'd be hurtin' her sisters if she opened her fat mouth, so I think she'll keep quiet. But I wasn't takin' no chances, an' that's why I done run outta there." He gave a loud curse and spat.

"Don't be spittin' on my floor, you big ox!"

"Fine, just tell me what you found out in town."

"All right, all right. There's this auction goin' on t'night at the community hall, some sort of benefit t' raise money for that women's shelter. It's bein' sponsored by that stupid temperance union."

"I know all that. I seen the posters around town. Keep goin'."

"Wull, there was a mess o' folks settin' up goods an' wares for that auction sale. Looks like they're goin' t' have a good turnout. I figure we can pay some little hoodwinker t' go in search o' Miss Kane and woo her outside, maybe tell 'er someone needs to see 'er. We'll figger that out later. When she comes out, we'll grab 'er and haul 'er off to 'er own store. I'm thinkin' that's the best place to do the deed—right there where Jacob will always see her with his mind's eye. The store'll be closed, an' nobody'd even think t' go lookin' for her there."

"Good, good, I like that. Did you see Jacob today?"

"That hoardin', clench-fisted money-grubber? Naw, I didn't see him roamin' the streets. I tol' him long time ago that I was goin' t' find a way to make him pay for my downfall, though, and this here is the best way to go about it, selecting his baby daughter. Killin' Jacob woulda been too kind. There wouldn'ta been enough hurtin' on his part, but this here—this here'll make him suffer 'n' bleed on th' inside for the rest o' his born days, jus' like he's made me suffer. Blame fool owed me big. I earned that insurance money, fair and square, but he found some stinkin', no-good, rotten loophole."

"You burned your own barn with all yer equipment in it, y' fool. Y' even tol' me that."

"Shut up! I had to. It was the only way I was goin' to get myself back on my feet, gettin' that insurance money due me after the fire. He don't know I burned it, and neither does nobody else, so it don't make no matter. Fact is, he owed me. Because o' him, my wife left me, my kids disappeared, and I plain ain't got a life. Never did catch myself up financially, and I plan t' make him pay for my lifetime o' sufferin'. It's time. Shoot! It's past time!"

"It's good we're both on the same page. I can't stand that little she-cat daughter of his for her nosin' into other folks' business, puttin' ideas into my Arlena's head about the way a woman ought t' be treated, her tryin' t' shut down saloons an' push this idiotic prohibition notion down people's throats, an' her thinkin' she can influence the women of the town with her narrow-minded religious views." He cursed again. "Time someone silenced that little shrew."

"Yep, we're on the same page, all right. So, we're agreed tonight's the night?"

"Pfff. Tonight ain't soon enough, far as I'm concerned."

They shook on it to seal the deal, then proceeded to drink themselves into stupors.

❧ *K* ❧

All afternoon, Abbie and a large number of other volunteers packed and stacked the community hall with items donated by local individuals and businesses. She could hardly contain her joy at folks' generosity. Why, they'd collected everything imaginable: baked goods, bicycles, hardware supplies, household items, trunks, carpets, curtains, women's accessories, toys, books, clocks, cameras, sporting goods—and the list went on. Looking around, Abbie found nary a spot or space left in which to lay one more article, and yet folks continued dropping things off, excited about the opportunity to give to a good and worthy cause. To her knowledge, every church in town had banded together to help make the evening a success. It appeared she wasn't the only one who sensed the need for a women's shelter in Sandy Shores, and her heart swelled with pride—not the sinful type, but the kind that makes one bubble up with gratitude to see such generosity.

Along with her joy, though, came a hint of uncertainty and discontent. She missed Noah, even though it'd been only two days since she'd broken her ties with him, and he would, no doubt, be part of the crowd of folks coming to the auction. Would he try to talk to her as he had at church yesterday? And what of Toby, the precious, blameless boy who'd already suffered so many losses? How would she explain to him that adults sometimes found themselves in tangled webs of their own making, and, as a result, sometimes had to sever ties with innocent loved ones? The thought even crossed her mind that she ought to give up teaching her dearly beloved Sunday school class, at least until Toby passed on to the next grade. Had she been smart, she would have avoided all contact with Noah, thereby ensuring that Toby would not get his hopes up about her becoming his mother. He already had a mother—one who'd traveled by train from Connecticut to see him, obviously filled with regret for the mistakes she'd made. Gracious, for all Abbie knew, the Lord had plans to bring her and Noah back together, and who would she be to argue with that? Wouldn't it be within His perfect design to reunite the parents of a dear child?

As she answered questions posed by volunteers—"Where should I put this?" "Where are the tables of baked goods?" "Do we have a place for musical instruments?" "What in the world would you call *this*?" (Abbie had no notion, herself)— her mind meandered to the other events of the day, namely, her talk with Gabe and her visit with Arlena Rogan.

By the time Abbie had arrived at City Hall earlier that day, Kitty Oakes, Gabe's secretary, had done a good job of settling Arlena down, actually putting her to work on sorting files. When Abbie had come through the doors, Arlena had shed some tears but managed to keep herself from falling to pieces. Abbie had led her to a back room, where they'd sat and talked for a good half hour or more, Abbie asking what, exactly, had prompted Virginia to run away, and whether Arlena had any idea where she might have gone. Arlena had shaken her head, sorrow contorting her face. "Shamus beat her bad. I walked in whilst he was hittin' an' kickin' her. Me an' the girls were out at the chicken coop collectin' eggs when we heard her screams." She'd shuddered, then had gone on in a wobbly voice, "I tell you, Miss Abbie, I never been so all-fired mad at that man in all my born days. I don't know how he could beat his own child. He's a monster, that's all there is to it—a monster. And what really got me fuming was that thickheaded, half-witted neighbor of ours. He could o' helped, but he just stood on his front porch listenin' and doin' nothin' at all. Nothin'!"

A memory had sprung to Abbie's mind, a memory of eyes watching through a window at the house next door when she and Hannah had paid Arlena and the girls a visit, and, later, when she'd gone there again with Noah.

"Who is your neighbor, Arlena?"

"Angus Clemens. He used to be married, but his wife took off a number of years back. He had a couple o' kids, too, but they'd be grown by now. I got no idea where they all went off to, but I'll tell you, they're better off wherever they are. That man and my Shamus make a ruinous combination."

"Do they associate with each other?"

"If you mean socialize, like in a friendly way, no. I wouldn't call them friends. But if you mean do they ever talk and connive, then, yeah."

"Connive?"

"Oh, they get these notions about buildin' a still if prohibition ever takes effect…stuff like that. They's both bad drinkers. They ain't friends, though, just acquaintances. I'd have to say neither one of 'em is the type to draw friends."

"Why do you think Shamus beat Virginia?"

Arlena had shrugged. "Don't know, exactly, but I'm thinkin' she got in his hair, maybe overheard him talkin' to that buzzard next door, and he didn't like her eavesdroppin'. When I put 'er to bed after that beatin', she kept sayin', 'Mama, he's got a bad plan up his sleeve,' an' I jus' said, 'I know, honey. He's always got some plan or 'nother.' After that, I kissed her forehead where I'd dabbed her cuts and bruises with a cold cloth, and she went off t' sleep." She'd let go a little sob. "That was the last I seen of 'er. Next mornin', must've been about five or so, she was gone."

"Why didn't you tell the sheriff right off that she'd run away?"

"I didn't want him thinkin' bad of her. As you saw, she's been known to stand out on ar porch with a gun in hand. She's a good girl, though. She never caused me any trouble."

While Abbie pondered her earlier discussion with Arlena, she tried to recall why the name Angus Clemens rang a bell of familiarity. She told herself that when Gabe arrived at the auction, she'd ask him if he'd ever heard the name.

That evening, May 9, 1907, the citizens of Sandy Shores crowded into the community hall like herded sheep, rubbing shoulders, waving greetings, and shaking hands with neighbors and old friends, their voices charged with excitement. Noah clung tight to Toby's hand, realizing how easy it would be to lose him in the crowded space.

"Is there anything here for kids, Pa? I don't see anything, do you?"

"Not sure, son. We'll have to keep our eyes peeled." *Where is Abbie?* They'd been there for ten minutes already, and Noah still had not caught even a glimpse of her.

"Look at everything, Pa. What is all this stuff? Hey, what's this?"

"That's a salt and pepper shaker set."

"They look like little kittens."

"They are. Probably porcelain. Put them down, Toby."

"What's this?"

"That's a camera."

"A camera! Can we get one?" He started examining it.

"Don't touch anything."

But how did one expect a child with eyes as big as saucers to keep his hands in his pockets when the temptation to touch everything in sight was almost more than he could bear? Noah tried to keep one eye on Toby and another out for a beautiful brunette with eyes like melted chocolate.

"Noah!" He caught his name over the hubbub and swung around to wave at Gabe, who was maneuvering his way through the crowd toward Noah and Toby. He must have been still on duty, judging by the look of his crisp police uniform.

"Quite a turnout, isn't it? How are you?" Gabe asked as he and Noah shook hands.

"Good, thanks. You on duty?"

He gave a light chuckle. "Let's just say it's been a long day. I've been looking into some things, doing a bit of digging with regard to…well, what you told me this morning about your encounter with Rogan on the sidewalk a couple of days ago."

"Yeah? Did you find out anything?"

Glancing over Gabe's shoulder, Noah finally got a glimpse of Abbie mingling with folks, smiling, talking, even throwing back her head in laughter, as if she hadn't a care in the world. And, perhaps, she didn't. Maybe breaking things off with him had been a relief.

"Well, a couple of things. I talked to Ab—"

"Could you excuse me—just for a minute?" he asked, pressing Gabe's arm.

"Uh, sure."

"I'll be right back. Stay put. Come on, Toby." He took his son's hand and pulled him along through the maze of people. By gum, he would make it clear to Abbie Ann Kane that he could not be forgotten so easily.

K

Abbie spotted Noah working his way through the crowd, towing Toby along and excusing himself as he bumped shoulders with several people. Her heart began to beat wildly. Oh, how she wanted to throw caution to the wind and leap into his arms! But her practical side reminded her that his beautiful, former wife was in town, and it would be prudent to keep her distance from the entire situation. She turned and purposely headed in the opposite direction, pretending not to have seen him. Besides, she had to find Gabe before the auction got underway so she could tell him what Arlena had relayed to her.

As the auctioneer climbed onto the stage, Jane Emery, Abbie's very capable cochair for the event, took the stairs at the other side of the stage. She had a megaphone in one hand for the purpose of making introductions. Suddenly, Abbie felt a hand clamp down on her arm, forcing her to turn. The warmth of that grip sent a tingle down her spine. "Hello, Abbie," Noah said, his sapphire eyes speaking louder than his words. Slowly, he released his grasp.

"Hi, Abbie," Toby chimed in. "Did you see all the stuff that man up there is goin' to try to make everybody buy?"

She put on her friendliest smile for the lad and crouched down to his level, thereby avoiding Noah's scrutiny. "Indeed, I did. I helped organize all these items. It was quite a job."

"I coulda helped."

"But you had school today, remember?"

"Oh, yeah. Do they gots anything here for little boys?"

"Hmm...." She pressed a finger to the center of her chin. "I think I saw a couple of wooden wagons parked at the front, and, oh, some building blocks on that table over there, along with some books and a mishmash of other items. There's also a doll or two, but I have a hunch you're not interested in those."

"Yuck!" he exclaimed. "Can we go look, Pa?"

"In a minute, son. Abbie, I...I've missed you." He kept his voice to a whisper.

"Noah, this is not the place to—"

"Where, then? And when? We need to talk."

"Is *she* still here?" she whispered back.

"I'm assuming."

"You haven't talked to her since Saturday?"

"Abbie, I don't want to see her. She spells trouble for me."

"She is Toby's—" Catching herself growing agitated, she paused and lowered her voice even more. "She's Toby's mother, and pretending she's not here won't solve a thing. You need to face this situation and make some joint decisions." Thankfully, the surrounding noise drowned out their conversation so that even Toby had no inkling of its topic.

"Are you going to wait for me to sort things through?"

She swallowed and answered point-blank, "No."

"No? Just like that? Without even considering what it might be like to share our futures?"

"You're getting ahead of yourself, Noah. Toby's mother is in town, remember? And I take issue with that. Who knows? She may consider moving here to be near her son. And maybe the two of you—"

"Don't even think it."

Her shoulders slumped as she sighed heavily before going on. "I've prayed about this, Noah, and I just don't—"

"I'll have you know I've prayed about it, too."

"You have?" This news both pleased and alarmed her.

"And I'm inclined to think the Lord—"

Someone tapped her lightly on the arm. "Ma'am?"

Abbie turned to see a boy of about ten, perhaps a trifle younger than Jesse. "Yes?"

"Are you Miss Abbie Kane?"

"I am. Did you want to ask me something?" She'd never seen the brown-haired, rather shabbily dressed boy before and instinctively wondered to whom he belonged.

"Yeah, somebody sent me to tell you you was needed out by the back door. They got a piece o' farm equipment like a tractor or somethin' they want t' put in the auction, but 'course they can't bring it inside. They want to know if you'll come out an' tell 'em how you want t' handle the sale of it. They heard you was the one in charge."

"Uh, could you please tell them I'll be right there?" The boy nodded and ran off, disappearing into the crowd. She looked at Noah. "I have to go."

"When can I see you again—so we can talk about this some more?"

Lord, what am I to do with this persistent man? "I just… can't see you right now, not while you have unsettled family matters. It wouldn't be right."

His face screwed into a disapproving scowl. "Just so you know, Abbie Ann, I'm not done pursuing you." He touched the tip of her nose. "And that, my dear, is a promise you can take straight to the bank. Well, maybe not Sinclair's bank, but a bank."

She giggled and gave him a push. "Go on with you. Can't you tell I'm busy?"

He gave her a long, hard stare, his lips turned ever so slightly upward, then reached down and, finding her hand, gave it a gentle, promising squeeze. "I'll see you later, young lady."

She watched Noah and Toby vanish like that disappearing boy into the sea of people.

When Abbie stepped outside, she noted that the evening had a springlike quality, aromatic, cool, and damp; aromatic in the sense that it held the scent of a mixture of flowery bushes, grass, apple blossoms, and horse dung. A dusky sky still provided plenty of light, but all Abbie had to look at were a bunch of wagons and horses parked clear up the block. If there was a pair of farmers out here wanting to donate a tractor, she certainly didn't see them loitering around, nor did she see any tractor. As a matter of fact, it appeared the whole of Sandy Shores had gathered inside the four walls of the community hall as she gazed up the empty, silent street.

Perhaps the boy had sent her to the wrong door. She started to go back inside when a thumping sound and a fleeting glimmer of movement off to one side caught her attention. Before she had a second to react, though, two hands flew up from behind, one quickly plastering itself around her chest, the other across her mouth and face, crowding out what felt like her last gulp of air. "Gotcha!" hissed a raspy, wheezy voice, its whiskey breath hot against her ear, as the man started dragging her to the side of the building.

Panic shot like a bullet through her veins, hot, cold, hot, cold. "Hmmmmm!" came her muffled scream into his cold, rough hand. He pressed the harder, pulling her up tight to his body. "Let me go!" she tried to scream, though a muffled "Lll eee ohh" is all that came out.

"Shut up, or I'll kill you on the spot, and I ain't kiddin'."

Instinct took over, and she started to kick and flail, but then a second person emerged from the shadows and swept her up by her thrashing ankles so that each end of her jerking, squirming body was bound.

"She's a wild li'l beast, ain't she?" the one at her feet said with a wicked hoot.

Her heart went into triple time as her mind shot in several directions. *Lord God, what's happening to me?*

"She's more'n that, she's a b—" In a desperate grasp at self-preservation, Abbie got a chunk of skin between her teeth and chomped down on the hand pressed over her mouth. Wrong move—the brute yelped and dropped her on her head. Torturous pain suddenly seized the back of her skull, and, for a second, she wondered if it hadn't cracked open right there on the hard ground, but then her thoughts started fading and drifting to a point of dullness.

"You dropped her, you idiot!"

"She bit me. Ow! You little she-devil!"

Their words came off sounding strange and oddly distant as the pain at the back of her head clouded her senses. *Scream!* her survival instincts urged her. But even the act of opening her mouth, let alone emitting a sound, seemed insurmountable.

"Pick 'er back up, blockhead, before somebody comes out here. The wagon's over there."

The fight having gone out of her, her body sagged in the middle when the man lifted her up by the shoulders. Now, it was a matter of keeping her brain alert enough to tell her body not to go to sleep.

Jesus, Jesus, help me! she screamed in her head before utter blackness completely enveloped her.

Chapter Thirty

Noah met up with Gabe again after speaking with Abbie. "Sorry I left you like that. I saw Abbie and wanted to say something to her."

Gabe's brow creased. "You two still courting? I noticed you weren't sitting in the family pew this Sunday."

Without going into the whole sordid story of Suzanna's sudden emergence on the scene, Noah explained that they'd come to a crossroads, of sorts, and needed time to work things out.

"Ah. Well, I hope you do. I'll tell you, that Abbie's a little spitfire. I thought Hannah had all the grit until I met her youngest sister. Maggie's a fiery little wisp, too. All three of them will give you a run for your money, but one thing's for certain: the men who manage to win them over find genuine treasures."

Noah wanted to be one of those men with every ounce of him. "Well, back to our discussion. You started to tell me you'd found out something?"

"Yeah, for starters, Abbie encountered a couple more... umm, odd situations a while back but chose to keep them to herself. I told you, she's a spitfire."

"And a little too independent for her own good," Noah added. "What kind of situations?"

"Well, apparently, someone followed her after one of her temperance meetings."

"What?" A cold chill raced up Noah's spine. "Did she get a look at the person?"

Gabe shook his head. "She saw nothing more than a shadow. In another instance, she found a note addressed to her, stuck under a paperweight next to the cash register at the Whatnot."

"Another note? What'd it say?" More chills and a kind of sixth sense prompted him to glance around the room to see if she'd returned from her dealings with the tractor donors, but either they were still figuring out where to put it, or she'd slipped back inside, unnoticed, which wouldn't have surprised him, considering all the commotion.

"Pa." Toby tugged at his sleeve, but Noah ignored him, his eyes and ears fixed intently on Gabe.

"I went over to her house today and got it out of her bureau drawer. Thank goodness, she had the sense to save it. Here, have a look."

Noah studied the crumpled paper and swallowed a hard, sickening lump. "It's the same handwriting."

"Yep."

"Pa."

"Just a minute, son. I'm talking to Sheriff Devlin."

At the front of the hall, a woman started speaking into a megaphone, capturing the crowd's attention. Folks started herding closer to the front, paddles in hand, poised in case they wanted to raise them up to bid on an item. Noah, Gabe, and Toby stayed put.

"So, the culprit had the gall to march right into the store and lay this note on the counter?" He waved the paper under Gabe's nose. "Unbelievable."

"Pa."

Yet another yank to the sleeve had Noah looking down at Toby with irritation. "We'll get to the auction in a minute, but—"

Suddenly, Gabe crouched down on one knee and gave Toby a curious gaze. "Did you have something important you wanted to tell us, young man?"

"Yeah, if my pa will give me a chance."

Now, Noah got down, too. "I'm sorry, son. What is it?"

"I saw the guy what left the note."

"You—what? But how could you have?" Noah asked, his pulse pumping crazily.

"I was there that day 'cause I di'n't have school."

He remembered now. "Did you get a look at him—this guy?"

"Sure. I even talked t' him, but he wasn't very nice."

"How do you mean?" Gabe asked.

"All I did was ask him about the scar on his face, and he got all mean to me."

"Scar? Rogan," both men said in unison.

Gabe's face took on a wan expression with the dread realization. "It doesn't all fit, though. The guy was sitting in a jail cell the night that rock went through the church window, and yet we discover it's the same handwriting?"

"Obviously, somebody else is involved. Did anyone visit him while he was in jail?"

"Abbie asked me the same thing this morning. I told her I hadn't admitted a single visitor. I asked a couple of my deputies, but neither of them had seen anyone, either. The only one I didn't check with is my night man, but, naturally, he wasn't in today, and he doesn't start his shift till ten o'clock."

With his eyes keeping a constant lookout for Abbie and his heart racing, Noah continued to speak aloud his swirling, internal thoughts. "How would anybody have known we were passing by on the street that night the bottle landed in the back of my rig?"

Gabe scrunched up his brow and rubbed the side of his nose. "No idea, unless the fellow was watching the whole time, knew Abbie's every move, and stayed one step ahead—or behind. We'd better put that young lady under lock and key after this. No more freedoms until we figure this thing out. Shoot, I'll tie a leash to her if I have to. Where is she, by the way?" Gabe started searching the room just as Noah had been doing.

"I got a bad feeling, Gabe. While I was talking to her, some kid came up to us and told her there were some men outside, wanting to donate a tractor or something...." He hit himself alongside the head as panic set in. "Good grief, what's wrong with me? Why didn't I have my feelers out? Stay here, son." He set off on a run to the back door, nearly knocking into several people in his rush, took a good look around for a donated tractor, and, seeing none, ran back inside. "Just what I thought," he said, breathless from fright as much as from running. "Nothing. Where is she?"

"All right, now, calm down, Noah," said Gabe. "We're probably jumping the gun here."

"Pa, is Abbie okay?" Toby's eyes welled up with huge tears.

"She's fine, son." Noah crouched down again, his emotions raging in a calamitous war, his heart threatening to jump clear of his chest. He pushed the hair off his son's forehead and bluffed calmness. "You did real good, Toby, remembering that man in the store. Real good. I'm proud of you. But I'm going to have to go find Abbie right now, so I need you to stay here, understand? Let me see." He stood up, looking for someone, anyone, whom he could trust to watch over Toby. Unfortunately, his aunt and uncle had decided to go with his father to Mill Point to look at the house he planned to rent.

"Sheriff Devlin?" said a man who looked to be about Noah's age, pointing past the huge cluster of people. "Some young woman just came through that side door over there, asking where she might find the sheriff."

At the front, the auctioneer had started the proceedings, and the excitement grew as the first item up for bids, a lamp, started at a dime and immediately was raised to a quarter.

"A girl?" Gabe asked above the din.

"Yes, sir. She's all banged up and seems a bit disoriented. I got no idea who she is. Just thought I'd better let you know."

"Okay, thanks, I'll check on her." Having done his civil duty, the fellow walked away.

Just then, Noah caught a glimpse of the back of Jacob Kane's head in the middle of the throng. Next to him stood Rita, and behind them were Donald and Esther Clayton. The four were bantering back and forth, laughing. At first, he breathed a sigh of relief, knowing he could safely leave Toby with them, but then the realization set in that Jacob had a right to know his daughter could be in danger.

"There's Jacob," he said, pointing.

Gabe nodded. "You go pull him aside and tell him what's what, then meet me at the side door over there. I have to see if I can find the girl that fellow was telling me about. I have a sneaking suspicion of who it is, and if I'm right, she may be able to fill us in on a few things."

"All right, I'll meet you in a minute. Come on, Toby."

⟋ *K* ⟍

Little by little, Abbie started coming out of her dense, dark fog, slowly growing aware of her surroundings, which were strangely familiar—she was lying face-up on the floor at the back of Kane's Whatnot. Why had they brought her here, of all places? And who were *they?* She was certain she'd never seen the man who'd carried her by her ankles. As for the other, she'd not gotten a good look at him, as he'd carried her by her upper body, with her back toward him. A searing headache awakened the memory of her attack and accentuated her urgent desire to escape. With the back door mere feet away, she could probably roll over and maneuver her way along the floor by slithering like an inchworm, but then what? Her bound ankles and hands made accomplishing anything nearly impossible. *Lord, I know nothing is impossible with You. Please direct me in what to do. Grant me wisdom, strength, and courage to face whatever lies ahead,* she silently prayed.

Be still, and know that I am God.

"I see that Carson feller fixed up this front window like new," one of the men said, his voice coming from the front of the store. "Too bad yer aim wasn't any better when you turned into him that day. You was supposed to make him go sailin' clear through the buildin' with the hopes that Kane woman would be standin' nearby to take the brunt of it."

So, Shamus Rogan and his cohort had planned the accident in front of the Whatnot? Those big, dastardly rats! A surge of anger made her squirm to get free from her shackles, but to no avail. They'd tied her fast.

Be still....

"Well, how was I s'posed to know how the whole thing would turn out? It's not every day I plan a near head-on collision." He snorted. "I thought I done pretty good, right down to my pretendin' to be drunk, drinkin' just enough booze to make my breath stink and spillin' some of it down my front. 'Course, I didn't know Carson would be the one I'd veer into. Maybe if an ol' codger like you had been drivin', he wouldn't've had quite the control."

"Shut yer trap, you stinkin' bonehead," the other male voice groused. "I ain't no codger."

"You ain't no young rooster, that's fer sure."

While they argued, Abbie sought to loosen the ropes around her wrists. If she could just break free of them, she'd be able to untie her ankles. *Lord, help me.*

Again, the inclination to simply be still whispered to her spirit.

"We better get on with this shootin', don't y' think? Who's gonna do the deed?"

"You are, you dumb horse's hiney. You been beatin' on your wife for years, and now your own kid. Seems to me you ought to be used to doin' violent acts." After a slight pause with no response, he said, "You ain't scared, are ya?"

"'Course, I ain't scared. It's jus' that we didn't really discuss this part. Yer the one what's carried the grudge fer Jacob all these years after losing that insurance claim. You said yer-self you wanted to watch 'im suffer. Seems t' me you'd get the most satisfaction from doin' it."

"Ain't you the one what holds the most hate fer that li'l busybody who's been stickin' her nose in where it don't belong, runnin' a campaign to do away with saloons, puttin' dang'rous ideas into women's minds? Wouldn't surprise me none if Arlena up an' left you one o' these days, just like my Martha took off on me, haulin' off my own kids and not givin' me any idea where she went. Like I said, if Jacob would o' gave me my money, I could've turned my sorry financial lot around and kept my family intact."

"Arlena's too scared to run off. She knows I'd come after 'er. Don't matter where she ran to—I'd hunt 'er down."

While Abbie worked to untie the knots that bound her, she kept her ears attuned to the conversation, still battling an excruciating headache and fighting off a bad case of nausea. Her fuzzy mind started putting pieces together—the scrawled notes, the mysterious occurrences, and, now, the name Angus Clemens resurfacing in her mind after hearing Arlena mention him earlier. Years ago, Angus Clemens lost in a lawsuit against her father to collect on an insurance claim. His barn had burned, along with many valuable possessions, and, while the story had been tragic, Angus had failed to pay his monthly premiums beforehand, despite many reminder notices from her father and an extended grace period he offered. Eventually, her father had canceled the policy. Shortly thereafter, the barn had gone up in flames. Angus's only defense in the lawsuit had been that he'd never received the notices. Judge Bowers hadn't bought it, saying Angus knowingly fell behind on his payments. It had been a clear-cut case. Unpaid premiums equated to no insurance policy, but, from then on, Angus Clemens had held

Jacob Kane responsible for his loss, even going so far as to cast the blame on him for his family's departure, which was ridiculous, considering Angus's long-held reputation for mistreating his wife and children.

But that had been years ago, and, while he'd threatened to make Jacob pay someday, everyone in the Kane family had eventually dismissed his threats. Was Abbie to be his means for finally evening the score with Jacob Kane?

"Hey, looky here," said Shamus, Abbie now distinguishing his voice from that of Angus. "Think we can crack open this wall safe before we do away with her? I bet they put all their day's earnings in here. Alls we need is a hammer to break the lock."

"Forget it. We didn't come here to rob Jacob Kane of his money; we came to rob him of his baby daughter. That'll make a far greater impact on his heart and body than losin' a little hard cash. Like I said, I want 'im to suffer." An evil cackle came out of him, making Abbie's nerves quake. They were going to kill her.

Lord Jesus, *"Thou art my rock and my fortress…I will fear no evil: for thou art with me….O my God, I trust in thee…I will not be afraid what man can do unto me….Yea, though I walk through the valley of the shadow of death…."* Her convoluted mix of Scripture verses lent a small measure of comfort, even as her heart thumped against her ribs.

"Let's see if she's conscious yet," Shamus said. "I wanna see the terror in her eyes when we come at 'er."

At the first sound of approaching footsteps, Abbie pressed her eyes shut, thankful she hadn't tried to slither away.

K

"My pa is mad as a rattlesnake when he's drunk and mean as a bear when he ain't. He beat me a good one 'cause I listened in on him an' that ol' brute Angus Clemens, our rotten neighbor. I was hidin' around the side of the house an' heard their whole plan. I'd a'come right to ya, Sheriff, but my pa seen me when I accidentally sneezed, and he came chasin' after me. I ran in the house and tried to lock the door, but he got to me 'fore I had a chance and started beatin' the tar right outta me. Woulda kilt me if my ma hadn't come in when she did and screamed at 'im. He tol' me if I breathed one word of what I heard, he'd kill me first and then my sisters, and I believe 'im. He's crazier than a coot, Sheriff."

Gabe had sat Virginia Rogan, who bore bruises on her face and arms from her beating, in a chair by the door so she could rest, and he, Noah, and Jacob listened to her with rapt interest, if not impatience. *Angus Clemens*. Noah had never heard of him; not surprising, since he still knew hardly a soul in Sandy Shores, but his recollection of having seen Shamus's neighbor running through the yard in the drenching rain that day when he and Abbie had gone out to the Rogans' place made him plenty suspicious now that the fellow had tampered with his wagon wheel. How could he have been so foolish not to think of it earlier? For the second time, he wanted to bust himself alongside the head.

"I had a run-in with Angus Clemens some years ago," Jacob spoke with a reflective tone. "He lost out on an insurance claim he swore I owed him. Fellow didn't pay his premiums, so I had to cancel him. He was plenty sore at me, even threatened to do me harm, but, good grief, that was a long time ago."

Gabe pondered that bit of news, looking as if he were trying to put together a giant puzzle, then set a hand on

Virginia's shoulder. "Your mama and sisters are safe now, and we're not going to let your father hurt them or you again, you hear?" Her eyes dripped with tears. "Tell us what sort of plan you overheard these men discussing, Virginia."

She raised her head slowly and looked at him with a solemn face. "They said they was goin' to murder Miss Abbie right in her own store on the night of the auction."

Chapter Thirty-one

While Abbie pretended to lie in an unconscious state, the men grew drunker and louder, the stench from their whiskey bottles stretching across the room. "We oughtta go do the deed now, 'fore someone misses her and grows s-s-suspicious. Don't matter if she ain't awake," said Angus, ending with a loud belch. At least their stalling gave her time to work on her hand shackles.

"You goin' to do it, then?" Shamus asked.

"I thought we decided you was."

"We ain't decided no such thing," Shamus retorted. "Sheee-oot! I think yer the one what's scared."

A skirmish followed, and Abbie heard something hit the wall and shatter. A mirror or a glass vase, perhaps? Of all things, she thought about the mess someone would have to clean up later.

"What'd you go and do that fer, you thickheaded dolt?" Shamus hollered.

"I don't appreciate being called a coward."

"I never called you— Shh, what's that? I heard something." More rustling, only, this time, it sounded like the two of them were scuffling to take cover. Dare she hope that someone—Noah, perhaps—had missed her at the auction? Might he and Gabe be coming to her rescue?

"I didn't hear nothin', you fool," Angus said. "Your head's plain muddled from the sauce."

"I swear I heard somethin'."

While the room fell silent, Abbie ceased trying to loosen the knots at her wrists, disheartened by her lack of progress. *Be still, My child....*

"I tol' you we should've h-hauled 'er up them s-stairs and outta sight," Shamus whispered. "But, no, you wanted her blood splattered all over the f-floor for Jacob's eyes to s-see. I say, let's go back there, both shoot her, and then sneak out the back door."

"Don't both of us need to shoot 'er, you fool."

"You just don't want to be the one with the blame pinned on 'im. Yer goin' to double-cross me, ain't ya? Try to make me do the shootin' so's you can get a lighter sentence?"

"Don't be stupid!"

A rustling sound ensued, and then a loud click—or maybe two. To Abbie, the sound resembled a gun cocking. Were they going to shoot each other, then? Her heart nearly hammered straight out of her chest.

Lord Jesus, please....

When overcome with terror, trust Me, My child.

I'm trying, Lord, I truly am.

Someone slammed into something, and another loud crash resulted—more broken glass, from the sound of it. Her body jolted. Had one of them pushed the other? She wished for a longer neck to see what was going on.

"You clumsy ox!" Angus said. "You're drunker than a skunk. Put that gun down."

"Y-you put yers down."

"You, first."

There must have been a stare-down, for several seconds passed without a single sound. Finally, Angus cleared his throat. "All right, all right, guns down...together. Let's not be stupid, here. Easy...does...it."

They must have lowered their guns, for she heard heavy sighs coming from both of them. "I ain't gonna double-cross you, Shamus." It was the first time she'd heard one of them refer to the other by his first name. She suspected that while they had a joint mission in mind (wiping her off the planet), they truly hated each other.

Slow, encroaching footsteps had her heart skipping in triple time. Oh, if only she could just break free of these lousy ropes, maybe she wouldn't feel as helpless as a bat without ears.

Be still, and know that I am God.

"She awake yet?" Angus asked.

She prayed for total composure as Shamus bent down and flipped up one of her eyelids. They looked each other straight in the eye, and by God's grace alone, she managed not to move a muscle. If he detected anything, he didn't let on. Silently, she thanked God for the setting sun and the deepening shadows. Satisfied, he dropped her eyelid and stood. "She's still out cold."

"Maybe you already kilt her," Angus said.

"I ain't never seen a dead person breathe, idiot," Shamus shot back.

She heard a rustle of wind stir the trees outside, followed by a snapping sound. Opening her eye a tiny slit, Abbie witnessed both men nearly jumping out of their dog-eared boots.

"What was that?" Angus asked.

"See? I told you I heard somethin' earlier," Shamus said.

Angus raised his rifle, resting the butt of it on his shoulder. Shamus took out a pistol from his pocket and pointed it at the back door, then pivoted on his heel to point it at a front window. Angus moved toward the front of the store, behind a shelf, and out of Abbie's line of vision. Drops of sweat dotted her forehead, and her breath caught and held while she silently prayed. Something impelled her to look at the rear door—and there stood Noah, his finger to his lips in a shushing gesture. Unqualified relief that she wasn't alone mixed with utter terror when she realized that Noah could well lose his life at her expense. She gave her head a violent shake. He tried to relay something to her with his eyes, but she missed the message.

"You see anything?" she heard Shamus ask, his back still to her.

"Nothin'. I think it was just the wind." Abbie felt the floor vibrate with Angus's hurried strides to the back of the store, and she shut her eye. "All right, here's the plan," he stated. "At the count o' three, we are both goin' to raise ar guns an' fire, you hear?"

"I ain't goin' to take the blame by myself, Clemens."

"Are you deaf? I just tol' you, we're goin' to do this together."

Again, she opened her eye a tiny slit and saw two pairs of boots facing her, five feet away. Had they raised their guns yet? She clamped her eyes shut and prepared her soul for meeting her Creator when, suddenly, she heard the front and back doors break open, and "Drop your guns!" "Do it!" and "Now!" shouted in a voice she recognized as Gabe's. Guns and knees hit the floor, and Abbie finally dared open her eyes to see Shamus and Angus with their hands raised to the ceiling. Noah was kneeling at her side.

Thank the Lord she was safe and virtually unharmed, save for the noticeable bulge at the back of her head and the matted blood tangling the hair around it. Noah cradled her close after loosing the twine from around her ankles and wrists and untying the kerchief that had been swathed across her mouth and tied in a knot behind her neck. He kissed the top of her head and whispered into her hair, rocking her gently while her tears dampened the front of his shirt. "You're okay, sweetheart. Everything's going to be fine. It's over now. Are you all right? Did they hurt you? How did you get this bump on your head?" His words poured out in one long sentence, a mixture of inquiries and assurances.

"Abbie." Breathless, Jacob crouched down beside his daughter. "Are you all right, honey? We tried to get here as fast as we could. Virginia Rogan overheard her father and Angus Clemens plotting to kill you, but we can tell you about that later."

"Papa!" she wailed, so Noah relinquished her to her father, albeit reluctantly. She heaved herself against his chest, her tears turning into outright sobs. "I was so frightened, but God just kept whispering in my ear, *'Be still, and know that I am God.'*"

Jacob gave a relieved smile and rested his chin on her head, his own eyes tearing up with a well of emotions. Noah couldn't begin to fathom as the thought of what might have been shook him to his core.

Deciding it prudent to give the two their privacy, Noah stood and walked to the front of the store, where Gabe and Randall Cling, the deputy whom someone at the auction had sprinted off to fetch and send to the Whatnot, had already handcuffed and gagged the vultures before plunking them in a couple of chairs, their feet fettered to prevent escape. No way were they going anywhere. He'd have liked to throttle them both, but his better judgment ruled and, instead, he silently thanked the Lord that no harm had come to Abbie, other than that bump on her head. Her quiet sobs at the back of the store gave his heart pause. What if he had lost her?

Noah tried to make eye contact with Shamus and Angus, just so he could give them a spiteful look, but both kept their gazes pointed downward, no doubt realizing they'd seen the last of their freedom for a good, long while. Kidnapping and holding a woman hostage with the intent of killing her did not generally go over well in a court of law.

After Gabe and Randall quietly discussed police procedures and recorded details of the crime in a black book, Randall hauled the creeps, one at a time, to the police wagon parked in front of the store.

Next, Gabe stuffed his little, black tablet in a back pocket and then turned, weary-eyed, to look at Noah. "Good work," he said with a slow grin.

"You mean, my not strangling them?"

Gabe chuckled. "For allowing me to assess the circumstances and decide the proper course of action. I know how much you wanted to act on impulse when you saw Abbie lying on the floor. I'd have been chomping at the bit myself if that'd been Hannah."

En route to the Whatnot, Gabe had instructed Noah and Jacob not to barge into the store, no matter how tempted they were, but to let him do his job, which involved a cautionary, investigative survey of the situation. Any false moves, he'd explained, could precipitate erratic action on the part of the criminals. To Jacob, he'd issued a warning to hang back; to Noah, he'd given permission to sneak around behind the store for a look before returning to report his findings. At no time was Noah to burst through the door, unarmed. He'd followed the directions to a tee—until it had come to the bursting through the door part. As soon as Gabe had broken through the front door, barking orders at the men to drop their weapons, Noah had come crashing through the back door, quickly kneeling at Abbie's side and making fast work of the trappings that bound her mouth, ankles, and wrists before hauling her into his arms. Now, he swiveled his body to look at her again, still sitting on the floor and cuddled in her father's arms, her cries having settled down to a quiet whimper.

"She'll be fine," Gabe was saying. "But for my own peace of mind, I'll call the ambulance wagon to come and take her to Dr. Van Huff's clinic before I deliver those creeps to their individual cells. I think the doctor should at least check that bump on her head." Noah agreed, and Gabe headed over to the counter to use the telephone. "You planning to go with Jacob and Abbie to the doctor's office?"

"You bet I am."

But when Noah announced his intentions a few minutes later, Abbie shook her head. "I thank you for all you did for me, Noah, but I…I think it's best if just Papa takes me. You understand."

He did and he didn't. In the worst way, he wanted to be with her, but there was the matter of Suzanna's presence in Sandy Shores, and, of course, Abbie's stubbornness.

First thing tomorrow, he meant to march over to the Culver House and tell Suzanna and her mother to take the next train back to Guilford.

He didn't have to do that, though, because at eight o'clock on the dot the following morning, his former mother-in-law showed up at the doors of the warehouse, dressed to the nines, as usual, but wearing a less than collected expression. If anything, her face expressed agony. Beyond the open double doors, he saw a dark-skinned man perched high on one of Enoch Sprock's rental wagons. He thought he recognized him as Jeffries Davison, the Dunbars' butler.

Noah dropped the wrench he was using to tighten a bolt and stared at her from inside his boat, quickly finding his manners and jumping out to go greet her. He'd always liked Ellen Dunbar, even admired her for putting up with her beast of a husband, Carl, all these years.

"Hello, Noah." She stepped through the doors. "You're looking very good."

"Ellen, you are, as well. I'm…surprised to see you." He met her at the center of the room, then abruptly stopped. Did he give her an embrace, a handshake, or a simple touch on the arm? He went for the embrace, making it quick.

Stepping back, he studied her face, which was more worn-looking than he recalled. "How are you?"

She hesitated for all of five or six heartbeats, then exhaled. "I have been better, Noah."

Guilt for not having at least sought her out in the past few days gnawed at his conscience. "I'm sorry. I know this is probably a difficult thing for you—not being able to see your grandson, coming all this way—and, well, whiling away your time in a hotel room. Truth is, Ellen, I haven't even talked to Toby yet about you and Suzanna's being in town. I'm a little worried about the impact it might have on him."

She looked at the floor and swallowed. "I'm sure you are, and I understand your worry."

He stuffed his hands in his hip pockets and glanced out at the sunny day. Coming through the door was a gentle springtime breeze. Birds whistled in the flowering oaks and maples that peppered the property. "Frankly, I wish you and Suzanna would've written or called ahead of time. Then, I could have at least had the chance to think things over, consider the prospect of a visit."

"That is what I suggested to my daughter, but she said you'd tell her not to come, so she insisted on making the trip unannounced. I'm here to ask you to reconsider letting her—us—see Toby."

Noah took in a deep breath of air, then slowly let it back out. "Suppose I did allow it. How would it change things, in terms of Toby's future? Suzanna's never shown any interest in raising him, and now, suddenly, she pops into town and wants to see him? It makes little sense to me. Why now—almost nine months after the divorce, and after as much time having no contact with him—is she whining about wanting to see him?"

Ellen removed her flowery hat and looked around the room, probably seeking a place to sit down. He'd intended to bring over a couple of chairs but still hadn't gotten around to it. "I see you're building a grand boat," she said, evading his question. "It's beautiful. You surely do have the knack." She walked over to run her hand across the smooth outer surface. "It looks nearly finished. Is it?"

"I have a lot of interior work to do yet, but it's coming along nicely. The fellow I'm building it for plans to enter it in this year's regatta. He hopes to win. I just hope she floats."

Ellen smiled halfheartedly and looked down at the boat again, seeming to ponder how to proceed. "She has many regrets, Noah. Especially now."

"Especially now? How do you mean?"

Ellen's gray hair, normally done up to perfection, had a few straggles falling from a not-so-neat bun at the back, and her signature smooth skin bore more wrinkles than when he'd last seen her. Had her daughter's divorce, and, now, her withering second marriage, affected her physical well-being? Unexpected sadness at the situation swept over his soul. She'd lost her only grandson, and her daughter's life lay in shambles. In many ways, she must have considered herself a failure as a mother.

She bit down on her lip as a tear rolled down her cheek. "There is just no easy way to say this, Noah, so I'll just come out with it. Suzanna is dying."

"What?" Shock bombarded his senses, stunning him into utter silence. He knew his mouth was hanging open, but he couldn't seem to bring his jaw back up. He sucked in several measured breaths and stared at his former mother-in-law, trying to discern whether he'd heard her correctly, her steady succession of tears convincing him he had.

"I know it's…very hard to…believe," she said between sobs. "It has taken me weeks and weeks to persuade myself it's true."

Weeks? They'd known for weeks and hadn't thought to tell him? But, then, their final parting had been anything but genial. "How did—? What—? Are you sure?"

"Yes, quite." She dabbed at her cheeks and regained a measure of composure, no doubt having already shed a river of tears. "We have sent her to several physicians, and all have come up with the same diagnosis. She is dying from an irreversible form of blood cancer. The destructive cells have spread throughout her body."

"C-cancer?" Had he heard right? "How did she get that? It's not—that common."

"It is more common than you think, Noah, it just often goes undiagnosed. With the invention of the X-ray machine and several other devices, scientists have gained much knowledge in the field, but, unfortunately, in her instance, treatment options are very limited, and a cure—well, outside of a miracle, it's quite improbable. All the doctors agree it's reached a very advanced stage. You saw her on a good day. She does have her good days, but the last two—well, they've been most difficult for her. Because she can't keep anything in her stomach, she's grown very weak." Ellen's voice trembled with emotion, but she held herself together.

"We have a few doctors in town, one whom I know somewhat, a Dr. Van Huff. Perhaps you should—"

"Yes, yes, he came up to our hotel room and administered some sort of liquid medicine to help with her nausea, then instructed me to continue giving her fluids. He said there really wasn't much else he could do for her. She did sleep much better last night and seems much improved this morning, so, for that, we are thankful."

"Good, that's good." He exhaled a heavy sigh of relief.

"We're going back to Guilford in the morning. I…I thought you would like to know that."

"Yes. Thanks for telling me." He grappled for the right words but discovered their complete absence. He turned to look at his boat.

"Well." She rubbed her hands together. "Don't let me keep you a second longer. I just—"

"No, wait." He touched her arm and made a hasty decision. "I'm going to go get Toby out of school."

Just thirty minutes later, he found himself knocking on Toby's classroom door. The teacher greeted him in a cordial manner. He explained the situation in its most abbreviated form, minus any details, that Toby's mother was in town and would like to visit her son. He could tell by the middle-aged woman's uplifted brows how very much she wanted to know the circumstances surrounding Toby's mother's arrival in Sandy Shores, but she had the prudence to keep her questions to herself.

Outside, Toby skipped up the sidewalk. "Pa, this is plain wonderful, you takin' me out of school. I get to miss my spelling test."

"I'm sure you'll have to make it up later, son."

That thought gave him pause, and he turned up his nose. "Where we goin', anyway? You got a surprise for me?"

"I do, actually."

"What is it?"

The excitement in his son's voice made Noah's chest constrict into a tight ball of pain. He spied a bench at the end of the school yard and directed Toby to sit down. "I have something very important to tell you."

"Are you goin' to marry Miss Abbie?"

"What? No, I...." Of all things to come rolling off Toby's tongue! "It's nothing like that."

"Oh." His chin dropped, hitting the top button of his shirt.

"It's about, well...your mother."

Chapter Thirty-two

Abbie found herself doing a good deal of sleeping the next day, listening to the phonograph, and sipping on Grandmother Kane's herbal tea. Reading was completely out of the question, due to her continuous headache, which also meant she couldn't write a letter to Maggie. She could, however, talk to her on the telephone, which she'd done that very morning while propped in Papa's favorite chair, her feet on a stool, and a light afghan thrown across her lap, something her grandmother absolutely insisted on, even though she wasn't the tiniest bit chilled.

Hannah had wanted to know every last detail of the events of the night before, having already heard them firsthand from Papa but wanting them repeated by Abbie on the chance that Papa had left out something important. Unfortunately, most of the details had turned to a muddy haze due to the concussion Ralston Van Huff said she'd suffered, so Papa's account had been more accurate. She remembered the important parts, though—particularly, Noah's rushing in through the back door, untying her, and pulling her into his arms. She recalled his indiscernible whispers of endearment and the sense of safety and strength she'd found in the circle of his strong yet tender embrace. She kept that precious secret to herself, though, not quite ready to divulge it even to Maggie.

She also remembered denying Noah the right to accompany them to the doctor's office and the flash of disappointment that had skipped across his brow. Oh, how torn she'd felt, wanting him with her, yet knowing there remained a number of unsettled matters in his life that kept her from loving him wholeheartedly.

Katrina Sterling arrived in the early afternoon, bearing platters of sugar cookies, peanut butter fudge, taffy, and a blueberry pie. It had always been Katrina's contention that when met with sickness, hard times, sadness, or pain of any kind, a sweet delicacy went a long way to cure the problem. Between Katrina and Grandmother Kane, Abbie had no excuse for not recuperating in short order. While she reclined on the sofa, Grandmother and Katrina kept up a constant flow of conversation in the two wingback chairs, exchanging recipes, critiquing last Sunday's sermon, talking about Cora' and Clara's latest antics, and discussing how Katrina's pregnancy was progressing. When Grandmother asked her if she thought another set of twins was in the making, she said she'd decided that whatever came out would suit her fine, as long as he, she, or they had all fingers and toes intact. A little hair would be nice, too, she tacked on.

Hannah and the children, minus Jesse, who was still in school, stopped by after Katrina left, and after they took their leave, Norma Barton, the next-door neighbor, came with a covered casserole, some sort of cheesy potatoes and meatballs over which Grandmother Kane oohed and aahed.

At the precise time Abbie confessed to Grandmother she couldn't handle one more visitor, a knock came at the door.

Grandmother peeked through the curtain, then cast Abbie a mischievous grin. "Are you sure about that?" she asked.

"Who is it?"

"Only Noah Carson."

She sat up too quickly, producing an awful wave of dizziness, tossed off the afghan and slung it over the sofa back, then fiddled with the combs in her tangled mass of hair, trying to make fast work of straightening her mussed appearance—all to no avail.

When Grandmother opened the door, she greeted him warmly, ushered him inside, and offered him something to drink. When he politely declined, she quickly excused herself to the upstairs quarters.

The first thing Abbie noticed when Noah entered the living room were the weary lines drawn into his handsome brow, the hint of red in the corners of his sea-blue eyes, which were perhaps even swollen, and the sag to his broad, strong shoulders. Had he slept as much as a wink last night? Not by the look of him.

He walked straight to the sofa and dropped into the chair next to it. "How are you, sweet girl?" he asked, the simple endearment turning her to mush.

Lord, I fear there is no hope for it. I've fallen seriously, irrevocably, utterly, and madly in love with this man.

"I'm fine." He looked into her eyes as if trying to reach her soul. "Truly, I am."

"Your headache?"

"Almost gone," she fibbed.

He gave a slow nod. "I hear those headaches can hang around for a few days with that sort of injury." He reached up and tenderly touched the bump at the back of her head. "It's gone down quite a bit."

His gentle touch produced a tingling sensation that made her visibly shiver. "Yes, it's barely there." She knew her voice was quaking and quivering, but there was no stopping it.

Noah leaned over and kissed her cheek, his lips moist and warm, lingering. He stole one of her hands from her lap and held it to his firm chest. "I want to tell you something, need to tell you something," he said, close to her face, his breath warm—no, hot—against her skin.

"All right."

He sat back, and silence fell, except for the sound of Grandmother Kane's quiet moving about on the floor above them.

She swallowed. He swallowed. She turned her body so that she faced him square on, then immediately grew mesmerized by his Adam's apple. "What is it, Noah?"

He pulled back his head and looked at the ceiling, then squeezed his eyes shut for ten seconds. Of all things to happen, two tears rolled out of the corners of his eyes, down his cheeks, and onto his collar.

"Noah!" she gasped. Without a second's thought, she freed her hand from his and wiped his whiskery cheeks with the pads of both thumbs, but then more tears rolled down to cover the ones she'd wiped away. "Dear, gentle Noah." Hastily, she reached into her apron pocket and took out a lace-edged handkerchief with a rose pattern. At least it was clean. She dabbed his eyes and cheeks with it, then made a bold move and leaned forward to kiss both sides of his face, tasting the salt of his tears. "What is it?"

"I've just come from visiting Suzanna. Toby's there now."

Her hand stilled. "Oh."

"No, it's not what you think. It's...she's...." She tried to probe the deep shadows that suddenly fell across his face when he lowered his head, his hair falling haphazardly over his brow.

She pushed the hair away, then dipped her face lower than his to see up into his eyes. "What?"

"She's dying. Toby's mother is dying."

Another gasp escaped, this one louder and more pronounced. "Oh, no! How is that possible? She looked so beautiful the other day. I'm ashamed to admit I was even jealous of her."

Noah attempted a chuckle but failed. Clearing his throat, he proceeded to explain Suzanna's condition, a sort of incurable, cancer-like disease that all the doctors said could take her life in a matter of months, perhaps even weeks, but one that still gave her days when she could function almost normally.

"How did Toby take the news? You said he's with her now?"

"Yeah, I picked him up at school, sat him down on a bench, and tried as best I could to describe her illness. Strangely, he's taking the news better than I am. He was actually excited about seeing her—and his grandmother, of course. I don't think he's fully grasped what's going on. He sat up on her bed and held her hand like a little man, told her about his school and the friends he'd made, and even sang her a little Sunday school song he learned from you. 'Jesus Loves Me.'"

She smiled, scratched an itch on her forehead, folded her hands in her lap again, and cleared her throat. "Do you still love her, Noah?" she asked outright.

She felt his surprise before seeing it. "What?" His head jerked up. "No."

"Then what do you feel?"

His eyes filled again with tears, and he wiped his nose with the upper part of his hand, then remembered the handkerchief she'd given him and gave his nose a quick swipe. There was something so vulnerable about a broken man using a woman's handkerchief that made Abbie's own eyes well up. "Regret, I guess. We were married for seven years, so there's something there, but it's not love—not in the way you'd think." Their damp eyes communicated for several intense seconds. "Things are going to be strange for a while, Abbie. I mean, I want to see you, but, I don't know…. My heart is mangled and ripped, and I feel like I'm holding Toby's heart in my hands right now—like it's my responsibility to make sure it doesn't break into a million pieces."

She reached out and gently squeezed his muscular forearm. "You feel that way because he's your son, but, ultimately, he's God's responsibility, Noah. Can you grasp that? Can you hand him over to the Lord? I have felt for some time that if you would relinquish those things over which you have little control—your father's mistakes and the early loss of your mother, the failure of your marriage and the inadequacies you surely must feel from raising a son on your own, the bitterness you hold for your former partner, not to mention Suzanna's father—all those things that control your mindset—if you could learn to let them go, give them over into God's very capable hands, you would finally experience true freedom in Christ.

"I don't want to be a distraction or a hindrance to that happening for you, Noah, so when you say that you want to see me, and yet your heart is too mangled right now, I completely understand that. In fact, I strongly believe we must distance ourselves from each other for a time."

He hung his head and pinched the bridge of his nose as Abbie dried a lingering tear under her left eye with the back of her hand. "You need to settle several things, Noah—some serious matters—and I pray you'll find the strength and will to do it. You do know that all the answers lie right within the pages of God's Word, don't you? That's where you'll find your comfort."

He sniffed, handed over her rose-patterned handkerchief, and gave a slow, deliberate nod, then put his hands on his knees in preparation for standing up. Before he did, though, he whispered, "Pray for me. And for Suzanna."

"You know I will. Every day, every hour, every minute."

He nodded again, then, quite without warning, drew her into a tight embrace. How good it felt to be pressed against his solid bulk. For one long, lingering second she yearned for his kisses—his warm, moist, heart-stopping kisses—but then, prudence swiftly reminded her of all that she'd just finished saying, and she very gently pulled away from him.

"You'd best get back to Toby—and Suzanna."

She saw him struggle with inner turmoil before finally getting up. Standing, he looked down at her, slipped a finger under her chin, and stared into her eyes for a moment. "You are an amazing woman for only twenty-one years."

She gave a half chuckle. "Almost twenty-two, I'll have you know, Mr. Carson."

One dark eyebrow shot up. "Really? How soon?"

"Next week. May 14."

Surprise glimmered in his velvety, blue eyes. "You're kidding, right? That was my mother's birthday."

She gasped. "No! Really?" She could barely believe the coincidence, but then she quickly checked herself. God was full of surprises.

Both of Noah's eyebrows shot up now, accompanied by a tiny, impish grin. "Could be some kind of divine sign."

K

Noah, Toby, and Gerald spent the evening with Ellen and Suzanna, Suzanna in bed, lying down or propped up with a pillow, her face drawn and ashen. He realized now she'd probably used rouge to give her face some color that first day he'd seen her. Aunt Julia, bless her heart, had prepared a meal and had Noah's father bring it up to their room around six o'clock. He'd not intended to intrude, just to hand over the basket, but Ellen and Suzanna both invited him to stay a while, so he did. *What a strange set of circumstances*, Noah mused, sitting and carrying on civil conversations with people who'd caused him measureless grief while Toby sat on the floor, coloring a picture for his mother. Every so often, his eyes caught Suzanna's, and he held her gaze, their unspoken apologies hanging in midair. For, while she had committed the adulterous deed, he knew he'd also contributed in less obvious ways to the death of their marriage.

They talked about the community of Sandy Shores, the beautiful lakeshore, the shops and businesses, and the small home in Mill Point that Gerald planned to lease.

"You seem so different now, Gerald," Suzanna said. "What turned you around?"

"Ah, I'm glad you asked," he said with a chuckle. The question provided him with the perfect opportunity to tell about his personal conversion experience back in Guilford, how he'd walked to that same little church his wife had attended to meet and pray with the preacher. Ellen and Suzanna listened with rapt attention to the miracle of his transformed life, and while he talked, Noah recalled Abbie's challenge to renounce those things he couldn't control and surrender his life into God's strong, capable hands.

He wondered why he didn't just choose to jump headlong into it, like his father had. Was there something still keeping him from making that commitment? Something told him there was, and he no longer thought it was his father, or even Suzanna, for that matter. It was Tom Grayson and Carl Dunbar.

Somehow, he had to figure out a way to forgive them.

K

Wednesday morning brought cumbersome, gray clouds and downright cold temperatures, the east winds threatening to push a storm across the Big Lake, typical of a spring day but unsettling to Abbie's mood. She opened her Bible in the hopes of picking up where she'd left off last Sunday night, but her eyes refused to focus, and as soon as she pressed them to try harder, her headache returned in all its ugliness. Impressed to pray, she got down on her knees and thanked the Lord for her circumstances, recalling that Scripture instructed believers to rejoice in all things, good or bad. Next, she prayed for Noah, that God would give him eyes to see beyond his pain and courage to place it all in the Father's loving hands. She prayed for Suzanna and her mother, for her father and Rita, and for Hannah and

Maggie. The greater her fervor became, the lighter her spirits grew, so that when she heard Grandmother Kane open the front door and usher in the Plooster sisters, she nearly leaped to her feet in utter joy. Could it be that the sisters had picked the gloomiest of spring days to ride into town just to see her?

While sipping on hot tea and partaking of every variety of cookie Grandmother Kane had piled on her silver platter, Erma and Ethel Plooster asked numerous questions about the dreadful incident on the night of the auction, having already heard a number of versions of it, which included everything from Angus Clemens shooting Shamus Rogan in the leg to Abbie being the one who did the shooting, from no one actually getting shot but Shamus falling on his rump when Abbie clobbered him on the head with a hammer straight from the Whatnot's shelf to Gabe and Noah knocking down the doors, attacking the no-good bums, and overtaking them with their fists. The latter rang the truest, but even that tale missed the facts by a country mile. Abbie tried to set the women straight, though her memory was still a bit foggy on some of the details.

After the sisters took their leave, various women from the W.C.T.U. and the Third Street Church began dropping by to wish her well, most of them bearing food in some form. Even old Erv Baxter sent his greetings by way of Gabe, saying he truly was glad nothing more serious had transpired and going so far as to tell her she and her fellow temperance ladies were welcome to come back to resume their hymn sings and prayer meetings, just so long as they conducted them outside, preferably across the street from his establishment. Gabe and Abbie shared a good laugh over that one.

"Mercy! If one more person brings a casserole or a cake, I'm going to start getting a complex. Don't folks know I can bake circles around most of them?" Grandmother Kane said after making space on her kitchen counter for yet another plate of goodies, this one of fresh-baked muffins.

Around noontime, after downing half a sandwich and another cup of tea at Grandmother's insistence, Abbie begged off any more visitors and went upstairs to her bedroom to take a nap. At least, that was what she told her grandmother. In actuality, she planned to kneel at her bedside first and pray again for Noah and Suzanna.

Chapter Thirty-three

After spending the morning together—Noah had kept Toby out of school for the day—Noah, Toby, Ellen, Suzanna, and Jeffries, the butler, headed to the train station, all with their varying degrees of weighted hearts.

Conversations had run the gamut all morning, from the events at the Whatnot and Abbie's encounter with two of Sandy Shores' worst bums, both now locked up tight, pending their formal indictments and eventual move to a larger prison facility, to Toby's fishing expeditions with his grandpa and uncle. Suzanna was having one of her better days, which was good, considering the long trip she was about to make back to Connecticut. According to Ellen, the drugs the doctors had prescribed for Suzanna only masked her symptoms, giving her a measure of relief and thereby strengthening her will but doing nothing to slow or stop the dread disease's progress.

"The doctors will be very surprised if she sees the first snowfall," Ellen had whispered to Noah earlier that morning while Suzanna and Toby had played a game of Old Maid on top of the bed. Never in a thousand years would he have pictured Suzanna playing a game with Toby, but now, she seemed to relish every moment of it, gazing lovingly at Toby while he chose a card from her deck, as if memorizing his every feature to store in her mind for future retrieval.

Noah had steered Ellen out into the hallway to ask her a few things. "How is Carl handling all of this? I notice there's been no mention of him."

"Ah, Carl. He's a hard soul, as you know; keeps his emotions tightly bottled until the pressure of holding them in creates an explosion, of sorts. He's always been this way. I know his true self better than anyone else, though, and I recognize the pain and regret in his eyes. He's as much as said he wishes he'd handled things differently with you, Noah, but at the time, all he could do was think about protecting his name and his image." She'd shaken her head. "Such a waste, considering Tom's treatment of Suzanna through all of this."

"What do you mean?"

"Oh, well, as soon as the doctors diagnosed her, he moved right out of that house for fear of catching her illness. Some still have their suspicions that cancer is in some way contagious. He's shown very little compassion for her situation, hasn't even visited her in the past three months. Rumor has it he's already found himself another woman to replace Suzanna as soon as…well, you know."

Utter disgust had wrapped itself around his lungs and nearly squeezed the breath right out of him. All he'd been able to do had been to shake his head.

"He never did get the house put in his name," Ellen had gone on to say. "Although he pestered Suzanna something fierce, she somehow had the fortitude to deny him her signature on several documents. Upon her passing, the house should revert back to you—if you want it, that is."

"What? I don't want it or need it."

"You may want to reconsider that, for Toby's sake. You could always sell it to retrieve your investment, I suppose. You are the one who initially purchased it, and it was plain wrong the way Tom swept Suzanna off her feet, stepping into your very shoes and taking over your company—which is failing, by the way." She'd said that with a degree of satisfaction.

"Suzanna told me."

"We all saw it coming," she'd said. "I suppose that is my vindication, if you will. Something in me wants to see Tom pay for his evil acts against you and, now, Suzanna. He is a charming man, but conniving and mean-spirited. I don't know how you hooked up with him in the first place."

"I don't think I ever truly knew him, Ellen, and we were both young when we got the business off the ground. As it grew, his goals and aims for the company changed, as did his values. It became a power struggle, looking back, his constant desire to hold the reins, to be the one making the decisions. He claimed he knew the best distributors, best buying sources, and the best cargo shippers. I didn't care, as long as I could get my hands dirty in the shop. He had his strengths, and I had mine, but in the end, he wanted it all—and got it, right down to my wife. I carry much of the blame for turning a blind eye, neither tending to my company or my wife with proper care."

"At least you have Toby. How very smart and selfless of you to give it all up without a fight so you could have the best of everything—your son. He's a fine, fine boy, and you're doing a good job raising him, Noah."

"Thanks. I have to agree, he's a fine boy." He'd gazed down the long hallway lined with red, velvet carpet, its walls plastered with some sort of dark, ornately textured wallpaper, and with crystal chandeliers suspended every dozen or so feet apart and casting long shadows from their low light.

"But, getting back to Carl, his heart is heavy for the future. I believe he fears that once Suzanna passes, there will be nothing left to hold us together."

"So, really, he's still thinking only of himself."

She'd sighed. "You're right, of course."

"Speaking of ill-fitted, poorly matched partners, Ellen, I don't know what you ever saw in Carl."

She'd chortled. "I suppose we've both made our mistakes in judgment, right?"

He'd been able to accept that. She'd started to turn the doorknob, but he had stopped her with a hand. "Ellen, you are welcome to return to Sandy Shores anytime to visit Toby."

Wetness had gathered in her eyes. "Noah," she'd muttered, her voice thick with emotion, "thank you. I would like that ever so much."

Passengers and other people milled about the station dock at noontime, holding satchels and bags of every size in their hands and under their arms, some dressed in formal attire, others in overalls and muddy boots, some setting off on twenty-mile jaunts, others on journeys of two hundred miles or more.

Toby held tightly to his grandmother's hand, no doubt sensing the imminent moment of good-byes. Tonight, perhaps, Noah would speak to him about the brevity of life. Or not. He had no idea how Toby would handle the whole process of Suzanna's passing. He supposed one day at a time was the best way. *"Be still, and know that I am God"* was the Scripture that most stood out to him now. He'd read it while lying in bed the other night, and its message lingered in his mind like an ever-present light on a dark, winding road.

A tap on his back made Noah turn around, finding himself face-to-face with Suzanna. "Thank you," she said in a tiny voice. He reached up and touched the paper-thin skin of her cheek. How had he not noticed her utter frailty just four days ago? "I needed this chance to see Toby, and you gave it to me. Thank you," she repeated, her tone choked and wobbly.

"Come here, let's sit you down." He led her to a bench, where they sat down with their knees turned in, almost facing each other. "I'm glad you made the effort to come all this way in your weakened state. You held up well. It was good for Toby...and me. It was good for me."

"And for me." She reached up to fiddle with his top button, letting her fingers linger there as she shook her head. "I was such a fool, Noah. You realize these things when life begins to run out."

"Don't talk about it now, Suzanna. I don't want you to have any regrets about us. We both carry blame. You asked me to forgive you a few days ago, and I told you I already had. Would you forgive me, as well?"

"Oh, Noah, of course." Tears sprang to the corners of her eyes. It seemed that a lot of tears had fallen over the last few days. Compassion prompted Noah to dab at her tears with the pads of his thumbs. Afterward, he bent and kissed one cheek, finding it icy-cold. He took her scarf and wrapped it more securely about her shoulders, as if that would take care of everything.

"I saw the way you looked at her, that Kane woman." His lips parted in surprise. "Are you going to marry her?"

"If God wills it, yes," he answered without hesitation.

She didn't flinch, just nodded. The flowers on her hat swayed in the chilly breeze, and he found himself focusing on the purple one, in particular. "I like your answer. It's the right one," she whispered.

Not quite sure what to make of her response, he asked, "Have you made your peace with God?"

She smiled. "Indeed, I have. Your father's account of his conversion experience challenged me to pray the prayer of salvation while I lay in bed last night. Tell him that, would you?"

Noah took both her hands and held them loosely. "I'll be sure to tell him."

"All aboard!" the conductor called, dragging out the word until it echoed from one end of the train to the other. Farewells rose up along the platform, accompanied by hugs and handshakes.

Toby ran up to the bench and into his mother's open arms, not fully aware, Noah knew, that this truly was good-bye. Yes, Toby knew his mother had a grave illness, but his six-year-old mind had not yet grasped the implications.

They all exchanged hugs, and Jeffries received a parting handshake from Noah. "Thanks for taking good care of them, Jeffries. You're a good man."

The fellow looked plain flummoxed. "Yo' mighty welcome, suh."

When the locomotive sounded its shrill whistle and the chug-a-chug of the mighty engine started pulling the cars over the steel tracks, Noah and Toby raised their hands in one final wave.

"When are they comin' back to see us, Pa?" Toby asked, his small body leaning against Noah's thigh. He set his hand atop his boy's sandy head of hair, raised his face to the sky, where a tiny patch of blue had broken through the gray, and breathed deeply.

"I can't tell you that, son," he said with all truthfulness. They set off on a walk uptown. "What say we go have a bite to eat and, afterwards, walk to Marie's for some ice cream?"

"Yippee!" Toby squealed, setting off on a skip beside him, his young mind already transitioning to a happier, more care-free frame. "Can I stay home from school for the rest of the week?"

"Absolutely not. I have a boat to build."

"Aw, shoot. That means I prolly gots to take a dumb spelling test tomorrow."

Abbie's birthday came and went with little fanfare, not that she'd expected any at her age. Oh, there'd been the usual Kane birthday dinner and presents, the traditional singing of the birthday song, and the blowing out of candles, but, beyond that, turning twenty-two had not been particularly exciting; certainly nothing like turning sixteen. And it didn't help that when her sisters were her age, they were either married or well on their ways, never mind that she'd spent her life telling her sisters, her friends, and her grandmother that she didn't need a man to fulfill her. "Men are the fluff of life!" she'd announced on a whim to Katrina one day. "If you happen to land one, it's sort of like getting that extra little fluff in your pillow. But if you don't, no worries, 'cause a thin pillow often means much less pain in the neck."

"Oh, for crying in a bucket, Abbie Ann. That is the worst analogy I've ever heard in my life. Imagine my referring to Micah as my pillow!" Katrina could sometimes be slow on the draw, but, looking back, it had been a ridiculous statement, Abbie was willing to admit.

True, a man could not fulfill a woman's heart and life. Only God could do that. But a birthday card never hurt. Fiddlesticks, she'd half expected Noah to send her one, particularly since he knew very well she shared a birthday with his mother.

"What do you want, Abs?" Hannah had said the other day when she'd complained about his failure to acknowledge her birthday. "You told him you needed to distance yourselves from each other. He's honoring that."

"And a birthday card would have broken that rule?"

Hannah sighed. "You can't have it both ways, sister dear. On the one hand, you won't commit to a man not fully surrendered to God, and rightfully so. But, on the other hand, you're not willing to wait on the Lord to finish doing what He started."

As usual, her older sister's wisdom far surpassed her own, and it silenced her complaints for the rest of that day.

And now, here she was, heading out the door to work an afternoon shift at the Whatnot and stewing over the matter yet again. It'd been ten days since she'd seen Noah, unless she counted last Sunday, when she'd seen him across the church lobby, talking to Donald Clayton, no doubt discussing the boat's progress and the upcoming regatta. Did he even miss her? More important, had he been praying, reading his Bible, and seeking God for guidance? And what was the status on Suzanna? So many questions on her mind, yet all of them unanswered. She had half a mind to march over to the warehouse and ask him why he'd kept her in the dark.

She closed the door on an empty house and headed up the street, thankful that, at least, her headaches had all but vanished, that glorious sunshine graced her path as she walked along without fear of being watched or followed, and that Shamus Rogan and Angus Clemens were now locked up tight in jail cells, awaiting sentences that most believed would land them in the Jackson State Prison for at least the next twenty years.

Arlena Rogan and her girls were flourishing out at their place and had started making a number of new friends, their plight having helped to raise awareness of the needs of other abused women and children. Dozens of volunteers, including Arlena, had been showing up almost daily at Hope House, the auction having raised more than enough money to pay for all the improvements and also deposit a surplus in the bank. Praise the Lord for blessings, great and small!

As Abbie walked along, listening to the birds sing at the tops of their lungs, she wondered how in the world, with all these blessings, she could possibly have even an ounce of discontent. But, of course, it didn't take a brilliant scientist to figure that one out.

It was that dratted Noah Carson!

⌘ *K*

"You getting impatient to set sail?" Gerald asked Noah one day as they worked amiably together. He had graciously offered to take off a day of work so he could help Noah with the interior work, the hardware, and the rigging. The manufactured sails had arrived from Chicago by special shipment, and, for all involved, excitement for moving the boat out to the yard had risen to its highest peak.

"It's going to be a grand day, I'll admit that," said Noah, who always felt distracted these days, despite his eagerness to finish the boat.

His distraction came from the constant, rocklike lump resting at the bottom of his stomach. The latest telephone call from Ellen revealed that since their return to Connecticut, Suzanna's disease had progressed, resulting in her sleeping more than usual and eating less than ever. "It won't be long, Noah. I'm sure of it."

"Do you want me to come?" he'd asked.

"No, you've said your good-byes. It's best this way, and I'd especially not want Toby to see her in this state."

"I wouldn't bring him."

"I think Suzanna wants to preserve what bit of dignity remains. It's enough that Carl and I are at her side."

Carl. Some comfort he was. Noah told himself he ought to cease work on the boat and simply go, but he had his responsibilities here, was up against a time crunch, and Ellen was right; Suzanna had just enough pride left not to want anyone to see her in this state. She'd always prized herself on her regal, classic beauty. Being seen gaunt and frail would humiliate and embarrass her, and he didn't want to do that to her, especially in her final days.

"Has Clayton decided on a name for this pretty lady yet?" his father asked as he bent over to attach a brass fixture.

"If so, he hasn't mentioned one."

"He'd better start thinking. And what about a crew for the regatta?"

"Well, now, that he has determined. There's a fellow out of Chicago, a Todd Seabert, some forty years of sailing experience under his belt, whom he's asked to fly the spinnaker. He's chosen Chuck Rycenga, who's in my Sunday school class, to be the pole setter and jiber, and Gary Slager—belongs to the yacht club and is an apt sailor, according to Don—to tend to the mainsheet. Don says Gary sails like he was born with a tiller clenched in his hand. Don and I will skipper it together; he wants it that way, and I'm in favor. It's his boat, after all, but he wants my expertise. I suspect he'll be following my orders rather than the other way around. He wants you acting as board man. You're competent, Dad, and, next to me, most familiar with the boat's design."

His father stood up, pivoted his body, and stared, open-mouthed, at Noah.

"What?"

"It's nothing. Just...."

"You don't want the job?"

"No, no, not that. I'm honored he selected me. It's just—I never heard you call me Dad before. I like how it sounds." He shrugged as a sheepish grin popped out on his face. "That's all."

Noah gave his head a jaunty toss. He wouldn't admit it, but the word had come out as naturally as if he'd uttered it a million times. And, of course, he had, but only in his head.

They resumed their individual tasks, Noah's spirit somehow lighter. The sun, mingled with clouds, still gave off plenty of light to work by. At lunch, they sat on the floor under an open window and enjoyed the gentle winds of late May. Bites and chews of their bacon and cheese sandwiches were interspersed with occasional talk, mostly boat-inspired but also touching on family, friends, and church. Gerald inquired after Suzanna, as he did almost daily, and said how gratified he'd been by the news that his humble testimony of God's faithful love and forgiveness had prompted her to pray a simple prayer of repentance and accept Jesus as her Savior.

"How is that courtship with Abbie Kane progressing?" his father asked while sipping coffee from his thermos, steam still rising from the insulated bottle.

"I haven't seen her in a while."

"I suspected as much. What went wrong?"

He rubbed the side of his nose. Thoughts of the woman had been another source of constant distraction. Between her and Suzanna, complete opposites in every possible sense, his head came close to erupting nearly every day.

"Nothing went wrong, per se, but we both agreed to put some space between us. This matter with Suzanna's illness and my trying to protect Toby against the pain of losing his mother, plus, the need to finish this boat on time—it's all been a bit much to juggle."

"It's got you all in a dither, I can see. You love her, this Kane girl?"

"I…yeah, I do, actually."

"Then it's all going to work out. God's got it under control."

"I like your simple logic," Noah said, grinning.

"It is simple. Simple and true. Your life's in His hands. All you have to do is surrender it."

"I've been trying, I really have." He drew up his legs and rested his arms across his knees, letting his hands dangle.

"Abbie challenged me to start reading my Bible more. Most of it doesn't make much sense, though."

"Ha!" Gerald threw back his head and laughed. "You think it's hard to understand, you ought to have my brain!" Now, they both chortled. "Here's my thinking on that. The Lord's going to reveal to you exactly what you need to know for that day. His Word is inspired, which means He wrote the book, even if a human put it to paper. Therefore, He knows it inside and out, and He'll help you understand the parts you need to know. And here's another thing: the more I read it, the more I catch on to it. It's quite an amazing thing to me."

"That's good," Noah said, nodding in agreement.

Gerald drained his thermos with a few swallows, wiped his mouth on his sleeve, and breathed out, casting a look at the beautifully varnished boat. "We'll have her finished in plenty of time, son. I'm convinced of it. Look at that lady, would you? She's as spotless as your Aunt Julia's kitchen." More good-natured chuckles. "When she wins that regatta, you'll have more orders than you can keep up with."

"You think so?"

"I know so."

"What would you say to starting up a boatworks with me—down the road, I mean, if I do get orders coming in?" Noah nearly fell over at actually having voiced what he'd only been thinking for the past several weeks. The very notion would have been nothing short of ridiculous a year ago, but that was before he'd come to know the new Gerald Carson.

Gerald gawked at him as if he'd lost his mind—and, maybe, he had. "Are you joshing me?"

Noah cocked his head. "I'm as serious as a surgeon."

"What would we name it? Not Carson & Son. It would be your company."

"How about just Carson Boatworks? And, who knows? Maybe someday, Toby would want to learn the business. He's been awfully interested in the process so far."

Suddenly solemn-faced, Gerald stared at his pant leg, then picked up a piece of lint and rolled it between his fingers. "The Lord sure has been answering my prayers, son. You don't know what a dream this is for me. Even in those days when I treated you so bad, I loved you then, I did. I just had a rotten way of showing it. But I'd have done anything back then, anything, to have my own boatworks with you. And to think it could actually happen—well, I don't know what to say."

Noah swiped a crumb off his chin, his lunch complete. "It's in the talking stages now, mind you."

"As it should be. I'll not hold you to anything. You want to change your mind about me joining you, there'll be no hard feelings whatever. I want what's best for you. Matter of fact, I've been meaning to show you something, but I didn't know if you wanted to see it or not. I know Julia told you about the letter your ma wrote, and I've sort of been waiting to see if you would ask to read it."

His heart skipped. "I've actually been waiting to see if you would mention it."

Gerald chuckled. "Well, I guess we both been waiting, then. Did you want to read it? I have it with me."

"Now? I'm not sure...."

"No, no, not now. I'd want you to take it with you and read it when you got a minute to yourself. It's in my Bible. I take my Bible everywhere, as you probably know."

"Yeah, I've noticed." Noah swallowed, the lump in his stomach stirring again. "I'd like the chance to read the letter."

Gerald rose and crossed the room, a lightness in his step. Blast if even that limp hadn't all but disappeared.

Chapter Thirty-four

The rest of the week brought doses of rain and cooler temperatures but then an abrupt turn with plenty of sunshine and downright hot air, typical of a Michigan spring. Old Alden Lawhorn hobbled into the Whatnot two days ago between a heavy patch of rain and a clear, bright sun and said Michigan reminded him of his wife—cold one second, warm the next, and as changeable as a doctor's schedule.

Today's weather had evened out, making work at Hope House a pleasant experience. With efficiency, Jane Emery, the project coordinator, walked from room to room with a perpetual smile, notebook in hand, inspecting progress and thanking volunteers for their time and effort. Already, the four small bedrooms and bathroom upstairs had fresh coats of paint, new carpet, and donated beds and dressers, albeit mismatched. Serviceable best described each room, but the bright, cheery colors were bound to attract and comfort any woman or young girl in need of refuge and support. The downstairs had a bright kitchen, a dining room, a large living area, a small library, a tiny bathroom, and another good-sized bedroom, which would serve as the live-in couple's quarters. Here, again, donated furniture, rugs, lamps, framed art, tables, and bookshelves filled each room, but the lovely wall colors in some rooms and wallpaper in others tied everything together in a most homey, welcoming way.

Delbert Huizenga donated new windows and doors to the project, sending over several of his men to install them, a generous move on his part, especially considering the magnitude of his own project: putting a much-needed addition on the building that housed his ever-expanding door and window company.

By mid-afternoon, several workers had left and new ones had come in, making for a constant shift of volunteers, lively conversation, and a generally lighthearted atmosphere. Abbie was stationed in the front yard, where she'd been assigned to paint a small coffee stand black, and she was certain more paint had wound up on her than on the little table. Of all people, Peter Sinclair came up the sidewalk, a briefcase tucked under his arm, looking dapper and dignified, as usual. A strange awkwardness came over her. Since they'd parted ways, not one complete sentence had been said between them; their communication had consisted of merely short, brief hellos and how-are-yous in the church lobby, with Charity Keeton typically hanging on Peter's arm. This time, however, Peter actually stopped to smile at Abbie and survey her work.

"Hello, Peter," she said, standing up and blowing the hair off her face, then mopping her damp brow with the back of her hand. This was a bad move, considering the black paint she saw on her hand afterward and the smear she'd evidently made on her forehead.

He threw his head back and laughed, which was rare for Peter Sinclair, unless something truly had tickled his funny bone.

"What?" she asked. But, for the time being, all he did was point at her and keep up his silly spurt of laughter. "It's just… I'm sorry, Abbie." He held his stomach and straightened his mouth, but only temporarily, soon letting loose another burst of mirth.

She giggled and looked down at her blue skirt with the pink flowers and her pink, scoop-necked shirtwaist, completely ruined, of course. "I look a sight, do I?"

When his laughter finally wound down, he shook his head. "I'm sorry to say you do. But your table looks nice— except, here." He pointed, taking care not to touch the wet paint. "You missed a spot."

"Oh." She dabbed the area with her paintbrush, then made the mistake of scratching an itchy spot on her cheek.

"Oh!" He pointed again, this time at her face. "Uh, you shouldn't have done that."

"More paint?"

He nodded, cutting loose another round of chuckles. She joined in. Mercy, it felt good to laugh. Had it taken breaking up with her for Peter to learn how to have fun?

"How've you been?" he asked.

"Wonderful. Good," she amended. If he'd noticed, he appeared to pay no heed. "And you? Are you well?"

"Wonderful. Good," he mimicked her. My goodness, how they laughed again. He quickly sobered. "I've meant to tell you for some time now how thankful I am that you escaped that awful experience with Rogan and Clemens. I hope you came out of it relatively unscathed." He reached up and touched her hair. "I hear you got quite a bump on the head."

"I did, but I'm quite fine now."

"Haven't seen you with that Carson fellow lately."

"Yes, well, we...." How did one respond to such a statement? "I've seen you sitting in church with Charity Keeton," she ventured. "Are the two of you seeing each other?"

"We are, yes. She's a lovely person. I'm—well, *we're*—very much...you know."

She leaned forward, arching her eyebrows as high as she could. "Goodness! It's serious, then? Well, wasn't that—quick!" She giggled nervously and laid a hand on his arm. "I'm truly happy for you, Peter." But was she really? Not two months after parting ways with her, Peter had wasted no time in finding someone to replace her, not to mention someone with an art for making him utterly giddy. Oh, not that she wasn't thrilled for him, no, but it bothered her that she did not seem to possess the same kind of power to thrill Noah Carson to his toes.

Oh, forevermore! There she went again, putting her heart before God's, laying out her plans ahead of His, wishing for things she had no business wishing.

When would she ever learn to trust the Lord completely?

K

Well, this is just dandy, Noah thought, finding Abbie and Peter sharing an intimate conversation on the front lawn of Hope House. He knew he should have picked a different day to volunteer, even though Uncle Del had asked him to help install the donated windows and doors. He reined in Ruby

Sue, slid off his saddle, and tied her to a tree, then started up the sidewalk just as Sinclair was reaching up to pull a strand of Abbie's hair off her face—her black-smudged face, he might add. Jealousy ripped through his veins at the sounds of their private laughter, each leaning into the other as they talked, Abbie looking down, then back at Peter, as if something he'd said in their exchange had meant a great deal. As a matter of fact, his presence so engrossed her she hadn't even taken one second to glance in Noah's direction.

Well, it certainly hadn't taken her long to fall back into Sinclair's arms. And here, Noah had been foolish enough to think the man had found another woman, someone he'd seen him sitting with in church. Ha!

He cleared his throat on his approach. A simple, brief hello would be sufficient.

"Hello." There. He started to pass.

"Noah!" Abbie nearly shrieked. "Hello."

Man, she looked good, even with black paint smeared every which way on her face, arms, hands, and clothes, her shirtwaist only halfway tucked into her tiny-waisted, floral skirt, the other half hanging out like a farmer's shirt. If ever he'd seen a sight that made him wish for a lingering second look, it was now, but he fought down the urge and looked at Sinclair instead, giving him a curt nod. Talk about a contrast! Did this fellow ever dress down? Of course, the briefcase under one arm indicated he had come on business, waylaid by one beautiful Abbie Ann Kane.

"Peter." He reached out a hand and managed a minute smile for good measure.

"Noah," he said, looking down his nose in an assessing manner. "Come to offer your services?"

Evading eye contact with Abbie, Noah said, "I'm here to help install the windows and doors. You?" He eyed the guy's spiffy attire and fine, leather briefcase.

"Me? Oh, I came to talk to Mrs. Emery about some financial matters regarding this house. In fact, I should probably go see if I can locate her. Would you excuse me?"

"Sure." He stepped aside.

"I'll talk to you soon, Abbie," Peter said, reaching up and tweaking her nose, then turning and skipping up the porch steps as if he'd just won a million bucks.

"Well, good to see you," Noah said to Abbie, trying to cushion his heart with curtness.

Her face quickly lost its glow when Peter disappeared. "And you."

"I'm sorry I didn't check on you after—"

"What? No, that's fine."

"Are your headaches gone?"

"Completely."

"Good, that's good." He stuffed his hands in his pockets. "You have a nice birthday?" He wondered what Sinclair had bought her. Good thing he'd decided against sending that card he'd picked out for her. In light of things, he would have looked like a fool.

"Lovely, thanks." Her hands went behind her back, and he imagined them tightly clasped. "I'm twenty-two now," she announced, like some young girl approaching adolescence might do. She made him want to smile, but he had his heart to think about. "How's Suzanna?" she asked, changing tunes, her childlike face suddenly solemn.

"Not good."

"I'm so sorry. This must be hard on Toby. I haven't wanted to ask him about her in Sunday school."

"Good, I'm glad. It's going to be tough enough explaining it to him once she passes on. Right now, he's just living like a normal six-year-old, with hardly a care."

"And that's how it should be. How about yourself?"

He put up his guard and fortified his emotions. "You know, taking a day at a time. The boat's keeping me busy."

"Oh! Is she beautiful?"

"Yes." He looked at her. "She is beautiful."

"We'll look forward to watching her take first place in the regatta."

He couldn't help but notice her use of *we*.

They'd reached a dead end. How could it be? "Well."

"Yes, well." Her laugh came off shakily.

He thumbed over his shoulder. "I better get inside."

"Don't let me keep you."

He turned to go, then paused. "Nice seeing you."

She gave a tight little smile, though he thought he detected a quiver of her lips. She probably had no idea how to tell him she'd lost all interest in him—that is, if she'd ever had any.

She cried all the way back to her house, bending as she walked to lift the hem of her skirt to wipe her eyes and blow her nose, then crying the harder. To anyone watching out a window, she must have looked a sight. Walk, bend, raise skirt to face; walk, bend, raise skirt again. And, if they'd heard her sobs, why, they might have supposed someone had died. In a sense, someone had—or *something*. Abbie felt overwhelmed by deep, dark disappointment to discover Noah had no feelings left for her. Clearly, he'd wanted nothing more than to escape her presence the second he'd seen her, the way he'd spoken to her in brief, emotionless sentence fragments. And to think she'd imagined they might someday love each other—assuming he made a true, heartfelt commitment to Christ. No wonder she hadn't seen him in several days. He'd been avoiding her. Avoiding her! Why, he hadn't even come into the Whatnot, which meant he'd been purchasing his supplies elsewhere, perhaps at Frank's Mercantile. With that notion, yet another sob sputtered out of her.

She tiptoed up the porch steps and tried to slip through the door unheard, but when she came inside and reached the staircase, Grandmother Kane called from the kitchen, "Who's home, Jacob or Abbie?"

Abbie sniffed and grabbed hold of her resolve, clearing her throat and putting a chipper tone in place. "Me, Grandmother. I'm going upstairs to take a bath and change these awful clothes."

She set off on a run, but her grandmother's voice at the bottom of the stairs brought her to another halt. "Why are your clothes awful?"

Without turning, she said in as casual a voice as possible, "I've been painting at Hope House. Don't worry, I wore my oldest things."

"I'm not worried. Let me see the damage."

With all her might, she hoped Grandmother wouldn't spot her red, swollen face in the shadowy stairwell when she slowly turned. The last thing she wanted to do was discuss her tattered heart. "Goodness gracious, child, not only can you not cook; you can't paint, either."

Well, if that wasn't the last straw—and from her own grandmother, no less. She burst into sobs loud enough to reach Grand Rapids. Then, making an about-turn, she lifted her paint-covered, tear-washed skirt and ran up to her bedroom.

"Sweetheart, it was a joke!" Grandmother called after her.

Abbie slammed her door and threw herself facedown on her bed, sinking into the old mattress's rock-bottom depths. It came as no surprise when, ten seconds later, the door opened, and a warm body plunked down beside her, making the mattress springs moan. A hand came up to caress her matted hair. "You cry as one with a broken heart," Grandmother said.

If her sobs had been loud before, well, the next one came out as a yowl.

K

After tucking a sleepy-eyed Toby into bed and standing at the door to watch him drift into a deep sleep, Noah dragged his heavy-hearted body to his own bedroom, pulled the string on one of the few electric lights in the house, and started to climb out of his clothes, tossing all but his drawers in a heap on the floor. He could have picked up Herman Melville's *Moby-Dick*, his cherished, antiquated volume with original binding, which often soothed his cluttered head after a busy day, but he reached for his equally antiquated Bible, instead—the one his mother had given him on his tenth birthday. His father had told him God would illuminate to him the Scripture He intended him to read. He wondered if it really worked that way.

Pulling back his blankets, he dropped onto the bed, his large, muscular frame making the mattress groan with displeasure. Laying the old book on his chest, he closed his eyes and took in a heavy breath, not as much from physical fatigue as from a weary soul.

"Lord God," he heard himself whisper, "I don't know where to start with what I want to say to You. All I know is, I'm confused. I feel like a cracked, broken, useless boat with no rudder, no sail, no means for steering."

Boats were what he knew best, and they were all he could think to use to draw a comparison to his life. He opened his eyes and stared up at the ceiling, discovered a big spider walking just over his head, and, for a second, let his mind soak up the wonder of it, a creature walking upside down with no fear of heights or falling or losing its way.

"I'm plain lost, God," he said, closing his eyes again. "I've made a grand mess of my life, spending a good share of it being bitter and hateful. He hurt my mama, God. He hurt her bad, and yet, I'm starting to feel something toward him that isn't hate." A tear rolled down his cheek.

He thought about his passion for boatbuilding, how it consumed his every waking moment; how, in many ways, he'd used it as a cover for his pain, a means of escape. He thought about Suzanna, how he'd married her just out of high school, not having the first idea about what marriage was supposed to look like, and certainly minus Carl and Ellen Dunbar's blessing. He was the son of a useless, other-side-of-the-tracks boozehound, and the Dunbars practically owned all of Guilford. The thought occurred to him that he'd probably contributed to Carl Dunbar's mean-spirited manner.

With his eyes opened again, he looked for the spider and found it working away in a dimly lit corner, purposefully, some mission in mind. A piddling spider had more direction than he did!

Something Abbie had said came back to him, something about all the answers to his questions lying within the pages of God's Word. He'd read conviction in her eyes when she'd said it.

But, today, when he'd looked into her eyes, he'd seen something else. Sadness? Self-consciousness? Regret that he'd caught her with Sinclair? He shook his head. He couldn't think about her now. It only contributed to his confusion.

Open My Word, came the message to his heart.

He did, and his mother's letter fell out. He thought he'd put it in his top drawer, but, apparently, he hadn't. He'd been meaning to read it for days but kept putting it off, worried, really, about how it would impact him—seeing her flowery handwriting, wondering if he'd discover her scent miraculously embedded in the paper.

In a spontaneous act, he slipped out of bed and onto the floor. If he was going to read his mother's letter, he was going to read it on his knees. It just seemed the appropriate, honorable thing to do. Gingerly, shakily, he unfolded the worn, frayed edges of the precious missive, curious yet fearful of reading it, but determined, as well.

My Dearest Heavenly Father,

> *This is a love letter to You. I figured, since You wrote one to me, the least I could do is write one in return. I know I won't be long for this earth, and so I don't want to miss my opportunity.*
>
> *I love You, Lord; I love You for bringing me a husband who has drawn me closer to You. I know it sounds strange because Gerald is not a godly man, and yet, because of that, it's made me look to You for strength, courage, and comfort. I wish that I could convince Gerald of*

the difference You can make in a surrendered heart, but he will have nothing to do with You; he hates even to hear Your name, which grieves my tired spirit. He has hurt me, Lord, but then, I have hurt him, as well. It's been a hard, mixed-up marriage with lots of disappointments. I pray that someday he will see I did not mean those hurtful things I said to him, and he did not mean the things he said and did to me; that he will discover Your deep, unfathomable love and redemption.

I love You, Lord, for the way You've taught me that even in the darkness, Your light never stops shining, that even in pain and sickness, there are plenty of reasons to rejoice. I've lost seven babies, Lord, but because I've surrendered my life to You, I'll get to hold each one of them someday. Oh, how I do look forward to that.

I love You for teaching me that You do answer prayer, even when the road seems bleak, bumpy, and uncertain. I'm proof of it, for in the midst of my greatest discouragement, You brought me precious Noah Gerald Carson. Who would have dreamed that, after all those miscarriages, I would have carried a perfect, bouncing baby boy to full term, and pushed all eight and a half pounds of him right out of me? It's a miracle of the highest degree.

I've done the best I could to plant Your seed of love in Noah's heart, but I sense a seed of bitterness growing up right beside it, one that tries to choke and strangle the life right out of the good one. I pray for the life of that good seed, that it will sprout strong branches overflowing with bountiful fruit, and that the bad one will die away for lack of watering and nurturing.

This is my love letter to You, Lord, but I am going to hand it over to the reverend for safekeeping. Perhaps, one day, someone who needs to read it will be encouraged by the words and discover Your love for himself. Therefore, I pray for a special blessing upon the words in this letter, that they might reach out and touch the very souls that need to read them.

It is in Jesus' holy and precious name that I bring my requests to You and send this letter of love.

Your daughter,
Sarah May Carson

PS: I hope You don't mind that I wrote this letter without all the thees and thous. I wanted to make it more personal.

Noah folded the letter and gently placed it back within the pages of his Bible. Next, he pulled open the drawer in his bedside stand and took out a handkerchief to blow his dripping nose and wipe his tear-drenched face. And then, he did what he'd been needing to do for the better share of his life: he repented of his sins and surrendered his heart to Jesus.

Chapter Thirty-five

May quickly slipped into June, bringing in a whole band of tourists, which meant more traffic, more people, more business, and more work. At the Whatnot, each employee's hours increased, and Jacob considered hiring yet another clerk to help out for the season.

He'd already hired Jesse to help stock shelves, and one would have thought he'd been hired to work in the White House, the way he took his job so seriously. It just went to show how motivational two dollars a week could be to a boy his age. Hannah said he'd been going through the Sears, Roebuck and Co. Catalog, listing all the items he could buy with one month's salary: a drum, a single-barrel muzzle loader, a new fishing rod and reel, a trumpet, and, apparently, his list went on. Hannah had told him that if he saved every penny of his earnings, with the exception of the 10 percent tithe that went to the church, he'd earn almost enough to buy himself a new bicycle at the end of the summer, and that she and Gabe would make up the difference. "I can't abide a drum or a trumpet," she'd told Abbie the other day, "and I hate the idea of his getting a gun. Why, he's not even an adolescent, for heaven's sake. The fishing pole would be all right, I suppose, but he has a perfectly good one now. What does he want with another one? I say a bike is the best bet." Abbie went along with her reasoning, not much in the mood for senseless chatter these days, which was unusual for her, considering it was something she was known for.

Donald Clayton strolled into the Whatnot at mid-morning on a day Abbie was working with Rita, his ruddy face grinning. "Mr. Clayton! You're looking your usual, chipper self today," Abbie said, glancing up from the cash register after handing change to a young female customer whom she'd never seen before—a tourist, no doubt, by the look of her lightly freckled, sunburned nose. Many Chicagoans moved their families into the cottages in Highland Park, a scenic settlement along Lake Michigan's coast, for the summer months. Abbie grew accustomed to seeing some of them, but there were others whom she might run into only once or twice throughout the season.

The young lady picked up her purchases and headed to the door, where several of her giggling, babbling friends were waiting, and Don Clayton stepped aside to allow the girl a passageway in the cluttered aisle. At the door, she divvied up the candy she'd purchased among her friends, handing out licorice sticks, chocolate bars, wrapped taffy, and a bag of gumdrops. Then, still chattering up a regular storm, they all exited through the squeaky screen door, allowing it to flap shut with a loud thwack.

"Listen," Don said as they left, cupping one of his ears. "Do you hear it?"

Abbie perked up and listened. "What?"

"The silence."

She reached across the counter and tapped his arm. "Oh, you, don't try to tell me you never caused a ruckus at that age."

"Me? Never. My mother always used to say, "Donald, why don't you ever get yourself into some trouble? You're just too saintly for your own good.'"

"Uh-huh. I happen to know better, Mr. Donald Clayton. My papa's told me a few stories about you from when you were younger, something about climbing the school's fire escape and tossing rotten apples through the principal's second-story office window; tying a long, transparent string around a shiny, silver ring, then hiding behind one of those big rocks down by the lighthouse to wait for someone to bend down and get it before you yanked it away...." He looked ready to protest when she raised a forefinger and added, "Oh, and what about the time you were hitting nice, round, smooth stones with sticks in the middle of Park Street and you sent one sailing straight through Mr. Metzger's front window?"

"Oh, that."

"Then, to make matters worse, you ran away!"

He chortled. "You notice it's your father who feeds you these tales, my dear girl, which means he must have played some part. I could tell you a few stories about him, if you're ever of a mind."

"I'm of a mind," Rita called from the back of the store, breaking her silence.

She and Don laughed. "Another time, Mrs. James, another time," he returned. "But, just let me say, Jacob Kane could be a scoundrel in his day."

The banter continued a bit longer until Don handed over his usual short list. Abbie perused it, recognizing Esther's fine handwriting. "I'll get these ready for you right away."

She set off, he following. "Aren't you going to ask?"

She paused midway to the center aisle, where Jesse had stacked the bags of sugar, and turned to look at him. "Ask what?"

He raised his eyebrows suspiciously at her. "How Noah's coming on my boat?"

"Oh, the boat." She'd been dying to know, of course. "Is it nearly finished?"

He chuckled. "Why don't you come and see for yourself?"

Warmth traveled up her spine and caused a prickly sensation where her collar touched the back of her neck. "I will do that—sometime."

He touched her on the nose, a fatherly gesture. "How about now, after you fill my order? You don't look overly busy. I can have you back within the hour."

"Now? I'm work—"

Rita stepped out from the back aisle. "Go, young lady. I can handle things just fine."

Confound it! Where were all those tourists? "Is…is he there?"

"Noah, you mean?"

She wriggled her mouth into a frown. "No, Santa Claus. Of course, Noah."

"Oh, well, he might be. Noah, not Santa, that is. Anyway, what does it matter?"

She dabbed at her perspiring forehead. "It's just that I figured if Noah had wanted me to see the boat's progress, he would have…you know, invited me. We haven't spoken for some time, and I don't want to impose on his work schedule."

"My dear," Don said, his eyes intent on her face, even as he lowered his chin to his chest, "you really must learn to relax a bit."

K

Noah couldn't stop whistling "Amazing Grace" as he put a dusting cloth to the boat's fine finish, *finish* being the defining word. He could hardly believe it as he stood back to admire his work—his and his father's work, he amended in his head. They'd finished her together, neither one of them getting much more than a couple of hours of rest a night for the past week or so, Toby falling asleep on the mattress Uncle Del had brought over so he could at least go to bed at a decent hour. Some nights, they'd worked round the clock, Gerald catching an hour here or there on the mattress next to Toby before waking up and diving in again before heading off to Mill Point and his "real" job. At the hottest part of the day, Noah and Toby would walk up the sloping street to his aunt and uncle's house for some lunch, and Noah would take a nap in the back bedroom while Toby played a game of Old Maid with Aunt Julia or helped her bake a batch of cookies. Afterward, back down the street they'd go, Toby's pockets full of cat's-eye, blue-sky, and wave-streaked marbles, with a few prized devil's-eye boulders from Uncle Del's collection thrown in. Two little boys who lived a block behind the warehouse and went to school with Toby often came over to play in the yard with him while Noah worked, his masterpiece now perched outside on a platform under the sun by day and the moon by night, a perfectly fitted canvas thrown over her if as much as one threatening cloud rolled past.

Noah couldn't explain exactly how he and his father had come to bond so closely during the building process, other than to credit divine intervention. The conversion experiences had put them on a different plane, a common ground that gave them freedom to convey their feelings about the past—and the future. Literal joy flowed between them as they worked, affirming in their minds that joint ownership in a boatbuilding company would work for them.

He had not seen Abbie since that day at Hope House, other than to catch a glimpse of her at church, and his heart grieved to think she might still carry a torch for Sinclair. He wanted to tell her about his mother's letter, the impact it'd made on him, and how he'd finally decided to follow Christ with his whole heart, but then, he worried that she'd think he'd done it primarily for her, with the purpose of winning her over. True, that *had* been her stipulation for resuming any kind of courtship. How was he supposed to convince her his decision had been genuine and not a result of his desire to capture her heart?

Then, there was the matter of Suzanna and the question of how many more days remained for her, what to tell Toby when her time came, whether to attend the funeral, and how all that would transpire. One thing he knew: her impending passing had played a major role in the speed with which he and his father had worked to complete the boat. And he would be forever grateful to Gerald for helping him meet the deadline. Now, all that remained was to put her in the water and watch her skim the surface.

He ran a hand over the boat's fine grain, sanded and varnished to perfection, and chuckled at the name Don Clayton had chosen for the ship: *Abbie-Gale*. The little play on words was clever, he supposed. He would love to be there to see Abbie's expression the first time she laid eyes on it.

If that hadn't been a premonition, he would eat shoe leather for supper. For, lo and behold, up the drive came Don Clayton in his fancy, motorized vehicle, honking his crazy-sounding horn, with Abbie Ann seated proudly beside him.

Noah's heart gave a kick, and he wished to high heaven he had shaved that morning.

K

When Don parked the automobile, he and Abbie stepped down and plodded up the drive to the warehouse. Rounding the corner of the building, she stopped dead in the dirt at her first glimpse of the boat. "My, oh, my!" she whispered.

"Like it?" Don asked, placing a hand to the middle of her back to urge her forward.

"Absolutely. It's the most beautiful thing I've ever seen. Where's…?"

As if he'd read her mind, Noah emerged from the other side of the boat, a cloth in hand. He stuck the rag in his hip pocket and approached. And if she thought the boat looked good, well, mercy, just look at its builder—tall, broad, and rough around the edges, with his trouser pants clinging to his thighs and his short-sleeved shirt revealing rippled muscles she'd never had the privilege of seeing before.

"Hello, Noah," she managed. "Mr. Clayton invited me to see the boat. I hope you don't mind."

He took a tentative step forward, the gentle wind ruffling his dark hair, and he swept a hand over his face, the shadow of a beard adding to his ruggedly handsome appearance. "Hello, there."

"Well," Don said, "go have a look. Noah, show Abbie your boat. And start at the back."

Noah grinned. "Yes, sir." He hitched his arm for her taking, so she placed her hand in the crook of it, her fingers tingling when they made contact with his skin. Glancing down, she noted the fine, dark hairs on his arm when she should have been admiring the boat instead.

He explained the details, using words like *jib* and *spinnaker pole* and *sideboards* and *tiller*, none of which made much sense to her, but she nodded and pretended to understand. She was completely distracted by the deep tenor of his voice, recalling the curtness in his tone the last time she'd seen him at Hope House but not detecting it now. Dare she hope that something had changed? That, perhaps, he did care for her in some small way, after all? Hadn't he invited her to take his arm? That, in itself, should stand for something, she figured.

"You want to climb aboard?" Noah asked.

"Really?"

"Go ahead," Don said. "I've seen it plenty of times."

Noah led her around to the other side. "I'll go up first."

He climbed the few steps like a gazelle, then turned and extended a hand to her. "Where's Toby, by the way?" she asked, looking up into his eyes while placing her hand in his. My, what a contrast. Her hands were as smooth as sea glass, his as rough as cowhide.

"He's got a couple of friends who live one street over. One of the boys' mothers came over and asked if Toby could go down to the beach with them."

"Oh, I'm so happy to hear he's making friends."

She climbed the rest of the way up and then, with his help, stepped down to the floor. Standing there, the breezes kicking up her hair, she half imagined herself surrounded by blue waves, with nothing but water for miles around. "She's absolutely lovely, Noah. Perfect."

"Yes, she is."

She felt his eyes on her, and when she looked up, he immediately averted his gaze.

"Tell me where we're standing right now."

"We're standing in the hull."

"Oh. The hull. What's this?" She grasped hold of a long, pole-like handle.

He grinned. "That's the tiller. It guides the rudder."

"Which is...under the boat, right?"

"Uh...." He gave his head a toss. "I think you need to experience it before it will start making sense to you. I'll take you out...I mean, if Sinclair—"

"What?" She brushed a few strands of hair off her face and stared up at him. "What about Peter?"

"I saw the way you two were gazing at each other that day at Hope House, laughing, talking, enjoying each other like old times. I mean, it was pretty clear to me."

Realization dawned on her. "Peter's in love."

Noah's lips parted for a moment. "I figured as much," he said, his shoulders dropping a notch.

"With someone else."

He blinked once. Twice. One corner of his mouth turned up, and his face tilted first one way and then the other. "You're not...you and Sinclair...?"

"No! Absolutely not. You thought...?" She let the sentence dangle, unfinished, thinking of the possibilities—and uncertainties. What did all this mean?

"Abbie, I have something to tell you." He took her hand and led her to the lower deck, three steps down, going ahead of her and turning to guide her below.

Once there, she stepped on the solid floor and stared at her surroundings, awed by the rich woods, the cushioned benches, the little table. "Oh, my goodness! Noah, this is— simply—I'm speechless. It's so beautiful." She touched the fine, mahogany cabinets, running a hand over the brass knobs. "Look, you have real cupboards down here. And a sink? It's like a little dollhouse!" she exclaimed.

He chuckled and cradled her face in his hands, touching a thumb to her mouth to silence her. "I have to tell you what's happened to me, Abbie."

She grew serious. "All right."

He swallowed, and there went that fascinating Adam's apple. She just couldn't help watching it bob up and down when he swallowed again. He began rubbing tender, little circles on either side of her chin with his thumbs, gazing down at her with those velvety, blue eyes and giving her a chill, despite the warm, summer air. "Everything you've been telling me about God's Word is true," he said huskily, as if his emotions were teetering on a tightrope and about to topple. "It's a treasure trove of promises. It took me a while to get it through my head, Abbie, that I needed a Savior to help me get past…well, my past. Yeah, I had to get past my past, if that makes sense."

She nodded, numbed almost to her bones by the sheer impact of what he was saying. "It does," she assured him. *Lord Jesus, can it be? Has he finally discovered You in all Your fullness?* She caught her lower lip between her teeth and put on her listening ears.

He started telling her in great detail about a letter his mother had written many years ago and given to her pastor for safekeeping, a love letter, of sorts, to God, thanking Him for leading her through the darkest stages of her life, and how, so many years later, that very letter had miraculously wound up in the hands of Noah's father, having been kept for years between the pages of a big, church Bible, discovered only recently by the church's current pastor. His eyes misted over as he told her of the impact that letter had made on his father and, later, on him—how it had finally opened his eyes to the truth and mystery of God's divine plan for his life, and how he'd reached that pivotal point of learning to let go of his past hurts and hand them over to God's competent, healing hands.

He led her to one of the cushioned benches, and they sat down, shoulder to shoulder. He spoke about the miracle of his newfound feelings of love and forgiveness toward his father, of how the Lord had started a work in their relationship—a rebuilding kind of work, one that would take time and probably some effort on both their parts, but also one about which he was optimistic.

He even revealed the final conversation he'd had with Suzanna—how she'd come to know the Lord because of Gerald's testimony of God's love and grace, and how they'd both decided that forgiving each other was the only thing that made sense.

His words made tears spill out of the corners of her eyes and run down her cheeks. She cried for the pain his mother had endured—the heartbreak of countless miscarriages, the misery of a marriage wrought with misunderstandings and heartache. She cried for all the setbacks young Toby had already braved, wanting to walk with him through the impending sorrow of losing his mother. It was strange how both she and Noah had lost their mothers at a young age, and how Toby now would have the same experience. Strange, too, how the One who knows, sees, and understands every person's needs marvelously orchestrated it all.

They sat a while in silence, wrapped up in their own thoughts, as the breeze above them whistled in beautiful harmony with the birds' songs. Somewhere in the distance, a dog barked.

In time, Noah reached down for her hand and held it against his heart. "Do you know that I love you, Abbie Ann Kane?"

A tiny gasp quietly escaped her lips. "I had hoped you did. Do you know I love you?"

He moved his arm around her shoulder and gathered her close. "What took us so long?"

"So long? We met exactly four months ago."

He kissed the cheek closest to him. "Then, we'll have to court some more before…."

She turned to look up at him. "Before what?" It felt as if her heart had moved up to her throat.

He gave her a long, tender kiss, making sure it glimmered with promise. Both adjusted their bodies, enabling a sweet embrace. Her hands opened on his broad back, then slowly moved upward to muss his hair. His hands cupped her head, messing with the tidy hairdo she'd spent many minutes perfecting just hours ago. They couldn't get enough of each other in their struggle to become a part of the other's heart and soul.

Finally, he tore himself away from her, held her head in both his hands, and then moved in for another passionate kiss.

She drew back next, taking his face in her hands and looking him square on. "Before what?" she repeated.

He kissed her again, then spoke against her lips, "Before I ask your father for your hand in marriage."

Her heart sang to the heights. "Don't you have to ask me first?"

He sighed, pretending to be annoyed. "Ah, you are one ornery little woman, aren't you? All right, then." He pulled away and stood up, then suddenly dropped down on one knee, taking her left hand in both of his. "Abigail Ann Kane," he said in a voice husky with emotion, "will you marry me?"

She straightened, pressing her back against the wall, and held her breath before letting it out with a shrug. "I can't cook, Noah," she confessed.

"So you've said."

"I'm not very domesticated."

"You mean domestic."

"That, either. I like being a part of the W.C.T.U., but I think I'll relegate my responsibility as president to Jane Emery."

He gave his head a toss of approval. "She seems very capable."

"I want to spend as much time as I can with Toby."

"He could use the nurturing." He bent forward to kiss the tip of her nose. "Now, who's stalling?"

She giggled. "If you don't mind eating the same thing every day, and if you don't expect a completely tidy house every minute, and if you don't mind my visiting the Plooster sisters—oh, and Katrina—and if you don't mind my running home to Grandmother's every now and again for recipes, and visiting Hannah, and...."

He plastered another kiss on her mouth, this time nearly stealing her last breath. "You'd better give me an answer before I change my mind," he teased.

She raised her chin. "I might be hard to live with."

He stared at her, silenced by his own impatience. It appeared that she'd taken him to his limit.

Finally, she said, "I will. I absolutely, definitely, positively will marry you—after we've courted."

"After we've courted," Noah agreed. He leaned in for one more kiss, but the sound of footsteps overhead brought a halt to it.

"Everything all right down there?" came Don's voice.

Noah pulled Abbie to her feet. "Nothing could be better, Mr. Clayton," she called up.

"Excellent! Say, you'd better come up here and see what name I've given to this boat, Miss Kane."

She looked at Noah, and he shrugged. "I had nothing to do with it."

Chapter Thirty-six

Over the stretch of the summer, life held a most amazing range of emotions, from jubilant euphoria to the utter depths of sorrow, from the *Abbie-Gale's* victorious finish in the Sandy Shores Yacht Club Regatta to the devastating death of Suzanna Dunbar Carson Grayson.

Of the regatta's win, the *Sandy Shores Tribune* had this to say:

> No finer vessel graced the waters on that bright, blessedly sunny Saturday of July 21 than the beautifully crafted *Abbie-Gale*, so named by owner Donald Clayton for his kinship with an old friend's youngest daughter, Abbie Ann Kane. Her curved, fair lines skimmed the water's surface like an old pro, even though this year's regatta marked her first-ever race. The Sandy Shores Yacht Club sponsored this open regatta, in which 18 yachts entered for a chance at the purse and trophy. The course was 26 miles extending from off the clubhouse at the Saugatuck Yacht Club and moving up the coast to Buoy 13, then to Holland's Robbins Reef Buoy 61, then widening

offshore to Buoy 47, heading straight north for five miles to Buoy 34, then traveling northeast and ending at the stake-boat at the Sandy Shores Lighthouse.

An unusually strong tide ran at the start, making sailing difficult for even the most experienced, the stiff southeast wind adding to the challenge. The yachts were restricted to jib and mainsail, and were not allowed to shift ballast. The sound of gunshot, signaling the start, was given at 10:10 a.m., and 20 seconds later the first boat, the *Abbie-Gale*, crossed the starting line. Following closely on her tail were the *Tom Olson*, the *Esther Marie*, the *Lily R.* and the *Harbor Queen*. Next came the *Albert J*, *Crosswinds*, *Mary Heart*, *Eaglewing* and *Sea Jewel*. The other eight yachts straggled behind, and the last boat to cross the line, the *Poor Boy*, was aptly named.

At the start, the yachts had to beat up shore and indeed all the way to Buoy 13. Off Holland's Robbins Reef, the yacht *Albert J*, while standing over on the starboard tack for Buoy 47, collided with the tug *Betty May* and carried away her bowsprit. Unfortunately, that compelled the crew to put back, thus costing them the race.

At Buoy 34, the *Tom Olson* took a very brief lead, with the *Abbie-Gale* falling into second place and the yacht *Harbor Queen* trailing at third. As soon as the yachts rounded this last buoy, they freed their sheets, bowed out their jibs, and went home flying into the wind. The *Abbie-Gale* easily passed the *Tom Olson* on the run home, crossing the finish line well ahead of the rest and at a record time of 2 hours, 52 minutes, and 41 seconds.

The *Abbie-Gale* was designed and built by Noah Carson, former owner of a shipbuilding company out of Guilford, Conn., presently residing in Sandy Shores, Mich., where he and his father recently launched Carson & Carson Shipbuilders. The prize for the winning yacht was $25 and a trophy. The tug *Wildwood* conveyed information pertaining to the race to the Sandy Shores Yacht Club throughout the course. Please see page 2 for the official record of the race, that is, the exact start and finish times in hours, minutes, and seconds, and for a complete list of participating yachts and the order in which they finished.

On a chilly, rainy night in early August, Suzanna Grayson had passed quietly in her sleep, her mother and father at her side. It had been a large funeral, attended mostly by friends and colleagues of Carl Dunbar, attorney-at-law, and his faithful wife, Ellen. Oh, and Noah and Toby, of course. Noah and Abbie both had seen it as a means for bringing Toby a sense of closure and setting him on a path to healing much sooner than if he'd been denied the opportunity to say good-bye in his own way—however that happened for a six-year-old. Since then, he'd bounced back to his usual, jovial self, and one never would have guessed that his mother had just died, perhaps because, in his young mind, she'd died in bits and pieces due to their prolonged separation.

In some ways, it had been good to return to Guilford, where Noah had sealed up some matters and gained a sense of closure, as well. Running into Tom Grayson at Suzanna's funeral and then at the Dunbar home afterward had proved nothing short of awkward, but it hadn't been as he'd expected it to be, either. Months ago, he would have slugged the fellow in the gut had he seen him on the street. Instead, he'd extended a hand, making sure to look him square in the eye when he told him he was sorry for his loss, something he never could have done were it not for God's far-reaching grace and tender mercies. Of course, his words had rendered Tom speechless. In a just world, it would have been the other way around, with Tom uttering his condolences and pleading forgiveness for wreaking havoc in Noah's business and personal life. But, alas, the world is neither just nor fair, and the people inhabiting it are far from perfect. Noah had accepted that fact and even found peace in the midst of it, perhaps due in part to Tom's having to turn over Suzanna's house and a good deal of her holdings to a trust set up by Carl Dunbar on Toby's behalf. Noah had thanked the Lord she'd had the foresight to do that before passing. God knew Noah had no desire for her earthly possessions, but it was a relief to know that Toby's future was secure.

The true miracle of his return to Guilford had come about when Carl Dunbar had motioned him over to a secluded corner in his massive home, filled with people paying their respects and carrying on quiet conversations in small clusters while maids in frilly aprons moved about with platters of sandwiches, and, in a gruff manner, offered an apology. "No need, sir. We all erred," Noah had assured him.

"Just the same, I'm…asking your forgiveness."

"Then you have it," Noah had said.

After they had shaken hands, Carl had reached into the inside pocket of his dress coat and pulled out an envelope. "This is yours," he'd said. "Take it and don't argue."

"But…what is it?"

"It's what you would have earned, had Grayson done the rightful thing and bought out your share of the company. It's going into foreclosure, in case he hasn't already told you, and I'm buying it from the bank."

"What?"

His face had contorted in a half grin. "I'll sell it, of course, since I have no interest in shipbuilding, and I'll make a profit doing it because I'll seek out a proper buyer, perhaps a larger conglomerate, and I'll take my time. At any rate, for my part in helping to make your life miserable, I'm repaying you everything due you, and then some, and, like I said, don't try to offer up any kind of argument. I won't hear it. Besides, I heard about this vessel you built that easily took first place in some Michigan regatta and the number of orders already coming in from folks out of Chicago for similar designs. Fact is, I have a couple of clients I'll send your way." He pointed at the envelope pinched between Noah's fingers. "That'll give a solid launch to Carson & Carson Shipbuilders."

Upon Noah's return from Guilford, this article had appeared in the *Sandy Shores Tribune*:

> The Sandy Shores chapter of the Woman's Christian Temperance Union is proud to announce the grand opening of the fully renovated Hope House, a home specifically designed to provide refuge to women and children suffering domestic abuse. It is capable of housing as many as one dozen women and/or children and will be operated by Mr. and Mrs. Lester Emery. Jane Emery is the newly elected president of the W.C.T.U., having assumed her post following Miss Abbie Ann Kane's recent resignation, and Lester Emery is a manager at Sandy Shores Bank and Trust. The home, located on the corner of Fulton and 6th Street, was donated by a former Sandy Shores resident, Ann Franklin, now of Florida.

The building will be open to the public for tours August 26-30, and a jar to collect cash donations will be located at the front door.

As autumn approached, Toby prepared for second grade, turning seven at the end of September. He'd spent many hours that summer fishing with his grandfather and Uncle Del and making friends in the little Sandy Shores neighborhood where Noah had purchased a new house for them—nothing elaborate or overly sophisticated, but a comfortable two-story big enough for a growing family, something he often dreamed about with Abbie. Once he'd obtained Jacob's blessing to marry her, they'd set a date for a December 28 wedding. Granted, it seemed like the worst time of year to get married, but they simply didn't have the ability to wait any longer. Besides, it being the Christmas season, her sister, Maggie, and brother-in-law, Luke, planned to bring their brood of children on the train and stay at the Culver House, thereby making a regular vacation out of the trip. "I cannot wait for you to meet Maggie. You'll love her," Abbie said one night while she and Noah cuddled on the sofa in her living room.

He leaned over and kissed her temple. "If she's anything like you, I'm sure I will."

When she turned her gaze up at him, devilish amusement flickered in her eyes.

"'She is no more like me than Hannah is, but you will love her, anyway, because all of us Kane sisters are downright irresistible."

The Christmas season ushered in a flurry of activities, everything from shopping for just the right present for everyone in Abbie's family, including nieces, nephews, and Noah and Toby, to helping Grandmother Kane in the kitchen, from finalizing last-minute wedding details to picking out paint colors for the house Abbie would soon be sharing with Noah and Toby. Already, they'd started moving Abbie's personal items from the Kanes' house to Noah's, and the very act of walking into his house and realizing it would soon be hers made her breath swoosh right out of her like a sweeping windstorm. She loved Noah more than anyone or anything she'd ever loved before, more than her own sisters, more than her father and grandmother, more than her own heart.

And she loved Toby, her soon-to-be stepson. My, he was a sweet thing, precocious and animated. She could hardly wait for the snow to accumulate so that she could take him over to Duncan Woods, where the best hills for sledding in all of Michigan could be found. Of course, Jesse would want to come, too, probably as would an assortment of other kids. That was fine by her, considering she wasn't much more than a big kid, herself.

Grandmother Kane had been giving her a crash course in domesticity. She knew how to clean, wash clothes, scrub a wood floor, and iron a shirt to perfection, but she hadn't gotten down the art of cooking, and she knew why: eating had never been her passion. But Grandmother said, passion or not, she'd better start getting used to the fact that a growing boy and a strapping man needed nourishing meals.

Well, put like that, the pressure was on, and so, with her wedding date nearing, Abbie started collecting and copying as many of her favorites from Grandmother's recipe box as she had time to write. And the ones Grandmother Kane kept stored in her head—the best ones—she had her dictate.

Then, every night, she worked feverishly in the kitchen, Grandmother Kane at her side, to prepare the evening meal. Noah and Toby started joining them each evening, Toby often bringing his homework along so she could help him with it at the table after they'd cleared away the supper dishes.

And, during this period, a most amazing thing happened. Abbie developed an uncanny love for cooking!

Two days before Christmas, Luke and Maggie Madison arrived with their four children, ranging in age from sixteen months to almost sixteen years. Abbie couldn't imagine how Maggie remained so beautiful, vibrant, and carefree with all those children to tend, not to mention the orphans she and Luke fostered, whom they'd left in the care of their two live-in employees. Hannah had insisted the two boys, Ricky, fifteen, and Stuart, thirteen, stay with her family, thereby giving Jesse a chance to get to know these cousins he rarely saw. Luke, Maggie, nine-year-old Rose Marie, and little Lucas planned to stay at Culver House, despite Grandmother Kane's desire to put them up.

"You have enough on your mind, what with Christmas and Abbie's wedding, Grandmother," Maggie had stated. "Believe me when I say that you don't need an excessively busy one-year-old following after you, especially when his entire goal in life right now is undoing everything you've set to rights. I don't even recall what it felt like to have all my pots and pans remaining neatly stacked beneath my stove or my knickknacks and books staying put on shelves and tables. I sometimes find them in the oddest places—under beds, in his toy box, or in drawers. I have even had to fish a few things out of the toilet bowl. I will say, he also has quite a talent for breaking things."

After that, Grandmother had quietly dropped the subject.

The entire Kane clan and extended family members, including Rita and Noah, convened at the home of Norma and Ambrose Barton, the Kanes' neighbors, for their annual festive gathering. This year did not include a formal dinner, however, not with the way children kept multiplying like ants in a colony. Instead, Norma had prepared a delicious fruit punch and several trays of small sandwiches, cut fruits, and fresh-baked goodies, all of which the children eagerly partook, even though their parents said, "Just take one of each," or "Mind your manners, now." "Oh, bosh!" Norma declared. "I made enough to feed the whole town. Let them have their fill. As for fallen crumbs, no worries. I'll have Ambrose up late sweeping the floor and cleaning the kitchen," she kidded.

Informal talk and excited chatter filled the house while the children played with toys and games in one of the rooms. Lucas Madison and Alex Devlin remained under their parents' watchful eyes, even caught up in their fathers' arms for settling-down periods, and the ever-growing RoseAnn crawled everywhere, sticking whatever she could fit into her mouth. The women exchanged ideas on various subjects, and, of course, Abbie and Noah's wedding consumed a good share of their discussions; the men talked about everything from politics to last summer's regatta to the latest local news. All evening, if Abbie and Noah weren't standing next to each other, touching, they were sending silent messages to each other in code. One wink meant "I want to kiss you," two meant "I can't wait to get you alone," three meant "I love you," and the number of fingers discreetly held to their sides or in front of them indicated the number of days until Rev. Cooper would pronounce them husband and wife.

If anyone saw them making eyes at each other, they made no fuss about it. After all, they'd been there, themselves, all starry-eyed and thunderstruck by love. Even Rita and Jacob wore that love glow, and one never would have guessed it to be the second time around for both of them. Of course, it was the second time around for Noah, as well, and Abbie sometimes feared she might disappoint him, but he always shushed her with a heart-pounding kiss if she so much as mentioned her fears of inadequacy. "After falling headlong in love with you, Abbie Ann, I've reached the conclusion I have never truly been in love before," he'd said. That was quite a statement, coming from someone who'd been previously married. "So, really, for both of us, this is all brand-new. We'll walk it together, one day at a time."

As always, his calm, patient demeanor settled her qualms.

In accordance with tradition, the evening ended on a musical note in the big living room, with Norma at the pump organ and everyone gathered around, arm in arm, singing Christmas carols and then holding sleepy children who weren't necessarily their own. Abbie couldn't help remarking how the bonds they shared tied them together in a beautiful bouquet of love, much like the aromatic, pine wreaths and colorful garlands hung about the Bartons' home.

K

Christmas Day dawned bright with rare December sunlight in the sky, and a thin layer of snow that had fallen in the night covered the ground just enough to qualify it as a white Christmas. "Is it the kind to build a snowman in, Pa?" Toby asked.

"I'm afraid not, son, but you can still traipse through it and make your very own fresh tracks."

"Can I do it now?"

Noah laughed. "We both will, and afterward, we'll come in and make pancakes.

They had their own private breakfast, their last one as just two, and enjoyed every bite. Pancakes with maple syrup was something Noah had mastered the art of making, and so he and Toby had them often.

"When we goin' to Uncle Del and Aunt Julia's house?"

"Right after you open your present from me."

"You got me a present?"

"Well, what did you think? That I would have left out the most important boy in my life on Christmas Day? Of course, I got you a present."

Toby frowned. "You're the most important boy in my life, but I di'n't have any money to buy you somethin'."

Noah reached over to tousle Toby's freshly-cut-for-the-wedding, blond hair. "You are all the Christmas present I need, son."

They arrived at his aunt and uncle's house about the same time Noah's father got there, Toby running to his grandpa to throw his arms around his waist and tell him all about the new fishing rod and reel he'd gotten from his pa. "An' he says much as he doesn't like t' fish, he's goin' t' give it a whirl next summer, 'cause he wants to spend more koala-ty time with me."

Over Toby's head, Gerald caught Noah's eye and winked. "Koala-ty time is a very good thing."

Although Noah had wanted to spend every second of Christmas Day with Abbie Ann, they'd decided to reserve some personal time for their individual families before joining each other at noon for the big Kane celebration, thereby allowing Noah and Toby a few hours with the Huizengas and Gerald. Next year would be different, as they would launch their own family traditions.

He could hardly wait to begin.

𝒦

Noah and Toby fit into Abbie's family like hands into an old, familiar pair of weathered gloves, Toby immediately taking to his new cousins and they to him, Abbie's sisters and brothers-in-law pulling Noah into all their conversations. A pile of presents rose up at the base of the big fir tree Papa and Abbie had cut down together at the Fett farm out on South Beechtree Street three days ago. They'd had a grand time, just the two of them, trying to choose the perfect one—a tall, straight, sturdy tree with branches long enough to handle Grandmother's wide assortment of ornaments. "Be sure to look at the trunk this time, for heaven's sake," Grandmother had said, handing them each a thermos of piping-hot cocoa before they'd headed out the door. "That one you cut down last year leaned something awful. It was a pure embarrassment." They'd laughed at the recollection as they had skipped down the steps and toward the wagon, Bessie already hitched and waiting.

There was nothing to be embarrassed about over this year's tree, though. Even Grandmother Kane, particular as she was, said it was the finest one they'd ever had.

It had been a day full of laughter and cheer, presents, family games, and enough food to last them through the winter! But, as all good things must end sometime, Hannah and Gabe announced their leave-taking when a weepy, fussy RoseAnn had had just about enough of being bounced and passed around for one day. That precipitated Maggie and Luke's gathering of their troops, as well, and so the business of collecting opened gifts, baby bottles and diapers, leftover food, and other paraphernalia took precedence.

In the midst of all the clamor, Jacob gave a loud throat-clearing that completely stilled the room, producing the same results an army general might if he suddenly marched into a dining commons filled with soldiers. He grinned. "Now that I have your attention, I'd like to make an announcement before you all go your separate ways. Rita and I do not want to overshadow Abbie and Noah's celebration in the least with our news, but we've decided we simply can't wait to tell you that...well...."

The room remained as quiet as an empty church as the Kane sisters, especially, waited with bated breaths, their mouths agape. Rita stood beside him, a hopeful expression written on her pleasant face. "Are you going to say it, or shall I?" she asked, feigning impatience.

"Papa, say it!" all three sisters said in unison, as if they'd practiced it a million times.

"Well, if we have your blessing, Rita and I would like to be married next spring. We were thinking April."

Joyful whoops filled the house as everyone gathered in for hugs of congratulations. When the excitement died down, Jacob continued, "And, just so you all know, Mother is not going anywhere. Rita and I have decided this place would not be home without Helena Kane here to run it."

It was one of the few times Abbie had ever seen Grandmother Kane blush.

That night, Abbie and Noah could barely say good-bye to each other. Jesse had begged to have Toby spend the night with Ricky, Stu, and him at the Devlin household, and Hannah had not had one objection, saying she had plenty of extra clothes, so Noah had consented. Jacob had driven Rita back to her house, and after giving the kitchen one final sweep, Grandmother Kane had retreated to her bedroom. That left just Abbie and Noah standing in the middle of the blissfully quiet living room with nothing but their own breathing and the crackling fire to listen to. "I love you, honey," Noah said, gathering her in his arms. The curtains were still wide open to the world, but neither of them cared who might witness their embrace. "And I love your family. This is all new to me, this big-family concept, but I like it. I never knew it could be so…fun."

She smiled, her heart too full not to, and pulled away, leading him over to the sofa. "Let's sit a while and just dream about our special day."

They fell into the softness of the old sofa, the same one Hannah and Gabe and then Maggie and Luke had sat in before them, equally enamored of each other, in love to the point of nearly bursting. "Oh, my," Abbie said with a long sigh. "If this old couch could talk, what stories it could tell."

She reclined against his arm, and he played with the puff of her sleeve, making little goose pimples pop out all over her body. She watched the flickering flames eat away at what remained of the two logs Papa had thrown on the fire two hours ago. "I love you, Noah Carson."

He leaned close and kissed her temple, then her cheek, and then the corner of her mouth, teasing her. More goose pimples erupted. "Do you know that in three days, you will be fully mine?" The meaning of that simple statement made her pulse quicken to new heights, and his warm breath on her ear did not help the situation. "You do know I'm not letting you out of my sight for at least the next twenty years, don't you? After that, I may give you a little leeway."

"Oh, Noah," she said with a quavery giggle. "How did I get you?"

He rested his head against hers and took in a long breath, drawing her closer to his side, his gaze pointed toward the fire, along with hers. "Well, let's see, here. It first happened back in February, when I peeked my head through a hole in the Whatnot and spotted this thrillingly beautiful brunette."

$\mathcal{K}$

They were married at three o'clock on a cold, blustery day. Freezing drizzle made negotiating the sidewalks and drive-ways treacherous but did not present enough of a threat to discourage folks from filling the Sandy Shores Third Street Church. My, how Michigan's weather could turn on a dime! Sunny one day and gloomy the next, but no matter; nothing could possibly dampen the spirits of Noah Gerald Carson and Abigail Ann Kane.

The bride wore a cream-colored, long-sleeved silk dress with a sheer, scooped neck and lace inserts, the six feet of her matching veil flowing behind her as she strode down the aisle on her father's arm while her bridesmaids, consisting of her sisters and Katrina, and the groomsmen—Gerald, Gabe, and Luke—all watched her grand entrance with speechless amazement. Of course, no one watched her quite like her groom, whose eyes misted over at the very sight of her. And who could blame him?

"Oh, my stars in glory!" Norma Barton whispered into her husband Ambrose's ear when Abbie passed their pew.

"Have you ever seen a more elegant bride, Mr. Barton?" She clutched her throat to keep a rising lump at bay, fearing it just might cause a rush of tears to spring forth.

He gave a slow smile and leaned over. "That's three down now, Mrs. Barton," he said of the Kane sisters' weddings. "And we got to witness them all."

"Indeed, we did. What a blessing. And to think Jacob and Rita will soon follow with vows of their own. It's the circle of love, Mr. Barton." His smile still in place, he reached down to take his wife's wrinkled hand.

Rev. Cooper seemed to take his sweet, precious time in moving the ceremony along. Never were two people more anxious to get on with the proceedings. "Do you, Noah?" "Do you, Abbie?" *Yes, yes, yes!* they both wanted to shout. Of course, they waited with forced patience. Like school-children restless for that final send-off in late May, with the entire summer strewn out before them and miles and miles of plans for how to spend it, Noah and Abbie thought about their own treasured dreams, beginning with their five-day wedding trip to New York City, where Luke and Maggie had secured for them a lovely hotel room overlooking Central Park. Whether they would spend much time gazing out their window remained to be seen.

In the front row, Toby sat with Helena, Jacob, Rita, and Jesse, all the other children relegated to a cry room at the back of the church, where Ricky and Stu Madison were watching over them—along with a couple of young girls who'd happily volunteered their services upon meeting the boys. Toby had looked forward to the wedding ceremony about as much as he would look forward to getting a tooth pulled. Not that the prospect of having a mother didn't thrill him to bits, but he plain didn't like to sit still, not when a full five days at Aunt Hannah's house with Jesse and the others awaited him. Shoot, it would have tickled him pink if his dad and new mom had decided to stay away a little longer, but they'd both said they would miss him far too much to do that, and, the truth was, he would miss them, as well.

When the reverend finally issued the words, "I now pronounce you man and wife," Noah cupped Abbie's face in his hands and leaned forward for a possessive kiss that compelled several women to fan themselves, despite the chill in the sanctuary. "You may now kiss the bride," Rev. Cooper said, almost as an afterthought, which produced a number of chuckles from those who heard him. He pressed his closed Bible to his chest with a smile and waited for the kiss to end. When it finally did, he turned the couple to face the congregation. One would have thought the bride was oblivious to the onlookers from the way her eyes never left her husband's face.

"Ladies and gentlemen, it is my pleasure to present to you Mr. and Mrs. Noah Carson."

To the pipe organ's rousing rendition of "Joy to the World," the bride and groom stepped down from the platform, making sure to stop at the front row to grab hold of Toby's hands so they could all walk out together. Or, in Toby's case, skip.

My, what a glorious Christmas!

An Excerpt from *Tender Vow* by Sharlene MacLaren

A Contemporary Novel

Coming in Fall 2010

Prologue

I cy breezes whistled through the trees in Fairmount Cemetery, prompting the faithfuls gathered there to pull their collars tighter and button their coat fronts higher, as the tent that had been set up for the occasion did little to protect them from the elements. Just two days ago, northern Michigan had experienced a warm front, unusual for late November, but today's temperatures made a mockery of it. Twenty-nine-year-old Jason Evans shivered, no longer feeling his fingers or toes, and wondered if the numbness came from the dreadful cold or from his deliberate displacement of emotion. He still couldn't believe it—it was just two days after Thanksgiving, and his brother, John, two years older than he, was gone. *Gone.*

As Pastor Eddie Turnwall from Harvest Community Church pronounced the final words of interment, sobs and whimpers welled up from the mourners. His mother's guttural cry among them gouged him straight to the core. Jason's father pulled his wife closer while Jason placed a steadying hand on her shoulder. His girlfriend, Candace Peterson, stuck close by, her hand looped through his other arm. His sister-in-law—John's widow, Rachel—stood about six feet away, clinging tightly to her father and borrowing his strength as tears froze on her cheeks. Her coat bulged because of her pregnancy of eight months, and Jason worried that the added stress of her grief might send her into early labor. Meagan, John and Rachel's three-year-old daughter, was the only one oblivious to the goings-on; she twirled like a ballerina until Rachel's fifteen-year-old sister, Tanna, bent down to pick her up. *If she knew the significance of this day*, Jason thought, *she'd be standing as still as a statue*. What a blessing God kept her shielded—at least, for the time being.

"And now, dear Father, we commit John Thomas Evans into your hands," Pastor Turnwall declared. "We know—"

"No!" Rachel's pitiful wail brought the reverend to a temporary halt. In the worst way, Jason wanted to go to her, but he had his mother to think about. Mitch Roberts supported his daughter, whispered something in her ear, and nodded for the reverend to continue. Pastor Turnwall hastened to a finish, but the last of his words faded in the howling winds.

At the close of the brief ceremony, many of the mourners stepped forward to give the family some final encouragement. Jason went through the motions, nodding and uttering words of thanks. While he longed to linger at the bronze casket, the weather made it impossible, so, as the last of the small crowd left the tent, he followed, Candace's quiet sniveling somehow disarming him. He didn't have the strength to comfort her, especially since she'd barely known his brother; she barely knew his family, for that matter.

"Are you all right?" Candace asked in a quavery voice.

"I'm doing okay," he muttered, his gaze pointed downward as they walked along the frozen path. How did one explain how he really felt on a day like this?

In front of them, mourners scattered in various directions, heading for cars covered in a thin layer of freshly fallen snow. Despite the cold, Rachel walked with slow, faltering steps, sagging against her father. Even from ten or so feet back, Jason could hear her sobbing moans. The sound made his chest contract.

Without forethought, he left Candace to her own defenses and raced ahead to catch up with them.

"Rachel." Breathless, he reached her side. "I'm so sorry."

"Jay." She turned from her father's supportive grip and fell into Jason's arms, her sobs competing with the sighing winds.

They stopped in the path, and he held her sob-racked body, feeling his eyes well up with tears. Through his blurred vision, he noted both families halting their steps to look on. One of Rachel's girlfriends took Meagan from Tanna and headed toward one of the cars. "Shh. You can do this, Rachel," he whispered. "Think of Meagan—and your baby."

"I—I c-can't," she stammered, her voice barely resembling that of the Rachel he'd known since high school, when he and John would argue over who was going to win her in the end. Of course, it'd been John, and rightfully so. And not for a second had Jason ever begrudged him. They fit like a glove, Rachel and John.

"Sure, you can," he murmured in her ear. "You are Rachel Evans, strong, courageous, capable—and carrying my brother's son, don't forget." He set her back from him and studied her perfect, oval face, framed by wisps of blond hair falling out from beneath her brown, velvet, Chicago cuff hat. Her blue eyes, red around the edges, peered up at him from puffy eyelids without really seeing. Chills skipped up his spine, and he didn't think they came from the air's cold bite. "Come on, let's get you to the car," he urged her, thankful when Candace stepped forward to take Rachel's other arm, and they set off together. Rachel barely acknowledged Candace, and he wondered if she even remembered her, so few were the times he had brought her home.

"I can't believe it, Jason, I just—I can't believe it," Rachel kept murmuring. "Just last week, we were making plans for our future, talking about John Jr. coming into the world, wondering how Meagan would feel about having a baby brother...."

"I know."

"He just finished painting the nursery, you know."

"I'm glad."

She frowned. "Tell me again what happened."

His throat knotted. "What? No, Rach, not here."

She slowed her steps to snag him by the coat sleeve. "I need to hear it again," she said, punctuating each word with determination.

"We'll talk later, but first, we need to get you out of the cold."

"Jason's right, honey," Mitch said, coming up behind them. "Let's go back to the house."

"But I don't understand how it happened. I need to understand."

"We've been over it," her mother said as she joined them. Tanna came up beside her mother and held her hand as they walked. Like everyone else's, Arlene Roberts's face bore evidence of having shed a river of tears.

"I don't care!" Rachel's voice conveyed traces of hysteria. She stopped in her tracks, forcing everyone else to do the same. "John was a good skier," she said. "He knew the slopes on Sanders Peak like the back of his hand. You said yourself you guys used to ski out there every spring." Her seascape-colored eyes shot holes of anguish straight through Jason—critical, faultfinding eyes.

A rancid taste collected at the back of his throat. "We did, Rach, and he was the best of the best, but it takes a champion skier to navigate Devil's Run. Come on, your car's just ahead."

Her feet remained anchored to the frozen ground. "Did you force him, Jason?"

"What?" The single word hissed through his teeth. "How could you even suggest such a thing?"

"Rachel, now is not the time for such—"

But Rachel covered her dad's words with her own. "Did you provoke him into taking Devil's Run? Witnesses heard you two arguing, Jay. Why would you be fighting on top of a mountain?"

"We weren't fight—"

"You've always been the risk taker, the gutsy, smug one, ever looking for a challenge. You pushed him to do it, didn't you?"

"What? No! What are you saying, Rachel? It was a stupid accident, that's all."

She stood her ground, her eyes wild now. "John isn't like you, Jay, never was. Why drag him to the top of Devil's Run if only a 'champion skier' can handle it? You of all people knew his capabilities—and his limitations."

Jason wanted to shake her but refrained, merely giving her a pointed stare instead. "I did not drag him anywhere, Rachel, and we've both navigated Devil's Run before. It's just…the conditions were extra bad that day. I told him not to try it. You have to believe me."

"Then why, Jason? Just tell me why he'd take the chance! Why?" she wailed, thumping him hard in the chest. Shock pulsed through his veins as he grabbed her fist in midair to prevent another assault. Everyone gasped, and Candace took a full step back, looking bewildered. Blast if he wasn't dumbfounded himself. Where did she get off blaming him for the accident? Didn't she realize his heart ached as much as hers over John's death?

Mitch stepped forward and put his arm around his daughter. "Witnesses say John went down of his own accord, honey, and the police ruled his death accidental. No one forced him down that slope."

Now she threw her father an accusatory glare. "How do you know that, Dad? Were you there?"

Mitch frowned. "Well—of course not."

As if that should have settled it, Rachel pulled away and marched up the snowy walkway, albeit with stumbling steps. In robotic fashion, everyone else followed, shaking their heads in dismay. Taken aback by her insinuations, Jason fell in at the tail of the procession. "She blames me," he muttered.

"She's completely rude," Candace said, taking his gloved hand in hers with a gentle squeeze.

"No, she's just not thinking straight."

"I don't see how you can defend her. She just hauled off and hit you square in the chest."

He cared very much for Candace, but she sometimes annoyed him with her snap assessments. "She just lost her husband, Candace."

Mitch reached the car ahead of Rachel and opened the front door for her. "Where's Meaggie?" she suddenly asked, almost as an afterthought, turning full around to scan the cemetery.

"Emily took her back to the house," her mother said, climbing into the back with Tanna.

"Oh."

Before climbing into the car, she glanced about, focusing on Jason. "He was a good skier, Jason."

Jason nodded his head in agreement. "Yes, he was, Rachel. No question about that."

"As good as you?" she questioned with a cynical hint.

"Yes. As good as me," he lied.

Seeming pacified, she bent her awkward, pregnant body and eased into the seat. Mitch closed the door behind her and went around to his own side, nodding at Jason's parents, Tom and Donna Evans, and the rest of his family before climbing into the driver's side and starting the engine.

When the car disappeared from view, Jason murmured again, "She blames me."

"It will pass," said Tom, removing his keys from his coat pocket. "Give her time."

As they approached his father's late-model Chevrolet, Jason asked, "What about you, Dad? Do you think I'm to blame?"

"Son, please, let's not talk about this anymore."

"Well, do you?"

"Get in the car," his father ordered in a tone Jason hadn't heard since his youth. Even though he was a grown man, he felt compelled to obey. Candace climbed in ahead of him, and they all rode back to the house in icy silence.

Chapter One

Ten Months Later

M ommy, will you play with me?" Meagan asked for at least the dozenth time.

Rachel scanned the kitchen, overwhelmed by the sight of empty juice bottles, a spilled box of baby cereal, a pan of lukewarm potato soup, and a pile of several weeks' worth of mail. A quick glance at the clock on the wall told her it was already 8:05 p.m. Her pounding head and jangling nerves were additional reminders of her upside-down life, and Rachel shot Meagan a weary look. "Mommy can't play just now, honey. It's already past your bedtime, and I still have to get you and your brother in the bathtub." She wiped her damp brow with the back of her hand. It had been an unusually warm day for September, and the heat and humidity still lingered in the house, despite the open windows. In fact, the entire summer had been the hottest and driest Rachel could remember.

"I don't want a bath."

"I know, but you played hard today. A bath will feel good."

"Uh-uh. Baths stink," Meagan whined.

Rachel had a good comeback on the tip of her tongue, but she kept it to herself.

"Can you read me a book?"

"Not this minute, no." Suddenly, it occurred to her that things were too quiet in the living room, where she'd left John Jr. Setting down her dishcloth, she headed toward the other room and found an assortment of magazines scattered about, their pages ripped out and thrown helter-skelter. Johnny looked up and grinned, his mouth jammed full with something. She ran across the room, knelt down beside him, and pried open his jaws, using her index finger to fish out a glob of wet paper. "Oh, Johnny-Boy, you little stinker, you'd better not have swallowed any of this."

"If he did, it'll come out in his diaper," Meagan stated.

In spite of herself, Rachel laughed, something she'd rarely done since becoming a single parent. In fact, more often than not, she laid her exhausted self in bed each night and cried into her pillow, counting all the ways she'd failed at her mothering job that day, wishing John were there to ease the load.

She whisked Johnny up and headed for the stairs, deciding to leave the kitchen mess alone for now. "Come on, Meaggie. It's bath time." She lifted the latch on the gate and allowed Meagan to pass ahead of her, patting her on the back to urge her up the stairs.

"Noooooo," came another expected whine.

Mustering up a bright voice, she said, "Remember, Grandma and Papa Evans are picking you up in the morning

to take you to the circus! You'll see elephants, tigers, horses…
and I bet you'll even see some clowns. Won't that be fun?"

"Is Johnny goin', too?"

"Nope. Tomorrow is strictly a Meagan day."

"Yay!" she squealed, her mood instantly improved.

Later, with the children tucked in bed, the kitchen
cleaned, and the house put back into a semi-ordered fashion, Rachel collapsed into her overstuffed sofa and heaved
a mountainous sigh. Her chest felt heavy, a sensation she'd
come to expect these days.

Be still, and know that I am God.

"I know, Lord," she whispered, breathing deeply. "But
it's hard. Sometimes, I don't feel Your presence. I will never
understand why You took John."

Be still.…

She leaned down and pulled John's Bible from a stack of
books beneath the coffee table, guiltily wiping off a fine layer
of dust. "Lord, I've been so busy, I haven't even opened Your
Word for weeks. What kind of a Christian am I, anyway?
Shoot, what kind of a *parent* am I? I can't even find time in a
day to read Meagan a book."

Be still.…

"I'm trying."

She opened the leather book, noting many highlighted
verses interspersed throughout the slightly worn pages. John
had been an avid reader, putting her to shame. She knew
God more with her head than her heart, but John had known
Him with both. She missed his wisdom, his courage, and his
strength. Most days, it felt like she was floundering without her other half. If only she'd had the chance to say good-

bye—then, maybe, she'd have fewer gnawing regrets. She gave her head a couple of fast shakes to blot out the memory.

I will never leave you nor forsake you, came the inner voice. It sounded good, but could she truly believe it?

***

Saturday morning dawned bright and full on the horizon, the skies a brilliant blue. The heady scent of roses wafted through her bedroom window. If John were still alive, he'd have headed out at daybreak and picked her a bouquet for the breakfast table. She smiled at the thought. Gentle, cool breezes played with the cotton curtains, causing shadows to dance jubilantly across the ceiling. She hauled her downy comforter up to her chin and turned her head to glance at the vacant pillow on the other side of the king-sized bed. *His* side always remained unruffled, no matter how much she tossed and turned in the night.

Two doors down, Johnny stirred, his yelps for attention growing by decibels. On cue, her breasts sent out an urgent message that it was feeding time. "I'm coming, Johnny Cakes," she called out, then sighed as she tossed back the blankets, donned her robe, and stepped into her slippers. She padded across the room, stopping briefly to touch the framed photo of her and John on their wedding day before continuing to the nursery, where her towheaded, nine-month-old baby was waiting in his Winnie-the-Pooh pajamas. Oh, how she thanked the Lord she still had her beloved children. Yes, they wore her to a frazzle, but they also kept her grounded.

When the doorbell rang at nine o'clock on the dot, Meagan sailed through the house in her pink, polka-dotted shorts and matching shirt, her blond hair flying, and made a running leap into her grandpa's waiting arms, wrapping her legs around his middle. Tom Evans laughed heartily and planted a kiss on her cheek, and Donna smiled, tousling the child's head.

"Papa!" Meagan squealed, reaching up to cup his cheeks with her hands. "You and Grandma are taking me to the circus!"

"No! Are you sure?" He feigned surprise. "I thought we were just going for a walk in the park."

"Uh-uh. Mommy says we're goin' to the circus. What's a circus, anyway?"

Tom laughed and began explaining what she should expect at the circus, while Donna took Johnny from Rachel's arms and moved to the bay window for a look at the gleaming sunshine.

While her father-in-law talked to Meagan, Rachel looked on, getting glimpses of John in his father's every gesture. Tom's manner of speech, his pleasant face, his lean, medium build, the way he angled his head as he spoke, and even his rather bookish, industrious nature put her in mind of John.

She then thought of Jason, sort of the black sheep of the family, only in the sense that he was just the opposite with his tall, strongly built frame, cocoa-brown hair and eyes, and reckless, devil-may-care personality. And he was terribly likable to everyone—except Rachel, even though she, John, and Jason had been almost inseparable during their high school and college years. They had stuck together despite Jason's penchant for weekend parties and John's utter dislike of them; Jason had spent so much time socializing, it was a wonder he'd even graduated. But Jason and she had grown apart, especially after the accident, and Rachel hadn't seen him since last Christmas—her own choice, of course.

Tom stepped forward to plant a light kiss on Rachel's cheek. "How are you doing these days, Rachel?"

"I'm all right," she said with a mechanical shrug and a wistful smile. She never felt like discussing her innermost feelings.

Tom narrowed his gaze as he set Meagan down. The child scooted over to her grandma, who smiled down at her, then looked up at Rachel and said, "Say, why don't you stop by the house tomorrow afternoon? You haven't been over for such a long time."

Visiting her in-laws' home was like walking into yesterday, and Rachel didn't know if she was ready to pass over the threshold again. The last few times had been too painful; she'd found herself glancing around the house and expecting John to come barreling out of one of the rooms. Silence followed as she bit down hard on her lip.

"Jason is coming home," Donna went on, bouncing Johnny as she moved away from the window. "He called yesterday, and I convinced him to come for dinner. He hasn't been home for a couple of months. I know he'd love to meet little Johnny. He asks about him every time he calls, and you know how much he loves and misses Meagan."

Just hearing Jason's name incited painful memories packed with guilt. For a time, Rachel had hated Jason, even blamed him for John's death. Now, she just resented him for reasons she couldn't define. In high school, the phrase "Three's a crowd" had never applied to them. Instead, "All for one, and one for all" had been their motto—until she and John had become a couple, that is. After that, the chemistry among the three of them had changed. Oh, she'd had warm feelings for both brothers, and she'd even dated Jason off and on, but John ultimately had won her heart in his final two years of college with his utter devotedness to her, his promise of a bright future, and his maturity and passionate faith.

"What do you say, Rachel?" Donna asked, turning her head to keep Johnny from pulling on one of her dangling, gold earrings.

"Yes, you should come," echoed Tom.

"I—I'm not sure. I think my parents are stopping over."

"Oh, no—they're coming straight from church to our place for lunch. They didn't mention that?" Donna asked, bobbing Johnny in her arms. The two families had always been close, having lived in neighboring towns and attended the same church for years. Then, when Rachel and John had gotten married, the bond had grown tighter still.

"Um, I guess they did, but I...I forgot." Panic raced through Rachel from head to toe. She didn't want to see Jason, couldn't picture him in a room without John there, too.

"Rachel." Donna touched Rachel's arm, her eyes moist. "We miss John more than you can imagine, but—we still have Jay. His birthday is Tuesday, remember? Won't you come and help us celebrate it like old times?"

Jason's birthday. She'd forgotten all about it. Yes, she did recall celebrating it as a family, just as they'd celebrated hers, John's, and every other family member's.

"I'm sorry, I just don't feel like celebrating anything or anyone."

"But he's your brother-in-law, sweetheart. Don't you want to see him? Remember how the three of you used to be so inseparable?"

"Mom, please," Rachel warned. "It's all different now."

"Of course, I know that. But—"

"Leave it be, Donna," Tom said sternly. Meagan, growing as restless as a filly, tugged at her grandpa's pant leg. "I can understand why Rachel wouldn't want to see Jason. Too many memories, right, Rachel?" He reached up and touched her shoulder. "It's probably for the best—you two keeping your distance, at least for now."

She swallowed a tight knot and released a heavy breath. "Thanks."

Donna blinked. "Well, if that's how you feel...but, at some point, I hope you'll reconsider." She shifted her fidgety body and frowned at her husband, then smiled down at Meagan and tweaked her nose. "Well, we should be getting to that circus, don't you think, pumpkin?"

"Yes!" Meagan jumped with unadulterated glee. *Oh, to be that innocent*, Rachel thought.

"We'll try not to be too late getting her home. How 'bout trying to get some rest when you put Johnny down?" Tom asked as Donna handed Johnny off to Rachel. "You look plain tuckered out."

It sounded wonderful, but also completely unrealistic, considering the overflowing baskets of dirty clothes in the laundry room, the teetering pile of dishes in the kitchen sink, and the brimming wastebasket in every bathroom. *Whoever said, "A woman's work is never done" must have been a single mom*, Rachel thought. Then, nodding with a forced smile, she saw the circus-goers to the door.

About the Author

B orn and raised in west Michigan, Sharlene MacLaren attended Spring Arbor University. Upon graduating with an education degree, she traveled internationally for a year with a small singing ensemble, then came home and married one of her childhood friends. Together they raised two lovely daughters. Now happily retired after teaching elementary school for thirty-one years, "Shar" enjoys reading, writing, singing in the church choir and worship teams, traveling, and spending time with her husband, children, and precious grandchildren.

A Christian for over forty years and a lover of the English language, Shar has always enjoyed dabbling in writing—poetry, fiction, various essays, and freelance work for periodicals and newspapers. She remembers well the short stories she wrote in high school and watched circulate from girl to girl during government and civics classes. "Psst," someone would whisper from two rows over, always when the teacher's back was to the class, "pass me the next page."

Shar is an occasional speaker for her local MOPS (Mothers of Preschoolers) organization; is involved in KIDS' HOPE USA, a mentoring program for at-risk children;

counsels young women in the Apples of Gold Program; and is active in two weekly Bible studies. She and her husband, Cecil, live in Spring Lake, Michigan, with Mocha, their lazy, fat cat.

The acclaimed *Through Every Storm* was Shar's first novel to be published by Whitaker House, and in 2007, the American Christian Fiction Writers (ACFW) named it a finalist for Book of the Year. The beloved Little Hickman Creek series consists of *Loving Liza Jane*; *Sarah, My Beloved*; and *Courting Emma*. Faith, Hope, and Love, the Inspirational Outreach Chapter of Romance Writers of America, announced *Sarah, My Beloved* as a finalist in its 2008 Inspirational Reader's Choice Contest in the category of long historical fiction. Following *Hannah Grace* and *Maggie Rose*, *Abbie Ann* completes Shar's latest trilogy, The Daughters of Jacob Kane.

To find out more about Shar and her writing and inspiration, you can e-mail her at smac@chartermi.net or visit her Web site at www.sharlenemaclaren.com.

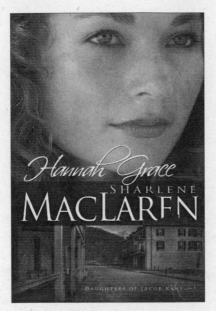

Hannah Grace
Book One in The Daughters of Jacob Kane Series
Sharlene MacLaren

Hannah Grace, the eldest of Jacob Kane's three daughters, is feisty and strong-willed, yet practical. She has her life planned out in an orderly, meaningful way—or so she thinks. When Gabriel Devlin comes to town as the new sheriff, the two strike up a volatile relationship that turns toward romance, thanks to a shy orphan boy and a little divine intervention.

ISBN: 978-1-60374-074-6 • Trade • 432 pages

WHITAKER
HOUSE

Maggie Rose
Book Two in *The Daughters of Jacob Kane Series*
Sharlene MacLaren

In 1904, Maggie Rose Kane leaves her hometown of Sandy Shores, Michigan, to pursue God's plans for her life in New York City. She works at Sheltering Arms Refuge, an orphanage that also transports homeless children to towns across the United States to match them with compatible families, and comes to love each child. When a newspaper reporter comes to stay at the orphanage in order to gather research for an article, Maggie is struck by his handsome face—and concerned by his lack of faith. Will she be able to maintain her focus on God and remain attuned to His guidance?

ISBN: 978-1-60374-075-3 ◆ Trade ◆ 416 pages

WHITAKER
HOUSE

![Yesterday's Promise book cover]

Yesterday's Promise
Vanessa Miller

Melinda Johnson has always felt called to ministry. So, when her father, Bishop Langston Johnson, decides to step down after thirty years, it seems only natural for her to take his place. But Bishop Johnson feels led by a God who has other things in mind, and to succeed him, he appoints Steven Marks—a man who is opposed to female pastors, not to mention the fact that he is Melinda's ex-fiancé. Can Steven and Melinda set aside past pains, forgive each other, and learn to love again? Or will their opposing positions regarding women preachers keep them forever at odds?

ISBN: 978-1-60374-207-8 ♦ Trade ♦ 240 pages

WHITAKER
HOUSE

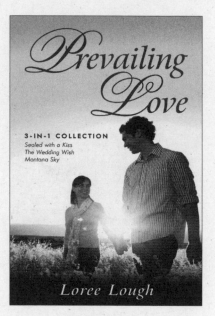

Prevailing Love
Loree Lough

In *Sealed with a Kiss*, bachelor Ethan Burke suddenly becomes a father to Molly, the daughter of his best friends, after an auto accident claims their lives. When he takes Molly to see Christian counselor Hope Majors, he gains optimism about her healing—and about a future with the attractive counselor. In *The Wedding Wish*, Leah Jordan is dying of cancer, and she's scrambling to launch a matchmaking plot to make her two best friends, Jade Nelson and Riley Steele, marry and adopt her two-year-old daughter, Fiona, before it's too late. In *Montana Sky*, cattle rancher Chet Cozart and veterinarian Sky Allen are caught up in a wolf war in the wild Montana woods, where they flirt with danger—and with each other.

ISBN: 978-1-60374-166-8 • Trade • 496 pages

WHITAKER
HOUSE

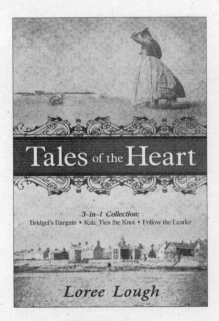

Tales of the Heart
Loree Lough

In *Bridget's Bargain*, Bridget McKenna dreams of bringing the rest of her family from Ireland to America. When she meets the tall, handsome Lance York at the plantation where she works, she finds herself falling in love. Might her British beau make not just one but two wishes come true? In *Kate Ties the Knot*, independent widow Kate Flynn realizes that her young son, Adam, needs a male role model in his life. But she didn't expect him to be a burly shipbuilder, much less to fall in love with him…. In *Follow the Leader*, Valerie Carter tries to put her life back together after the Civil War breaks it apart. When she moves to Maryland to be a schoolteacher, her heart is gradually warmed by her students' affections—and by the affection of one Paul Collins. Can he restore her faith in God and give her a new future?

ISBN: 978-1-60374-167-5 ♦ Trade ♦ 480 pages

WHITAKER
HOUSE

Love's Rescue
Tammy Barley

To escape the Civil War, Jessica Hale flees Kentucky with her family and heads to the Nevada Territory, only to lose them in a fire set by Unionists resentful of their Southern roots. The sole survivor, Jess is "kidnapped" by cattleman Jake Bennett and taken to his ranch in the Sierra Nevada wilderness. Angry at Jake for not saving her family, she makes numerous attempts to escape and return to Carson City, but she is apprehended each time. Why are Jake and his ranch hands determined to keep her there? She ponders this, wondering what God will bring out of her pain and loss.

ISBN: 978-1-60374-108-8 ♦ Trade ♦ 368 pages

WHITAKER
HOUSE